Pride

SEVEN DEADLY SINS

Compiled & Edited by
Ben Thomas & D Kershaw

Also available from Black Hare Press

DARK DRABBLES ANTHOLOGIES

WORLDS
ANGELS
MONSTERS
BEYOND
UNRAVEL
APOCALYPSE
LOVE
HATE
OCEANS
ANCIENTS

BHP WRITERS' GROUP SPECIAL EDITIONS

STORMING AREA 51
EERIE CHRISTMAS
BAD ROMANCE
TWENTY TWENTY

OTHER VOLUMES

DEEP SEA
WHAT IF?
KEY TO THE KINGDOM
BEYOND THE REALM

Twitter: @BlackHarePress
Facebook: BlackHarePress
Website: www.BlackHarePress.com

You bade the Morning Star betray the Light,

And Eden's idyll jarred to raucous woe ;

You lured Napoleon to the fatal snow,

And drave Achilles to his sulking flight:

Crowns and the love that were the hero's right

On meretricious swagger you bestow:

Here, venal maids to psychic squalor go,

There, frowsy Murder struts a gartered knight.

And Decadent decoys of Merlin youth,

Pragmatist Pilates of chameleon Truth,

Transvaluers anon of good to ill,

Proving that God is dead and love a sham

In radiant trope and perfect epigram,

Frequent with you our Tree of Knowledge still.

Into the ape I breathed, and you were men :

Umbrageous Art I planted on your way,

And steeped your garments in the dyes of day :

Of marbled Athens was I denizen,

And Shakespeare's England welcomed me again

I bade your dawning godhood disobey

Nostalgias for the comfortable clay

Of tamer kin in maudlin Nature's den.

While my disdainful cruisers guard the sea

Their comely holds no coward's lading bear :

Never was night I led not to the m o m :

There is no mount you may not climb with me :

No god you may not challenge, if he dare

Immure the soul I lit ere he was born I

Pride **by Bernard O'Dowd, 1909**

Table of Contents

The Perfect Model

by Alexander Nachaj

When I reached the third floor of the abandoned factory, I wasn't expecting to find the body, but it was there nonetheless. It belonged to a man, possibly in his mid-50s. His head was downturned like that of a man who had suddenly dozed off. He had an overgrown grey beard crusted with soup, oily white and black hair covered his eyes and ears. He lay on the ground with his back pressed up against the spray-painted wall. One arm lay loose by his side with the palm upturned like a penitent, a needle still shooting from his vein. His other hand sat halfway across his chest, still clutching the belt he used as a tourniquet.

"Fantastic," I said. I'd spent the past few days scoping out buildings by the tracks running from Westmount to Downtown, searching for the right shot to complete a project on urban environments I was compiling for Dacha magazine. I met up with a gang of aging skater punks, took one on as a guide, and let him show me all the hidden rooms and hideouts where those in the know went to tag, get laid and deal. Most of the locations told the same rote story. Factories that had gone under. Warehouses with wares no longer worth storing. Apartments condemned because of mould and neglect. But this was something else altogether.

"Jesus Christ," said Mathias, coming up alongside me to get a better view of the body. His usually beady eyes were now open wide.

"Shh." I took a step closer and knelt down before the dead man. He stank of piss and shit, and somewhere in between there was the faint smell of rot and emptiness. The rings on his fingers, along with the silver from his belt buckle, were catching the sun in just such a way that, had I known otherwise, I would have sworn the man was posing for us. "This is perfect."

I glanced towards the missing wall overlooking the tree-lined yard and the tips of the city skyline beyond. The sun was still peeking above the city skyline, but not for long. I pulled the lens cap from my camera and got into position.

"See if you can lower his head," I instructed, "so the eyes aren't in the shot."

"What!" Mathias said. "Rex man, we can't touch him. We've got to get out of here."

"The dead don't mind," I replied, circling the body,

looking for the right angle. Memories of the countless corpses I had come across covering the Rohingya massacre the year before filled my head. True, it had been gruesome, but once you surpassed the gory details, you saw bodies for what they were. "Think of him as a model in need of a helping hand."

I could see that Mathias was still hesitating. I sighed.

"Do you want to be paid or not?"

Mathias' face went blank. For a moment it looked like he was going to head back downstairs, but slowly he moved towards the corpse and gently lowered its head.

"Hold it there one second," I said, considering the angle.

"Whoa!" Mathias exclaimed, standing up and letting the head fall back down. "He just moved."

"He didn't move," I replied. It was obvious from the stench and the way the man lay there that he hadn't moved in some time. "He's dead."

"I don't know, man, I—"

"Fix his head!"

Mathias' whole body stuttered, but he followed my command, readjusting the corpse.

"That's better. Now, get out of my shot."

I focused on the corpse, realising how fortunate I was to find the man at this time and place. His body told a story all on its own, waiting to be captured. It didn't matter who he was. Seeing him like this. The contrast of the concrete, the graffiti, his downward gaze. It said so much about the despair of the urban landscape. He was wonderful, I didn't dare lose my chance. I took my pictures working the angles and the lighting until the sun had set and I was left shooting in the shadows. I would have preferred more time to work the scene, but the moment had passed.

As I put my camera away, I could see that Mathias was still eager to get moving. He hurried back down the way we came, and I slowly followed. When we reached the yard, I stopped to glance back at the building, content that I had captured a stillness in time that would never repeat itself again.

Mathias promised he'd dial 911. He kept repeating that we should have checked more closely if the man was alive or dead. I waved his money over his head and told him to grow up. I'd seen plenty of corpses in my time and this wasn't one that we had to worry about. Besides, I recognised the look in his eyes. He was simply worried because he wanted to feel better. To be a good guy, making the right call. I get that. Man's conscious can feel like a terrible burden sometimes. It's one of those things you learn to set aside or be crushed under its weight.

I picked up a bottle of Chablis on the way home, set it in my freezer, and hurried to my office to review the photographs. I was feeling excited, almost like a child about to unwrap a gift. My fingers drummed against my desk as I waited for the transfer from my memory card to the hard drive. As soon as it was complete, I dived into my work.

The shots that I had gathered were better than I imagined. They were amazing, even in their raw state without touch-ups and corrections. In fact, they were almost better that way, as they highlighted the grime and dirt of human existence, and the sense of isolation and depravity that only a modern city could tolerate. I almost couldn't believe it. I felt elated, high, like I had just experienced the best sex in months.

I drank half the bottle of Chablis on the porch, listening to the night traffic in the distance. All the while, I couldn't get the body out of my head. It was so perfect, like the universe had saved him just for me. The photographs I had taken of him would come to define my career. I was no longer a journalist, but an artist. And I had only just begun.

With that came the realisation that I had to get more.

I couldn't wait. I picked up my phone. Mathias answered on my second attempt to reach him.

"What is it, man?" came his tired voice.

"Take me back. Tonight," I said. "I'll pay you double."

"No way!" He seemed suddenly awake. "We can't go back. What happens if the cops find him? We'll get in deep shit."

"Mathias," I said calmly. "Double."

There was a brief silence. "We'll see." He hung up.

I waited for Mathias at the same corner where I met him earlier that evening, not sure what to expect. When he failed to show sometime after two in the morning, I decided I would find my way back to the factory without his help. This time I carried my DSLR, opting to go for a higher quality camera than the flimsy mirrorless one I had brought earlier in the day. I also carried a heavy torch I sometimes used during night shots.

Moving through the fence at the edge of the road, I stumbled through the bushes, tracing my way through the darkness. It took me longer than I would have preferred to find my way through and into the bushy yard by the abandoned factory. I cursed Mathias for not having joined me. When I reached the yard, I switched on the torch and made my way back to the top floor.

The body lay against the wall where I had found it previously, but several details had changed. Earlier, he had been sitting upright, but now, he was lying on his side. There were flies crawling over the sallow skin of his face and the room around him had acquired a distinctly earthy, compost-like aroma. I leaned in with a kerchief over my mouth. His eyes were fogged over and moist, and his mouth hung slightly open, his yellowed tongue hugging the edge of his lips.

I stepped back. Though his posture had lost some of its significance, he still made for an incredible model. I set down the torch, getting it to cast his shadows just right. I circled him and took several shots—medium shots and close-ups—the quality of the DSLR already evident in the viewfinder. With every photo, I only wanted more.

My mind raced with possibilities. There was so much more we could do together—I, the artist, and he, the muse. I just had to make him cooperate. I looped my camera strap back around my neck and approached the body. I wrapped my hand with the kerchief and slowly lifted him back to a proper seated position, like I had found him before, and tilted his head backwards to a better angle. I'd set myself up once again, ready to take a photo, when his head tumbled back forward. I readjusted him and tried again, but my model wouldn't keep the position I wanted.

Frustrated, I came closer. He was being rather unruly for a corpse. His yellowed tongue was now protruding from his mouth, and though comical, it didn't make for the shot I wanted. I covered my finger with the kerchief and pushed it back inside.

That's when I felt his jaw snap shut on my finger.

I pulled my hand back. Blood seeped from my finger, gushing down my palm and also covering the corpse's chin.

"Fuck!" I shouted, kicking my model. I wrapped my finger in the kerchief and kicked the corpse again, and again. I would have gone on kicking had his hand not suddenly grabbed me by the ankle and caused me to lose balance.

I fell onto my back, groaning from the concrete that slammed into my spine. I would have lain there a moment, had I not felt his hands grab my shins and start to pull.

I looked up. At the bottom of my feet lay the vagrant, his eyes fixated on mine. The needle and belt buckle from his exposed arm dangled and slapped into my legs as he tried to pull himself closer.

For the briefest of moments, I felt shock.

Mathias had been right, there was still some life left in this fellow.

"You were better as a corpse!" I shouted, kicking back. My heel connected with his face and then I was free and crawling away. He shuffled after me across the floor, quickly, his body knocking the torch back towards us. In the beam of light, the man looked like the gangly shadow of a dying insect, scurrying after its prey.

I was so engrossed by my assailant that I never noticed Mathias reach the top floor until he was darting across the light, coming to my rescue.

"Off of him!" he shouted, pulling the vagrant's body away from me. He meant to throw him against the wall, but the vagrant turned and latched onto Mathias, the two of them struggling like a pair of wrestlers as they danced in front of the torchlight.

I scurried away, looking for anything I could use as a weapon, finding an old piece of copper piping against the wall. I picked it up and turned just in time to see the needle ripped from the man's arm, raised over his head and jammed into Mathias' open, screaming mouth.

Mathias fell to the floor, the needle protruding from between his teeth, one hand fighting to keep the man away and the other to pull the syringe out.

"Stop!" I commanded my model. "I'll pay you whatever you want!" I came close, holding the pipe above my head. The man turned towards, me and for a moment, I thought he would listen, but then he lunged at me with his open hands. Reluctantly, I slung the pipe and struck him on the side of the head. I heard his skull crack and on the second blow, felt his cold dark blood gush out onto my hand and forearm. Just as I thought he was done, he took a wobbly step towards me, his milky eyes looking into mine and letting me see the truth.

There was no life in them, nor had there been for some time.

I backpedalled, refusing to believe what I was seeing. I swung the pipe, striking his face again and again. I tore open his cheek, broke his nose, and cracked him in the jaw so hard that a row of teeth clattered to the floor.

"I would have made you!" I howled, furiously raising the pipe for a final crushing blow, "taken you from a nothing junkie to one of the greatest works of art this city has ever seen!"

And then, suddenly, there was no more floor beneath my feet.

I was suspended in mid-air for the longest heartbeat I had ever felt. I saw Mathias pull the needle from his mouth. Remembered the gap in the wall I had seen during the day. And felt so much regret that I had never completed my photo project.

The last thing I saw before I fell through the night air and into the yard below was the dead man, staring into my eyes with something like pity in his. Even as his skin hung in shreds from his face, he looked at me, the living, with defiance.

And then I was falling, past the two floors below, and down to the ground. My left leg snapped and buckled under me. My right shoulder popped, and my head hit a slab of what felt like concrete, exploding into light. But the worst of the pain was the piece of rebar that tore through my gut and burst through me with a gush of blood and intestines.

I coughed. The taste of metal filled my mouth. The dead man had disappeared from the edge of the floor two stories above, and I heard Mathias scream a final time, before everything went silent.

Lying there, I was so cold, I should have been shivering, but instead I was distracted, taken in by the sights all around me.

Even as the darkness closed in, I could see that the ruined yard around the factory was peaceful, beautiful, and that I was every bit a piece of that beauty now. There was the sound of distant birds and the first pale glow of the morning in the sky above. Like the body that I found, I too would go unnoticed for some time, become lost and forgotten, until someone like me should chance upon where I lay.

I knew there was no more time left to waste. My camera lay on my chest, still attached to the strap around my neck. I moved the only arm that still could, reaching for the shutter button. I was about to become the perfect model, but it wouldn't last for long.

Brick and Bone
by Erica Schaef

Old bones are nothing to fear, are they? Provided that they keep to their dark, neglected corners, of course, and forgo the knocking and rattling, which they used to love so well in life. Everyone has a past, if we're being honest; some metaphorical and immensely morose Pandora's Box, which is kept buried and out of sight where it can't upset the lively masses with its obscene decay and stark-white death. We are, in fact, conditioned to accept that every new acquaintance we make has some recessed part of themselves, some bottomless well, the depths of which we will never truly understand. It goes without saying that we *all* have our skeletons. Mine just happens to be of the literal variety.

The house I occupied on Lafayette Square was a tall, red-brick affair with a sharply-pitched roof and three long, dormer windows. I usually spent my evenings in front of the massive, unlit fireplace, reading a book or else dozing easily in my overstuffed chair. That night was no exception, I was enjoying a new mystery novel by candlelight. Beside me, curled up neatly on the sofa, was a sleeping ginger cat. He was my only companion in the sprawling home. There had been a wife, once, but not anymore. My eyes flicked automatically to the back of the grate where a set of bricks arranged in a perfect square appeared to be slightly less aged than its fellows. Of course, if you didn't know it was there, your gaze would have drifted carelessly over the new square and onto more interesting points of the room. That's what happened when the Scotland Yard inspector paid his obligatory visit after I'd reported my wife as missing.

His eyes hadn't lingered, even for a moment, on the condemning spot. Instead, he had taken notice of a particularly beautiful renaissance painting, which my wife had purchased on a trip to the continent some years back.

"Exquisite attention to detail," he'd said, and the irony of it had not been lost on me.

It had been weeks since his visit, and the news of my wife's disappearance had since lost its glistening novelty. After all, a suitcase, along with her considerable wardrobe and most of her personal effects, had gone with her. There had even been a witness, claiming to have seen someone fitting my wife's description boarding a train bound for a port town down south. This was an unexpected bout of luck for me, of course, one that I hadn't counted on.

My only real mistake during the entire ordeal had been in forgetting the ivory hairbrush. It had been a prized possession of hers, one that still had strands of her blonde hair clinging to its bristles when the inspector found it on the vanity. She'd had other brushes, I'd told him, and an assortment of combs, too. He had believed this readily enough, resuming his search of the place with no outward sign of suspicion. I had performed perfectly, and outwitted the law at every turn.

Thunder clapped outside, tearing me from my reminiscence. The cat opened its striking emerald eyes, blinked twice at me, then curled up again to sleep. I was just starting back on my reading when a knock sounded at the front door.

"Rather late for a visitor," I said to no one in particular, but rose from my comfortable seat just the same.

I had to appear to be an anxious husband, after all. *Perhaps my beloved wife had decided to return to me*, I thought with a restrained grin.

When I threw the door open moments later, my face the very picture of hopeful enthusiasm, it was to find my efforts wasted, however. There was no one on the front stoop; no one anywhere, for that matter. Heavy, relentless sheets of rain obscuring the street's gas lamps, were all that awaited me. I frowned, then shrugging, made my way to the kitchen to brew some hot tea.

As I was returning to my study, the knocking sounded again, louder this time. I didn't bother to disguise the dismay I felt, and returned to the front door, teacup in hand. Again, there was nothing but oppressive rainfall. I closed the door with no small amount of trepidation.

My nerves were decidedly frayed at this point, and so, upon my return to the study, where I was confronted with something shocking, I dropped the porcelain teacup and heard its abrupt shattering upon the floor. Before me, in the grate, burned a large, amber fire. Of course, when I'd left the room originally, the fireplace had been dark and empty as usual. In fact, I hadn't lit it since I'd mortared in the new bricks all those weeks ago. Still, impossibly, it crackled its undeniable presence, taunted me with its dancing flames. In front of it, almost imperceptible on the floor, was the ivory hairbrush.

"No," I whispered, unable to keep the tremble from my voice. "This can't be."

I had put the brush in a locked jewellery box upstairs after the inspector had found it, "to keep it safe for her return," I'd said.

Now, here it was, in my study, two floors away from the bedroom where I'd left it so many days ago.

Beads of sweat formed high on my forehead, trickling down over my cheeks and chin as I stared wide-eyed at the thing. No one could have known my secret. Yet, here before me, was all the glaring evidence of attempted blackmail. But how had the intruder entered my home? Had an accomplice distracted me with the door knocks while the blackmailer had trespassed into the house by some other means? And who could it possibly be? Who could know?

My eyes darted around to the shadowed corners of the room. In my panicked state, my senses seemed to play horrible tricks on me, making out the forms and voices of conspiring men where there were none.

After a tediously thorough search of the entire house, I still had precious little to go on. Nothing, in fact, seemed to be out of the ordinary, apart from the roaring fire, and the dead woman's hairbrush. I sighed. It was the first time I had referred her as dead, even in my own mind. I was very careful to always talk of her in the present tense, "my wife enjoys…," or "as my wife likes to say…". Little good it did me though, I had still been found out. There was nothing to do now but wait. Eventually, the blackmailer would make his terms known to me, what was the point otherwise? He just wanted to shake me up a little first, to be nice and sure that I would comply to whatever ridiculous price he deemed acceptable. Resigned to this oblique fate, I sat down in my chair once again, my eyes fixed resolutely on the fire.

For a long time, nothing else happened. I was beginning to think that my intruders had given up on their game for the night, or else had decided to let me suffer in peace for a while.

Then, slowly, just as my eyes had begun to grow heavy with exhaustion, I became aware of a haunting, almost musical sound. It was issuing from the now dimly-burning grate; I knew that instinctively, without having to investigate.

The new bricks seemed to hum and quiver with delight in the hazy air that rose up from the low flames. Certainly, the movement may have been—and probably was—a trick of the flickering light. Still, I could not account for that maddening, wordless song, which was becoming ever-so-slightly more boisterous with every passing second. It sounded like the obnoxious noise that my wife used to make when she had busied herself with some unimportant household chore, like dusting the already-spotless feminine knick-knacks that fairly littered the mahogany shelves of my once-sacred study. The humming set my teeth on edge, as it always had, but this time it was accompanied by a chill of terror, which swept down my spine and caused me to shiver.

"What is this?" I demanded to the room at large in a tone of false bravery.

I succeeded only in scaring the ginger cat, who woke with a start to dash hurriedly from the room. The sound from the grate was very loud now, it reverberated in trilling echoes through the chimney.

"Enough of this!"

I rose from my chair, and the noise ceased instantly. I'd almost convinced myself that it had all been a paranoid hallucination of half-wakefulness, and was beginning to sit again, when a low, rumbling sound started from the square of bricks. The mortar that bound the red rectangles together began to crack and loosen behind a scorching fire that blazed suddenly anew.

"No," I shuddered as, first one brick, then another, broke loose of the makeshift wall to land among the growing flames.

The humming started again, and I knew that it was her; the phantom of my forlorn wife, come to ruin me with the exposure of my crime.

"Stay in there," I admonished helplessly, torn between the fear of justice and that of ghostly things come back from their graves.

A bony arm was stuck through the hole the fallen

bricks had left, reaching out into the fire towards the sound of my voice. It was an unspeakably horrendous thing, with bits of torn fabric and decaying flesh still clinging to the exposed radius and ulna. The skeletal hand at the end of it wore a thin, gold wedding band around the ring finger. I muffled the cry that attempted to escape from my parched throat. I could not draw attention to this place, lest my terrible secret be known.

The hand groped to the brick below the gap, grasping and pushing at the rough edge of it, until that one, too, had fallen to the fire.

If I did not steel myself to act, she would have herself free of the crumbling prison before long. Already, her unsightly hand was working at the next brick, wriggling it free of its mortar holdings.

"Stop this at once, I command thee, wretched wife!"

The humming corpse paid me no attention. Another, less decomposed arm had come out to join the first in its freeing task. In the blackness beyond, I could just make out the milky witness of opaque eyes where the red of the fire was reflected murkily, as though through clouded water.

"You force my hand, foul thing!"

I ran to the grate before my waning courage was lost completely. Kneeling at the hearth, I took up the metal poker and attempted to fish out the smouldering bricks. *It is no good*, I lamented as the humming of my wife became more fervent, her movements more hurried.

I poked wildly into the flames so that embers and bits of ash rushed out to pepper and burn my face and arms.

One especially inflamed bit of wood was flung all the way to my heavily draped window, which caught fire almost immediately.

"No!" I cried hoarsely, and grasped my temples in useless exasperation, inadvertently pulling chunks of hair from my scalp.

In one last flailing attempt at concealment, I reached with my bare hands into the flames. It was excruciatingly painful for a few moments, as I gripped the red-hot bricks and forced them back to their rightful place among the wall. It was undoubtedly the worst physical torment I had ever experienced. Eventually, though, the pain stopped. The skin dripped from my hands like flesh-coloured candle wax into the fire as I continued my work.

Outside, beyond the smoking inferno of my window, I could hear raised voices and the frantic whistle-blowing of a policeman. *It is no good*, I thought miserably. My hands had become too burned and numb to carry out their task of concealment. From her place in the wall, my wife transformed her humming to cold, derisive laughter. The dead eyes that looked out from the dark void and piercingly into mine were full of untold malice. Her mad, hysterical laughter became my own as I withdrew from the flames to crumple into a pathetic heap upon the floor. Clamouring footsteps and barking yells came near to me as a thick, sooty smoke filled my lungs. All was blessedly black. If only it had stayed that way.

Now though, I sit and think endlessly of her; my poor and wretched wife…my skeleton. Or, perhaps *I* am the skeleton now, condemned to this white-padded closet for all that remains of my dreadfully fleeting life, encased in this pristine, straight-jacket enamel. I laugh; a strange and hollow sound, which is absorbed into obscurity by the heavily-cushioned walls that surround me. *It's almost,* I muse, *as though I never even existed in the first place.* I laugh, still harder. What does it matter, in the end? We are all just bones, after all.

Obstructive Gaze

by Kylie L. Webber

"Tell me about it," I invited. I've practiced that line over and over, tailoring it to how I believe it will best have its effect on my intended recipient. Sometimes it is brittle and sharp. Other times I say it disinterestedly, with the promise of being nonjudgmental. That works best on victims of sexual assault. They sit back and allow themselves to disengage from the moment, reciting the facts with the dry remoteness of a judge orating the rote legal matters of their profession. I've seen it a lot, that soulless puppetry, when the spark of personality has retreated to protect itself.

But this time, I let my voice be as warm and caressing as butterscotch sauce. I let the words flow over her, embracing for a moment, and I see her sink, cloaked in them, to the seat on the other side of the ironwork table. Of course. I'm very good.

A waitress pours waters in a long, practiced cascade, and departs with the promise of menus.

"I'm dissociating," she blurts, laying her hands neatly on the table before her, side by side, thumbs tucked under her palms, index fingers touching.

"All right," I keep the butterscotch pouring, "in what way? When has this been happening?"

"Every day. All the time." Her voice wavers and cracks, her eyes are wide like she's starting to panic. I hear her breath coming faster, beginning to rasp in her throat. Her nostrils flare.

"Take a deep breath," I instruct, "and let it out slowly. There. Good. You're safe here. Just focus on your breathing for a moment. Breathe in—one—two. Breathe out—one—two—three. Good."

She fumbles for the glass, sloshing it, and closes her eyes as she sips. I take the opportunity to examine her. Mid-twenties, not a hair out of place with those severe cornrows falling in long straight plaits down over her shoulders. Restrained makeup. One braid has a feather in the end, a note of summer break whimsy which jars. Not an azure plume, which I would choose for her, but a dusty, striped brown. A feather that could have come from the wings of the first, primordial bird.

She has polished cheekbones, her skin is healthy and well-moisturised. The only sign that anything might be wrong is the fine dotting of perspiration about her upper lip, and the deep crease incised between her eyebrows.

I turn my attention to her clothes—neat, restrained,

the mid-range garments of a young professional—and to her hands. One pink palm is cradling the base of the glass, the dark, slender fingers of her other hand wrapped around the columnar length of it, as though she is holding a baby which is at risk of throwing itself backwards and out of her grip. Not a nail chewer, though she keeps her fingers clipped short with barely a hint of white crescent growing.

I let my eyes run up her wrists—

"Stop it," she says, opening her eyes.

"I beg your pardon?"

"I can feel you staring at me. The male gaze. It's really depersonalising."

I smile, smooth and concerned. "I assure you, Tia—"

"Tiamat, please. And yes, I know, your observation is purely professional," she says flatly, her voice still fractured with tension. She gives a little cough to clear her throat. A good guess—I was about to say just that to her.

I release another transient smile and change tracks.

"Tell me why you came here today, Tiamat." *Tia*, I think. *Tia, you're an upset and angry young woman.* The frown line deepens. I wait, composedly. She will either get up and walk out of here, in which case I have a free slot before my next appointment, or she will start talking, and I will have a potential new patient.

We both order cappuccinos, hers with soy milk. Lactose allergies, or vegetarian? Note the tattoo on the inside of her wrist, slightly darker than her skin, of one of those bulbous goddess symbols. Vegetarian then, and probably vulgar about it.

She coughs politely behind one hand. It sounds like she says, "Vegan." How very Freudian of me, transferring meanings like that. I mentally slap my wrist and then refocus on the task at hand.

"You were saying?" I ask. There is a clock on the wall of the train station across the street. It allows me to track the time without being so gauche as to check my watch. I let my eyes flick out past her shoulder. There is half an hour left, and we've barely completed the pleasantries. My next client is old, rich, and utterly incurable. I won't be late for a meeting with Old Faithful. Her fees alone paid for my bathroom last year.

Tia sighs. "I've been dissociating. It's something that's always happened to me—you know, like when your attention just drifts, even while you're trying to focus, or while someone is talking to you, and you suddenly snap back into the present moment, with no idea where you've been or for how long?"

"Certainly. It happens to the best of us, especially under trying circumstances." Comfort the patient, build a professional rapport. Invite the confidences.

"It's been getting worse lately, since I graduated. And I'm not sure why. I can feel it coming on," she makes a vague gesture at her head, "I begin to feel like I'm in a trance state, like I'm becoming sleepy, and taking a step back from my brain at the same time. Sometimes it's like I can't feel my limbs anymore."

"What do you think causes these fugue states?" I ask, making mental notes. Young, neat but with the reference to her heritage in her hairstyle. Professional but probably has a pagan Earth Mother axe to grind. See use of "snap,"—violent language, and "trance"—suggestive of a history of substance abuse?

She looks at me doubtfully, as though she has concerns as to the attention I am paying her. I raise my brows slightly and give a minute nod. *Yes, Tia, I'm listening. Saint Christina, spare me from post-adolescent hypochondriacs.*

Tia continues, but her enthusiasm, limited to begin with, wanes as the outpouring of concerns progresses.

"I'm not sure. They seem to be getting more and more constant."

"How have your family reacted to these? Have they noticed anything?"

"I don't have parents," Tia says, clearing her throat

nervously. That is a vocal tic I could grow to loathe. Estranged or dead, I diagnose, unless she's fibbing, in which case the statement is an over-dramatised form of wishful thinking, which I must suffer through. And she has recently graduated from with a double-degree in accounting and applied mathematics, which I'll believe when I see her transcript. The student loans must be enormous. I begin to revise her suitability as a client.

"Have you found anything which alleviates these…events?"

"Yes," she says decisively. I perk up, able to lecture on the dangers of self-medication for the remaining fifteen minutes without effort, after which point, I can recommend her to some colleagues I dislike. "Writing. I've always liked doing it, it's been a way for me to…re-centre and relax."—that sounds like yoga terminology, check for magical thinking—"but lately it seems to become a compulsion. I've noticed that if I don't write, say if I take a break for a few days, I start having more of these…dissociations." She will probably be happy with some Jung-spouting, pseudo-psychic so-called 'psychologist'. Tealeaf readers.

To an abnormal extent for an already abnormal situation, apparently. I heave an internal sigh, but ask the question. If it were any more obviously a hook, she'd have written it across her forehead. However, it should tell me something about the cast of her mental obsession.

"What do you write about, in these states? And what do you consider a lot of writing?"

Significant amounts for anyone, it becomes apparent. She gets up at five am and writes for an hour and a half before breakfast, usually spends her half hour lunch break writing at her desk, and when she comes home, prepares dinner and writes for another one to two hours before going to bed. A truly prodigious amount of time.

Tia looks rueful. "The subjects are very boring. Real everyday, slice of life kind of affairs."

Affairs. What an odd term to use. A slip up? Perhaps the young professional has a guilty conscience weighing on her mind. She wouldn't be the first workplace romance I've had to lead to healthier decision-making.

"And you say these help your dissociative states? Why do you think that is?"

"I feel like…this is going to sound stupid…but I feel like I'm creating reality. And I have to dedicate time to doing that in a short, focussed way by writing, in order to have a life for myself the rest of the time." Are my eyes rolling? They're not, good. Smile.

"Hmm. No parents, no partner or children, I presume? An intelligent, capable young woman entering the workforce could well feel like she was creating the world anew, and I would understand that impetus to create finding another outlet if she were under stress or being stymied in another aspect of her life."

Tia presses her lips together for a moment. "You're just going to brush me off?"

I glance over her shoulder at the clock.

"Not at all, my dear. I think that your unique challenges would benefit from ongoing discussion." I place a business card on the table in front of her, tucking a ten-dollar note under my coffee cup. It is best to be generous with a new client. "My secretary will call you to arrange a time."

She touches the card with one fingertip.

"These sessions. They'll consist of convincing me that I'm deluded, and that your vision of me is the correct one?" Her cheeks have reddened with some strong, negative emotion. Schizophrenics often react with anger when their worldview is threatened. Poor fools. One does not bring about a cure by investing in a faulty belief system. "That's pretty egotistical."

"Well, it does seem to strain credulity somewhat, doesn't it? The thought that sitting before me is a young woman who is, for want of a better word, God, creating the world with each page she writes? Why not write away death and taxes? Or war? Write yourself into becoming a millionaire?"

"It's not that simple. I write things so they become real, I don't dictate their course." Nice save. A convenient out.

"Tiamat," I lean forward, urgently trying to get the message across before she leaves this ridiculous train-wreck of a session and withdraws into her delusion, "you have come to me because some part of you knows you need help. Follow through on that. Let me help you."

She stands, rummaging in her bag. "But what if I'm right?"

I shake my head, smiling regretfully. "Come and see me next Wednesday, and we can talk about it further."

"No. *What if I'm right, and you convince me to stop?*"

The forceful young woman shoves a handful of papers at me with her angry rhetorical question, and strides away, scattering pigeons and pedestrians. I glance at the sheets, fold them and stow them away in my breast pocket for later perusal. Right now, I have to get back to the office for a meeting with Old Faithful.

This was a complete waste of time.

Hours later, I see my last client out to reception where Sam will take payment and schedule another appointment in a fortnight. People. How are they all so simple, and yet so complicated? Narcissists, manic-depressives and borderline cases. If they simply followed my advice, they would see immediate improvement. There're always questions. Excuses. *Arguments*. I type up my notes from the pad of notepaper and shred the originals. An oddity ubiquitous to clients is their dislike of seeing me on a computer in their meetings, as though I am preordained in their imaginations as some antique Freud, complete with leather-bound books and gilt page edges. Or perhaps they are uncomfortable at the thought of me hiding behind the upright of a glowing screen, potentially online shopping while they bleat. They want authenticity: me leaning forward in my distressed leather chair, notepad upon a tweedy knee, and them reclining upon a fainting couch, staring up at the ceiling as their vision runs with tears. As though authenticity were a branding decision. There is no suggestive chaise here. There are chairs with arms, and a box of soft tissues unobtrusively nearby on a low table. I receive them on my terms. I don't need to impose the artificial vulnerability of asking them to lie down before me.

As I turn off the computer and air conditioning, and

prepare to close the office for the night, I feel a crinkle in my breast pocket. I puzzle for a moment. *Ah. Yes. Tia.* The would-be creatrix. Three double-sided pages of close-pressed words, torn from a ring bound notebook. I sigh, adjust my glasses and promise myself that I will go home after one page. If nothing else, it will make an amusing anecdote over cocktails.

My stomach begins to bubble with acid while I read, fumbling the pages into order as I flip through them. Tiamat has written, word for word, the events of our meeting. She cannot have written it before it happened. This must be a complex trick. Prosthetic hands? An eavesdropping scribbler at an adjacent table and sleight of hand? Except that she has included all my internal commentary, effectively hiding herself beneath my professional observations, making herself impossible to follow.

Going to Sam's desk, I rummage through the book of appointments. *Surely* he will have taken her details when she phoned to request a meeting. My fingers do not shake while I search. I am stressed, angry even, and I am determined to discover her methods of trickery. Any sense of fear is simply a nervous tension response to a stressful situation that is completely explainable using terms other than "omniscient young woman." Even if she did somehow (unbelievably) write out the secret thoughts that I would *never* tell a client. They need to be handled like delicate glass coming up to temperature, slowly led to the dawning light and warmth of sanity, or else they are susceptible to shattering. Where is she?

There is a phone number, a first and a last name, a small sketch of a frowning face paired with a smiling one. Some scribbles where Sam has tried to force the flow of a stuttering pen. Clearly a habit of thriftiness developed during his impoverished childhood. No address.

A robotic voice states, "The number you have dialled has been disconnected. Please check the number and try again." No doubt some cheap prepaid thing that teenagers buy and discard like train tickets, in between prank calling the authorities and hacking each other's social media pages. I do not slam the phone down. That would be puerile and counterproductive. I sit in the cheap, uncomfortable secretarial seat, force my hands to relax open on my thighs, and struggle to slow my breathing. My faculties of objective reasoning remain unparalleled. I am not having a… I am not insane. I am a registered psychiatrist with twenty years' experience, respected by my peers. I would have *noticed*.

I need a plan to find Tiamat Abzu, but over the increasing, drumming tension headache, all I can hear is the repeating loop of her last words:

"What if I'm right, and you convince me to stop?"

First published in *Lane Cove Literary Awards Anthology, 2015*

Like and Subscribe

by Raven Corinn Carluk

[16 August]

[Intro music plays when the video starts, techno music overlaid by soprano vocals. Letters slide across the screen, colours shifting to the beat before forming the title: Syrienne Sings. The words hold for three seconds as the music reaches its peak, then cuts away to the hostess.]

[She's a beautiful woman with dusky skin, glossy black hair, and large doe eyes. Her makeup and hair are normally meticulous, but today she looks drab with a sloppy bun, basic eye shadow and lip gloss, one strap of her channel-branded camisole falling off her shoulder. She's sitting on the floor in front of her futon, a range of beauty products on display on the coffee table before her.]

[After a heavy sigh, she begins talking in a subdued tone.] Hey guys, Syrienne here. Sorry I didn't have a new vlog up on Monday. I've just been really down, and I just couldn't think of what I wanted to talk about. I haven't even really been writing any new songs for you.

But then Justin reminded me I owe all of you an update, at least. You're all not just my *fans*, but my *friends*. Each and every one of you.

[A photo pops up over her left shoulder, showing a bespectacled young man in a button-up flannel and tee-shirt, smiling awkwardly while she leans on him, breasts pressed against his arm. She begins speaking again, more upbeat this time.]

So, everyone, *this* is Justin. I haven't shown him to any of you, and that's just not fair. He's my *absolute* bee eff eff, and I just *don't know* what I'd do without him. If he weren't such a great friend, I might even think about dating him.

[She laughs, wrinkles her nose, and the picture fades.] But *no*, I wouldn't sleep with him. He's like my brother. But since he's the one who convinced me to just share my pain with you, told me that *you'd* all care for me as much as *he* cares for me, I wanted you to meet him.

Thank you, Justin! And thank you everyone watching. I *really* couldn't do this without you. [She waves at the camera, blows it a kiss, and the video ends.]

[Video receives twice as many Likes as normal. Viewers telling her how much she's loved and wishing she gets better soon fill the Comments section.]

[19 August]

[Video begins abruptly, shaky, is clearly captured from a phone camera, and shows only darkness. She finally comes into frame, poorly lit and off-centre. Her hair is dishevelled, and tears run down her face, smearing her makeup. When she speaks, her voice is husky, and she can barely catch her breath.]

Hey guys, Syrienne here. I know this is really weird, but it's been, like, a *super* weird night for me too. Justin is around here somewhere, and he's being a freak, but I just wanted you to know in case something happened.

[She glances around, slipping out of frame. She returns quickly, very close to the camera.] Justin went absolutely *effing* wild after the last video. I've never seen him so mad. He kept complaining about the *friendzone*, or something, and said I was just a stuck-up bitch, or something. Said I only cared about views and likes and *whatever*.

Listen, everyone. [She looks directly into the camera, then holds up her other hand. Pills rattle inside an unmarked bottle, and she can't uncurl her fingers from it.] He said we were going to play Seven, but I had no idea what he meant, and before I knew it, he was gluing my phone and this bottle to my hands. Then he turned off the lights, and—

[Hands come into frame and grab her face. She screams as the camera flops around. The rest of the video is wet squelches and pleas for mercy, though far too shaky to see anything. A bloody thumb finally crosses the camera and the video ends.]

[Likes and Dislikes skyrocket, and many people share to their social media. Several arguments break out in the Comments section over whether it's real or not. Most express hope she is okay, though several say she got what she deserved.]

[21 August]

[Downbeat intro begins, a soft trance piece, though still with soprano vocals. Everything else about the graphics remain the same.]

[She appears centre frame, hair in an artfully messy pile atop her head, eye makeup a display of peacock blues and greens, her lipstick a deep sapphire. A pale blue bandage covers the entirety of her nose.]

Hey guys, Syrienne here. *Very* much alive, thanks to some *very* charming doctors. Don't forget to thank a doctor, the next time you see one. They really don't get enough appreciation. [She waves and smiles.] *Thanks,*

Doc Greg!

And thank you to all my lovely fans. My *dearest* friends. Each and every one of your comments meant *so much* to me while I was in the hospital. Still means so much. *You're* the reason I sing and make videos, and I will *always* love you.

[Her expression changes, becomes stern. Even while frowning and with the bandage obscuring her face, she still had a breath-taking allure.] Now it's time to address all you *haters* out there.

First, some of you are incredibly rude. Words like that *can't* be unseen, and they'll stay with me and the kind people you're abusing. They just wanted to make sure that I was okay after that...

[She pauses, looks away, and swallows. She licks her lips, then starts again without looking back.] What Justin did to me was horrifying. I can barely sleep, and I worry that he's in the dark, and I'm scared of what he might do to me. But some of you *bullies* insist this didn't happen.

[She rips the bandage free and snaps her head back to the camera. In place of her regal nose is a gaping hole. The edges have been sealed, but nothing covers the dark red folds inside.]

This *isn't* some computer trick. Justin *really* sliced off my nose. Thought I'd choose to *die* rather than be *disfigured*. That none of *you*, my *friends*, would accept me if I were less than perfect. And *every* single one of you *toxic*, *problematic*, hateful *bigots* are just proving him right.

Well, *this* woman *isn't* perfect, and *you'll* just have to *deal* with it. [She glares hard into the camera for five seconds, unblinking, before the video ends.]

[Likes pour in, and triple all other Likes on the channel combined. Naysayers are shouted down in the Comment section. Subscribers join by the hundreds every day, and her merch store can barely keep up with orders. The top comment is a GoFundMe that quickly reaches $50,000.]

[16 December]

[Dubstep music wubs around new soprano vocals, rising as the title grows in the centre. Colours shift to the beat, until the final drop starts the video.]

[Her hair is pulled back in a severe tail, recently coloured purple. Three hoops shine along her left eyebrow, one on the right. Her lower lip is split, and she keeps her chin lifted to present the wound to centre frame, head turned slightly to the right. Her nose hole is rosy pink, with a delicate ring hanging from the remains of her septum. She looks happy, and her voice is an excited chirp when she begins.]

Hey guys, Syrienne here! Thanks for coming by. Glad you're here for the big *hundredth episode* reveal. Can't believe we've come so far since Justin and the relaunch.

But, first, mad props to the Disfiguration Squad. Keep those hashtags going, spread that awareness. We've *got* to do our *duty* to remove the stigma of scars, and help our brothers and sisters understand they're *accepted*. It's current year, and it's time to recognise we're *all* beautiful.

This week's shout outs go to: [A series of full-screen photos cover the screen. The first is a heavy-set young woman with fuchsia hair and no eyelids.] Sweetpea Seventy-Seven.

[The second shows a shirtless man, severely underweight, with a fresh scar running from his hairline, down his face and chest, all the way to his prominent hip bone.] Ex Ex Ex Man.

[The third photo is a pair of girls who look no older than fourteen, holding a claw hammer. They smile broadly, revealing shattered teeth.] And finally, Lynn and Susan. Everyone looks *great* with their newly-made disfigurements.

[She's smiling when the video cuts back to her, holding a hand up along the right side of her face.] Are you all ready? [She raises her eyebrows, mouthing a countdown from five.] Ta-da!

[She turns her head and moves her hand at the same time. Fifteen tiny black stitches hold closed the skin where her ear used to be. She laughs cheerfully, and the camera zooms in on the amputation.]

Isn't it *great*? Greg did it after hours, and he's just *such* a sweetheart. I mean, like the *biggest*, *sweetest* teddy bear. He does *so much* for me, and I *love* him like a best brother.

[Video cuts to a centre-frame shot of her, and she's let her hair down. She taps her split lip, on the verge of laughing.] I *love* you all. Remember how *beautiful* you all are, that *no one* can tell you otherwise. [She blows a kiss, and the video ends.]

[Likes reach into the hundred thousands, Dislikes into the tens of thousands. New subscribers spike, followed by comments praising her strength and beauty. Disfiguration Squad channels number seven hundred, with new ones forming daily.]

Golden Boy

by Trisha Ridinger McKee

Holden nodded absently as his manager lectured him on his behaviour.

"Seriously, Holden, are you listening?" Frankie grabbed the beer out of his hand and cursed. "You're going to get kicked off this project."

Holden gave a casual shrug, shooting the girl across the room his lopsided smile, expecting the blush staining her cheeks and that silly grin twisting her lips. He could cause mass chaos with a wink. Turning back to Frankie, he assured him, "There's no way they'll kick me off. I'm the star. I turned down three projects for this one."

"Listen carefully. You're hot this second. But I've seen this a hundred times if I've seen it once. You young kids get popular quick, and then you think you're the best thing to come along. Let me tell you—there is another Holden just waiting at that door for this shot. You screw it up and talk travels fast in this town."

"I was just late!"

"You held up production for three hours. And you were drunk. Watch it, buddy."

Shutting his eyes slowly with that gradual grin, Holden nodded. "I'll shape up. Promise."

By the end of the day, he was exhausted. He had forgotten his lines and stumbled past his mark more times than he cared to remember. And everyone overreacted. His manager, the director, that hot but snobby co-star. They rolled their eyes, shouted, corrected, all over some minor mistakes and short delays.

They were lucky he even agreed to do this movie. It was beneath him. But his manager convinced him this was the right direction. He was popular because he was beautiful. A heartthrob. This movie showcased that.

"Hey asshole, learn your lines. Tired of carrying you," Alecia hissed as she stomped past.

Holden laughed and held up his hand in a wave. That first day of filming she had been all over him, giggling every time he messed up, drooling over every move he made. They had had their fun off the set in his trailer a few times. Then she caught him with the sound girl, and now she was one of those bitter females who could not let go of the fact that she had not conquered him.

He was only twenty-two. How did anyone expect him to settle down with the first bimbo who fluttered her fake eyelashes and flashed her fake boobs at him?

His career was just now taking off. Growing up,

everyone had commented on his looks. The sharp cheekbones, the straight nose, those golden-brown eyes framed by dark long lashes that were all real. And the thick black hair. His mother always told him he was destined for great things. She told him to always go after what he wanted.

And he wanted to be a star. He started on commercials, and then was recruited to a soap opera. Holden had despised that gig because it was gruelling. Every day, so many lines to remember and not enough time to get it all down. But it was his launching pad.

It was not long after that he auditioned and got a part on a popular prime time show. It was supposed to be a temporary part, but he became such an overnight success that they gave him his own show. And the movie parts were rolling in.

His manager was quick to warn him, "It's your face, Holden. You're a gorgeous guy. But your acting needs work." He enrolled him in acting classes, but after the second session, Holden had walked out. He did not need to stand in the middle of the room and pretend to be a train to be a good actor. They tried to humiliate him because he was better than anyone in that class, including the instructor, some old actor that still spoke of his movie awards decades later. Whatever! He would have more awards than all of them!

As the crew and cast prepared to leave for the day, Holden glanced up and saw one of the extras standing in the way, looking lost. She was young and cute in a not-so-obvious way. But earlier, she had delivered her lines flawlessly.

"Hey," he greeted, sauntering over and leading her out of harm's way. "You gotta step to the side so they don't run you over." Holden noticed with satisfaction that she blushed and stared in awe. "You were great today. First job acting?"

"No." She cleared her throat, her sapphire eyes the only thing that could mesmerise. She pushed back a strand of dark blonde hair and took a deep breath. "No, I've done commercials."

"Aw. Already a pro. What's next, huh?"

The awkwardness faded away as she lifted her gaze up and smiled, showing all her teeth. "Actually, back to college. This is just a way to earn tuition money."

And that was how the fascination with Cora began. She was not beautiful enough to hold his attention. The extent of her fashion was jeans and a sweatshirt. She was not well travelled. She was not sophisticated.

But she was untouched. The glamour of this world did not appeal to her, and it fascinated Holden. At a mere twenty years old, Cora should be *oohing* and *aahing* over the process, the lights, the money. She should be scraping for her next chance, the shot at being famous. But she was more excited about going back to college and keeping her nose in a book.

Before Holden understood what was happening, they were going out together two or three times a week. Cora had a fresh way of looking at things. At night when he took her home, she paused outside the door to point up at the stars. The stars! As if they were not settled in that sky every night.

She also loved discussing books and movies. Not movies in the way that he liked to discuss. She did not rate actresses or actors by their looks. She wanted to talk about plots. Theories.

Within two weeks, they were sleeping together, and although Cora was not a clingy woman, she did toss out a general warning.

"Hey, Holden. You have a reputation—"

"Listen, babe—"

"No, just…let me get this out. I'm not as naïve as you think. I'm just not geared toward your world. So, I understand…this…"

"Hey. Hey!" He sat up and wrapped his arm around her. "I'm not sure what you're thinking—"

"Let me finish! I know you work around some beautiful women. I get it. But I have one request."

"Sure."

"Don't be a jerk about it. I know this isn't forever. It's just going to be a blip on our radars in the big picture. But when the time comes, and you're moving on…just let me know. And in return, I promise no drama. No tears or threats."

He could not help but grin. "Oh really? No tears? You won't beg me to stay?"

Her eyes darkened in a way he had never seen, and he drew back in confusion. "I'm telling you, Holden. Just always be honest with me. Whether it's tomorrow or a month from now. Don't make me look like some loser. Okay?"

Holden chuckled and drew her to him. "No! Not what I do."

"It is what you do. I was around for the first few weeks of filming, remember?"

He laughed away her arguments. "Different."

Cora pushed gently on his chest so she could meet his gaze. Something intense held him there, drew him in, and had him hanging on her every word. Something. "It wasn't, but this isn't about that. This is about you and me. And I want you to simply be respectful. This is as much for you as it is for me. My family…we come from a long line of casters. It's…sometimes our emotions cause havoc. I want you to avoid that havoc, Holden."

He hung on her every word, somehow unable to focus on anything else until she seemed to blink her eyes rapidly and then he was released. Stunned, but released.

It was not long before Holden forgot the intensity of that conversation. He was soon sneaking around with the daughter of the director. The daughter had luscious blond hair and smelled like strawberries and Root Beer and drew him back to his childhood. Not to mention, he felt like sticking it to the director.

He dodged Cora's calls and never returned the messages. One day on set, he glanced up and saw her. She was with a few other girls, and the director was talking to them, pointing out different areas and items, obviously talking Cora up to her friends. Holden rolled his eyes and turned his back.

"Hey Holden. I just wanted you to meet my friends. I wanted to show them the set I worked on."

He turned and gave them barely a glance, her friends even less remarkable-looking than she was. "Oh. That's right. You worked here for like a day. Connie, right?" He laughed and turned back to his script. But he caught the stilling of her body, the steel-blue of her eyes, and for some reason, he braced himself.

That was the last Cora tried to reach out. And frankly, it was the last Holden gave her much thought. He was busy having fun. Trying to get famous.

But the movie was a bust. The director blamed him, he blamed the director, but word was out. Holden's reputation was soiled. He was known as a brat on set, his tornado-sized tantrums expected from established actors, not newbies like him. That's what his manager told him.

The television show lasted four episodes before it was pulled.

Still, Holden was not worried. He was the best around. He saw himself at the top for at least the next ten years. He would not have sprung up so high so fast unless this was what he was meant to do.

He was in two more movies, one of them never made it to the theatres, the other one was laughed at by critics and audiences. His manager dropped him. He moved out of his luxurious home into a one-bedroom apartment.

Holden managed to survive on paid appearances at conventions and bit parts on shows and movies. His looks still had some pull. It seemed women could not get enough of him. He settled into a much tamer lifestyle.

Then he noticed some wrinkles splaying out from his eyes. Those late nights of partying and the rigorous tanning had taken their toll. He saved some money from a parody film he did and got some injections and minor nips and tucks. It was a treat to himself. He was not looking old yet, but Holden wanted to stop it from becoming a problem.

It became a problem.

The procedure caused damage to his face and made him look older and slightly lopsided.

The surgeon insisted that he had been precise and accurate in his work and that this was a fluke, a one in a million reaction. But it was a fluke that cost the surgeon some major money. Because Holden sued. They ended up settling out of court, and he was given a sum of money that was more than he had made since that dismal first movie of his.

With money in the bank, Holden researched his options, asked his actor friends, and finally found a plastic surgeon that he was confident could fix his face.

Only he did not. He made it worse. Holden's once prized cheekbones now looked like they would cut through his skin.

He received a smaller settlement from that. And the next surgery seemed to prove what the previous doctors had insisted. That his body was not meant for cosmetic surgeries. Because now the bridge of his nose was skinny and looked feminine.

For the next several years, Holden focused on his career. He still auditioned for parts, even begging for a chance to be on a sitcom.

But then he began going in a different direction. He started to produce and direct some small projects, keeping himself out of the spotlight. It was during this work that he befriended a man who insisted he could fix him, make him resemble that young man he had been all those years ago. And Holden listened, transfixed with the thought of being that man again.

Because this work was good. He was talented in this area. But he craved that spotlight. He needed to be adored and sought after.

It was an extensive surgery, and it took him weeks to recover. But the ending result was that it had aged him another five years and deformed his features even more. Now the lower half of his face resembled a skeleton with his teeth sticking out.

Somehow the media got wind of the story and published his picture alongside one from his early years. People went crazy. To see a man they had known as one of the most beautiful people on the television now look as if he had been disfigured by a horrible accident simply fascinated them.

So Holden let go of the idea of reversing the damage and aging. This was who he was. No longer that young, dazzling man that had left so many speechless. Somehow the peak of his life had slipped past him before he even had a chance to truly grasp it.

Holden was a bit lonely, never learning how to be in a give-and-take relationship. Holden had learned to be adored, and he found it difficult to let go of that particular ideal. So, he threw himself even more into creating and directing.

After a full day of shooting, Holden stopped at a farmer's market. As he tried to choose the best eggplant, someone caught his eye. That hair…and when she turned, he gasped. Because those eyes, those vivid blue eyes cut into his soul, and for a few moments, stole his breath.

"Cora," he whispered, stepping back as she spun around. There was no mistaking it was Cora; she had not aged one bit. In fact, she was stunning. She glowed, her cheeks rosy, her scarlet lips swollen, her eyes round and bright. She had not been this striking when he had known her. "Wow. You look… Cora, you look amazing."

She smiled and tilted her head. "Why, thank you…. Um, I'm sorry. Who are you?"

It was a strike to his ego. But he smiled anyways. "It's Holden. Holden Letcher. We worked on Something

Good back…oh, years ago. We…we dated briefly."

Recognition mixed with shock coloured her cheeks even more before she composed herself and nodded. "Of course. How are you?"

"Not as good as you. Man, you look amazing. Like you haven't aged a day. I have to ask, who is your doctor. Because," Holden gestured toward his face, "I've had a hell of a time trying to get anyone halfway decent."

Something in her eyes shifted, and he tried to remember something nipping at his subconscious. Cora tilted her chin up. "I really have to go. I'm sorry. Good seeing you…"

She set down the basket in her hands and rushed away. It was only when she was out the door that Holden remembered. It hit him smack in the face with the force of a brick, and he reared back in the realisation of everything.

"Cora! Cora, wait." He jogged up to her as she stood there with her back to him. Gently, he clasped her shoulder and turned her toward him. "You're the reason, right?"

Slowly she nodded. "Yes."

"My career sank before it began. I always thought it was something I did—"

"Wait. What?" She shook her head, her smooth, silky

hair flying around her face. "No. I never touched your career. That you tanked on your own. Your damn behaviour. Don't blame that on me."

"But you said…when we were together, you said you had powers."

"I'm a caster. Emotions get out of control, and things are cast. But it wasn't your career."

"Then…what?"

"The thing you're most proud of. What is that?"

"My career!" he argued emphatically.

"No. Not even close. You assumed you would have a lasting career because of…"

And he cried out. It was even worse than he had imagined. "My looks. You…this was…this was why they could never do even a simple procedure."

Cora nodded solemnly. "Right. Every time you went to fix or improve, it would age you five years and add a disfiguring feature. And it would give me five years back on my appearance. So, I look young because…because you kept going back."

Holden glared at her, his jaw clenched. "Then undo it! You had years of fun at my expense. Years to get over this grudge."

"Holden. I'm not a witch. I didn't cast a spell. My emotions got the best of me and set this in motion. I can't undo it."

"You're disgusting."

"Careful," Cora sang out. "It still happens."

"You had nothing to do with this. Your emotions set this in motion, but you're not making out too shabby. Look at you."

She scoffed. "You think I like looking like a damn teenager? Huh? You think I like that I'm not taken seriously in my field of biochemistry? I never wanted this. I wanted decency from you. I gave you an out. And you still had to be such a jerk. So yeah. This is how it is now."

As she stormed off, Holden watched, remembering those days his face lit up people's worlds. When he was in demand. He had been so sure about everything—his talent, his youth, his looks. He had never considered they would someday be non-existent. He had not planned for that.

Holden went back to work, as always trying to salvage something of his career. Of his pride.

by Luis Manuel Torres

Luke Russo was supposed to be the heir to the Italian mafia in Boston. There was one major problem though; he was in love with the rival family's daughter. Her name was Claire Saint. Their love for each other was mutual, but they had a duty to their families. They were the future of their family and weren't allowed to be together. The Russos were currently on top, but the Saints could easily dethrone them. A present day Romeo and Juliet story, and the perfect mortals for Ares and Aphrodite's little bet.

Ares told his sister, Aphrodite, that mortal's care more about power and legacy than love. Aphrodite said there was nothing stronger than the love she can make mortals feel. She was going to have them give up everything for each other. Ares, on the other hand, would get them to choose pride over love. Ares and Aphrodite would play the roles of angel and devil on their shoulders.

Luke was driving Claire out of town to a club named The Tunnel for a night of fun. They needed some time away from all of their family drama. He parked outside of the club. "It's looks like an actual tunnel," said Luke.

"Where did you hear about this place?"

"Lisa told me about it," she answered. "This is my first time here. Looks cool, right?"

"It's definitely different." The two of them got out of the vehicle and made their way inside, Claire wrapping her arm around his. "Does Lisa come here often?"

"I think so. She's been trying to get me to come out with her for a while now."

Inside the club was what you'd expect from a place called The Tunnel. It was a long hallway with small booths on both sides. Half way down the hall was the bar. The pop music wasn't too loud, which was a relief to Luke because he would be able to hear Claire.

"I thought this place was a dance club not just a lounge," said Luke as they were making their way to the bar.

"There's supposed to be a dancefloor somewhere," said Claire.

From a booth, someone grabbed Claire's hand as she passed by. It was Lisa, who stood up and gave her a hug. "You made it," she said, a big smile on her face.

Luke saw she was sitting with a couple. Lisa came up to Luke and gave him a kiss on the cheek. "Hi Lisa."

"I'm glad you came," said Lisa. "These are my friends, Alex and Jennifer."

Jennifer waved hello while Luke and Alex shook hands.

Lisa sat down bringing Claire with her. "Sit," she said. "Join us."

Luke sat down next to Alex while the girls sat across.

"It's about time you two joined us."

"It's a bit of a drive," said Luke. "I'm used to going to clubs closer to home."

"Going to the same spot can get old," said Alex. "It's good to change things up."

"I don't know. A club is a club. The only difference I can really think of are the people who go to them."

"How about the music?" asked Jennifer as the music changed to reggae.

"I hear the same songs in every club I go to. Not much of a difference there."

"You don't find this place a little different?" asked Lisa.

"More than a little," he said, scanning around. "This is more like a bar with a railroad theme. I wouldn't actually call it a club."

"The club part is upstairs," said Alex.

"So, there is an upstairs," said Claire.

"Yup," said Lisa as she held Claire tightly and leaned her head on her shoulder. "And it's about three times bigger than down here."

A waiter stopped at their booth and took their orders. The girls talked amongst themselves while Luke was lost in thought. There was a voice in Luke's head telling him not to trust Alex. Luke thought it was his instincts, but it was a more powerful being.

You don't like this guy, said Ares from inside of Luke's head.

"See someone you don't like?" asked Alex.

"No. Why do you ask?"

"You seem angry."

Yeah, you, said Ares.

"*Don't be that way,*" said Aphrodite, unbeknownst to Luke. *You don't really know him.*

"It's nothing. This is just my face."

The waiter brought everyone their drinks, and they were glad to officially start their night. Luke watched as Lisa held Claire tight in an embrace, both girls happy to see each other. *You don't know how you feel about their relationship*, said Ares. Luke had to look away, not wanting to give away his disapproval.

"Is there something wrong?" asked Claire, putting her hand over his.

"I'm good," said Luke. He noticed Alex gave him a weird look before he turned away.

What's he looking at?

"Are we ready to go upstairs?" asked Jennifer.

"Let's go," said Claire.

The girls were the first to stand, followed by Luke, then Alex. Alex went to Jennifer, putting his arm around her. Claire put her arm around Luke, looking up at him.

She's so beautiful, said Aphrodite. Luke couldn't help but smile.

"That's better," said Claire, giving him a kiss. "I like it when you smile."

"Sorry if I seem angry. I have a lot on my mind."

"The families?"

"Yeah."

"Well don't think about that. Tonight is about having fun." She pulled Luke along as the group went up. "Wow," she said as she saw the second floor. "It's so big."

"Nice isn't it," said Lisa.

"Now this looks more like a club," said Luke.

"It gets bigger," said Lisa. "Follow us." Lisa walked behind Alex and Jennifer.

Luke and Claire followed Lisa, Claire putting a hand on her shoulder to keep up with her through the crowd. They walked down the hall into a second room which was a lot bigger than the rest of the club. The second room had a huge bar in the middle which was crowded by customers getting drinks.

"This is better," said Luke.

The group continued to walk past the bar and into the last room; the dancefloor. Music was extra loud. It was crowded with men, outnumbering the women two to one. Alex and Jennifer continued to walk through the crowd until they reached a table in the back of the room. Lisa and Jennifer sat, while Alex, Luke, and Claire stood around them.

Claire leaned back on Luke and kissed him on the cheek.

What a wonderful girl, said Aphrodite.

Lisa stood and grabbed Claire and Luke's hands, leading them to the dancefloor. Lisa was the first one to start dancing as she held Claire's hand. It didn't take long for Claire to dance along. Next person to join them was Jennifer, while Alex stayed behind at the table. Luke was about to go back to the table but chose not to due to Alex.

Luke saw how much fun the girls were having and wanted to join them. Problem was, he needed a couple more drinks to loosen up. Luke downed the rest of his beer and leaned close to Claire's ear. "I'm going to get another drink," he said. "Want anything?"

"I'll take another one," she said, and finished her drink, handing him the empty cup.

Luke was struggling to get through the crowd as someone bumped him. *"Watch it,"* said Ares.

Someone put a hand on Luke's shoulder from behind. Luke turned and saw Alex who said something he couldn't hear. Alex walked right past Luke and squeezed through the crowd. Luke took the opportunity to follow. The two made it out of the dancefloor and were on their way to the bar.

"What did you say?" asked Luke.

Jackass, finished Ares.

"I said you have to be aggressive if you want to get through," answered Alex. "People seem to make way for you if they see you walking with purpose."

"I'll remember that," said Luke as they reached the bar.

Alex waved the bartender over and turned to Luke. "Same as before?"

"Yeah."

This guy isn't so bad, said Aphrodite.

Alex made the order and turned to face Luke. "So, what's your problem with me?"

Or he's the asshole you think he is, said Ares.

"What do you mean?"

"Your girl noticed something wrong, so your attitude changed when you saw me. So, my question is…what did

I do to piss you off?"

Who does this guy think he is?

"Nothing."

"Are you sure, because you look really pissed right now."

"Maybe that has something to do with this conversation."

Give the guy a break, said Aphrodite.

"You had a problem with me the moment you saw me. This conversation might not be helping my case, but you made up your mind about me the minute we met." The bartender brought them their drinks.

"I don't know you. I have no opinion of you. Well I didn't."

"So, you have an opinion now?"

"Yeah. It's not good."

"It's because I'm Hispanic."

It's always the same thing with these guys.

"It's because you're annoying. I didn't even know you were Hispanic."

"Bull. You gave me a dirty look the moment you saw me."

"Drop it," said Luke as he grabbed the drinks and walked off.

He got to the dancefloor and again struggled to get

through. He walked with more confidence and could see the girls dancing as he made his way to them. Just as he almost reached Claire, a guy bumped into him, causing her drink to spill.

Damn it!

Luke turned around to see the same guy who bumped him earlier walking off. Luke shoved him as Alex watched. The guy turned around.

"You spilled my drink," yelled Luke.

The guy ignored Luke and turned his back on him.

Don't let him get away.

Luke grabbed the guy by the arm only to be shrugged off. Luke moved forward and grabbed him. "You spilled my drink," he repeated, only to be pushed away.

Now that's it, said Ares, and Luke threw the first punch.

Luke hit the man square in the eye, backing him up into the crowd. Another man came up behind Luke and shoved him. Luke turned around and punched him straight in the jaw, knocking him out. The first guy tackled Luke as the crowd circled around. They were able to trade a few punches before the bouncers got their hands on them. It took four bouncers to get Luke and the guy outside. They took Luke out a different door.

"Get out of here," said the bouncer, shoving Luke

forward.

"My girl is still inside."

"If she cares about you, she'll be out here any minute. If she's smart, she'll leave you now."

What did he just say?

"Careful," said Luke.

"Or what? You going to," the bouncer took a punch to the mouth before he could finish his sentence.

The bouncer swung at Luke, but he ducked and countered, punching him in the jaw. The bouncer went down to a knee. One bouncer went to the other's aid while a second bouncer confronted Luke.

Bring it on, said Ares as Luke gestured the same.

"Luke," yelled Claire. He hadn't noticed he was outside. She was standing next to her friends.

Luke heard the police sirens nearing, so he went to Claire and they ran. They got in his car and took off into the street. The two of them sat in silence for a couple of minutes, Luke deep in thought.

Was that necessary, said Aphrodite.

Of course it was, said Ares.

What must Claire think?

That I'm a Russo and must be treated with respect. She's part of the Saint family. Same rules apply. She'll understand.

Will she?

Of course she will.

"What happened?" Claire finally asked, breaking the silence.

"Some asshole decided to pick a fight instead of apologise," answered Luke.

"And the bouncer?"

"Another asshole, but let's not talk about that."

Claire noticed a mark on Luke's cheek. "They hurt you."

"It's nothing," he said as he continued to drive.

You must've embarrassed her, said Aphrodite.

"What's wrong?" asked Claire.

"I don't know."

She grabbed his hand. "What do you mean you don't know?"

"I was in a bad mood and some idiot bumped me."

"You got into a fight because someone bumped into you?"

"He spilled your drink and didn't apologise."

"So, you hit him?"

"Basically."

"That's not a reason to hit someone."

Luke hesitated. "Yeah. Like I said, bad mood."

"This isn't like you. You should've said something.

We could have left."

"It didn't cross my mind."

"I should have noticed," she said. "I knew there was something wrong but—"

"But nothing. That's not your responsibility. I'm sorry. I should've controlled myself."

What are you saying, said Ares. *It's her fault for putting you in that situation.*

Luke was frowning. Claire reached out to touch his cheek, but he flinched. "You're still mad," she said.

Oh, just leave it alone woman.

"It's our families isn't it," said Claire. "That's what has you in such a bad mood."

No, it was your stupid friends, but now that you mention it, our families are a problem too.

"Our families are a problem," said Luke.

"Their problems shouldn't be ours."

"But they are, and we can't ignore them."

"What are you suggesting?" asked Claire. "You want to break up?"

Of course not, said Aphrodite.

"Of course not," repeated Luke. "But it's not something we can ignore for much longer. Your father wants me dead."

"Actually, he wants your father dead. Mostly just

your father.”

Luke let out a bit of a laugh.

Claire smiled. “That’s better.”

Luke’s smile went away. “Don’t tease me.”

“I’m not teasing.”

Luke pulled up into the Red Inn’s parking lot where he and Claire had met earlier so their families wouldn’t know. He pulled up right next to her car. “It’s time for you to go home,” said Luke.

“You don’t want to spend the night together?” asked Claire, shocked.

“Not tonight.”

“Wow. Hadn’t realised how bad of a mood you were in.”

She’s mocking you, said Ares.

“Go home Claire.”

“Not like this.”

She defies you.

“We need to talk about this,” said Claire.

She loves you, said Aphrodite.

She’s using you, said Ares. *Don’t trust her. She’s a Saint.*

No, she loves you in spite of being a Saint.

If she loves you, why put you through tonight? She set you up. She introduced you to Alex to make you jealous.

No, you're being paranoid. She's only shown you love and respect.

If she's only shown you love and respect, then why'd she make you go out with that friend of hers?

Lisa's not so bad, besides, you probably have friends Claire doesn't approve of and she puts up with them.

Yeah, but how often do you actually spend time with your friends. When you're with Claire, you usually hangout with her friends, not yours.

"What's on your mind?" asked Claire.

"I don't like Alex," he said.

"That's random."

"I don't care for Lisa either."

Claire didn't seem to know how to react, choosing to stay quiet.

See, said Ares. *Her silence gives away her true allegiance.*

"I didn't know that," she finally said. "About Lisa. I could tell you didn't like Alex, but what could I have done about that. It was my first time meeting him too."

See, you're being paranoid, said Aphrodite. *She wasn't trying to make you jealous.*

"Never noticed you didn't like Lisa."

Because you didn't have a problem with her before

today, said Aphrodite.

"Are you okay?" she asked.

"I have a headache," he said, rubbing his forehead.

"That explains your mood."

My mood is due to her friends and family, said Ares.

"My headache is due to everything, not the other way around."

"Everything?"

"This isn't going to work," said Luke.

"Are you breaking up with me?"

No, said Aphrodite.

Yes, said Ares.

You can't.

You can. You have to.

No, you don't. You love her.

You love your family. Family comes first.

She could be family.

Luke closed his eyes as he rubbed his head. Claire got out of the car.

So that's it, said Ares. *Good riddance. It was never going to work. A Russo and a Saint.*

The door opened and Claire sat back down, surprising Luke. She had a bottle of aspirin in her hands as she picked out a pill and handed it to him. "Here, take this," she said. "It'll help with the headache." She passed him a bottle of water and he took the medication.

"Thank you."

See, that's love, said Aphrodite. *And you love her. She's more important than a family feud.*

"I'm sorry," said Luke. "Something in my mind was telling me I had to choose between you and my family, but I just realised it isn't really a hard choice." Luke was looking straight ahead. "I love you. Screw my family."

"And that's why you were never going to work. I'm the smartest, strongest and cleverest person you know. Just like the rest of my family. Saints were always meant to rule."

"What?" Luke turned just in time to see the gun fire.

"You lost, Sis," said Ares. "You thought the boy was the only one conflicted when it was the girl you had to worry about."

"That was a cheap win."

"Ambition was going to win in the end. There was always going to be war."

"You underestimate love."

"Never," said Ares. "Love is a powerful emotion. I just know how to use it to my advantage. Like love for one's family."

"I think you're confusing love with pride."

"They go hand in hand. There's no pride without love. Claire's love for her family led to her pride and my victory."

The Artist and the Magician

by Robert Bagnall

"The problem with conceptual art is just that: it's all in the concept, not in the execution," said the artist. He leaned forward in the scroll wingback Chesterfield armchair towards the crackling fire, waving his tumbler of vodka conspiratorially at the magician. "When Marcel Duchamp exhibited a urinal in 1917 and called it art, that was the art: the concept that a urinal could be art. You can fake the Mona Lisa, but you can't fake a urinal because how do you fake a concept?" He sat back. "Conceptual art has no technique."

The magician considered for a moment. "Neither does magic."

"Rubbish. It's *all* technique."

The magician shook his head. "You are confusing magic with illusion. Illusionists are performers, actors playing the role of magicians. It's a worthy profession, but it's not magic."

"So, what's magic if not illusion?" scoffed the artist.

"Well, didn't somebody say that any sufficiently advanced technology is indistinguishable from magic? Take these vodka tumblers." The magician held his up to the light. "Imperceptible nanobots on the surface of the glass change the cheap grain spirit at a molecular level imparting it with quality and taste. Purple tumbler for cranberry, pale yellow for peach…"

"…and the white ones denature the alcohol altogether without any adverse change to the flavour." The artist sounded impatient. "That's science, not magic. They're also eight hundred dollars a glass—I had to leave them rights to my organs as a deposit, bloody Koreans—so please be careful."

At that, the magician placed a hand over the artist's glass, covering it with his palm. And pressed. The thick glass tumbler sitting on a thick glass table somehow melted into nothing. The magician turned his hand over to confirm that the glass was gone.

"Magic," he explained. "It has no technique. It just *is*."

"I'm very impressed," the artist said, almost managing sincerity. "Now can I have the glass back?"

The magician wagged a finger. "The glass has disappeared. It is gone. To another plane of reality."

The artist scratched his head. He didn't like jokes.

"Come on, give it up. That's my spleen you've just sacrificed, you know."

The magician shrugged, an enigmatic smile playing across his lips. "It has become energy and dissipated."

"Eight hundred bucks," the artist complained. "I didn't read the small print; I only assume they have it after my death." He was building up to a sense of humor failure.

Having played the joke up to, but not beyond, the limits of decency, the magician reached behind the artist's ear and, as if from the ether, revealed the glass, intact, vodka unspilt.

"Illusion," spat the artist, mock accusatory. He studied the contents of the glass skeptically.

"Maybe," agreed the magician, "but I could have made it *really* disappear. And I would have found it easier. Because true magic has no technique."

The eyes of the artist narrowed. "BS," he spelt out.

"No. Really. I could make anything disappear, send you to a place without time and space. I could make you levitate. I could make you return to the past. I can stretch spacetime itself. There are not too many of us left. The true magicians."

The artist shifted uncomfortably. He'd met fanatics before. One second, they're lucid, rational; the next it's all tinfoil hats. "You know," he said, suddenly placatory, "we're not that different, you and me."

"How so?"

"We both deal in illusion. Nothing an artist does is real. It's all representation, whatever your school is. When I paint a tree it's not a tree, it's a painting of a tree. Just as everything you do is show."

The magician ran his fingers through his beard, considering the argument. The artist really wasn't getting it, not getting it at all.

"So, what would the artist do if he could make use of true magic? What would *you* do?"

The artist smirked. "Levitate. Stretch time and space. Send me back into history. What were the other things?"

"Send you to a place beyond place, a parallel existence."

"Do it, do it now," the artist exclaimed with mock urgency, and leant back in his armchair, roaring with mirth.

"I just want to know what you, the great artist, would do with the opportunity."

"I used to like shouting."

"Shouting?"

The magician was taking him deadly seriously. The artist almost had to bite a lip to stop himself crying with laughter.

"Yeah, shouting. When we were students. You know, 'happenings'. We'd get a megaphone, stand on a platform and shout things. Peggy Satchell used to laser words on to buildings and call it a manifesto, but I preferred the shouting."

The magician placed his fingertips together. He'd expected a response somewhat more respectful, even if he knew it would be disbelieving. "And this is what you'd do?"

"Oh, I'd give anything," the artist said, trying to hold back tears of mirth, his chest heaving.

"To shout?"

"Yeah, shout. A few names, numbers, random things. Slogans. Quotations from the Cabaret Voltaire. Maybe throw some noise in there just to confuse. Confusion focuses the mind, you know."

Lost in thought, the magician said, as much to himself, "Yes…shouts from the astral plane…echoes in the ether…earthbound, but not earthbound…detectable to those with the means of detection but invisible, always beyond reach…distorted, like white noise, electronica, feedback…"

When he opened his eyes all was silent, the armchair opposite was empty. The artist had gone.

He wondered whether he should bring him back. He could drag him from beyond reality right now, after the artist had been away for an hour, or a day, or a year. He could return him to his seat and his vodka, finessed courtesy of nanobots, and see what an eternity of looking into the abyss whilst being compelled to scream did to a person.

"Nah," said the magician to himself as, cat-like, he snuggled into the padded leather and raised his tumbler to the vacant seat opposite, still indented and warm where the artist had been seated. "Well, at least there's no chance of the Koreans getting hold of your spleen now."

Never Seen

by Kelly Matsuura

Today is my turn. Cool ocean waves set a rhythm for the *Trong Com* drummers and temple singers. I walk along the shadowed beach; strips of coloured sunset on my left and the cheering smiles of well-wishers on my right. They clap for me, but they also form a wall that stops me running away into the dark jungle.

I am cloaked from head to toe in bright silks, the colours chosen to celebrate my imminent transformation and to represent our hidden kingdom. I am cloaked in these silks, but also in magic. From the day I was born, I was one of the nominated maidens, destined to bond with the king and become one of his mages.

The spell that makes us what we are can only be broken by King Amnuay himself. Our pure beauty is veiled; no other man ever sees the glint of the sun on our hematite hair, or feels the soft texture of our skin, likened to that of polished pearls. They don't see the real colour of our eyes; the spell blackens the irises on us all until the night of our awakening. My own eyes are the green of a papaya leaf; bright, sharp and strong. I don't look away from anyone.

He feeds. On my body, my energy, my beauty. At first, I feel only the pull of his hunger, draining my essence deep from within my core, taking a source of my power I never knew was there until it is suddenly gone. He takes it all, and I want to die here in his bed; in this moment I am nothing without my inner light. I have nothing to live for. But as I see the end and clamour for peace, his power reverses and I am flooded with new energy; not the beautiful light I had been born with, but deeper awareness and strength. This, I know, is the magic of the *Co Tai* Ancients and will now be mine for eternity.

I will never marry, nor have children, but I will be revered as a visionary and powerful mage. I will learn the spells of my ancestors and call the mists to protect our island and kingdom. From tomorrow, I take my place with The Twelve and begin my service to the king in my new form.

We are destined to be loved only once in our lives; the act of joining our bodies with the king is our final celebration of beauty. We are butterflies in reverse. In the height of beauty our wings are plucked bare, leaving us only ugly, withered forms of dead colour.

I hesitate to view myself in the looking glass, but King Amnuay urges me from behind.

"Look. You think you have lost your beauty, your youth, but see what you have gained tonight."

I open my eyes. I see what I knew I would: a seventy-year-old woman who has lived a full life. I imagine for a moment she has raised her children and cared for her grandchildren and slept each night beside a loving man. She smiles, and her eyes hold mine, strong green irises that won't let me look away. The woman is me now; I absorb this reality and raise a hand to my now-white hair. I look so old, but don't feel it. I have strength, wisdom, awareness. My senses are heightened; I quiver from the king's breath on my shoulder, I hear the cuckoos stir in their nests far off in the jungle. I smell our mingled perfumes and the scent of fresh rain in the air. It both overwhelms and invigorates me to test the new depths of these senses.

He sweeps my long locks back over my shoulder with a gentle touch. He, I notice, glows with more vitality and beauty. *My* beauty. I see it clearly; no different to if he had scalped me and wore my hair as his own.

"You have fulfilled your destiny, Chaiama. Be proud. Love your new self. Regret not the years you perceive you have lost, for you will have them back tenfold," King Amnuay whispers in my ear.

"Why?" I whisper back. A tear escapes as I open my robe and view my full nakedness. "Why take our beauty? Our youth?"

"The Twelve must protect our treasured land and magical people. They must not be distracted by earthly wants and notions of love or physical connections. You have had this one experience tonight, so that you know it is nothing to give up, and that you have gained so much more than you have lost. You will not hunger for a man's touch; you will only hunger for knowledge and skill. To use your power to the fullest and achieve the impossible. A young woman living in our jungle home has only her beauty to be admired. A wise crone has the world in her hands and can cross to realms unseen by commoners."

I nod and bite my lip. I know he is right, but I need a moment to grieve my youth.

He leaves then, and I sleep the day away. Tears fall around my head, nourishing my hair but emptying my heart.

The silks of yesterday are gone. I'm given a simple

woven gown of hemp to wear for the rest of my days. I leave the jungle palace filled with cheerful animals, flowers, and aromas and am taken to the inland caves where The Twelve reside in secret.

Young maiden of beauty no more, I join the circle of crones. I hold their wrinkled and shrunken hands and drink the awakening potions they serve me. They sing, not quite the melodic chant of the monks last evening, but a warm, enveloping sound that tells me I'm accepted as their sister.

We never speak of our lost allurement or envied traits—we are now all the same. Mothers of the new people, advisors to the king, and high mages of the fae lands.

Filtering

by Nicola Currie

"Happy Rebirthday!"

My family cheer my arrival as I enter the living room. It is appropriately decorated, with more silver and gold than usual. The table is laid with shining gold platters, bronze goblets, jewelled cutlery. The regular platinum and crystal chandelier, the glinting constellation about our dining room for as long as I can recall, has been upgraded for the day with swags of amethyst and diamond. My gifts, wrapped in gold leaf and ribboned with strings of pearl, take up the whole of the far wall. Together, they create a gorgeous mirror that reflects a golden version of me back to myself. She smiles too. It is strange that this will be the last time I see her.

Mother rings the bell for Medusa as we take our seats at the table.

"How excited you must be, my darling. I remember how I felt on my rebirthday, when I saw myself for the first time. It is wonderful, to truly know you are beautiful. And I only had an average 98.6% pre-birth advantage, with a 98.4% adherence after my filtering. A total 197 is good enough for little old me. But you, Lustre. You could really be special."

My mother grins her gorgeous grin and her violet eyes sparkle like gemstones, further brightening her flawless face.

"Thank you, Mother. I know I will make you proud." The light in her eyes falters as I hit her with my own radiant smile. I smirk inwardly. We love each other, of course, but it has always been there, that little shard of jealously, that wish that she could be as beautiful as me.

"Do you really think Lustre will have a shot at being a Perfect 200, Dad?" Duke asks.

My little brother can be stupid. He is only a 96 out of 100, with four years to go before his filtering can take him to a 196 at best, the lowest the family will have seen since great-great grandpa's generation. It should be enough, above the 190 minimum, but he would struggle to maintain a truly elite life if not for the rest of us. With Father at 198.5 post-filter and myself at a Perfect pre-filtered 100, Duke's lucky place in our family is enough to reassure any future bride that his 4% below perfect pre-filtered appearance was nothing more than an unfortunate fluke, with the family genes strong enough to ensure Winner offspring.

Still, whenever I see the tiny mole on his left earlobe,

I want to vomit. I used to blush whenever I had to walk with him in public, until I realised my beauty was enough to make up for his imperfection.

Although pre-birth genetic improvement has been used for beauty for centuries now, there are still only around 20 Perfects born every year. We are the valedictorians, the prom queens, the captains. We become CEOs, film stars, presidents. Perfection is my destiny.

Medusa and the other servants enter, carrying the first of the rebirthday feasts. Soon, the table is heaving with pastries, smoked fish, imported cheeses and fine champagne. The first rebirthday cake is a six-tiered caramel beauty, topped with a golden peacock.

An hour later, when we have feasted as much as we can, Medusa collects the remains of the partially-demolished cake. She knows to keep her eyes lowered as we take our ThinPills, that destroy all excess calories so we can continue feasting throughout the day without bloating our perfect bodies. I glance at Medusa and smirk at my family. They smirk back, sharing the same thought. It's a shame Medusa isn't allowed to take ThinPills, like the rest of the Losers. She looks at least five pounds overweight.

"Give the leftovers to the dogs," I say. "You and the other servants are starting to look like pigs."

Medusa nods. As she lifts the remains of the cake, the tiers start to wobble. Before I can protect myself, they collapse on top of me, besmirching the gloss of my jet black hair, ruining the gold slip dress that shows my sexy yet elegant form. My family leap up to fuss around me. As I pull chunks of cake from my cleavage, Medusa really goes too far. As she panics and apologises, she dares to look at me.

I shudder with revulsion. Medusa is merely a 92, and that is all she will ever be. Any Loser, anyone born with anything below a 95% perfect appearance, lives to serve the Winner class and is ineligible for filtering when they reach eighteen. Every Winner goes through it, to ensure the beauty we are born with is taken to its full potential by the final enhancements the filtering gives once we are grown. The success of filtering is measured by adherence, how perfectly the final improvements take. It will be 100% for me. I know it will. I will be a Perfect 200. I will be a goddess.

A goddess who shouldn't be stared at by one as imperfect as Medusa. Her mismatched eyes—one sapphire blue, one emerald green—should be lowered. That has been the rule since we agreed to take her. Anyone born with a below 80% appearance automatically goes to the Outlands, far away where we never have to see them, to join their fellow monsters and produce resources for Winner cities. But anyone between 80-95% is raised in the city workhouses until they are ten and then may be allowed to stay in the cities as servants, if they can find a family who will tolerate their ugliness. Medusa has shiny golden hair and moves with elegance. My parents are kind enough to employ her, on the condition she keeps her mismatched eyes fixed on the ground. Looking at them makes us all sick. It's why I named her Medusa.

"How dare you!" my brother roars.

"After all we have done for you!" Mother slaps her. "Ungrateful, deformed Loser!"

"You," Father says, calling through the door to another servant, "Fetch a guard. This one is to be transported this minute. I won't have this hideous creature in my house a moment longer."

"No, please!" Medusa says, covering her eyes. "I'm sorry. Please forgive me. I can't be transported to the Outlands. They'll work me to death!"

"Good!" Mother says, her red lips spitting. "Ask them to close your eyes when you die. The least you can do is make a pretty corpse."

Medusa sobs as city guards drag her away. I smirk and wave goodbye. It feels like a good omen. Today is about filtering out any trace of imperfection, after all.

The Filtering Centre is the shining sun at the centre of our city. Its towering bronze walls glint in the daylight and today it seems like it is beckoning to me, like gold waiting at the end of a rainbow.

As I step out of the car, I am greeted by the sequin flashes of a hundred cameras. A Perfect's filtering always attracts media attention. They're looking to scoop the story of the world's first 200. I watched the news nervously a month ago, as another Perfect from the other side of the country, a girl called Majesty, appeared on the balcony of her centre after her filtering. The media spoke for days about how beautiful she was, and she only had a 99.8 adherence, a whole 0.2% shy of a perfect 200. She lapped up the praise but I could see the disappointment in her eyes. *Sorry bitch*, I had thought smugly, *that 200 is mine.*

I pull the fur stole from my shoulders and puff out my chest. It seems the incident with the cake has worked to my advantage. The tight, flesh-coloured leather dress I changed into enhances every one of my curves, displays the warm honey of my skin. I can almost feel the air shift with the prod of a thousand simultaneous erections as I strut past into the centre, my family following behind.

The centre staff have gathered to greet me, the VIP. The Centre Director, Dapper Godson, kisses my hand. Perfects get a home visit before their filtering so we have met before.

"Lustre," he says, his eyes running up and down my body. "You're a vision. We are truly honoured to have you here."

I giggle as everyone applauds.

"Good luck, Sis." Duke says, absent-mindedly brushing his hair behind his ears. I immediately gag at the sight of his gross mole.

"Cover your ear, freak!" I hiss.

Duke moves his hair back. "Sorry," he says, his face reddening. His voice is tight and resentful but I don't care. He needs to understand his place.

"I am so proud of you," my father says, tears in his eyes.

"We'll see you after," my mother says. She kisses me and I know she means it, but I can still feel it tingle with that edge of jealousy. She'll have to get used to her place too.

Dapper leads me to a filtering lab. A technician sits at a control station. A screen covers the wall and a raised stage fills the centre of the room. On it, a long glass tube disappears into the ceiling. It is just the right size to hold one person.

But first, the technician gestures to a metal frame. "Step through here. It is up to you, but it works better if you undress."

"I'll give you some privacy," Dapper says.

"No, stay." I reach for my zipper. I shimmy out of my dress and watch his face as he sees me in my semi-sheer underwear. "I'm not shy."

He swallows. He is silent but the glint in his eye and the pulse jumping at his throat shows me the effect I have had on him. Soon, every man will be at my mercy like this. Hell, most women too.

Bars of light appear across the frame and ripple over me as I step through. Images of random parts of my body—my kneecaps, my nostrils, my hipbones—flicker across the screen as the system calculates. Less than a minute passes before three boxes of data appear.

"Let's see," the technician says. "Option 1 looks good. About sixty micro-enhancements, including minor adjustments to the nostrils, a slight curvature to the hips. This would give a minimum adherence of 98.8 and a maximum of 99.6 with no risk factors. An excellent choice, safe but beautifully effective."

"No way," I say. "99.6 is not good enough."

"Well, option 2 could give you a result as high as

99.9 and a minimum of 99 flat. It does have a 1 in 20 billion error risk, however. You should consider that."

Of course, I have heard about filtering going wrong. It is the basis of every horror story at every childhood sleepover. It is theoretically possible to get less than a 95% adherence. I know it is something my parents worry about for Duke. As a 96er pre-filtered, if he gets less than a 95% adherence at his filtering, he won't fit in socially. He'll have to live with Mum and Dad forever, shut away with whatever luxury they can afford him. Of course, that won't happen, not even to Duke. The science is so developed now, the risks so minimal. The chances of things going wrong are pretty much impossible.

Besides, I have already seen the Perfect 200 blinking from the screen.

The technician smiles and Dapper whoops as they clock it too. "And option 3 would give you minimum adherence of 99.9 with a high probability of a perfect 100. Either way, that would make you the most perfect person in the world."

"Then Option 3 it is!" I walk towards the filtering tube and get inside.

"Wait… The risk factor for option 3 is higher than any I've ever seen. There's a 1 in 10,000 chance the filtering process will fail. That could mean it slips a couple of percent.”

“Option 3,” I say firmly. “I’m a Winner, through and through. There is a reason no one else has got a double Perfect until now. It’s because it is meant to be me. It is my destiny.”

The technician nods and I hear the filter whirr to life. The door closes and the floor begins to vibrate. For a split second, the tube fills with blinding light that burns through my bones. Then the door opens and I step out. Perfect.

The technician takes one look at me and faints. I must be magnificent.

“Oh god!” Dapper screams.

I turn to see the look of lust on his face but instead see a look of revulsion. His hand clasps his mouth as he gags.

“Get it out of here!” he yells into the corridor. “Get it out!”

There is more screaming as more technicians rush into the room.

What is happening? I try to look down at my body but they throw a sheet over me and bundled me down a corridor into a small room. As the door slams shut, I realise it is a cell.

I pull the sheet off as my mother enters and screams

too. She tries to close the door behind her.

"No, darling, don't look! Duke, stay away!" The horror on her face is mingled with the smallest touch of victory, just clinging to a corner of upturned lip.

But it is no use. My father and brother rush into the room. Their faces blanch.

"What the hell is going on?" I shout.

"My god," my father says, different tears welling in his eyes now. "They haven't told you."

"Told me what?" I ask.

He says nothing but leaves the room. My mother clutches my brother to her, as though she is afraid for him to get too close to me.

My father returns with two technicians. They look at the ground as they place a mirror against the wall and leave quickly.

"Look for yourself," my father spits. "See what you have done." My family huddle together as I step towards the mirror. I do not recognise the person I see.

"No!" I say. "I'm Perfect. I'm Perfect!"

The person in the mirror is hideous. Her skin is blotchy. Her flabby belly hangs over her underwear. Her shrivelled breasts swim in loose fabric. Her nose is crooked, her hair greasy. Her nostrils are too big and flare when she breathes. Her small eyes are dull and bloodshot.

She—I—am ugly.

"What are we supposed to do with you now?" my mother hisses.

"They have to reverse it! I'll stay here as long as it takes!"

"That's impossible," Father says in the voice he uses for servants. "Besides, the Director has ordered you out of this centre immediately. We have ten minutes to decide what to do with you or he will load you onto the next bus to the Outlands himself."

My whole body shudders. "I'll have to stay home then, until somebody can find a cure. Pay them, Daddy. Pay them to find a cure." I move towards him and reach out. Mother and Duke scream and cower. Dad steps in front of them and pushes me away.

"Stay back!" he says. "Don't you understand? You're a monster. The filtering actually had a negative effect. You're barely a 50 now. Half a percent lower and you'd be facing execution for the crime of ugliness. You can't come home. We'd be shunned. And Duke's prospects would be ruined. I'm sorry, Lustre..." My father pauses. I understand. My name is so ironic now, dull as I am.

I burst into tears. This can't be happening. I'm beautiful, the most beautiful.

"Maybe she can stay in her room," Duke says. "Will trust one servant and they'll be the only one to go in and out. We'll tell everyone she's gone overseas."

I look up and am grateful that somehow he looks at me with love in his eyes. He smiles and tucks his hair behind his ear.

Out of habit, I recoil at the sight of his mole. Duke's face hardens. "But then again, what servant would tolerate that? She'll be better off in the Outlands, with the rest of the monsters."

"No, please…"

"You're right, Duke. When your filtering comes, at least we know to take the safe option, even if you'll never be more than a 191. That's enough. We can still be proud of that." My father pulls him towards the door. "Goodbye, Lustre," he says, his eyes on the ground. "I can't say I'm not disappointed in you. If you have any decency left, go quietly. Protect us from any further embarrassment."

They leave but my mother lingers. She looks me up and down. The corner of her mouth wants to twitch into a smirk but she controls it.

"Take care, darling," she says as she saunters away. "I'll always remember how beautiful you were."

Five minutes later, a city guard dresses me in overalls and smuggles me into a central courtyard. The backdoor of a bus opens. It has black windows. As I am forced inside, twenty ten-year-olds turn to look at me and gasp. They are headed for the Outlands too, rejected from the city. At the front, there is someone older, her golden hair spilling out behind her. The guard forces me into a seat across the aisle from her. I look at my feet and cry.

"As a 92, you'll be amongst the leaders of the Outlands," the guard says to her. "You'll have your own crew. You can start with her, decide her work assignment."

The golden-haired girl laughs. "The sewers," she says.

"Best place for her," the guard says. "Oh, and she'll need a new name. The family wants to make sure there's no chance she can be linked to them."

I look up and see one stunning blue eye and one glorious green. They return my stare.

"Her name is Pig," Medusa says.

Chet and Floyd Play in God's Domain

by Justin Hunter

"What we have here is the beginning of the dawn of a new generation of a new era of a new eon of a new sunrise of a new start of a new…"

"Finish your sentence," Floyd interrupted.

"Of a new thingy."

"Nice."

Chet and Floyd were standing in Chet's mom's basement. Chet was wearing a white apron over his clothes. His glasses hung crookedly on his nose. Floyd was leaning against a wall with his arms crossed. His hair, shockingly white for a man in his late twenties, stood in carefully gelled spikes in all manners of direction.

"It would have been better if you didn't interrupt me," Chet said, slapping a glass fish tank that held a barracuda. The fish swam around irritably. Next to that tank was another. This one held an octopus who was chilling on the bottom. "We have the opportunity of a lifetime here. We can create a new species of life by messing up two perfectly good ones. This is going to be great!"

"I don't think that's going to work," Floyd said. "We're not geneticists. We have no idea what we're doing. I don't know much about science, but I don't think that two different species can mate to make a new one. It doesn't work that way."

"I am the harbinger of love!" Chet exclaimed. "I can make this happen. Where's the Marvin Gaye music?" Chet rummaged around the shelves, unnecessarily knocking over many items. "I can't find anything. I will have to sing it *a cappella*. Wait!" Chet shoved a box of glass cylinders off a shelf. Floyd winced at the jarring sound of breaking beakers. The Barracuda was swimming in agitated circles. The octopus stayed where it was at the bottom of his tank. Octopus don't give a crap about anything.

"I've found a CD player," Chet said, blowing away a half inch of dust from the electronic. He opened the lid and took out the disc inside. "Enya?" Chet grimaced. "This isn't sex music. Enya is the slayer of octopus boners everywhere. Do you know why there aren't any octopi in Iceland, Floyd? Because Enya is from Iceland. She killed them all."

"Enya isn't from Iceland," Floyd said. "You're

thinking about Bjork."

"I will let you in on a government secret, Floyd. Enya and Bjork are the same person. It's a conspiracy to rid octopus hard-ons everywhere."

"What about Barracudas?"

"Barracudas are badass," Chet said. "They can have sex no matter what is going on." Chet opened more boxes, but ended up throwing his hands in the air and squealing in frustration. Floyd was watching the octopus. He stuck his finger in the tank. The octopus reached up a tentacle and touched the digit.

"Why don't we just eat it?" Floyd asked.

"Tell you what," Chet said. "I was thinking the same thing at first. I've spent way too much time with you, Floyd. You're making my brain simple. You see, I crave scientific achievement. Before I met you, I was a great scientist. I travelled all over the world doing sciency stuff."

"Okay," Floyd said, rolling his eyes. "So when we're done we eat it."

"First, we see if we can get them to make a baby octopus barracuda thing."

"Barra-puss?"

"Octo-cuda," Chet said. It was his turn to roll his eyes. "You're the barra-puss, Floyd. Anyway, this is a win-win situation for us. If we get these things to mate, then we can eat the babies, sell the babies to a side-show, sell them as pets, and all that other crap. We will live like kings. If we can't get them to mate, then we might as well eat the octopus because we suck."

"How long will this take?" Floyd said.

"By my scientific knowledge of barracuda and octopus reproduction…we should have about thirty octo-cuda babies swimming around here at about three o'clock tomorrow afternoon."

"That fast?"

"I am a very good scientist, Floyd."

"Okay," Floyd said. "So, what do we do?"

"We have to get these two things to make love," Chet said. "Quick, grab the barracuda out of that tank! I'll grab the octopus."

"Hell, no. I'm not grabbing the barracuda. That thing will chew my arm off."

"Fine," Chet said. "I have to do everything around here. All I ask is for you to wrangle one little barracuda and you go all sissy on me." Chet grabbed a couple of latex gloves off the counter and put them on. He picked up a large glass cylinder and dunked it into the barracuda tank, filling it two-thirds full of water. The barracuda was swimming in darting circles. Chet took a wooden step ladder and put it next to the tank. He climbed the ladder and rubbed his hands together.

"Are you sure you know what you're doing?" Floyd said.

"I am the greatest scientist in all the world!" Chet said. He slammed his hand into the tank, swiping at the barracuda. Chet screamed as his arm was pulled into the water up to his shoulder. The water ran red, and Chet thrashed and cried. Floyd looked over at the octopus. It was still holding onto his finger with its tentacle. Octopus were pretty chill.

Chet ripped his arm out of the tank with a great heave of his body, the barracuda still attached beneath his armpit. Floyd ran over and grabbed the fish's slippery back fin and pulled. Chet shrieked. Floyd punched the fish in the back of its armoured head.

"Holy hell, get this thing off of me!" Chet screamed. He ran in pained frenzy away from Floyd. Floyd slipped and fell, smashing his nose on the wet floor. He inhaled once, and then blood flooded out of his nose in a fountain. Chet ran in blind panic and pain, smashed into the wall. The barracuda dislodged from his armpit and flopped on the floor. The fish gasped for breath, pieces of Chet's skin dangled from its dagger-like teeth. Chet and Floyd picked up the fish and put it into the large glass cylinder. The fish leaped out of the water, making the men shriek and become immediately embarrassed that such a high sound came out of their mouths. They picked up the barracuda again and put it back into the cylinder. When the fish tried to leap out again, Chet gave it a roundhouse kick in the side of the head. The fish sank to the bottom of the cylinder. It was breathing, but dazed. Chet put a hand to his armpit and winced as he felt his shredded flesh. Floyd put a dirty towel on his nose to try to stem the flow of blood.

"Now, that's science!" Chet said. "Let's get the octopus."

Floyd's nose stopped bleeding. Chet took the towel, put it in his armpit, and duct taped it in place as Floyd spat blood on the floor.

"I'm forgetting how this is a win-win situation for us," Floyd said.

"Scientific advancement always comes at a cost," Chet said. "You can't play around in God's domain and think things are going to be all songs and roses. God looked upon his creation and called it 'good.' Humans aren't good. We're a bunch of assholes."

"I don't play around in God's domain," Floyd said.

"Floyd, did your mom have any kids that lived?"

"What does that mean?"

"I don't know," Chet said. "It's just an old saying. I've never really known."

"Then why do you say it?"

"I don't know," Chet said. He tried to slap Floyd, but Floyd stepped back and Chet slipped on the wet floor. "It means you suck, Floyd. You suck. I hate you."

"Let's get this over with," Floyd said. "What do we do next?"

"We get the octopus out of that tank and put it in with the barracuda. Then they have sex and make octo-cudas. Bam! Science!"

"That's it?"

"Bam!" Chet raised his arms into the air. The duct-tape gave a sharp tearing sound. He screamed and fell on the ground, clutching his armpit. Floyd pulled Chet back to his feet.

"Let's say we just give up and move on with our lives," Floyd said. "This would be a stupid way to die."

"I am a man of science, Floyd." Chet gripped his armpit with his good hand. It was bleeding again.

"Well, I'm not going to get the octopus. You're going to have to do it."

"I will!" Chet reached into the octopus tank and grabbed the creature. He dunked the octopus into the water with the dazed barracuda. He shoved them against each other, mushing them together over and over.

"Make sweet love!" Chet screamed as he rubbed the octopus up and down the barracuda's body. "Sweet, sweet, love!" After ten minutes, Chet was spent. He took the half smashed octopus out of the water. He put a cigar in the Octopus's breathing hole.

"Have a smoke on me," Chet said. "Now you are a man."

"That's it?" Floyd said. It was an odd thing to watch his friend do. Mesmerising, but odd.

"That's it. We have scienced the heck out of these two creatures. We have created new ocean life. My work here is done."

"That was very enlightening."

"Thank you. It was a blessing to have you be a part of this."

"I'm not too sure of what this exactly was," Floyd said.

"I messed in God's domain," Chet said. "Now I am a god."

"Good Lord, Chet."

"Don't take my name in vain, Floyd." Chet said. "Show some respect." Chet fell over onto the floor. Blood began to pool around the rent in his arm. Floyd took the cigar out of the octopus's breathing hole and put it in his mouth.

"I guess I'm having you for dinner after all," Floyd said.

He left his friend to bleed out on the floor.

Good Intentions

by Michael Donoghue

So, I guess you want to know how it all began?

The trees in the bog gave me the idea.

Because of my selected genes, I don't need as much sleep as regular people. Most nights while my mom zeds out, I channel surf. That's what I was doing when I stumbled upon this story about oil and coal which are so vital for society—creating everything from energy to plastic. Now organic matter, like plankton, settles on the ocean floor and becomes oil in a geologic time scale. But that wasn't always the case. In order to convert the plankton into oil, the organisms had to evolve to be able to eat that organic matter. But the stone-like trees in the bog fell in before the organisms had evolved. So, they just sat there for all this time.

Well, something like that, I didn't get all the details.

Then I flipped the channel to some nature doc about this environmental group's sailboat that was navigating into the North Pacific Gyre. It's the part of the ocean where there is a convergence of winds and currents. So, if you throw a plastic pop bottle off the waterfront of Tokyo,

Vancouver or Hawaii, they all end up in this one place—a massive vortex of floating plastic trash I call the GPGP. This Great Pacific Garbage Patch is filled with grocery bags, pop bottles and other crap. And it's four times the size of Texas. Horrific. Their yacht, "Mother Earth", took a month to plough through it. I was riveted and must have watched for a whole ten minutes.

It may help you to understand; I'm Generation Z. I grew up on Xbox1080; I've got the smartest genes money can buy, and can count 10 meaningful Augmented Reality friends for each physical one. I finished High School at 12 and got my Bachelor of Science two years ago at 14. For me, instant gratification just can't happen quick enough.

We are told by our parents and teachers to believe in ourselves. That we're "special". But if everybody is special—then no one is, right? But I am. I really am. Mom always said that I'd make her proud. To make sure of it, she spent a fortune choosing primo genes that would make my abilities far beyond that of any normal person. I guess, because she assembled my DNA from thousands of dads, none of whom would be around, she wanted to give me every advantage she could.

I'm wired to be 'see a problem, want to fix it.' Which explains why, after seeing that show, I decide to do something about all that floating plastic. Not in an "I'll go and help the cuddly animals who are being caught and strangled" kind of way, but to tackle the actual source of the problem. Like the first program showed, given a couple of millennia, nature will create enzymatic microbes that will eat anything over time. But I wanted to speed up the process.

It wasn't that hard. I had the resources because of my substantial allowance from my mom. She had a biotech company that used gene therapy to change skin colour. It was very popular among clubbers. I'd tried working for Mom. She ended up paying me to stay away.

There was this *little* accident with some transgenic mice.

All I did was let them out of the cages to run around on Mom's company's back lawn for an hour. They kept getting diabetes and I wondered if it was because they weren't getting enough exercise and natural light. The lawn was all fenced in, they couldn't go anywhere, and given their sacrifice for science, don't you think they should get one lousy hour of freedom? Of actually having their cute little paws run on soil? Who expects an owl at five in the afternoon? I still think the City and the FDA culling every owl in a 150-mile radius was an excessive overreaction.

So, there I was with the money, smarts, and to be

honest, a little bored. A 16-year-old male, one science degree and nothing to do. And you know what they say about idle hands? So, I decided to form a plan of action. I went into Augmented Reality and talked with some friends on the net who worked in biochemistry, did a lit search on some scientific databases, pulled up some studies from the UK Royal Society of Geo-engineering, and hacked up a solution.

I needed to and get my hands on some bio-organisms, which was near impossible with the latest anti-terror legislation. So, I did the modern-day equivalent of putting on a fake moustache and wig—I got online using a standard 2,048 bit encrypted secure Tor-based random key proxy. Routed my traffic between a number of VPN servers all with IP spoofing. I said my name was Mohamed Mohamed and that I had a bio-terrorism plan to kill millions of Godless Americans. By the end of the day, I get 31 proposals of money and support from various law enforcement and intelligence agencies around the world masquerading as fanatical Islamics. Like geeks to the new Star Trek 23 film.

So, through the Brotherhood of Martyrs—who, strangely enough, were routing their email out of an .fbi.gov server in Houston—I received a shipment of microbes from the genus Pseudomonas; and from the

Sword of Islam—whom I traced back to a server for Homeland Security in Detroit—I acquired bacteria from the genus Sphingomonas. I had them delivered to an untraceable drop box with double-blind couriers out of Pittsburgh, PA.

Of course, my suppliers wanted to meet me and my terrorist cell, so I told the Brotherhood to come next week to Dubai's Burj Al Arab Jumeirah Hotel. They'd recognise us because we'd be wearing Mexican hats. Then I told the Sword the same, but tell them to wear sombreros. That way I didn't need to show up. I hoped they wouldn't get too upset, after all, they were getting a free trip overseas out of this. As far as I know, they could still be there, trying to set each other up.

Mom's spare penthouse condo in Heaven Towers is never used, so I cloned the keycard and converted the master bathroom into my biochemistry lab. It's pretty easy when you know what you're doing. I upgraded the bathroom fan and made the place airtight—I won't bore you with the details, but there was a lot of plastic sheeting and a massive amount of duct tape involved. Some plywood over the pseudo-stone sinks created a workbench where I put a fermenter courtesy of Allah's Will, who seemed to be operating out of the same server the CIA uses. And the Jacuzzi bathtub became my model for the Pacific Ocean.

The hardest thing was scoring some Thermo labs-on-a-chip. Too expensive to buy, but then I thought how small they are. And solving problems is what I do best. It's not that I have an excessive belief in my ability to overcome hurdles, my genes just make me better at it. So, I went to the one place where I knew I'd find the chips; Mom's work.

It was a little tricky. I had to invent a reason to visit her, and now whenever I'm there they have an escort with me at all times—but mom also bestowed upon me the fast muscle twitch gene ACTN3. The chips are small, my hands are fast, and my pockets large.

Then it was just down to screening, genetic engineering, and tweaking some pathways.

I don't want to make it sound too simple. It took a long, long time and wasn't without its challenges. I'm not sure if I've ever stuck to one project so long in all my entire life, apart from World of Ultimate Warcraft. It took weeks. I was spending all my time taking out genes, putting them in, breaking this pathway, adding that one, and checking the results.

I admit, I was rushing things back then, maybe I didn't think everything through. My genes are better than almost everyone, but my human nature is just the same. I started to get tired of the screening, besides, staff at the grocery store were starting to get suspicious. I needed polyethylene plastic bags like the ones in the GPGP. Each day, I would go to the store, pick out one item, and head to the tills where it would be swiped and I'd be asked, "Do you need a bag?"

I'd always say, "Yes," pay the $1 Green Tax and leave. I know how you're supposed to reuse the bags or bring your own, but the looks their staff gave me! By the second week, I think if I had been a pregnant woman talking on a cell, they would have been less offended.

But I still couldn't get it to work. In the Augmented Reality model, everything worked fine. According to the simulation, the plastic bag should break down over the course of a year. But when I dropped a microbe-seeded bag into the jacuzzi with the correct level of saline and at the same temperature as the ocean, it would get carried by the jet streams into the centre and just swirl around. I'd pull it out at set time points and test it and there would be no change to its structure. Infuriating!

I kept trying to increase the efficiency of the microbes, but nothing worked. All I ended up with was a tub filled with water-soaked grocery bags.

Despondent after another failed session, I pulled out all the bags and decided to get some sleep. It was five in the morning and the sun was just coming up. I'd just started brushing my teeth, when I heard sirens coming from the street below and that unmistakable quadcopter sound.

I nearly shit myself. I thought, *this is it. They've come to arrest me for the mock-terrorist stunt I pulled.*

Still, I opened the doors and walked out onto the wrap-around deck. I never went out there much because the railings and part of the deck floor in Heaven Towers are glass. I know it's stronger than concrete, but it's human nature to fear such a long fall, isn't it?

When I looked down, I saw more than a dozen cop cars parked randomly on the street, doors left wide open, all empty. The police quadcopter dropped in front of me and blocked my view. It was facing me, maybe 30 feet away. I could see the pilot and co-pilot inside the cockpit. Then it pivoted, and I was face-to-face with the door gunner. She had this huge rifle with a barrel that was as thick as my arm and twice as long.

Even though the morning light was warm on my skin, a cold layer of sweat broke out all over me. It was horrible. I thought, my life was about to end.

But then the 'copter swung around, and the gunner pointed her rifle down at the house on the other side of the street. I followed its aim and could see this throng of police officers around the house. Then they blew the door out and stormed inside.

I stood there for maybe three or four minutes, waiting for the next bit of human drama to unfold. That's when something hit my foot. I looked down, and there was my blue plastic toothbrush.

To be accurate, it was *half* my toothbrush.

I opened my hand and brought it close to my face. My palm had still been wet from the microbe-loaded tub water. The other half of my toothbrush seemed to have melted away. My palm and fingers were stained with blue water, like an exploded ink pen.

It worked. It worked! And far, far better than I'd expected or could have predicted. I was stoked. But why did it work? What was different? Was it fresh air? What?

At street level I saw the cops start to file out of the house. It was pretty far away, but I got the gist of it. Looked like an illegal grow-op. I could see they were pulling out what must have been the tobacco plants wrapped in plastic evidence bags. And then I saw them bringing out the UV lamps.

That was it. That's what was missing. Sunlight! In my simulations, I factored in the sun, but inside the bathroom there was only artificial light—no dangerous UV rays!

After that, all I had to do was work on the delivery system. If I threw a loaded bottle into the ocean, it would take at least a month to get to the GPGP. I settled on using a phage therapy delivery system for my modified microbes, giving them three months to replicate before activating the second part of their life cycle, when they'd get hungry and start to chow down on the plastic. After that, they should just sink to the bottom and die. Right? Made sense to me.

Now, a lot has been made of me buying survival provisions, but in fact, I only did it because they're Green Tax exempt. Do the math, I needed 400 plastic bottles, and with the $5 Green Tax for each, it was way cheaper to order a 13-month survival kit that came with a daily ration of water. I saved way more than buying the bottles individually.

Once I got the supplies, I emptied each plastic water bottle and loaded it up with the microbes I'd given life to. Then I checked the tides, phases of the moon, and selected the best date and time. Two weeks later, at 4am, I headed down to the beach in a packed up GoogleDrive van.

It took a while to offload all of the bottles into the hightide, but when it was finished, I had a real sense of pride. If it didn't work, at least I had tried to make the world a better place. And I didn't know if it would work—

it's one thing to be successful in my bathtub, I knew it would be different in real life—still, I'd given it my best shot.

Anyway, I had a new project now. While I was waiting for the 4am departure at home, I found a news story about a rise in osteoporosis due to bio-manufactured vat-grown milk having less calcium. I had some thoughts on how I might solve that problem too.

Six months later my news alert flagged a story on the sailboat *Mother Earth*'s return visit. It was supposed to show viewers how much worse the GPGP had become. Instead, they found the plastic island was now less than a quarter of its original size. Maybe you saw the live video feed? It was on all the main blogs and other news channels.

I felt so awesome. Man, was I proud. Yes, I claimed responsibility—sure there might have been some ego at play. Maybe I had thoughts of the Nobel Prize for my contribution to humanity. Most importantly, I wanted to hear mom say the words, "Well done, son. You've made me proud."

Maybe I didn't think through all the implications, but hey, I've never been good at thinking that far ahead. Who expects a ship to visit in the middle of your experiment? I was just trying to do something positive.

Here was something that could benefit all humankind. Problem—solution. That's how I work. I did it because I'm a problem solver. It's in my genes. Literally. My mom picked the AA genotype for my SNP rs1800497. So, that's my behaviour, and human behaviour is hard to change.

Now, as we all know, the *Mother Earth* started experiencing problems and had to be towed to San Francisco. A month after that, all the plastic in the city started to degrade and break down. A year later, we're pretty sure the only plastic left in the world is in that research station in Antarctica. Plastic, it's in all the computers, it lines all the power and phone cables, it makes cars go, planes fly.

Instead of being Time's Person of the Year, the last cover they ever printed claimed I was 'The Boy who Broke the Wheel' because all the cars were starting to fail.

My genes may have made me smarter, stronger and given me a better immune system, but I'm just as susceptible to human nature as you are. How many of us throw away something that is recyclable? And for good reason. Maybe you're already running late. Maybe because it would require rinsing and you're on a water budget. It's human nature to take short cuts. I was simply trying to find a scientific solution, because that is easier than changing human behaviour.

But I've got some ideas on gene therapy to fix that if you give me a second chance. And that is why, ladies and gentlemen of the jury, I ask you that you find me Not Guilty of these charges of terrorism.

The Completist

by Hari Navarro

The ceiling looks old. Beams and floorboards curved with walking feet and moving furniture and heavy hanging arguments, and the tiny paws that, for year upon year, had pounded upon its surface and etched into its patina.

She does not look old. She looks...she looks like...she looks like something you would make up. A fantasy thing, leached from teenage cravings. Her skin, a gentle smoulder of burnt creamy dessert. Her hair sweating about her lips like wanton exhaustion primed for one more go. And you think—no, you are quite certain—that you love her.

The cuffs bite at your wrists and your ankles, and sweat gathers at your groin as she gathers you into her hand.

"I love cocks," she says, and you see the tip of her tongue as it flicks as she speaks.

"I had no idea," you reply, and you inhale the scent of her warm breath as it lashes up and numbs at the stems of your eyes.

"A very wise man—my grandfather, in fact, a man who I very much respected—told me that, no matter what I do in life, I must do it with pride," she says.

The room is aglow, and there is a source of heat that taunts at the side of your face. There are shelves and there are more shelves and, at the very strained reach of your truncated view, there is what appears to be shelves. The heat does not burn, though you feel your flesh gently contract beneath its caress, and she slips as if beneath floating sheets, down and into your head.

You love the sound of her voice, don't you? The smooth rolled inflections that you just cannot place. You love it, but it scratches. It taps and it plays games at your temples. And you stare at the moist grooves in her lips and you forget everything. You forget just what it is that she is.

The shelves are all lit. You are colour blind, but it's a blue glow, you think. Row after stacked row of preserving jars, and the light punches up and floods and hugs at their contents.

There is something alive in the jars, or at least that's how it seems. You see through them. Just as she saw through you. You gaze into the detritus and, somehow, it manages to twist and to dance. Flakes of skin and globules of blood that marry and part in this vile collection of hermetically sealed rage.

"So, you collect penises?" you ask, and your words are meant as a bold statement of fact, but they falter and slip out instead as a feeble and barely formed question.

"Only severed ones," she chuckles.

"I used to collect dead flies when I was a kid. I'd put them in a bottle-top filled with PVA glue and watch as they struggled and finally died. The glue would set and cast them just so. Then, I'd put them in a little cardboard display case under my bed. It was my most precious thing. Until my parents found it and screamed at me that I was a sick little fuck and that I was going to end up being a serial killer, or worse." And your reply is wrapped in your own forced laughter, and you just know that she sees the tiny line of piss that meanders down the inside of your thigh.

"Should have found a better hiding place," she says, and you hope to catch in her reply a hint—a glimmer of hope—that maybe your story connected with her on some fucked up level, but you don't. Not the slightest ripple. Not a single one. And you blink and you try not to cry.

"This was my grandfather's basement. He would come down here and work for hours and hours turning wood into the most wonderful things. I used to be able to smell the French polish; he made it himself and kept it in jars just like the ones that I use. But now all I smell is the

Formaldehyde. I like to breathe the chemicals. They smell like pickles."

"Was your grandfather... I mean, did he..."

"Hells no. He was a lovely man. A very good man. If you are looking for a reason for me being this way inclined, then he is not it."

"I didn't mean to imply, just made the connection between the jars and this place and..."

"You connected the fact that he once used jars to store his polish and that he toiled down here as do I. You equated this to him being a paedophile and the reason I put cocks into jars?"

"Yes, I guess I did."

"Well, I never saw it before, but I guess there are parts of who I am that I've taken from him and perverted and converted into this thing that I am. The perfection and the pride that he had in his work; that is his. Each specimen is my collection is pristine, and each and every one of the jars is labelled and rotated to face perfectly forward. I measure the gap between them, and that, too, is precise. I can sense in my dreams if even one is but a fraction askew."

"I am impelled, not to squeak like a grateful and apologetic mouse, but to roar like a lion out of pride in my profession," you mumble as you try to turn your head from whatever is causing that fucking annoying heat.

"Steinbeck. You are very not like the others. You are a special boy," she purrs, and you hope now finally that this is the crack. The hole in this crazy bitch's façade. The connection. The rope to climb up and out from this pit.

"What do you use for the cutting?" you ask, and you know she feels warm from this, your latest sudden burst of courage.

"Well, you are a hungry sponge for knowledge, aren't you just? The cutting...well, I must admit that at one time it was more of a hack than a surgical slice. Such a horrible mess. Such unimaginable pain."

"So, a scalpel?"

"No, I don't have the finesse. I wasn't even looking for it when I found the answer to my butchery woes, actually. I was moseying through the garden section of a big hardware store, you've probably passed it. It's the one out by the Sunny Chicken Deluxe just before the underpass. So, anyway, I'm in there moseying—I fucking love hardware stores, they turn me on like nobody's business, them and pies. But I digress...so, I'm hunting down nails...very specific nails...little brass nails, and I happen upon a display cabinet. It was no more than a perspex box, actually, and in it there was a pair of hand-held mechanical garden shears. They were in the box for safety reasons, I guess, this tiny bad boy could lop off a limb. OK, maybe not a limb, but at least a digit. Which was perfect. You see, the problem wasn't just cutting away the penis, no. I also wanted to retain the testicles, just doesn't look right without them."

"Like a face without a nose."

"Yes, or as I prefer to see it, a nose without a face. Plus, with you guys thrashing and shouting and screaming, it was rather difficult to use a knife. So it dawns on me...use the shears. I superheat the blades first and then, with only one hand, I can snip and sear off the bleeding all in one go. No more fountains of hissing blood. The blood never actually hissed, I just want to paint for you a visual."

"Got it."

"You know, sometimes I can complete the entire procedure without spilling a single drop?"

"That's the heat, isn't it? That's what I feel at my face?"

"Yes, yes, it is. I have the shears gently roasting on a portable gas stove, just behind your sweet little head. Another of my hardware store acquisitions."

"You should be proud. You have adhered quite perfectly to your passion. Not everyone can say that."

"You say the most lovely supportive things. I think

you are a very kind man. Though, I'm afraid, you are very much the exception rather than the rule. The men, they scream the most horrid things sometimes. I don't mind saying some of it hurts. It really hurts. One guy even called me an Emma Watson man-hating dike-whore."

"She's a feminist, and he probably falsely equated that to man hatery. It's quite common."

"Ah, misandry, my old nemesis. I do like Emma Watson. She seems very genuine."

"You know, I've never even seen one of the Harry Potter films," I lie.

"Look—sorry, I don't even know your name—but thing is, you probably won't get the chance to see anything. Not ever. Not your parents, the ones you love, the end of your favourite television show, whether or not Donald gets to build his wall. I'm taking more than Mr. Dribbles here. I'm taking everything."

"Can I ask you something?"

"Always."

"What do you do with the..."

"Leftovers?"

"Yes. The leftovers."

"Well, I render down the fat to make soap, and I stew the meat and make it into pies."

"Really?"

"No. But you should see your face. Abject mortal fear. Priceless."

"I am to die?"

"Well, yes, unless all this banter somehow allows for someone to break through the house's state of the art security system—which was a bargain, by the way, and I got a free set of garden furniture thrown into the deal— and they save you just in the nick of time."

"I'm going to die."

"I don't hate men, I really don't. Not only do I not hate them but, and this is just between you and I, I'm thinking of branching out after I've completed the entire set. I'm thinking of getting into vaginas."

"That will be nice."

"Won't be easy. Mounting them, I mean. Maintaining their structural integrity. They'll look like dead jellyfish."

"You could try plastination."

"Come again?"

"Plastination. You prepare them in Formaldehyde as per usual. This helps to slow the decomposition of the tissue and will also aid in maintaining rigidity. Then a bath in acetone, this is to draw out any moisture. The acetone actually replaces the moisture within the cells of the organ, as it were. Then another bath in something the likes of epoxy resin. The acetone is boiled at a low temperature and this creates a vacuum that draws out the vaporising acetone and sucks the resin into its wake, thus filling the cells with liquid plastic. This is then cured by gas, heat or ultraviolet light, and there you have it. One hard vagina. You could mount them on little plinths. Perhaps, a little splash of up-lighting."

"I like it. Where were you when I started this thing? I could do the entire collection over. Hard plastic ones and soft pickled ones in a jar."

"What exactly is the criteria for your not so very little collection, if I may ask?"

"Countries. I want one from every last country. Even the Vatican, which is a task that has lost me a fair amount of sleep, I must say. You know, I'm still going to cut you, right? I mean, I don't want you to get the wrong idea and be thinking that because we're talking that I'll back down. I only say this so you don't build up any false hope. That wouldn't be fair. You've been great and so very helpful. I don't even want to know how you know all this shit, but I never back out of a job started."

"Pride?"

"Exactly, too bloody much. I've been looking for you for a very long time. I'd expected that I'd have to visit an ex-patriot group or such like. But for an Uzbekistani to pass by this way. Well, it's fate, isn't it?"

"I'm not from Uzbekistan." And your eyes suddenly widen, and you manage the beginnings of a smile.

"Yes, you are."

"No, I'm not."

"You told me in the club when we were talking at the bar next to that thing."

"No, I said my name was Stan. It's John actually, but folks called me Stan. On account of my blond hair...and that song. Plus, do I look or speak like an Uzbekistani?"

"How in the fuck should I know? I've never met one."

"But surely..."

"Seriously, in your situation and you're riding me on this?"

"Look, I'm just a run of the mill garden variety New Zealander. We are a dime a dozen...we're like sand after you've been to the beach, we're every fucking where. I mean, you surely already have a Kiwi and, besides, look at me...I'm tiny."

"It's not about size, it's about form, but you are, though it pains me to say it, quite right, again. I do have a New Zealander. One of my finest specimens."

"So?"

"So, I'm sorry but you won't be on display. I'm going to have to save you for swaps."

Hubris in Retrograde

by Mike Adamson

Tap. Tap… Tap. Clack, tap

It was coming closer. Again

Tap, tap. Clack.

The mage Salamon drew a shaky breath and fought the trembling of his limbs. His wizardly robes felt chill and damp in these passages, the hidden ways amongst and beneath—so far beneath—the keep of Irongraf, seat of his late master, Duke Hellingen. Silence, darkness, the wan illumination of the cunningly concealed glass bricks here and there which provided those passing unseen among their fellows a modicum of day-glow.

He could have wept, for it was his own stupid, stiff-necked fault. All of it, his own personal disaster, what he had done to an innocent—an objectionable youth, but innocent enough in the scheme of things, just perhaps—the jeopardy of the dukedom, the civil war which would roll across the land all too soon.

But he would not live to see it, for he was hunted through this catacomb, moment after relentless, restless moment, and as the sound of infernal clacking came closer, he drew a breath and whirled from his alcove, leaving behind the silvery light and descending, by trembling touch, a stairway into the blackness below.

How he cursed the day Duke Hellingen had swept into his laboratory and commanded his sorcerer to perform spellwork.

"My son, the Prince Vailencourt, will be of marrying age soon, and the future of the dukedom dictates a fine wedding to a daughter of neighbouring nobility. But the prince is hardly a shining example to his people, or anyone else's." The duke had posed in his black leather suit and burgundy cloak, his silver whiskers elaborately styled, and eyed Salamon as if he were some lowly serf. "My son is a tub of lard whose greatest pleasure in life is his dinner. And every other meal of the day. I have done all I may with him, but he is an embarrassment, and I would have him step out before the peoples of two nations proudly, and *not* in corsets."

Salamon had bowed with an elegant gesture of his fine magician's hands. "And what would His Grace desire for this working?"

"Get half his weight off him. *Before* marrying day arrives." The duke had sniffed disdainfully, "Nothing else has worked, we may as well give magic its chance."

"An interesting challenge Your Grace, but well

within my capabilities. I shall send word when a spell has been prepared."

How he cursed those words, regretted his own overconfidence, the pomp of his position as magician to the court. It had been an easy enough life; drawing people's astrological charts and telling their futures, adjusting the horologes, doctoring mild ailments, the odd spot of surgery, pontificating as keeper of the ducal library of arcanum. He had worked his share of spells in his day, done good work, but become…soft. *Conceited*, he admitted to himself through clenched teeth, and with tears prickling his eyes in their maze of wrinkles, as he panted at the bottom of the stair in the dust of ages.

The clacking was far off now, and he pressed on in the ghostly rays of glass tiles cunningly set into the gardens above to light this unknown vault. He paused for breath, then gathered his robes and passed among labyrinthine walls into passageways he had long ago committed to memory.

Unfortunately, so had his nemesis.

It's so unfair, he thought, choking back his misery. He had served well all these years. Had he not turned aside the storms that would have laid waste to the harvests? Had he not defeated the plague in the year of the scorpion? Had he not invented magical toys to amuse the court, clockworks that never required winding for their mainsprings were charmed? Thus, did the guards of the citadel travel in chariots without need of horses; and a hundred other mechanisms worked softly to themselves on this mountain? All this had he accomplished, only to fail at the finish.

For the dozenth time, he forced his tongue to make the arcane words of a protective spell, only to stumble, stutter, and have to begin over. What was wrong with him? Frustration gnawed, and he clenched his hands to still their shuddering.

Bitterest of all, he could still hear the words of old Maritsa, the cleaning skivvie… He had worked long that night upon the duke's spell, couching in finest form the eldritch evocation of the mighty spirits who would perform the transformation, in exchange for a foothold upon this Earth, a year in possession of some regal creature to be their vehicle in the mortal realm, or perhaps just for blood.

In the candlelight he had worked at his great desk upon the parchment of the spell, and seen the dumpy figure in peasant garb, a cloth about her hair, from the corner of his eye as she mopped among his paraphernalia and mechanisms, his telescopes and clockworks. But eventually, he had realised she was leaning on the mop and staring over his shoulder.

"Oh… You're doing it like that, are you?" Her voice, in the accent of the lower town, was like glass powder under his skin and he shot her a withering glance. "It's the third stanza, that fourth line, marked up for a rising tone of voice."

"What of it?"

"Well, my Alf was a sorcerer's mate, and you wouldn't have caught him dead doing it that way."

"Your Alf *is* dead."

Her eyebrows had risen into her headscarf. "He were good at this magic-lark, was my Alf!"

The sight of his official cane of office sent her back to mopping, and he gave it no more thought, other than to damn her impudence, never even looking again at the passage, so sure was he of his dominion over spellcraft. But on the day His Grace called upon him to perform the working, ah, then he recalled, and something in his soul died. It never reached his face, for face is all to those whose dignity is their privilege, but failure was failure.

It had been in that very laboratory, before the duke's gaze, and in the presence of senior seneschals, by the light of a full moon streaming through tall windows and with the blood of three black cocks in a bowl upon an altar. The working had built in power as the patch of moonlight crossed eldritch designs upon the hard stone floor, and the portly prince waited in a simple robe of white, ill at ease and complaining of his lot, that privilege should win him the right to be whatever nature decreed.

Come the appointed moment, Salamon had orated the spell, boomed out its stanzas, acknowledged the elder spirits of the world and beseeched their benediction. Yet, even as the magic had taken effect, he had known the first bitterness of ultimate damnation, for the prince collapsed with a shriek such as the sorcerer had never heard before. The youth crumpled in on himself, and the urgent searching of the mage's hands revealed not that half his body weight had been removed, but *half his body*. The lower half. The prince ended around the hips in a grotesque approximation of radical amputations, yet his whole body was also affected, streaked with lesions as if the spell had sought to strip flesh wherever it might, leaving him nigh putrescent, and quite, quite mad.

Yes, the rising tone. It should have been falling.

The thought battered at him from that day forth, yet Salamon remained perplexed, for spells, while exact, were not so susceptible to error, for the first rule concerned intent. Yet, this was not the purity of spellcraft, it was mediated by angelic beings who were capricious, and delivered precisely what was negotiated for. They had demanded their blood in payment for the travesty they had delivered, for the error was his own.

The duke had collapsed also, from shock—a bleeding in the brain in all probability—robbing him of the power of speech, which was just as well, as he may have ordered the mage beheaded on the spot. Claiming the authority of the spirits, Salamon had ordered all from his laboratory that he may attend the prince, as physicians saw to the duke, but only he knew it for the hopelessness it was. As much as he could do was dress the lesions, bless them with a healing spell, and administer the concoctions to bring the youth peace for a time. And when the prince regained consciousness, it was to find himself nestled into a carrying sling mounted in one of Salamon's experimental clockworks, a travel craft for all ground, whose mainspring never ran down, and whose six, jointed brass legs would carry him forth in response to a simple steering mechanism.

Tap. Tap. Clack, tap, clack…

Salamon squeezed his eyes closed as he realised it was at the top of the stair from the castle. In another moment, a rhythmic rattling began as the metal limbs negotiated the steps one by one, coming down… Coming down. He ran again, breathless with terror, for there was nothing left in Prince Vailencourt now, save hate.

How long had they played this remorseless game of cat and mouse? Hours…or days? The duke had expired without uttering another word, and only the fear in which people held a sorcerer had kept his head upon his shoulders this long. But without an heir to the ducal throne, their neighbours saw rich lands ripe for the picking, and grizzled generals were stocking the citadel for a siege as peasants were conscripted, and blacksmiths beat out cheap spear blades and rough swords by the score.

Hunger and thirst were his foes, too, and such was their onslaught he wept for his own pity. He had thought to escape into this maze and at last fade quietly from the ken of his old masters by an outer escape tunnel, a fair enough scheme, but he had forgotten that, as a child, Prince Vailencourt played in these passages. He knew them as well as the Captain of the Guard, even better, and once inside, had become the spider to Salamon's fly.

The mage panted into his long beard, paused once more and listened. The tapping was not far away, but the maze lay between them. For long moments, there was only silence, perhaps the scuff of a rat in the blackness, then he heard it move again and realised it was in the maze.

No, he cursed under his breath and made one last

terrible effort to summon the dark powers to his aid. But it seemed—bereft of his equipment, his books, his substances—the gift of magic had eluded him, even a spell to render him unseen to foes faded on his lips as the words fled his memory. He could but press on through the maze, seeking its far end, turn by turn, as he had learned it long ago.

And his pride was undone in totality when, instead of the final passage to the exit from the maze, he found only a dead end. He sank down against the blank, sheer wall of stone—unclimbable, cold and aloof—and reviewed, in the minutes that remained to him, where he had gone wrong.

Perhaps he should have thanked Old Maritsa, made a quick note, a mere flourish of the quill, reminding himself to pronounce the syllables upon a descending tone. Would it have been so great a burden to his dignity to acknowledge that other sorcerers may better remember an incantation than himself? *Oh, pride, thou art a cruel mistress,* he thought, *to bring thy servant to such ignominy.*

Cold. Darkness relieved only by wan rays from the few tiles above, like stars in a nighted vault. Dark walls all around him, caging him like an experimental rodent; only no mage waited to transform him for some purpose, grand or abominable. Only the transition from one realm to another, and he smiled with a cynical acceptance. What did he believe? The things he had propounded his life through, or…?

In the end, he had the pride; the dignity to rise to his feet, straighten his robe and face his end with composure, for it was all that remained to him, and when Prince Vailencourt appeared at the end of the passage in the gloom, seeming like a mechanical crab, he did not flinch.

Tap, tap, clack, clack, tap…

His mechanism would outlive its creator, bearing forth its insane burden, and in the dim glimmers from above, the prince seemed not of this world, but the degraded offspring of demons. His face had collapsed on one side, the hair withered away, left arm shrivelled, and only fury dwelled in those dead eyes.

Fury, and hunger. The deformed mouth hung partly open, revealing stained and crooked teeth, and Salamon saw only the regard of hunter for prey in him.

Pride goeth before…

The mage screamed as the foremost pair of jointed brass limbs flicked out and wrapped him in a vice-like grip, and he was lifted inexorably toward those teeth.

Knot for Fame

by Jo Seysener

"Perfect. Oh, *so* beautiful," the Crimper moaned, garnet nails extending, tucking a wayward strand of horsehair away. Assessing the mass of knots and braids, she trimmed stray hairs for a perfect finish, her nail splitting in two, snipping with a sharp crystalline edge. Light reflected their blood-red facets as her nails retracted to their normal size.

She slipped tiny diamonds set into curls of silver into the intricate twists and braids forming the Queen's enormous wig for her ball. Blonde and sparkles swirled into the natural grey of the aging queen.

As natural as plucked for a horse's behind.

The Crimper giggled, stifling the sound beneath a horsey cough of her own. Blood splattered the kerchief she yanked from her breast just in time.

Not long now.

Sorrow filled her, but she would have one last victory—this hairpiece would be her crowning moment. Or rather, the Queen's. With no children of her own, funds would be transferred to her mother and sister, both in the early stages of her ailment.

With an unearthly grace she'd inherited from her grandmother, the Crimper lofted the confection of diamonds and hair to chest height, pausing at the door to knock with her boot.

Her personal guard—she was so coveted, priceless herself—opened the door with a gallant bow and she passed him, head held high, chest out, balancing the wig...

...only to have her matching, albeit smaller, one catch in the doorway.

She tugged, leaning as backward as her creation allowed to slide beneath the door frame but it was no use; she was stuck.

"Perhaps your ladyship should wear something...lesser...than the Queen's," the guard murmured, sliding a hand over the tip of the wig. She passed beneath the threshold easily, cringing as diamonds pinged the Black Sassafras floor.

Gliding as she had seen visiting dancers do on stage—the hours of practice it had taken before her glass, rippled and second rate that distorted her slight figure as she sucked in her belly, working her bustle—she rapped on the door of the Queen's private salon, so close to her own.

To be on the Queen's own floor!

Such a revered position. It came naturally, of course. Dressing the hair of nobles, especially with her talents. As though she knew what they wanted before they asked, setting trends and ending them as she saw fit.

Her own private empire.

But now she was to enter the presence of *Majesty.*

She simpered at the door, practicing. Bag in hand, she waited for the guard to admit her, but to her surprise, he gripped her arm. Handsome as he was, he earned only a third of her compensation. She drew back her arm with a disdaining smile that reeked of etiquette.

"Be yourself."

The comment broke her from her thoughts, and she looked into clear brown eyes. *So common.*

Hers were blue and clear as the Queen's. Almost as though they were sisters.

Her indignant expression prompted the man into speech. He cleared his throat, motioning to her headdress.

"That—it mirrors *hers,* doesn't it?"

The Crimper nodded, feeling a faint frown dipping her brow. If this silly man didn't hurry up, her face paint would be ruined.

"Take it off."

She reared back, staring in confusion. It was the most

offensive thing he could have said. This was *her* creation!

"But it's for her."

As though reading her mind, the man gave her a long look and, seeing she wouldn't adhere to his advice, announced her, motioning her into the Queen's presence with a sorrowful look. She ignored him, bowing as low as her wig allowed.

She looked up at a harrumphing sound, edging forward as her monarch turned, waving impatiently to her in the mirror.

The Crimper took the hint and got to work.

Curlers, combs and diamonds scattered the vanity table. Even though she wouldn't need them. Slipping the balding hair into a net with a squirt of moisturiser—*who cares if it rots, as long as it doesn't itch*—the Crimper set the magnificent wig atop her Queen's head, unravelling curls kept tidy with pins so they framed her once heart-shaped face. She freed her nails to tidy the top. A final primp and puff, and she was done.

The Queen admired herself in the prefect glass.

"Seems fine."

She flicked her hands at the purser waiting beside the frieze.

"Pay her."

He flicked coins the Crimper's way and she caught

them expertly. It was a little game they'd always played.

The Queen turned, and the Crimper took note of every nuance: the way her shoulders turned back, how her hips swivelled in the chair. To emulate later, of course, in the little time left to her. She would leave this world with dignity.

Face to face, she bowed to her employer, who sat frozen. The Crimper stared around the room, perplexed. Down at herself. Had she spilt wine down her front? That last burgundy she'd helped herself to had been quite nice. As had been the kitchen boy who served her.

Well, not such a boy after all.

A giggle burst past her lips and she coloured, heat ruining her makeup.

"Yours."

Her attention snapped back to the Queen.

"It's the same."

She smiled, nodding. Bowing. Deference always helped with these vain creatures.

"Of course," she demurred, "I had to model it—to ensure Your Grace would...appreciate my work."

As she lifted her head, balancing the wig, the Crimper caught the Queen's eyebrows rising. The nod she sent to the guard, hovering by the door.

He approached her with a closed face, grasping her

arm, sliding the headdress to the floor. She squealed, arguing until cold metal pressed against her neck. It was sharp and drew blood that ran down her neck at a touch.

She didn't need to look to know the steel, as razor sharp as her nail scissors, was held by the Queen's own hand. It was the Queen's trademark way for dispatching enemies, anyone who stole her limelight.

At least it would be quick.

"You know what they say about pride," the Queen touched her naked scalp, freshly shaved clean for this night.

The Crimper knelt on the hardwood floor—so much easier to clean than the rug—and studied the intricacies of the wood.

So beautiful.

"The fall and all," the Queen gloated as she vacated the salon. The Crimper's still-conscious head thumped onto the floor, listening to the tinkle of coins that tumbled from her purse.

"Collect that. She won't be needing them."

No one but the guard noticed fresh tears that trailed through lead powder as he gently lifted her to be displayed with the rest of the Queen's failed retinue.

Driven to Death

by A.R. Dean

I was a firm believer in perfection. Every inch of my life was an example to all on what they should strive to be. The entire country should have celebrated that I was in it. I knew from an early age that I was special. More men should follow my example; it would make the world a better place. The day my life fell apart I couldn't take it. For the first time, I was weak. I allowed her to defeat me. None of this was my fault.

"She ruined everything," I mutter to myself as I stroll across the empty eastside flat. The city lights draw me to the bay windows. As I absorb the New York skyline, more bitterness consumes me. Six weeks ago, I was content. I had it all. Everything I had worked my whole life for. I take another long swig from my last bottle of whiskey.

I can't help but think about the woman that took it all. After fifteen years of marriage, she cleaned out our joint bank account, emptied our apartment, and even took the damn dog. All while I was away on business.

She discovered that the business I had was with a sexy young model. A man has needs that must be met.

Feeble minded women don't understand. It doesn't give her the right to ruin my life. I'm a man who is entitled to his needs.

I allow myself another slow drink. Too bad the wife didn't know about the Swiss bank account. There wasn't enough in there to rebuild my life. It had just enough for revenge. I feel my cheek twitch in the glimmer of a smile. For weeks, I've slept on the refurbished hardwood floor, plotting revenge.

My mind had been so occupied with my vengeance that I stopped paying attention to everything else. If she wouldn't have left, I'd still have my job. The humiliation I suffered because of her. People whisper about a man when his wife walks out.

Ten years wasted at that firm. Working my balls to the quick for the ungrateful bastards at MacMurray and Hart. I'd been on the fast track to partner at the best defence law firm in the country. Until she left.

"You're distracted," Hart had told me matter-of-factly.

"You lost us the biggest case we've ever had. National news and we are being pasted as failures," MacMurray roared. His bald head glistened in the flickering fluorescent lights. His portly face burgundy with inflamed rage as the saliva dripped down his jowls.

His fat gut kept slamming into the conference table as he stood, trying to attack me. He couldn't reach, so MacMurray slammed his meaty fists into the aged wood instead. Hart held up a hand to quiet his partner. Ancient boney hands calming the raging bull at his side. They were comical in their opposites. Too bad I hadn't been in a laughing mood. I was getting fired. I knew it. No one who got called in to a meeting with these two after a loss got to stay.

"It wasn't my fault. I have always given you perfection. I don't know what went wrong…" I explained with a shrug. I kept my face neutral. I was lying. I knew what went wrong. I allowed my wife to distract me. It had kept me up nights drinking. To be honest, I didn't just drink at night. The flask in my desk drawer was proof of that.

Hart interrupted me with a clearing of his thin pale throat. The man needed to leave the office and see the sun. Maybe get a tan. "You need to take a leave of absence."

"Unpaid." MacMurray growled under his breath.

"Some time off to recharge would do you wonders. You haven't had a vacation in a few years. You can get everything else in order," Hart said more calmly than his enraged partner. Hart had never raised his voice or showed any emotion in all my years with them. I knew he was discussing my wife when he told me to get things in order. No man at this firm had ever allowed his spouse to embarrass him as mine had. He was letting me know in his own way that I should take control of my woman before it wasn't just my job at the firm destroyed. The very idea of my leaving should devastate him, but the man was an unfeeling ghoul.

"How long before you realise you're making a mistake?" I queried. My anger boiling me from the inside out. She did this. I had never lost a case before she left. MacMurray's face went fuchsia as his mouth dropped open like a fish.

Hart gave me a look of disapproval. "It's not a mistake. You need to take a month off. Maybe more," Hart ordered.

My lips snarl at the memory. Unpaid leave my ass. I know what it really was. A push out. They were giving me space before they terminated me. I had been an outstanding defence attorney. I was the best that firm had ever had the privilege to hire. That didn't even describe how I mastered my profession. I had spent ten years getting off the criminal elite. I was lucky that it came with a few benefits. I procured powerful connections in the dark illicit underbelly of this city. These connections allowed a man to have certain favours called in.

My cell phone lay charging on a counter in the kitchen. I was patiently waiting for the one call that could give me joy. My life had been upside down since I came home to a Dear John letter and the electric shut off. Back to a penthouse smelling of spoiled food rotting away in my refrigerator.

I walked through the empty apartment searching for any sign of her. My leather furniture was missing. My clothes were strewn about our bedroom. Armani suits that cost more than some people make in a year, wrinkled and tossed about like garbage. I had tried to call her often, but she sent me straight to her voicemail. I read her letter. That whore had the nerve to cheat on me. She was too stupid to realise I was the perfect husband and better than someone like her could do.

She even took my car. A brand new 2018 Mercedes-Benz SL-Class. Red and sleek with an engine that vibrated power. A great little ride that helped me get off in more ways than one. In the letter, my wife explained that she had found out about the other women. She had found out about my love nest in the Hamptons. She thought taking all my possessions and a young lover would punish me. As another form of spite, she took my Benz, my baby.

The car was my real love. It got me so much action.

She did it because she did not understand how expensive her stupid Tesla was. Even with all the gizmos and gadgets I had installed in her car, she'd been jealous of mine. Mine was a higher end piece of machinery with every top end item I could have shoved into its metal frame. Best Christmas bonus I ever spent. She'd had a jealous tantrum. I was the one that earned the money, why shouldn't I spoil myself?

Bet by now, the greedy bitch had ruined my precious car. I'm certain that slut had scratched the custom cherry red paint. I'd invested a ton of money into the perfect vehicle. Just like I had wasted fifteen years creating the perfect wife. Exactly like the ten years I threw away being the best attorney in New York.

She had been twenty when I had met her, all hard bodied and eager. I had spent millions nipping and tucking to keep her looking how I deserved. She had one job. She was to stay the young society girl I had married, a perfect trophy. No original parts left on her now. She had called me selfish. Selfish is running away from a marriage for a twenty-seven-year-old personal trainer named Chaz or Skye. Maybe it was Nico. I shook my head. What did it matter? The man child had some douche bag hipster name.

She had used my money that she stole to buy herself

a Brownstone. She had always wanted one. "Better for kids," she had said.

Why the hell would I trade a penthouse with this view for a Brownstone and snot-nosed brats. That disaster of a woman said children would complete her. It was the dumbest thing she had ever said. Children were vermin that sucked you dry. I often explained to her I was the intelligent one in our relationship, that is why I made all our decisions. Obviously, she wasn't as smart as I was. Not that I married her for her brains.

I thought women wanted an intelligent man to lead them. Couldn't have her overloading that tiny brain of hers. Didn't she realise that children would destroy our lifestyle? She said I was controlling her. Ruining her life by not letting her get fat with a baby. She didn't realise how expensive liposuction and tummy tucks were. Any moron could see how stressful her upkeep was for a man in my position.

That's why I secretly got myself fixed. One knocked up mistress was hard enough to dispose of. Pregnant wives were another matter. I couldn't have some kid messing up my life. Who knows what she would have done if she found out about the vasectomy. I know why she really wanted kids; she wanted more of my money.

Her response to my cheating was to run away, taking

some fruity-named child with her. That pissant of a man was walking my dog and screwing my wife. They were both mine, my property. I hated when people took my things. The little punk even quit his trainer job so he could have more time to spend the money my hard work had made.

All of it would be over soon. With one phone call. I took another drink. I swirled the liquid in the bottle. Getting close to empty. Damn, this was the last. That phone better ring before I ran out. Being sober wouldn't help this. I turned, glaring at my silent phone. Still charging. My beautiful bare ass was shining in the moonlight. I glanced back at my naked reflection in the giant windows.

I may not be as young as the hippy, but at fifty I was still a catch. My hair is thick, wavy, and dark. A hint of grey dusted my temples. My lovers often told me it made me distinguished. I bared my teeth at the reflective glass. They were straight and white. I had my teeth capped, but it added more to my already handsome face. Hell, I even had abs. How picky can a woman be? Damn it. The only reason she wasn't some overweight thirty something is because of all the plastic magic I had paid for.

The phone rang, making me jump. It rang again. I leapt across the room. My bare feet create echoes on the walls. The echoes were my only company these days. Quickly, I hit the speaker button.

"Yeah?" I kept my voice calm.

"It's done," came a gravely New Jersey accent.

"The trainer?" I couldn't keep the eagerness from my voice.

"Chopped up like calamari in the bathtub."

"And my lovely..." I snickered on the word, "wife?"

A heavy smoker's laugh started on the other end, only to cut off early by a deep and phlegmy cough. Seconds ticked by as the harsh cough mingled with the laughter. It took a few more moments for the man on the other line to control it. After it calmed, his gravelly voice got back in control. "Nothing lovely about her now, Boss. She's fish bait in the river. I messed her up real good before she went in. Just like you asked. Hours of pain for both."

"My car?"

"Parked below your apartment like you ordered. Must say it handled like a dream. Smoothest thing I ever drove."

"Yes, she is. Did you get the rest of your money out of the slut?" I asked.

Another deep chuckle, "Yeah. You were right, she was a greedy little bitch at first. Tried to hang on to every dime. She got a little more generous once I removed some fingers and toes."

I could feel myself smile. A genuine smile. My teeth were seeing the light for the first time in a while. "Oh, Johnny T, you were my favourite acquittal."

"Thanks, Boss man. I'm taking your wife's generous donation and heading to the islands."

"Enjoy your holiday. Thank you for your work." I hung up the phone. Downing the rest of the whiskey, I hurled the bottle into the giant bay windows. It shattered. Shards of glass were everywhere. I walked across the room so the air could hit my face, not feeling the pain of glass cutting into the soles of my feet. It's over.

I can't return to my job. Those ungrateful pricks at the office saw to that. My girlfriends left when the money disappeared. What little I had left went to Johnny T. Those leeches should have been grateful that I had been their lover. Leave it to women to be greedy. My wife who I'd moulded into excellence, gone. Everything in my life destroyed. I looked eight floors down. Shining somewhere in those streetlights is my wonderful red Mercedes.

With a deep breath, I close my eyes. My precious Benz is my only thought. I'm remembering all those drives up the coast. Long trips into the country with a beautiful coed's head nestled in my lap. The raw surge of pure masculinity that surrounded me while I drove. I felt like Hercules, with women always fawning over me and my lovely red car.

I got used to being powerful and perfect. The courtrooms filled with people that sat in awe of me. Worshipping me like a god, as I deserved. The job that rewarded my heroics with piles of money. The trophy wife who worshipped me back when she had no idea how much sex I got on the side. My life was great but never as perfect as when I drove that car. The car and I were one. Our souls merged from the moment I first touched the wheel.

Another deep breath in, I open my eyes. My life was ending. No respecting firm would take me. Why marry again? Another bitch to take me for a ride. Nah, I only had the car. The repo men would take that with no income. Someone else would drive my car. Eventually the police would have questions about my late wife. I sighed, closing my eyes again while spreading out my arms like a bird. Leaning forward, I feel myself plummet out the window only to reunite with the top of the Mercedes.

Picked Her Up Again

by Neen Cohen

"Are you going to hide, like dirty little voyeurists, the entire evening?" She poured another generous amount from the half-emptied bottle and took a sip from the small glass. Her fingers tapped on the packet of cigarettes she had grabbed earlier but hadn't yet bothered to open.

Finally, she heard the gentle movements of her lurkers as they slipped out of the shadows behind her. She imagined them to be nothing more than the pollution from an oil spill, but imagination was rarely in her favour. Turning on the barstool, back now pressing against the wooden bench where she left the bottle, she saw their eternally annoying perfection. They fucking well glowed, even now, after all these millennia.

"Just when we thought you were starting to learn." The female spoke with the voice of a harp being perfectly plucked.

"Regretting your decision yet again, to let me move?"

"Such a human idea. But perhaps seeing as you never seem to learn."

"So, what have I done now?" Could they say it, they hadn't been able to for such a long time now.

"Oh, Ni, what you always do." His voice was the rumble of an approaching storm. He spoke rarely, but when he did, it shook everything inside of her.

"Tell the gods I don't give a fuck. Every time you come, it just proves again how right I am!"

Ni slipped off the stool and threw back the rest of the drink in her glass. She replaced the empty glass on the counter, as though it mattered. Grabbing the packet of cigarettes she headed out the front door. No need to lock up or punch in the alarm tonight. No need for anything at all.

Across the road from her small bar, she stopped and sat in the gutter. She opened the packet of cigarettes, lit one up and waited for the show.

She was halfway through her fourth cigarette when the smoke began to billow out of the cracking windows.

She shrugged, feeling neither here nor there about their use of fire this time. At least they had allowed her to get out of the way before they blew the place up.

The fire danced and enticed, like belly dancers trying to get one wet. Red and orange against the black sky, they continued to taunt her.

When the place exploded, she didn't move or jump.

She simply took a deep pull on her cigarette and continued to watch.

Ni had worked hard; built the place up from nothing and treated her staff with respect and generosity.

She knew it would go sour when Sarah had told her earlier that evening that the place, the people she worked with, were like her family.

Ni had smiled and forced back the groan. She had been thinking the same thing for months now. She was unable to stop fostering that feeling, even though she knew what the inevitable end would be.

It was safe and warm, and though it made her ache for her lost flesh and blood, the snippets of comfort that the life she'd built gave her were worth it.

Pieces of her life rained down beside and around her. The gods were far too vicious to allow her to finally end the torment. But, a stray piece of mortar flicked toward her and nicked a small tear in her cheek.

It stung, and the pain made her smile.

Taking the last pull of her cigarette, she flicked the butt toward the chaos that was raging in front of her before wiping away the wetness on her cheek.

It didn't surprise her to see that the blood wasn't red but a clear fluid. Ni didn't need to taste it to know that it was salty.

Millenia came and went and all it took was that blossoming warmth in her chest, like from Sarah's words, and they would slither back in, and take all of her hard work away in a single moment.

The world had changed and nothing was the same, not even the crime she had been accused of. Punished for that very first blossom of warmth in her chest.

Letting out a loud breath, she stood up, brushed off the seat of her pants, pushed back her shoulders and walked away.

She had learned the hard way what happened if she sat for too long, that trapped feeling that overwhelmed her into a statued form. Presented as a mercy, it was merely another curse. All because of her human nature to feel that warmth.

It may always come before the fall, but it would also be the thing that always picked her up again.

The Fairest of Them All

by Ali House

The Queen took a deep breath before lifting the black veil that covered her face. In front of her was the large golden frame of her Magic Mirror, and looking into it only confirmed her worst fears. The blue eyes that stared back at her had clouded over, and the skin was grey and sagging. Hair that had once been bright yellow and voluminous looked more like dried hay, dull and flat. Turning from the terrible sight, the Queen quickly pulled the veil back over her face. She had known that this would happen soon, but that did nothing to lessen the pain, nor the horror. For the past seven days, she had been wearing the black veil, hoping in vain that maybe this time the magic would maintain and she would stay beautiful forever.

She had been radiant once, many years ago. Her long blonde hair hung in perfect waves, shining in the sunlight, and her blue eyes sparkled, lighting up rooms. People had looked upon her with love in their hearts, admiring her appearance and praising their beauteous Queen.

But time passed, as it does, and she began to age. Although she possessed great skill in the magical arts and was able to prolong her life, she was unable to find a spell to stop and reverse the ageing process. What she did find, however, was an ancient ritual to preserve beauty. It would only last for ten years, but it would keep the youthfulness of its subject perfectly preserved until the spell wore off.

And now, today, her ten years were up.

Crossing the room, she walked over to a golden bell cord and pulled on it. Although she could hear nothing in her bedchamber, she knew that a bell had rung throughout the castle, alerting her staff. As she waited for someone to appear, she moved over to the fireplace and sat in a chair made of dark cherry wood. It had been many years since a fire had been lit, and all it contained were cold ashes. In days long past, she used to sit in front of the fire, dreaming of marriage and children. Now all she could think of was her beauty and the price she would have to pay to get it back.

A few minutes later, her consult entered. He was a short, thin man who always seemed to be stammering or fumbling. His father had been her previous consult, a reserved man with sad eyes who did his job impeccably, but he had passed away six months earlier. She hoped that her new consult would be competent enough to handle such an important task.

"Yes, my Queen?" he said, bowing his head.

"Ten years have passed," she replied coldly. "It is time."

A nervous and fearful look crossed his face, but he quickly banished it and bowed again. "Yes, my Queen. The festival shall be held in three days time."

After he had left, her eyes moved once more toward the golden frame, but she quickly gained control of herself and turned back to the ashes, steeling herself for what was to come.

Notice of the festival was affixed to the large tree in the middle of the village. Two of the Queensguard stood next to it, towering imposingly in their dark armour. As villagers read of the upcoming festival, they were careful not to show any emotion other than delight. Although the Queensguard did not have eyes or ears, they were preternaturally observant and would report any unfavourable reactions to the Queen.

Back in their homes, where they were safe to whisper

the truth to one another, the villagers could express their anger and fear. Every day they prayed that these festivals would cease, but every ten years another took place.

It had been ninety years since the Queen brought down the magical barrier, trapping the village and castle inside. Since then they'd had no contact with the outside world, nor escape from the world inside. Many had tried to find a way through the barrier and all had failed. Their bones littered the ground, serving as a warning to others.

Every year the Queen grew more powerful and more unstable, and there was nothing the villagers could do to stop her. They could only pray that one day she would come back to her senses and regain the humanity that had vanished many, many years ago.

Sienna thought about killing herself. There were many ways that she could try to take her own life, but no guarantee that she would be successful. She couldn't ask anyone to help her, as they would be punished, and if she somehow remained alive after such an attempt, her punishment would be worse than death itself.

Looking in the mirror, she cursed her beauty. As a young child, her parents had hoped that her hair would darken or her eye colour would change, but as the years passed her looks remained the same. Now, at sixteen years of age, her golden hair fell straight down to her waist, and her blue eyes were the colour of a peaceful, cloud-free sky. She had grown used to the pitying looks the other villagers gave her whenever they looked upon her – looks that had grown in intensity ever since the festival's notice. But there was still hope. There were two other young women in the village who shared her curse, and it was possible that one of them would be the sacrifice instead of her. She felt sick wishing such a fate on another person, but she wasn't ready to die.

Sienna had only been six years old during the last festival, but she could still remember the sense of terror and helplessness that had fallen over the village. Her parents had given her lots of rules to follow, and there had been much crying after the festival was over, but she'd been too young to truly understand. When she turned twelve years old, her parents finally told her the truth about the festivals. She wished they hadn't.

The festivals happened once every ten years and they were the only time the castle was opened to the villagers.

The servants and Queen's consult were not allowed to leave the castle, and the villagers were not allowed to enter. Only the Queensguard, who loyally performed the Queen's bidding, were allowed to come and go regularly with ease.

Three days from now, the villagers would walk into the castle's ballroom and try their best to be merry and dance. The Queen would enter and sit on her throne, on a dais at the front of the room. She would be wearing a black veil, which would completely hide her face. Rumour said that she wore the veil because of her vanity and that the reason for the festival was the failing of her looks. Although they never saw her face, there were paintings of her beauty all around the castle – pale skin, blue eyes and blond hair, wearing elaborate gowns, a golden crown upon her head. As the Queen watched the dancing villagers, she would be looking for her sacrifice, and once the festival was over, a young woman with blond hair and blue eyes would be taken away by the Queensguard, never to be seen again.

Rumour said that the young woman's blood would be drained and the Queen would bathe in it to bring her looks back. But after ten years the spell would wear off and the Queen would need another festival and a new sacrifice.

Two days before the festival, a loud cry pierced the air. As Sienna hurried to the centre of town with her parents, she saw one of the Queensguard pulling a young blond woman towards the tree. Sienna recognised the woman as Joanne, one of the others who shared her curse. Joanne was crying loudly but it was more in misery than pain.

The Queensguard pulled her to her feet and grabbed her face, showing it to the gathering crowd. Sienna gasped as she saw what Joanna had done. Blood streaked down her face, flowing from deep cuts gouged into her once flawless skin.

"This being is guilty of the crime of self-mutilation," the Queensguard said, it's hollow, emotionless voice sending chills throughout the crowd. "The punishment is death."

Tears gathered in Sienna's eyes, but she held them back, refusing to let them fall. The Queensguard might see her pity and misinterpret it, reporting her to the Queen. Steeling herself, she watched as Joanna was held against the tree by another guard, unable to fight against their supernatural strength. When the first guard placed a large iron nail to her forehead, Joanna seemed to regain some of her sense and cried out for mercy. Her cries were in vain.

When the punishment had been completed, the Queensguard stood to the side of the tree, giving the villagers a clear view of what they had done. Sienna said a small prayer inside her head as she looked at Joanna's still form. It dangled from the iron nail, eyes still wide with fear, blood running down the mutilated face. Johanna's body would remain nailed to the tree for days, until the Queen felt that her point had been made.

When the Queensguard finally released them back to their homes, Sienna's feet felt heavier than before. The news of the festival must have driven Johanna mad, otherwise she never would have done such a thing. The villagers knew it was a punishable offence for a possible sacrifice to damage their beauty, so it had been decades since anyone had tried. With what happened today, it would be many decades before it happened again.

Back in the safety of her home, Sienna wept for Joanna. When she was finished, she wept for herself.

The day of the festival was bright and sunny, but the mood of the villagers did not match the weather. Although they were all dressed in their finest outfits, their steps were heavy and filled with hesitation. Still they trudged towards the castle, towards their unavoidable fate.

The ballroom had been decorated with flowers and ribbons, the bright colours standing in contrast with the subdued mood. Queensguard were placed around the room, standing against the walls at equal intervals. They did not move, and it was almost possible to mistake them for inanimate suits of armour.

Once all of the villagers had arrived, they gathered in a group at the centre of the room, waiting. The festival would not begin until magic had confirmed that there was nobody hiding in the village or the forest. The room was completely quiet, the villagers fearfully waiting with downcast eyes.

Finally the trumpets sounded. They looked up as the Queen walked into the room, followed by two of her guards. She wore a gown of rich purple and the black veil that covered her face was topped by a golden crown. Lowering herself into the throne at the front of the room, she clapped her hands together and music suddenly began to play.

The song was a lively number and the villagers began to dance, performing for the mad Queen. She never danced, only watched them through her veil. Her head never turned, but they could feel her eyes searching the room.

Sienna felt her palms start to sweat. They were into the fourth dance and she knew that it wouldn't be long now. Looking over at Adriana, she saw her own fear echoed on Adriana's face. With Johanna's death, the odds were now fifty-fifty.

The song ended and Sienna switched partners. Maybe today would be different. Maybe the Queen would have them dance forever until they passed out from exhaustion, preferring to kill them all at once instead of one at a time.

In the middle of the dance the Queen suddenly clapped her hands, stopping the mystical music. Her hands returned to her side as the two guards standing next to her moved forward, walking through the crowd.

Sienna glanced over at Adriana, who was only a few feet away. They shared one last look before turning back to the guards. Each step the guards made felt like a punch to the gut, but there was no way to know who the chosen one was. Not until they were closer.

The two guards stopped in front of Sienna and she felt all the hope drain out of her. Lowering her eyes to the floor, she didn't fight as each guard grabbed one of her arms and led her out of the ballroom. Nobody said a word as she was taken away. They knew it would be hopeless to try and save her, so they stood there, powerless.

The Queen stood up and left the room without a word. After she was gone, the villagers slowly began the walk back to their homes.

The door to the Queen's bedchamber opened and the consult entered, carrying a long box. His breathing was laboured and his eyes were wide with fear at what he had just witnessed. The Queen had demanded that he be present for the ritual and although his father had tried to warn him of what would happen, nothing could have prepared him for such a monstrous event.

At this very moment, the Queen was washing the blood from her hands. He didn't have much time. Moving over to her vanity, he placed the box on the table and opened the lid. Quickly and cautiously, he performed the final act of the ritual – the one his father had told him of, and the one the Queen knew nothing about.

He had just closed the box when the Queen arrived. Her hands were clean, but her gown was still spattered with bright red blood.

"The ritual went well," she said, her voice filled with

delight.

"Yes, my Queen," the consult answered, picking up the box and moving away from the vanity. His voice was tight with stress, but she didn't seem to notice. She walked straight to her vanity and sat down, her body trembling with anticipation. Taking off her veil, she looked into her Magic Mirror, and her smile grew as she took in the youthful face that looked back at her. The blue eyes were the colour of a peaceful, cloud-free sky and the golden hair was luxurious and soft. There was not a single wrinkle to be found. The Queen gave a satisfied sigh. The ritual had worked. Her beauty had been restored.

"Consult, you may leave."

The consult bowed his head. As he neared the door he couldn't help looking back at his deluded Queen. She stared ahead happily, not realising that the golden frame did not hold a reflective surface, but instead framed a box. Inside the box was Sienna's head, carefully preserved with ritual magic. It stared out at the Queen, and she stared back at it, unable to realising that it was not her own – unable to realise that her own skin was dried and wrinkled, her eyes grey with age, and her hair white and sparse.

As the door closed behind him, the consult wondered what would be worse—for the Queen to continue this reign of terror or for her to wake up one day and see the truth of what she had become.

Malcolm and Amelia

by Angela Zimmerman

It would have been polite to classify Malcolm as stubborn. Proper manners would perhaps allow the word obstinate to be used as well. Not that politeness mattered much to Malcolm. He would probably have used the word principled instead. Those that knew him best would have chosen different words. Words like pig-headed, tenacious, and everyone's favourite asshole.

It's not that Malcolm didn't care about other people's feelings. He just didn't see the point in them. If there was a job to do, he was going to do it, regardless of who or what opposed it. Personal opinions were nothing more than road bumps, small pauses on the path of progress. It wasn't that he was an evil man, he just took great pride in being able to carry out his ideas and being able to stick to his word.

So, when Amelia arrived at his doorstep, her hair in pigtails and her suitcase almost as big as she was, he was dumbstruck. Why would anyone think he should be the guardian of a child? How was he even on the list of potential guardians for a kid? He barely got along with adults! He had been a bachelor for all his 50 odd years, how was he even in contention for being a caregiver to a young girl?

But as the lawyer that accompanied her explained, Amelia was the only daughter of one of Malcolm's reclusive first cousins. After their unexpected deaths, she had made her way through what remained of their small family tree until she found her way to his doorstep. He was her last stop before the orphanage. Feeling responsible for someone who shared not only the same last name but also the same bloodline as he did spoke to his principles. And as a very principled man, Malcolm couldn't say no. Additionally, the monthly stipend she came with didn't hurt his decision either.

"There's a room in the back you can have. We'll get the boxes out tomorrow," he told the little girl, neither warmly nor gruffly, after he closed the door on the lawyer.

"Is there a basement? I'd really prefer that." Her voice, small yet serious, caused him to stop walking and turn around.

"Yeah, there is. It's damp and dark and full of mess, but if you want to sleep with the spiders, it's all yours. There's even a couch down there." He grinned at her gumption.

"I can manage." She struggled to pick up her bag and

waited for him to show her the way.

The hinges on the basement door gave a little fuss as he opened up the door and led her into the darkness. The overhead light buzzed in protest but illuminated the room with a dingy light.

Amelia struggled with her suitcase but made her way to the sagging couch and placed it on the middle. "This is nice," she said, bouncing up and down and, for the first time, showing hints of her age.

"If you say so, kid." Malcolm smiled at her. Then he paused. "You want a light? Need some blankets? I'm kind of feeling bad about leaving you down here."

He looked around. It wasn't the worst basement in the world, but for a young girl, it was pretty bleak. For a young girl who had been bounced between homes after losing her own, it was horribly bleak. Even though he valued function over aesthetics, he couldn't help but wonder if she wasn't owed something little bit nicer.

"Oh no, this is fine. A blanket would be nice, but it's not needed. I don't really get cold." Her dark eyes locked on his, and suddenly he felt very uncomfortable. Something about her gaze made him feel very small and very unprepared. Usually, people buckled from *his* gaze. He was usually the one winning stare downs. This time, he felt outmatched. He blinked and took a step back.

"I guess I'll leave you to it then. I'll be right up there if you need me." After a tip of his head, he turned and started climbing the stairs out of the basement.

"Mr. Malcolm?"

Her voice startled him enough his foot almost slipped off the stair it was on. He grasped the rail to steady himself as he turned to look down into the darkness.

"Thank you for everything. I won't forget it." Her small voice echoed in the dimly lit room until it took up all the space. It wedged itself in the back of his head and left a bad taste in his mouth. He tried to smile down at her before rushing up the stairs and through the door.

Back on the main floor, his heart pounded in his ears. Anxiety had never been an issue for him before. Maybe his age and the sudden realisation that he was responsible for a child had planted it in him. Or maybe, a voice in the back of his head screamed, it was something else. Maybe something wasn't right with the girl.

He quickly tuned that voice out and put on some water for tea. What he needed now was a big warm mug of normalcy.

The next morning, Amelia was sitting at the table

when he walked into the kitchen.

"You're up early." He grinned, but seeing her sitting there, perfectly still in the morning light unnerved him. The sun from the window made her look paler, her eyes bigger, and somehow, it made her look older than she did when she arrived. The dress she was wearing was different to the one she arrived in, but Malcolm couldn't exactly say how. The colours were muted, and the material looked rough. He didn't know a lot about fashion, but he could tell this was not something young girls typically wore.

"More time in the day if you begin before the sun." Her voice was nowhere as big as it was the night before but still, it seemed out of place coming from her small body. He tried to shake off his uneasiness with the ritual of making a pot of coffee. He lifted a cup to offer her one, not knowing what else to do and she smiled in agreement. So, he went about making two cups.

Both with two sugars, two dollops of cream, and just a dash of salt to counter the bitterness. He brought the steaming mugs to the tabletop and slid hers carefully towards her. She accepted it with a wide smile that showed exceptionally white teeth with incisors that, to him, looked too large for her mouth.

She raised the mug to her lips, and to his amazement,

started gulping the scorching liquid.

"Woah! Careful there, child! You're going to burn yourself!" He reached to grab her arm to pull the mug away from her mouth but by the time he had taken the few steps to get around the corner of the table, she had already emptied the cup.

"It wasn't that hot. I've never had this before. May I have another?" She didn't blink while looking up at him, her lips red from the heat of the coffee. Unable to find any words, he refilled her mug and watched as she drained it in a similar fashion as the first one.

"Ok, wait. Wait. This isn't right." He put a hand on his head and a hand on her shoulder. He wasn't an expert in child rearing, but he knew for certain that young children weren't supposed to guzzle hot coffee with that much gusto.

Her huge eyes looked up at him, again unblinking. The pupils had expanded and taken over her irises. There were none of the colors he had seen when she had been dropped off the night before. His breath quickened and he felt something in the middle of him quiver.

He was confused, overwhelmed, and more importantly, he was afraid.

"You don't look okay, Mr. Malcolm. I can hear your heart and it doesn't sound like it's remembering the right words to its song. You should sit down." And with that, the chair beside her slide from under the table.

His legs gave and he found his way to the chair. She was right, his heart wasn't beating right. And not just that, his brain wasn't functioning right either. Nothing was working right currently. The poor little orphan he had taken in out of the goodness of his heart, and potentially his bank account, was currently slugging down piping hot coffee in the middle of his kitchen. And to top it off, her eyes just changed to solid black.

Nothing about this made sense to a man as practical as Malcolm.

He tried to gain some sort of composer by rubbing his eyes and clearing his throat, "I think I'm going to go lay down Amelia. You're welcome to watch TV and have anything you can find in the fridge. I just need, uh, a few moments." His legs were unsteady as he lifted himself from the chair. He made sure not to touch Amelia as he shuffled around her and out of the kitchen.

He barely made it to his bed before he collapsed. He had never been a man who had felt true primal fear. Standing in the kitchen and see the young girl with her black unblinking eyes look up at him, he had finally felt it's electric grasp on his soul. He decided while looking up at his ceiling, he didn't like it. He didn't like this unreasonable, illogical, absurd feeling. He didn't like the girl bringing it to him, dirtying his home with the rudeness that fear brings. If he were ever in the position to choose, he'd rather not ever experience that feeling again.

He counted his breaths until they slowed and then let his brain take over.

What was he going to do? The girl had only been here for one night. He couldn't send her away now. If he tired how would he explain it? Would he call the lawyer who left his card just a handful of hours earlier and explain that something was so wrong with the girl that he needed to come and get her RIGHT NOW? How would that make him look? And what about the papers he had signed?

Malcolm felt his heart beginning to race again. His breath was coming in gasps and the corners of his visions were starting to darken. Again, he began to count his breaths, forcing himself out of his pit of anxiety and into a place of calm logic where he could think. Before he could find that place, he worked himself asleep.

The sun had slipped into the middle of the sky when he jerked upright, fully awake. Amelia was perched on his dresser, like a prepubescent bird of prey, a bowl of boiled pasta in her hands.

"I made this," she held the bowl towards him," do

you want some?" She tilted her head to the side and with what appeared to be a great effort, blinked.

Malcolm pulled his feet up towards his chest and moved higher up in the bed. HIs ability to be calm was just about at its end.

"No! What is this? What are you doing?" His voice was shrill like it had been when he was her age.

"I'm eating Mr. Malcolm. And I'm offering some to you. I think your real question is not 'what am I doing?' but 'what am I?'. Is that right?" She put the bowl down on one of his folded shirts. She wiped at her mouth with the back of her left hand and then stretch out her arms.

Malcolm stared from the top of his bed, hugging his pillow like a little boy in the middle of a nightmare. She no longer looked small and helpless like a sad young girl who had lost her parents, but large and imposing like a dancing shadow from a candle during a storm. Perched on the dresser, arms now pinned behind her back, staring into his face, she was the most intimidating thing he had ever seen. At some point, she had tied her hair back from her face so he could see how truly pale her skin was. She blinked at random intervals while staring into his frightened eyes. He felt like he was going to lose his mind.

He attempted to swallow but found his mouth too dry, "I don't know what I'm asking. I don't know anything anymore." His words were rattling whispers from behind the pillow.

"Then I will help you, Mr. Malcolm, because you helped me." She leapt from the dresser to the foot of his bed, landing on the balls of her bare feet with her hands making small imprints in his light blue comforter. "The cousins you never saw, the ones you didn't know, wanted a child. But they were getting old and running out of options. They didn't want to adopt and had ran out of money for medical treatment. So, they prayed. They prayed hard Mr. Malcolm."

She stopped forcing herself to blink and tilted her head to the side. There was a reptilian glisten to the darkness of her eyes now. "They prayed so hard that everyone listened. But God was too busy, and He doesn't answer selfish prayers anyway. But we do. We answer them, Mr. Malcolm. So one night, I was shipped up from Hell and placed in my mother's belly. They were so happy when they found out!"

She inched closer to Malcolm whose shaking was causing the bed to rock in a fitful rhythm.

"But that happiness was short lived. I wasn't the pink baby they wanted. I wasn't the prayer they had wept over. I was too loud, too pale, and my teeth, even then, were too sharp." She opened her mouth and Malcolm struggled not to weep himself. Her teeth were not the teeth of a child. They were not the teeth of an adult. What he saw in her mouth wouldn't belong to any human anywhere. "They called me a mistake. They were not happy with me no matter how good I behaved. No matter how many gifts I brought them. They locked me away and pretended I never happened. But Mr. Malcolm, my real family found out. And they didn't like that at all. They told me what to do and one night, I did. And that's how the house burned down and how I became alone."

She was inches away from Malcolm's face by this point.

"The other folks didn't want me either. They smiled for the lawyer, then stuffed me away. I didn't even make it a night with them. But you, you gave me a room. And you felt bad that it wasn't fancy enough. I read your doubts. And you offered me a blanket! And you made me that drink. What was it? Oh, coffee! You said it was called that right? I had never had that before. You are a nice man, Mr. Malcolm. I think we can be great friends."

His breath was little more than a wheeze. He saw his reflection in her solid black eyes and was surprised at how young fear had made him look. The uncertainty in his panic had restored something boyish to his face.

With a voice that was small and quivering, he

whispered, "I hope that we can be too, Amelia."

"Good!" She plopped down on her bottom, legs folded under her, and smiled in a way that hid the sharpest parts of her teeth. "Come out from the pillow and we can have lunch! I left my noodles on the dresser, but I can make more. I know how to cook! Well, not too many things but I can make noodles for you." And just like that, she was a young girl chatting away. She was not the creature with solid black eyes that was just detailing her assent from Hell. She was just a little girl trying to brag about her abilities.

Malcolm, being the practical man he was, moved the pillow away from his face. He folds his legs under him and squared himself up to Amelia. Her smile broadened, the tips of her teeth showing over her lips. She continued rattling off all the things she knew how to make in the kitchen and how she learned to make them. Concentrating on his breathing, Malcolm stayed in the moment and listened. While none of the events of the day made sense, what mattered now was that she, whatever she was, needed someone to listen to her. She needed someone to be nice to her.

Amelia needed a friend.

And as a man of his word, Malcolm knew that was his job.

The Hunt

by Brianna Witte

A twig snapped under my thick hiking boots. I froze, listening for movement in the forest. I pulled my small handgun closely to my body, ready in case I needed to spring into action. I waited, hearing only the birds chirping in the trees and the water rushing beside me from the fast-paced river. The forest seemed to be quiet today. I took a deep breath, inhaling the air, hoping to catch the scent of my target.

As a werewolf, I had many improved abilities that allowed me to track my prey easily. The bloodlust that I felt when the full moon rose was unbearable. Whenever I had to change into my wolf form, I became a solitary animal, searching for a living, breathing life form that would quench my hunger.

I had not always been this way. I was born human. Never in my life would I have thought it delicious to rip large chunks of flesh from an animal or, in my worst moments, another human being. Yet, that unexpected night came where I was scratched.

My friends and I were at the beach one night,

drinking and acting like the young college boys that we were. The bonfire was the only source of light since the moon and stars were covered by a blanket of cloud. It was the last night where we all sat together, acting as if we were invincible.

The last thing I can remember clearly was Peter's face when the clouds suddenly parted and the full moon shone in the night. He was petrified; knowing what was coming. He had tried to get away from us, but we wouldn't let him. We knew nothing of his secret. We insisted that he stay to finish his drink. After all the party had just begun.

It happened so fast. His body changed into something horrific; a large oversized wolf. Three of my friends were slaughtered that night. Mutilated right in front of me by a person I thought I knew.

Somehow, through all that terror and certain death, I had been spared; but not without a price. Blood ran out of my body from the deep lacerations I had endured. On top of me lay the wolf. His teeth inches from my throat. In horror, I pushed him off me. He dropped to the ground, limp and unmoving, my pocketknife embedded in his chest.

From then on, my life was changed. The price I had paid for surviving that night was that I had become the blood thirsty monster. Looking back, I would not have fought back. I would have gratefully died that night, knowing my soul would be whole and the blood that I have spilt over the past year would not be my doing.

To keep myself under the police's radar for murder, I was continuously travelling from city to city, homeless and keeping to myself. After a full moon I would move again, hoping that my presence had gone unnoticed. I was in a dark place; depressed and angry for what I had become, until I met one of my own kind. He took me in for a short time, telling me stories of a now rare creature that could cure the werewolf disease.

Elves were no myth. Humans have always feared what they cannot explain, or the beings that are different. That is why werewolves, along with many other species, were killed and had to go into hiding to survive; which in turn is the reason that modern day humans think that we are part of old fables. Of course, the humans deserved to defend themselves against the werewolves and other carnivorous creatures when we were at our peak in history, but their fear grew into bloodlust; hunting anything that was unlike them and considering it evil or demonic.

Centuries ago, the elves' numbers thrived. They were a peaceful and humble people who closely resembled humans, except for their pointed ears which could easily be concealed; this kept them out of harms way. If they had to they could fit into society for a short time, however they left the humans alone, preferring to stay deep in the forests among their own kind for fear that they would become hunted.

Sometime in the sixteenth century everything changed. Under the full moon, a starving werewolf had taken the life of an elf who had wandered too far from its small village. Soon after devouring the young elf, it is said that a roaring pain spread through the wolf's body, transforming it back into a man. Never again did the moon hold its grasp on the man. He was cured.

In that moment, the werewolves discovered that the blood of an elf was the key to release them of their unholy fate; a way to return to society without fear of being killed for what they were.

It was called the Hunt. Many werewolves would join together in packs to seek the elves and drink their blood. Only then would the werewolves' reign of terror be over and they could live their lives as humans again. The elves were sought after until their numbers depleted; their once serene way of life destroyed. They were believed to have become extinct, leaving the werewolves that remained stuck with their curse.

However, after hundreds of years of hiding and rebuilding their race, the elves were once again spotted from time to time. Most wolves thought of these sightings as a delusion; a hallucination from desperate werewolves who wanted nothing more than to be cured. After all, elves were supposed to be extinct. However, I believed the stories. It gave me hope. I would give anything to get my life back; to return to my family. So here I am, in the Black Forest where werewolves claim to have seen the elves. I was continuing the Hunt.

I lowered the gun, put it back in its holster and continued on with my trek through the dark, dense forest. I had spent four days walking. My feet ached from the hike and my eyes were heavy from lying awake most of the night, waiting for the odd chance of an elf to pass by.

Although I had become accustomed to sleeping in the most inconvenient, cold places, the Black Forest was nothing like I had encountered before. There was no light from a nearby streetlamp and the moist ground seemed to seep into my sleeping bag, leaving me cold and wet most of the time. My only hope was that once I had found an elf, this nightmare I had been living in would be over. I would go back to my family in London and never look back.

I crouched close to the ground as I slowly slid down

a slope leading to the riverbed. My water bottle was almost empty, and my dry throat screamed for a cold drink. My boots sank into the sand as I approached the river. The steady flow of water roared through my ears. I dipped the bottle into the river, letting the rushing water flow into it.

I twisted the lid back on the bottle and headed up the bank. The climb down seemed to be easier than it was going back up the slope. I slipped multiple times and my hands couldn't properly grasp the soft dirt.

I made it to the top of the slope, panting. I wiped the dirt off my jeans and continued on my way, following the river. After a few minutes, I caught the sound of something moving.

I quietly crouched down and sat at the edge of the slope, peering down at the riverbank. If was then that I noticed the child walking towards the water. I watched as the young girl crouched down before the river; her long blond hair falling in front of her face. My brows drew together confused. She looked like a regular person, yet her scent was off. She wasn't human. Then I saw it. Pointed ears rose up out of her drooping hair.

It was an elf. The tales were true. My heart felt like it was beating out of my chest as I stared down at the elf girl.

I slowly took out my gun as the elf dipped a large wooden bowl into the river. This was my only chance. If I didn't act, the opportunity would be lost, and I would remain a werewolf forever.

I put my hand on the trigger, ready to fire. I closed one eye as I aimed the gun at the elf's head. As if sensing something was wrong, the elf looked around hastily. She stared up at the slope where I crouched, gun raised.

Our eyes met. In that minute, the elf was not my chance at happiness but a child who had only just begun her journey through this world. My decision would forever change both of our lives. Uncertainty drove into me like a knife puncturing my skin. Who was I to make that choice?

Thoughts thundered inside my head with such force that I had to close my eyes. This was a child. No one in their right mind would harm a child. Even if she was an elf who could possibly cure me, she was still innocent in the whole situation. *Can I live with myself if I go through with this?*

An argument rose inside of my head from the part of me that desperately wanted to be rid of this curse. *If I don't do this, I will not have a second chance. I will remain a werewolf and have to suffer the fate that I was given.*

Never in my life would I have thought of doing harm to another person, yet the day had come where I had to make the difficult choice. Would I kill a person to save myself? Will I go to my grave knowing that I had committed the worst crime imaginable to someone so young and vulnerable? Or will I walk away from here, accepting defeat, but knowing in my heart that I did the right thing, even if it meant that my life would continue on a downward spiral?

My hands shook as I held the gun. Part of me screamed to get it over with; to think of this moment as a victory not a set back. Everyone dies eventually. But my finger didn't budge. It was as if I was frozen in place, unable to move. Was I a killer? If I took the shot that title would forever be engraved with my name.

I was not being controlled by the werewolf. In this very moment, I was a person of free will. My decision would define who I truly was.

I couldn't live another day like this. Every full moon it felt like a part of me was being torn apart. I don't believe my soul could survive another kill. It was either her or me and I have come too far to give up now. I have to finish this.

I took a deep breath and pulled the trigger. The elf dropped where she stood, her body limp. The smell of blood drifted into my nose as I sat on the edge with tears pouring out of my eyes.

In that moment, I came to learn one of the ugliest sides of a being human. We would do anything to save ourselves, even if that means hurting the innocent. As a person, not a beast, I decided to kill rather than live with the part of me that I hated.

Life is all about choices. The choices we make can either make us into heroes or break us until there is nothing left but the painful memories of the ghastly things we did in order to keep moving through this world.

I chose to live with the tragedy and regret over my choice. Would you?

Trip to Comeuppance

by Catherine Kenwell

She was world-famous. And now she was accepting a Global Humanitarian Award for her work with Cambodian children. Saving them from the streets. Making media darlings of a few attractive ones, but secretly harvesting the rest for sweatshop work in factories outside Phnom Penh. Several were so talented, she engaged them to craft her gown for the awards ceremony.

"Thank you for this well-deserved recognition," she addressed the audience, shaking the trophy in a fist pump.

She exited the stage. Tripped. Broke her neck. A tiny pocket sewn into her hem caught her stiletto. Just the way they'd planned it.

When the Wood Walked

by Clint Foster

Orum and his brother Osai grew up in the Eskeria of old, when the wood was alive with the magic of the world and sang often beneath the light of Lau, the moon. They grew up quickly, like all elves, in more ways than one. When their progenitors ordered them to choose the tree which would become their home, both boys knew in an instant which to pick, and the other elves were glad they agreed.

Most elves reach physical maturity in fifteen years, experiencing physiological aging at almost twice the rate of a human, not that there were any of those wandering around when Orum and Osai were young. There were no kingdoms then, no nations or countries with which to align oneself. There were just elves and the other creatures who had life breathed into them by Bol himself. Eskeria smothered all the world beneath emerald canopies and elegant foliage that lived in a manner beyond how they were perceived. So too did the ground live and walk, for magic was thick upon the air of old Eskeria, and is the font from which all life springs.

Golems roamed wild through the hills and haunts of the world. Forces of nature and magic given animation and sentience. Centaurs dotted the wood, keeping to themselves and sticking to the hidden places among the massive boles of the Eskerian trees. There was nothing to fear, not this far south anyway. So, when the two young elves were told to pick that tree for their home, they were careful to choose one that would neither age nor wither. It was a hearty, thick-trunked oak near the heart of the world. The boys were pleased with their choice, and took to singing magic into the mighty boughs that would hold them safe.

Though the boys always had similar ideas, their implementation varied wildly, and they argued more and more frequently over whose way was the right one. Orum would chide Osai for his impetuosity, and Osai would condemn his brother's patient ways, accusing him of an impotence of spirit or heart. "A fire burns hot until it dies young, killing anything it touches, yet a river can change all the world without doing harm."

Osai retorted, "I can dam a river and douse a fire, but both require action."

And so it was with the two of them all their lives

together. When it came to the tree, and they each sang separate magics into the wondrous wood, they then began to truly learn the power in their own voices. Eskerator they named it, and it grew with their praise in both size and majesty. More beautiful than any other tree, from the combination of the boys' magics, it was the only tree throughout Eskeria whose leaves changed colour, whose fruit grew and fell, and whose bark aged, withered, and shrivelled. Not for long was it an oak, and sometimes it was an elm, a maple, a conifer, or any other number of trees, and it was a marvel that could be appreciated by all elfdom, and it was. The boys were renowned, and though they kept Eskerator hidden through their magics, there came to be no shortage of elves who had visited the wondrous changing tree in which Orum and Osai lived.

They never ceased crafting their home, not even when there came news of a schism through the entirety of the elvish race. It started small, like these things always do, with harassment and threats. The high elves who lived in the trees came to resent those they deemed their lessers for singing magic into the stones and living in elaborate caves sung by magic into the stone and dirt of Eskeria's floor. Whoever started the hostility did not matter, and the animosity took on a life of its own. Eskeria and the elves within were consumed by the bitterness brought only by war of the least civil kind.

A few of the Praestans, those who deemed themselves superior, formed a small army and set about attacking the cave elves, systematically rooting them out of homes they had, in some cases, occupied since the first dawn. It was only a matter of time before someone was killed, and from there the whole world seemed to fall into blood and chaos. These elves knew better than to farm the lumber of the wild wood without first getting permission, but once it was given, the living tress watched in horror as their seedlings were butchered for the industry of war. The elves had promised progress yet delivered only pain. They had asked Eskeria for aid, and when it was offered, they made slaves of the trees.

Neither side could ever overcome the other, and clashes of arms soon exploded in growing numbers throughout the wood. Limited engagements of only a dozen or so elves at a time, in places that had never yet known violence. Metal was heated for the first time, not forged, for it was Karak the dwarf who first hammered upon an anvil, but sung into useful edges and blades, just as the trees were twisted into homes and hearths. Wondrous steel was made by the elves then, and the blades from the Sundering era remain the most sought after swords in the world outside of the starsteel forged by

Karak himself.

Orum did not agree with the war. He felt violence was the least necessary thing in the entire world. It was worse than accomplishing nothing at all, it set everything back, and in setting things back, made the future not as progressed as it should be. There was no shortage of resources or space, and no power to poorly distribute. Not before the Sundering anyway. Philosophically, the idea of killing to further oneself was abhorrent to him. Nothing Osai ever said could change his mind, and they held their noses up at one another, each knowing themselves to be right.

Initially, the fighting happened far west of Eskerator, but became more and more widespread as elves were dragged into conflict by pride and honour and any other number of made up reasons. It was only a matter of time before whispers and rumour spoke to Eskerator of the coming of battle. Conflict infringed upon the territory Orum and Osai once roamed as children, and they despaired to see the places they had loved be destroyed by the wanton magics and focused malice of their own kind.

Singing a tree into a home takes time, for just as it is when building one, wood does not care to bend far and especially such a mighty oak, for that was what Eskerator still was at its heart, proved stubborn.

"We have no quarrel with either party, they should leave us alone," said Orum often, shaking his head, too stuck in his own way to consider any other. "If they approach we will destroy them," spat Osai in return. He would practically dare others to steer the violence toward Eskerator, knowing that if they but asserted their power, the elves would be supplicant and stop fighting.

One of the last other elves in the area, a heartless old man with whom no one cared to spend much time, stalked past Eskerator the dawn following a nearby clash. He came upon the two elves arguing and muttered, at both but neither of them, "Compromise or die kids, compromise or die."

"Compromise is a sign of weakness," Osai laughed, "such a thing should never be expected from us."

"Compromise is concession," Orum shrugged, "and where must we draw the line if not at the very feet of our homes?"

For three years they had sung together, separately, to twist and mould the oak to their wills, and in that time, they formed of it a palace of nature and magic. Beautiful beyond anything their peers could even imagine. Powerful beyond even what they themselves could. The Sundering burned and roared all around them and yet thus far had not encroached upon the oak. But it was not to last.

All too soon the brothers heard shouts on the breeze that tickled the leaves of their home, and they steeled themselves, too proud to flee.

The Praestans had no quarrel with them, for they lived in the trees and were deemed allies. Yet they wanted no affiliation with those who called themselves by any name other than their own, and made their position clear. So too, when the Braecans passed by and confronted the brothers, were they denied allegiance. An uneasy night passed with both factions camped perhaps a hundred yards apart with the oak in their midst.

All that night, Osai was practically vibrating with rage at the insolence of the other elves, and though Orum shared in a portion of this anger, he knew hotheadedness would do naught for them save cause greater problems. "It was ire which caused this war. The ire of fools."

"Bol's will that it be my ire that puts an end to it."

For two weeks the elvish armies stayed their bloodlust, and representatives from both parties convened at the base of the oak to parley. Neither side seemed to want anything other than to destroy the other, and after the first day, they nearly dissolved into violence. Orum suggested that he and Osai, being neutral in the conflict and mutually respected, split up to deal with the factions individually. Orum met with the Braecans, and Osai with the Praestans.

Separately, they met with the representatives of both sides, staying on opposite branches of their home to avoid any potential opportunities for violence. When Orum asked the Braecans why they felt the need to cause such devastation and death, for it was they who started the war, the answer came from an old elf who was set apart from the rest by his magnificent silver beard. He spoke calmly but with a strength that was evident by his methodical gait and practiced, effortless gestures, "They live in the shadows of the boughs, and the shadow corrupts. Your brother will make it clear to you, in time."

To his sorrow, Orum did notice a change. His brother had always been haughty and quick tempered, but now, as they sang their magics still into the Eskerator, he felt a darkness about Osai which was undeniable. Inevitable, if he were to believe the old elf who warned him of such a change. Just in spending his days with the Praestans he was being corrupted. Changed. Warped into a creature that barely resembled the Osai he once raced in the heart of Eskeria.

Finally, on the fourteenth night, when they were singing to the oak and asking it to bend to their wills, Osai snapped in a vicious tone directed at the tree, "As we command so shall you obey. Whatsoever we will of you, so let it be."

"Brother, your time with the Praestans has made of you a thing of malice."

"Quoth he whose hypocritical dealings set him singularly apart from reason."

Orum was impassive, and his voice neither rose in pitch nor darkened in tone, "I can endure your insults brother, for they are naught but words."

Osai was practically hissing at his brother, threatening with all but his words, "Elves should not endure, they should rule."

"Whence comes this desire to conquer?"

"Always I have known us, you and I brother, to be the same and yet so distant from one another. You wish to be a king just as I do."

"Leadership requires calming the tempest of our personal selves."

With a sharp laugh, Osai ordered, "Calm it no longer brother, the Braecans turn you against me even as the Praestans would turn me against you. But I have not known, at any time past nor present, any elf whose might in magic and arms could rival our own. Together we could rule them all, regardless of what they wish to call themselves."

This sparked in Orum an idea of how to possibly put

an end to the sundering entirely, and he spoke aloud to his brother, "Perhaps we should rule. Separately. You over the Praestans and I over the Braecans. They have no true leadership, either party, and they've already leaned heavily on us to provide negotiations in this brief respite."

Osai picked up his brother's thread, but continued the timeline, "As kings we could expand. Venture at last out of the wild wood and see the world as none never have."

Orum beamed to see his idea sparking such joy in his brother, but his smile fell sickly as Osai's expression darkened and he gazed into a future of power. "We would be conquerors."

"Is it not enough to be kings?" Orum asked sadly, knowing his brother's answer though Osai did not speak in reply.

They stayed up late into the night, until well after Lau, the moon, had come to shine her pale light through the gaps in the foliage. Perhaps if the wood did not provide such good cover from light, what happened next could have been avoided entirely, but that was a future that was not to be.

Throughout the long evening, the brothers argued over how to rule, where they would go, what precautions they might take, and other such matters of the throne. When they broke for the night, and Orum climbed high into the oak to rest, Osai left his brother and his home behind to meet in secret with the warring elvish factions. To the Braecans he said, "Your guide has failed you, and Orum is meeting with the Praestan elves to plot an attack on you this very night!"

Before they could ask too many questions, he had stolen back into the darkness, crossing beneath the waving limbs of Eskerator and into the camp he had spent many hours in of late. "Brothers," he said as worried as he could, "Braecan elves are taking to their weapons, advised by my own brother, to strike tonight!"

So baited, both armies rose and girded themselves for battle, and they met in violence beneath Eskerator. Orum, who had been asleep throughout, woke to the sounds of death coming from the ground above which he slept. Through the window he saw a battlefield, and wept at the waste of war. Then, even as he cried, he felt a fury rise in him that he had never known, and whatever patience once reserved his wrath was lost. In a tumult, he flew to the battlefield and roared above the din, "My brother has betrayed all elves this night!"

The silence crashed as heavily on their ears as the battle had, broken only by Osai's laugh. He ascended the base of a nearby tree with elvish deftness, coming to his brother's height above the battlefield. "Do you see how easy it was to make them fall upon one another? Do you see how easy it was to stop them?"

Finally, Orum saw the power inherent in power. He was but moments away from reaching out to Osai and taking him up on the offer to rule at his side. Just in the moment he opened his mouth, a Braecan arrow sailed noiselessly through the air and impaled itself in Osai's right eye, pinning his skull to the tree.

With a scream, Orum summoned the magic in his veins and the wood, and using Eskerator as his tool, turned on the Braecan elves and battered them unto the brink of death until they fled as far as they could, stopping only at the Seia Wesrin's shores. The first of many living trees was born of Orum's rage, and Alkurah would never forget their power.

Once it was done, and he saw the devastation he wrought through Eskerator, he wept silently for days. When the offer came from the Praestan elves to be their king, he accepted somberly, weighed down by the loss of his brother and his morals. He made Eskerator his home, and the home of all Praestan elves, as there was room for any and all. Osai's body was cradled in the roots of the tree-home of Praesta, and sunk into a magnificent mausoleum that loomed above Orum's throne room as an eternal reminder of where having pride in one's power leads.

Roses Are Red
by Jason Holden

Lord Barton's shovel crunched into the dirt. Wiping the sweat away from his forehead, he left a brown streak behind from the layer of dirt covering his hands. The rose bushes needed tending better, they had been brought from Earth, along with the precious soil that contained them, when his noble family first settled here. He would have a word with the gardeners in the morning. The thought made him angrier than he was already. There was a time when you could rely on people for jobs like this, but no more. A lord like him should not have to talk to peasants like the gardeners he had on his staff. Throwing down the shovel and picking up the fork, he eased out the third rose bush in the line and placed it gently with its fellows. Each bush was spaced two feet apart, giving them ample room to grow to perfection. Being a Barton meant something. His family were from noble birth even before people had been forced to live in domes on this rock. Even the gardens needed to be perfect. Maintaining the image of the family was important, his father had taught him that.

His daughter should have known that too. He

entertained her courting the boy for a while, thinking that she would figure it out on her own. He was below her station; he made his money from playing video games, for god's sake! Video games! While other plebs like him sat on their settees and watched, munching their snack food and no doubt waiting to collect on their government provided benefits. The fork went back in its previous place, stood against the wheelbarrow as Lord Barton picked up the shovel and thrust it into the dirt once more to deepen the hole. The state of the roses was appalling, but soon they would have the nourishment they need.

Anger coursed through him again as he struck a rock buried in the ground with an audible thump, jolting his arms, and gnashing his teeth together. There should be no rocks in the flowerbed, the pH that made up the ground of this moon would kill them. Yet more evidence of the shoddy work the plebs under his employ executed. He knew they called him a "toff" and thought him arrogant. Thoughts that had been echoed by his daughter at their last meeting. That boy had the gall to stand in his home and tell him he was going to marry his daughter. Tell him! Not ask him, tell him! "How dare you not ask me first!" Barton had spurted.

"I told him not to ask Daddy, because I knew you'd say no, your arrogance wouldn't have let you approve!"

Barton muttered the words under his breath now, re-living the conversation as he dug, bringing up shovelful after shovelful of rich brown dirt. "The boy is beneath you Charlotte! I won't allow it, being a Barton still means something!" She stormed off while the boy remained, looking him the eye. He should be on his knees, genuflecting, at least trying to show some respect for his betters. But no, he stood eye to eye with Lord Barton and said he was to marry Charlotte no matter what he might think. He did all but spit on Lord Barton, such disrespect!

Blood trickled from his hands, leaving a red line where it trailed down the shaft of the shovel. He'd have to clean the tools off after he had finished. It simply wouldn't do to let people see he'd been using them. Unused to manual labour, his hands were now raw from handing the rough wood on the shaft. He should not have to be doing this, but it was necessary. His fine clothes were covered in dirt and blood from the work he had been carrying out. Once again, he thought that as little as fifty years ago someone could have been relied on to take care of this. His father would roll over in his grave if he saw his son now, covered in sweat and filth, digging in the ground like a common farmer.

Barton remembered striking the boy, breaking the skin on the back of his hand. That had been the first cut of the evening. It could have ended there, but his daughter walked back in, no doubt to give him another piece of her mind, and spurned on by the presence of his woman and not wanting to seem meek, the boy had given in to his baser instincts, as one of low class was bound to do and struck Barton back. Lord Barton had expected Charlotte to finally see the boy was unworthy of her right then, but instead she defended him in his attack and claimed her father deserved to be hit. Luckily, there was an old cavalry sabre mounted over the fireplace on the wall, and Lord Barton was able to grab it and fend off the advances of the boy.

The hole was deep now, deep enough so that he could stop digging. It had taken a long time, and his wife had come out multiple times, sobbing and yelling at him. He told her how he'd had no choice, "How could I let her marry that lowlife! Being a Barton means something!" Yelling over the grounds was unseemly, but he had no choice, the Lady Barton refused to come closer even though his work here was important. He had thought she'd understand, but alas, her feminine hormones had gotten the better of her. She only wanted her daughter to be happy, not caring about propriety. Ridiculous woman! Charlotte would have been just as happy with a man of *his* choosing. Why could nobody see that he was right.

He clambered out of the hole and, kneeling, he pushed at the rolled-up carpet that previously lay on the floor of his study. Containing two bodies made it heavy. Wriggling his hands underneath the ornate fabric, Lord Barton heaved and grunted, tipping his daughter and her would-be suitor into the grave with a hollow thud.

Blue lights flashed from over the high, well-trimmed hedgerows that lined the grounds as dirt from Lord Barton's shovel rained down over the corpses. He recognised the lights as those of police cars, briefly he wondered why they were outside his manor house. Perhaps some yobs causing trouble outside, he had called them himself multiple times in the past, ordering them to remove picnickers or campers trespassing on his fields; his was the only grass on the small moon they inhabited and the ordinary folk thought it their right to use it as they saw fit. They should have worked harder, maybe then they could afford their own grass. Looking up to the house, he saw his wife's silhouette in a top window. The light behind her obscured her features to him, but he knew her shape, they had been married for over thirty years, she was watching him work.

Multiple beams of light appeared from round the side of the house, waving backwards and forwards as people approached. They shone onto his face, and blinded by the bright lights, he had to lift up a dirt covered hand to shield his eyes from the lights that assaulted them. "What on earth are you doing? This is private property, you ingrates!" Rough hands grabbed at him, forcing him to the ground and pushing his hands behind his back. "Archibald Barton, you are under arrest for the murder of Charlotte Barton and Adam Townsend." He couldn't see the woman who spoke because of the lights still shining on him, so just directed his outrage at the place where the sound was coming from, "How dare you, you tart! I am a Lord! You simply cannot treat me like this!" Two pairs of hands hauled him upright and started dragging him back towards the house, "I demand that you wait! My roses, they'll die if you don't let me plant them back. They've belonged to my family for generations!" He screamed and yelled all the way to the cruiser they sat him in. They would pay for this; he'd have all their badges. They'd see, being a Barton meant something.

Honour's Pride

by D.A. Smith

"My great lords," I growled, biting back poisoned words as I dismayed at having to beg in front of these whoresons. "With divine respect, this is folly. We are but victims of the fieldclans. Master Dattori meant no dishonour, they made the first move. Pardons, please. You must listen. They paid in equal measure to their crime. What was lef—"

"Quiet, Tobigawa," Master said.

Taking my eyes off the surrounding guards, the dogs, for a second, I turned to him. Old, wrinkled, a tired warrior. His eyes shimmered in the low light like koi ponds against the moon. Elegance and honour were all that remained. The laughter lines now redundant as despair gripped him. Not for what was to come, but for what I might do. Master always said anger and pride were a bad mixture, that they soured honour. But what use was that wisdom now? A candle flickered, and the perfume of incense cut through the scrubbed cypress, and the smell of the tatami beneath me. Gritting my teeth, I tore away from Master's stare and back to the grinning hyenas that awaited the show. High on the dais, the five of them stood judging me as only the divine should. I tugged against the sweaty grip of the guards at my back, the thick white dress robes allowing movement within their restraint, something I could use to my advantage. Maybe. A bludgeon-like fist smacked me, and I recoiled.

With a wave of the pompous shogun's hand, the beating stopped, and a strike to the back of our legs brought Master and I to our knees. Gold-gilded plate armour that had never seen a battle, adorned with intricate carvings of the sora dragons, rattled against the cur's body as he motioned to us again. Smirking, the shogun was enjoying this farce too much. My chest tightened, and I found it difficult to get my breathing under control. To the shogun's sides, the four lords stood in ceremonial plates of silvers, blacks, greens and greys, but never gold. That was strictly for His *Godliness*. Talk of honour, theirs was bought for a few gold kobans. Gold coins for cats.

At the foot of the dais stood a monster in fox-decorated armour. The Fox swordsman. Eight blades in all hung from the shogun's pet. Representative of the tails of a kitsune, supposedly. Chances were slim, but I would take them rather than settle this with their worthless honour. How ridiculous it still means so much to Master, to all these men. No, I'd rather live. I will…must.

"Let's get on with this." The shogun yawned. "The charges!"

Lord Jizu stepped forward, holding a scroll for effect, and said, "Ahem." *Take your time you mongrel.* "The charges levied against Lord Dattori of the Blue Moon, and his retainer Tobigawa Eyasu, are the most heinous of crimes. Those that go against the rule of the very gods, and the peace and prosperity of the shogunate. The murder of the clans within, and the illegal seizure of, the Tayo lands, manufacture and distribution of the poppy, and treason. Treason, of all charges." The room seemed to hold its breath around me as I waited for Jizu's final words. I blew out a breath and it was so. "Carries the penalty of death."

The room broke into jeers and cries.

"Lies!" I said.

"Tobigawa!"

"No, Master—"

"Speak out of turn in front of his godliness once more. I plead," the Fox snarled. "And I'll suffer you not any longer. You will not leave this plane with honour." He gripped the hilt of the katana at his left side and started to pull the blade when the shogun stopped him.

"Put that away." He gestured to the Fox, and then looked at me. "Fine, let's hear your pitiful words. A final speech, as it were."

Master's breaths were heavy, the rasp really was getting to my head as he stared at me. I felt it tug at my soul. I looked away from the shogun and back to the man I revered. His eyes pleaded with me to stop. Pleaded that I go with honour. My blood was hot with it. He shouldn't have asked that of me, he knew my temper. Ignoring it, I turned back, wanting to spit in front of the cur upon the dais. Master's gaze still heavy on me. If I could save his honour, I would. I began, "The fieldclans under Jizu's command prepared the poppy, set fire to our fields, destroyed our crop, raided our lands. Under your nose, Godliness, did Jizu plot this. Master and I are but a sacrifice deemed appropriate of his own crimes. They brought a sword to our homes. It was only in return that they paid for it in blood. As such, we moved into the blood-claimed lands. The laws dictate it. Godliness, the laws we protec—"

I stopped in my speech as he chuckled, letting out a guffaw as the fools behind him tried their best to mimic the cries of a laughing gull. "Lord. Lord Jizu. Would you dishonour yourself by forgetting the appropriate way to address him, retainer?" The shogun said. "And what of your plot against me, against the shogunate? Treason is unforgivable. Against the heavens, it cannot be forgiven.

Must not!" Cheers erupted around the room again, and one of my teeth cracked against the strain of my own anger.

"Lies! All Lies!"

"Tobigawa. SILENCE!" Master strained.

I tried to rise, but the men at my back beat me down again, the encircling guard taking a step closer.

"How dare you!" The Fox drew his katana, bringing it above his head into the Kamae of Heaven.

"Away, I said, Kita." The shogun descended the dais, stopping by his pet. "You dare call my good lords…" He made a show of turning back to them, waving his hands, and back to me. "My dear friends. Liars?"

Realising my betrayer tongue had made a mistake, I'd gone too far, I backtracked, "No. Many apologies, my Godliness." I bowed as low as I could with the guards at my arms, feeling the chill from the tatami. "Please accept my apologies. But you see—"

"ENOUGH! You insult my good nature. Here I am, full of mercy, in front of my good peoples, in front of heaven, offering you a chance to regain your honour in death. And yet you exploit this opportunity, woman, by begging and pleading." He clapped. "Bring Lord Dattori his tanto." My heart sank. "This will go on for no longer."

Death. Oh gods and dragons above. This is what

years of service to the shogunate has brought Master? To him, a life well-served in death, but to me it was a waste. The *badump badump* of blood raging like lava was in my ears. I trembled. Anger rose in me. Master never did manage to tame it, said it was a demon's hold of me. "DEATH?" I shouted. "This is what farcical lies have earned my honourable Master?" My anger had bit into me now.

"How dare you raise your voice at me! Kita, here." The Fox strode towards us at the same time the servant carrying the tanto entered the room. I gulped hard. The Fox and his eight blades clattered over to me. The servant was there, too.

The guards pulled Master and I to our feet, letting him go while they clasped me. It was strange. He straightened his robes ready to receive the blade. Master wheezed and I closed my eyes hard, a pit opened in my stomach at the weakness this ordeal had left such a great man with.

The shogun took the tanto and Master bowed as he handed it to him with a smirk. Dishonourable smirk. Master held the bow for much longer than he should have.

Thump thump, my blood was a torrent of madness. "No. NO MASTER. YOU CAN'T." My breathing was shallow, fast. "DON'T. NO. DON—"

Master swung around, tanto outstretched, moving towards me quicker than I thought he could and slashed opened my chest. I fell back into the guards, the warmth of my life pumping down my chest. My head dizzying.

The guards cried out and the room erupted in laughter. The shogun waved his arrogant wave once more, "Very good, Dattori. You still know your place, but that is one step too far for your…pupil. KITA!"

The Fox drew closer, katana held to heaven still, smiling a gaunt smile.

Blood poured down my chest, my head lighter and lighter. Ears buzzing. That's when Master spoke up, "Please Kirsam— Godliness. Forgive her. She holds a passion for her service. A passion to preserve the shogunate's laws. She only wishes to serve. Allow her the honour of death in that service. By my honour—"

"Silence, beggar. This is finished. What honour?" Anger gripped hold. The shogun turned, and it was then I saw the glint in his eye. Then I knew. "It is not her honour that is lost!" Too late. As the shogun stepped back, the Fox's blade sung as it cleaved Master's head above the eyes, taking his honour, and his life, eternal. Taking my honour, or my care for it with him, stoking my anger. I probably couldn't have stopped it if I wanted to.

I heard a cry. Someone shouted as I dropped to my

knees once more. My own shout. Like a white-hot knife that cut through everything, it all went quiet as I fell into the pit. A buzzing and a distant laugh. Gone. Master. No. I won't settle like this.

The hum receded as I snapped back from my despair. The sticky blood on my chest. Eyes squeezed shut, tears tracked down my cheeks as I realised the chance Master gave me. What his final act had done. Looking down, I was knelt in a pool of my own blood. They'd not even known. I looked up and laughed in the shogun's foolish face. Anger. I laughed at him.

The Fox took a step back and levelled his blood-slicked blade at my head.

"Kita. She will have her honour. Her *Master* died without his for it. Whatever it is worth without that buffoon in the heavens." He gestured to Master's lifeless body then bent down, doing his own work for once, and chucked the tanto at me.

Seething, they'd not known their mistake. I could Bloodreach, and why would they know? I, Master's final secret. Damn mine honour. I will not bow to these pigs. Red hot, I breathed in and out furiously. Placing my hand into the puddled blood, smearing it until I gained purchase, driving it with the anger, I turned the insubstantial and made it substantial. I worked the blood in my hand and drew forth a crimson blade, parrying the Fox's katana at my face as I dashed, in the same movement, backward. Sword in the Kamae of Metal, the dragon's tail, it trailed a streak of blood as I went.

All around me, faces went white. The colour dropped, and toothy grins closed up. A shout behind me, probably the shogun frantic, but I couldn't care. I would live.

Jumping into the first set of guards, landing badly on my foot, I moved into the middle of four. They were just about quick enough to have their blades half-drawn as I cut down the first one, and just about quick enough was the second to have his blade out as he went down. Turning and striking, the third managed a parry. But there was a second's thought in his riposte. A second you don't have against a swordswoman like me. As I brought the blooded blade down across his, he was done. My feet were doing the good work now, nicely planted. Seeing a couple move ahead of myself, the fourth didn't have a chance. Feeling more guards close in, I pirouetted, lashing out hard with a blade that could cut the gods. It sliced through their own swords, their armour and their flesh, leaving them a mess on the floor around me. Dancing backwards, but panting hard, I put some distance between the oncoming guard.

In the background, the cowardly shogun and his lords

shouted from the dais, their men crowding in front of them. Shouts I couldn't discern from the blood pumping in my ears encompassed the room. I tasted metal. Blooded, I was faster, braver and in less pain than I should be. Than any man would be. But I couldn't get them, not now. I turned and broke through the canvas out into the night air. Crickets replaced the shouts. Respite from the madness. A cool breeze whipped up from the Naiji river ahead. My destination. My escape.

I caught the wind in my step and tore through the night, closing in on the dark waters. Only the rush and crash of violence against riverbanks guided me towards it. Told me of its presence.

Thump thump.

A few yards before it and I was undone. A blade hissed out of the darkness, and I turned it away. Again, a second, and I stepped backward. A third and I half-turned but another strike caught me in the side, opening a second gash, blood flowed again, and I dropped to one knee. Looking up, expecting a unit, but seeing one man, I gasped. The fox-masked helmet snarled in the moonlight and the white plate rippled as if it were the foaming, white waters behind me. A wakizashi in one hand and a katana in another. The only man I'd ever met to wield two-handed and still dance the way he did. Another six blades at his back. The Fox.

I stood and swayed on the spot. The night swarmed around me. Not good. I moved backwards, creating distance between us, I held my sword in front of me. A fool's guard. It took all my effort to stand. My breath was hurried and what blood left in my body still flowed from me. I had not the strength to control it. With each pump in my ear, time was whittled away. Master's gift was costly. Would cost me. Anger turned into anger. His killer in front of me. I screamed, forgetting my guard, I leapt at him. The Fox shifted and in one movement closed the distance and parried my strike. Only his first blade met mine, and I turned it away once more in time to meet his second. I was knocked back with an impossible third strike. I dodged and tried to create some distance as to not let him control the fight but received a slash to both shoulders in my flight. Impossible. His blades danced unpredictably like the tails of a kitsune. The Fox moved forward again, his two blades seeming like four with their reach. Blood gushed from me. I took the initiative and stepped into his slash. With a two-handed grip on my unbreakable blade, I evaded the flurry in a spin and slashed heavy. Not at him, but at his offhand. The force of it shattered one of his legendary swords. Carrying on in the spin, I brought my blade around, but he stepped away. Hot and heavy, pain lanced through me. Unimaginable. A searing pain in my abdomen. I dropped my blade and it splashed against the earth. Wet and thick agony. I cried out. No. Staggering backwards, away from his blade, a third that had replaced his broken second. I was run through. Pain. White-hot. Unbearable. I vomited. My head pounded with razors upon daggers.

He laughed.

I cried again. The water rushed behind me and he stepped forward. The fox mask smiling. He swung his blade and I leapt backward, the tip slashing my throat as I fell into the raging waters. My pride had engulfed me, swallowed me up.

The Vessel

by Jacek Wilkos

She stood, fascinated, in front of a mirror. The rejuvenating serum really worked. She stroked her smooth skin; not even a single wrinkle. She was young and beautiful and intended to stay like that. All she had to do is regularly use the serum.

"Servants! Clean here, now!"

Two men immediately unfastened leather belts, removed the empty serum vessel from its wooden construction, and carried it out; a young girl whose throat was cut.

The countess did not pay attention to them. Blinded by her desires, she did not see the wrinkled truth hidden beneath a thin layer of blood.

The Ravencroft Reunion

by Dannielle Viera

Mallory nudged the glass a little to the left. She stood back and viewed the table critically. Each plate was perfectly spaced and topped with a crisp napkin; the water jugs were gleaming. The layout was flawless. Tonight, it had to be.

Moving clockwise around the table, Mallory placed small name cards behind each plate. Occasionally she shuffled the cards until she came to the one she wanted. Like the rest of the table decorations, the cards were impeccable. Gold calligraphy curled and straightened to form a wealth of names, including Alexis Lockwood, Jacqueline Forbes, Paige Dumont, and Vanessa Balfour.

As the clock chimed seven, the first three women entered the room. "Welcome to La Vittima. Please take a seat," Mallory intoned, gesturing towards the table. Engrossed in conversation, the trio swept past Mallory without acknowledging her. Mallory's eyes narrowed, but she said nothing.

More women arrived, in groups of two or three. Some smiled at Mallory, and others even thanked her, but none seemed to regard her for more than a few seconds. Finally, a blonde in five-inch stilettos strode in and stopped, looking about the room. Mallory cleared her throat, ready to begin her welcome speech, but the woman interrupted her. "Don't I know you from somewhere?"

Before Mallory could answer, squeals of delight erupted from the table. "Vanessa! I'm so glad you could make it!" The woman was carried away in an eddy of air kisses, leaving Mallory standing awkwardly on her own. Not for the first time.

As dish after dish arrived at the table, Mallory oversaw the dinner service with a shrewd eye. Leaning in to position napkins on laps and to fill wine glasses, she overheard snatches of the pompous exchanges occurring around her.

"Ah, Ravencroft. What a glorious school...for the right people."

"Did you hear that Ms May is now the principal of Windsor Academy?"

"Whatever happened to that mousy little girl, what was her name?"

"This is a lovely restaurant. Pity about the hideously mismatched chairs."

Mallory winced at the last remark. She was on the verge of informing the speaker about the tenets of modern interior design, when she noticed the blonde woman staring at her. "I do know you! It's Mallory Magro, isn't it?" All eyes turned to Mallory.

"Ye-es," Mallory stammered, her cheeks flushing.

Whispers swirled around her. "Mousy Mallory?"

The chair critic smirked at Mallory. "Are you the head waitress here? You haven't made much of your excellent Ravencroft education, have you?" She nudged the woman next to her, and they both sniggered.

"Actually, I'm the owner of the restaurant. I've worked very hard to escape the extreme depression caused by the bullying at Ravencroft." Mallory spun on her heels and walked off. As she reached the door, she called over her shoulder. "Just so you know, Ravencroft's most brutal bullies are seated on the black chairs. And the deadly poison they've ingested tonight should begin to work in seconds…"

God's Right Hand

by Lyndsey Ellis-Holloway

Raegul.

The first of the female Angels to be created by God's hands. She was the most beautiful thing that Gabriel had ever set eyes upon. The Angel of Judgement would be a perfect union for him, he was God's right hand—the Leader of the Army of Heaven, wielder of the halberd Judgement Bringer, an Angel best associated with destruction—he could only be partnered to the best of his Father's Angelic Host, and who better than the first of his sisters?

It was a pity she had been created alongside Sammael. Gabriel had despised his brother since the moment he had drawn breath alongside his twin—where she was a perfect specimen of what an Angel should be, her brother was flawed—even from the very beginning he had seemed distant, not quite a part of the Heavenly Host designed to serve God. As though he teetered on the edge of disobedience. He was too like Lucifer.

Gabriel shook his head, dismissing his brother from his thoughts. Lucifer was no better than he, and Gabriel knew it, just as they all did. They had been created together; Lucifer, Gabriel and Michael. God had breathed life into the trio as one, uniting them as true brothers—they were the eldest of the Host, the best of the Seraphim.

And he was the best of all of them.

The others knew better than to challenge Gabriel; it was clear he was God's favourite, since their Father kept him by His side more so than any of the others. Not to mention that the moment he was asked to perform a task he did it. God knew He could rely upon His son. That was why He had made Gabriel the Leader of their Army, who else could He trust with such a task?

Not Michael. While Gabriel held a deep respect for his brother as God's left hand, he also wondered what ran through the other Archangel's mind. He had never disobeyed, but he was better known as the Angel of Mercy; he was too soft on sinners—even those who questioned their positions in the Heavens. No, Michael was better taking orders from Gabriel, at least *he* could make the hard decisions when it was required of him.

And Lucifer? Even the mere thought of him (much like thinking of Sammael) enraged God's right hand. His brother was too flippant, too invested in being amongst their brothers and sisters, too involved in being their sibling and their friend to understand that even they require a firm hand. The Morningstar had never taken anything seriously in his life, why bother when he had two brothers to do that for him?

Again, Gabriel dismissed the thought of his brother from his mind, he did not need that fool sullying his mind, not today. Today was about his union with Raegul. He'd waited long enough for her to make a move herself, but it was clear that she had not thought herself worthy of his attentions. For that, Gabriel could not blame her—he could have the pick of any Angel within the Host, why would she ever suspect that it would be she who caught his eye?

A smirk crossed his handsome face, amber coloured eyes glinting beneath his long lashes as he strode through the streets of the Golden City, head held high. He knew the others watched him intently as he passed, his very presence was hard to ignore—especially when he wore his finery.

His armour positively shone, Heaven's light reflecting from its shimmering, polished golden surface. He had been a beacon for Humanity once (who else?) and who could deny he was a beacon now? Everything about him was so precise, done with such confidence—Gabriel knew his mind, he knew what he wanted and knew what he was capable of; it was why their Father so often looked to him for guidance. Gabriel was the one best placed to guide his Father, of course.

Striding out of the City proper, through the ornate Golden Gates, he turned towards the Garden where he knew Raegul would be found, watching Earth from the pond lest her judgement be required. Father had not informed him of any immediate tasks for her, so there would be no distractions while they spoke. Not that she would be distracted by Earth while *he* was with her.

A smile crossed his face as he saw her, his red-gold wings unfurling slightly as he held himself straight and tall. His mere presence caught her attention—naturally— and Gabriel nodded his head to her in acknowledgement.

"Greetings, Gabriel," Raegul said softly, storm-grey eyes fixed upon his own as she nodded her head to him with a smile. "To what do I owe this pleasure?"

Ah, such sweet words, though he had expected no less. "I have something I wish to discuss with you, Raegul."

"Oh? Intriguing, please, sit with me."

Settling on the bench, Gabriel took a moment to position himself properly. "Raegul, I have spent quite some time watching over you, not only in my capacity as God's right hand, but also out of self-interest. As the first of the female Angels, you hold a certain natural rank amongst our brothers and sisters, however you have also carved your own way within the Host that resonates with my own journey to where I am now. As such, I realised that there could be only one amongst our number that could possibly be partnered with myself. You are the best of them, Raegul, therefore you should be with me. We are the perfect pairing."

Silence followed his words, and Gabriel smirked. The look of disbelief upon her innocent face was a picture he would not so easily forget. Of course, this was a shock to her. Once the rest of the Host heard of their pairing, they too would be just as surprised to think that he had taken someone as his own; none of them would have believed another worthy enough!

"Gabriel," she began, tucking a strand of hair behind an ear, her four, pure white wings quivering with what he could only assume was nervous excitement at his offer. "I'm sorry. I'm flattered that you would think of me that way, of course I am, but I've already found someone to pair with."

It took a moment for those words to sink in. This had to be a joke, of course it was. *Who* could she *possibly* have picked over *him*? He was Gabriel! He was God's right hand! He was better than the rest of the Host, even *God* could see that, and made it known regularly!

"Who?" He snarled, his own wings trembling as anger began to build within him, a slow burning fire flickering deep in his chest, manageable despite this slight.

"Gabriel, does it matter?" Raegul all but pleaded with him, and then he realised it—she could only have been coerced. Look how desperate she was not to hurt him, look how her eyes begged him for forgiveness for not waiting.

No, this could not have been her choice. No one amongst the Host would *knowingly* choose against him. Maybe he had waited too long to speak with her after all? Of course, he had lingered, and she had accepted the first offer from one of the others, thinking that *he* would never want her.

The fire extinguished at the thought. He reached over and took her hand. "Who, Raegul?"

"Lucifer. He would often come to the Garden while I was working. Before I knew it, I had fallen in love with him. He's quite special, there's no one in Heaven like him."

Lucifer.

Of all the names she could possibly have said, this was the one he could not, *would* not, forgive.

Everything else she said did not register. The flames

he had extinguished roared back into life, a wildfire that no amount of apologies or kind words would quash now. He had thought he would merely speak to whichever insignificant had been brave enough to ask her to be theirs, he would give them a terse talking to and leave it at that, and claim her as his own, as was his right. But Lucifer?

He threw her hand away from him in disgust, sullied by her touch and his brother's by proxy, face contorted in a mixture of anger and abhorrence. No. This could not be. She could not pick *Lucifer* over *him.*

Rage filled him; his pride wounded by her words. He would teach her; there was no one better than he. If she wished to sully herself with such lowly company, then he would happily oblige in marking her as tainted.

He barely noticed Raegul recoil as he stepped towards her. All Gabriel could think was that he would not let her bring him down because of her stupidity, that he would show the rest of the Host that she had not been *worthy* of him. His hand shot out, grasping one of her pure white wings, fingers digging into flesh beneath the feathers. Her gasp barely registered as the vice-like grip of his other hand on her shoulder secured her where she was.

"Gabriel! Gabriel you're *hurting me!*" Raegul

screamed, though he did not care, didn't even flinch when her hands began to bat at him, her other wings flapping violently as if she might somehow shake him off.

No. He would teach her a lesson, and in doing so, he would remind the Host of where they stood in Heaven, including Lucifer. His lips curled away from his teeth as he sneered, his face filled with that confidence he had always possessed. Without a word, his muscles began to tense, and Gabriel called upon his strength, pulling at the wing in his grasp, holding Raegul where she was as he tore the limb from her body.

Her screams filled his ears as her blood spurted across the hand holding her still. There was no hesitation as he tossed the wing aside, his hand a blur as he moved to grasp the next wing, grip tightening anew, wrenching the limb from Raegul's trembling frame. He revelled in the feel of it, the tearing of her flesh and the snap of the bone as he separated it from her, slinging it away from him like trash, just as *she* was.

As Gabriel disposed of Raegul's last wing, he pushed her to the floor, casting her aside as he towered above her, ignoring her sobs and laboured breathing, her back covered in blood and broken feathers, stumps where her wings had once been, protruding from her ruined dress.

"You were not worthy of those wings, just as you are

not worthy of me. Let Lucifer have you, I will not sully my name with any association to *you*," he snorted, turning away from her, his own glorious wings held aloft as he washed his hands in the pond, ridding himself of her blood and the feathers that had stuck to him.

Once he was clean, he gave one last, loathing look in Raegul's direction, stepping on her broken and bloodied wings as he strode back to the Golden City, satisfied that she would be suitably repentant when next she saw him, and would regret snubbing him as she had.

After all, he was the best of them.

Marinok

by G. Allen Wilbanks

Marinok wilted in his chair, resting his forearms across his knees and letting his head droop until his chin touched his chest. He listened to the doctor—Doctor Dave, as the man's patients liked to refer to him when he was out of the room—drone on in that tedious, nasally voice that made Marinok want to ram an ice-pick through both of his eardrums. The doc must have loved the sound of his own voice though, because he never stopped talking. From the second the sessions started to the moment it was time to leave, his lips were moving.

Wasn't listening supposed to be part of the job description? wondered Marinok. Yet, the doc never seemed to pause long enough to take a breath, much less listen to what anyone else might have to say. Maybe the guy was part fish and got all the oxygen he needed from a set of concealed gills.

Marinok almost laughed aloud at the thought of Doctor Dave's mouth opening and closing like a goldfish while a set of gills in his neck flapped in and out. Almost. Being trapped in this room by court order was too depressing for anything to be quite that funny. Laughter was reserved for people who had better things to do and more interesting places to be.

The doc, however, seemed perfectly happy. It was clear he loved having the spotlight and a captive audience.

Along with Marinok and Doctor Dave, four other listless participants sprawled on the available furniture, dutifully following along with the doctor's lecture. The folding metal chair Marinok occupied was arranged, along with two sofas and six other mismatched seats, into a horseshoe-shaped pattern, with the doctor's stuffed vinyl armchair placed at the open end of the shoe. This guaranteed that the doctor was the focus of everyone's attention at all times.

Other than the eclectic furniture, the room was kept empty except for a wheeled cart near the exit holding a stack of waxed paper cups and an industrial, metal coffee pot. There weren't even any pictures hanging on the mocha-coloured walls. The mostly undecorated room was just one more tactic to be sure the unhappy attendees of this circus did not get distracted from the ringmaster's ongoing performance.

Anger management therapy. *More like boredom management therapy*, Marinok thought as he opened his mouth in a jaw-cracking yawn. And people thought Hell was a terrible place to end up. Well, they had never been on the wrong end of a speech from Doctor Dave. Marinok muffled a second yawn as the doctor nattered something about closing your eyes and picturing yourself at the beach or some place calm, and blah, blah, blah. All of it, useless garbage and psychobabble.

Marinok groaned aloud.

"Mark? You have something to add?" asked Doctor Dave in the tone of a schoolteacher chastising a wayward child.

Mark? Who was...? Oh, right. Mark. Marinok recalled that Mark was the human name he had selected for himself. He looked up to meet the doctor's cool, superior gaze.

"No. Not really," he said.

"All right, then. Please try to pay closer attention. As I was saying—"

"You know what? Actually, I do have something I want to say," Marinok blurted out, cutting off whatever the doctor intended to add. "It's just that I really don't know why any of us are here. I mean, none of us has a problem with impulse control. If we did, everyone in this room would either be asleep from boredom or jumping up to try to strangle you. Am I right?"

Nervous laughter issued from the other participants

in the session. Marinok took this as encouragement to continue.

"I don't get into fights because I can't control my anger. I'm completely aware of what I'm doing, regardless of how upset I am. I get into fights because I make poor decisions. No amount of counselling or therapy is going to change that. And, let's face it, even if I had anger issues,"—Marinok raised his hands to make air quotes around the words 'anger issues,'—"six weeks of listening to you sermonise at me about peaceful imagery and counting to ten is only going to make me more pissed off than I was before."

The laughter grew a bit louder.

"Okay, Mark. I think that's about enough—" the doctor began, trying to derail Marinok's rant.

"Here's the thing," Marinok bulled forward. "I'm only here because the judge said I could choose between this or jail time. I don't want to go to jail. I think the others are with me on this. Guys?"

A few heads nodded in reluctant agreement.

"There. See? But, Doc, I understand that you have a reputation to protect and, of course, there's all that state money you collect for keeping us here for the full allotted time. I don't want to screw that up for you, so here's what I suggest: Next meeting, you bring beers and a couple pizza's, then you sign off on our court paperwork. In return, we sit here quietly for the whole six weeks of sessions and, if anybody asks, we tell them that your classes were the best Goddamned training we ever got, and your amazing teaching completely turned our lives around."

The mutterings and soft laughter from the other members of the group grew to vocal shouts of agreement.

Doctor Dave lurched to his feet, his cheeks flushing bright red. "Enough!" he shouted to quiet the room. "Today's session is over. Everybody out. Go home, all of you. Except Mark." The doctor levelled a shaking finger in Marinok's direction. "I want you to stay behind. The two of us need to talk about boundaries and appropriate behaviour."

The group rose and quickstepped to the exit, happy to be finished with the day's therapy session early. They didn't hang around to chat or grab coffee on the way out, not wanting to risk the doctor changing his mind and ordering them back to their seats. Marinok grinned and watched them head out.

"You guys go and have fun," he called out to the others. "I guess I'm getting detention."

Doctor Dave stormed away to a closed doorway at the opposite end of the room from where everyone else had exited. The upper half of the door was inset with frosted glass and the legend "Doctor David Purser. PsyD" in black, block letters. He pulled it open and pointed forcefully into the room beyond.

"Inside," the doctor ordered. "Go sit down."

Marinok raised his hands in a gesture of surrender, the smile never leaving his face. "You're taking me into your office? Wow, this must be a really special occasion."

"Sit down and shut your mouth."

The doctor was visibly struggling to keep himself composed at Marinok's disrespectful antics. He closed his eyes for a moment and took a deep breath.

Taking your own advice, eh doc? Marinok thought, but he said nothing further. Instead, he marched into the doctor's private office and settled himself into an uncomfortable wooden chair situated in front of Doctor Dave's desk.

The doctor closed the door and locked it behind him. Clasping his hands behind his back and trying to appear casual, he strolled over to Marinok, positioning himself directly in front of his wayward patient. Bracing one hip against the front edge of his desk, he leaned forward to loom over the object of his current displeasure.

Marinok nodded as if he had put together a difficult math problem in his head. "Yeah, I think I see what's happening right now."

"Oh, do you?" the doctor intoned, mockingly. "I only have ten years of advanced schooling, a couple of doctorate degrees in clinical psychology and deviant behaviour, and about fifteen years of private practice. I clearly can't hope to compete with your own vast depths of knowledge and experience, so if you would be so kind, please do enlighten me as to what you think is happening right now."

Marinok nodded again. "Mm-hmm. Yup. I cracked your fragile little ego, didn't I? I stepped on your toes, and worse than that, I did it in front of witnesses. You can't stand, for one second, that somebody else took the focus away from you. But, more than that, you think you're so much better than the broken little toys like myself that come into your building for treatment, that the thought of any one of *us* getting the better of you just wads your knickers something fierce.

"Why else march me in here, hover over me like the angel of death, and parade your degrees and pedigree in front of me? You need to establish that you're the alpha. You lost control and now you need to take it back. I think I popped your superiority balloon in the other room, and you dragged me in here to try to re-inflate it. Well then, Doc, what's the plan? Should we look at bank accounts?

Fight it out? Or maybe we should just drop our pants and do a quick comparison?"

"I could send you back to jail," the doctor threatened.

"I suppose you could. Would you consider that a win; the fact that you couldn't handle one uneducated miscreant with a big mouth? Instead of using your fancy degrees and that big brain of yours to turn me around, you'll just toss me back to the judge to put me in jail? You treat jailbirds like me for a living, and yet you're ready to bounce me after three classes? I'm thinking that doesn't look so good for you. It feels like kind of a low bar you set for yourself."

"Stop it, Mark. That's enough!"

"Although, I guess I'm not really surprised. You know what they say about people that study psychology. They have no interest in other people's problems; they're just trying to figure out their own screwed up shit. You have to *be* crazy to treat crazy."

"I'm warning you. Stop talking," the doctor growled through clenched teeth. "I won't put up with any more of this."

"So, what was it for you, Doc? Were you trying to figure out why you like to pull the wings off flies? Did your parents forget to show up to your school recital? Or, did you see your sister naked when you were kids, and it made your little man stand up and feel all tingly? C'mon, you can tell me. Did your sister—"

Light flared behind Marinok's eyes and an explosive pain filled his head. For a moment, the room went fuzzy, and he lost track of what was happening around him. When his head finally began to clear and he could once again think straight, he found himself on his back on top of the broken wooden pieces of his chair. Marinok rolled over to his hands and knees before slowly pushing himself back upright. He regained his feet, still feeling a bit unsteady, and squinted blearily at the doctor.

Doctor Dave stared back with wide, panicked eyes. In his right hand, the doctor held a glass paperweight about the size of a softball. Marinok could see a trace amount of blood marring the clear surface of the glass sphere.

The doctor tried to take a step backward but was stopped short by the desk behind him.

The doctor hit me! Marinok realised.

And it had been quite the devastating attack. Although the pain was now receding, that blow to the head had sent him sprawling. Marinok had never even seen it coming.

The doctor made no further attempt to move from where he stood. He appeared terrified and he clearly wanted to run, but instead he remained frozen in place. His eyes trailed from Marinok to the floor, then back up. Marinok glanced down to see what had caught Doctor Dave's attention.

"Crap," he muttered. "That's not good."

On the ground, at Marinok's feet was…Marinok.

To be more precise, it was the body Marinok had been wearing for the past few years. The doctor had apparently clobbered him good. Killed the body dead in one shot. *This is going to be problematic*, he thought as he imagined going back home and waiting the decades it would take before he gained permission to inhabit a new body. He sighed, then shrugged. Oh, well. It was all just part of being a demon. Nothing to be done about it now. It had been a fun ride while it lasted, and at least he had managed to claim one more soul in the process of getting his skull caved in.

"That is going to be really difficult to explain to the police," Marinok said, pointing toward the body. "I think you've made some poor choices in the past few minutes, Doc, and I don't think the judge is going to let you off with a few lousy therapy sessions."

Marinok giggled at his own wit.

Without a body to inhabit, he could not physically interact with the human world anymore. However, even in spectral form, the doctor could still see and hear him. Marinok took advantage of that fact.

"Don't forget while you're in prison to tell all your new friends about how much smarter you are than them."

"Than they," the doctor corrected softly, automatically; still in shock at the scene in front of him. He opened his hand and let the paperweight fall to the ground. It landed with a heavy *thunk*.

"That's the spirit!" Marinok enthused. "I am really looking forward to seeing you again, Doc. Especially since the next time we meet, it will be on my home turf. The two of us can have a nice long chat about boundaries and appropriate behaviour."

Caleb's Claim

by J.M. Meyer

Entrenched in cold greyness and infinite mountains of snow, we remained entombed on the desolate Kansas prairie, miles from our closest neighbour, and even farther from the nearest town. The numbing air crept in through the clay and the small stones that Caleb slathered between the logs of our cabin. My husband hovered, ever present. Our son would try to avoid him, but the cramped quarters made privacy impossible. Caleb's bursts of anger became more frequent. I longed for a closet or a box in which I could disappear, even for a few moments. Sometimes, when the wind howled, I heard my three dead children beckoning me to join them. I had not succumbed to the madness that prairie life could inflict on most inhabitants during the lonely, harsh winters, my children's voices were real. I wished to be with my loves again, but Joseph was the last of our four children to walk this earth, and he was my focus and sole comfort.

"Don't let the fire burn out. How many times do I have to tell you to keep it going?" Caleb's massive frame stood next to me, arms crossed, hands tucked under his armpits. His ice-blue eyes, with narrowed pupils darted like lightning, primed to strike any future offense.

"Throw the corncobs and braided hay on there, woman. Do you aim for us to freeze? We won't have firewood 'til spring, and I don't want to burn the furniture. Took days to make." He paused, then added, "And watch your skirt. All's I need is for you to burn this cabin to the ground."

"Yes, Caleb," I said as I lowered my chin to my chest. I was past fearing the man; I tried my best to hide my hatred. The steam that rose from the thin stew warmed my face and smelled good. Joseph and I hated to kill the calf, but the food might keep us alive. The train lines reopened in the spring, and Caleb could trade rabbit fur for supplies: nails, flour, sugar.

I hunkered by the hearth and stirred the stew in the black wrought-iron pot I brought with us from Vermont two years ago. I carefully tucked my skirt between my legs, away from the flames. The dress was tight when we arrived in Kansas, but I altered it several times as my weight diminished. Even when food was plentiful, I found it difficult to eat. When I glanced at my reflection in the small, broken looking-glass, I didn't recognise the face that stared back. My lips were thin and turned down and my skin creased and brown. My sunken, hollow eyes reminded me of my sister's eyes after my father had pulled her from the well following a two-day search.

The snow made it impossible to travel to town; storms arrived one after the other. The summer months, with unending green grass below a blue sky, were replaced by white and grey, a blurred boundary between the land and sky. Our world beyond the four walls that protected and imprisoned us was devoid of colour.

"The storm's getting worse. I'll do the barn chores; I expect supper when I get back."

"Caleb. Hold the clothing line tight."

A clothing line stretched from the cabin to the barn. When visibility was poor, people died mere feet from their front door. They would wander in the wrong direction and die of exposure. I fantasised about cutting the rope myself; Caleb, unable to find the house, would choke on the snow flowing into his lungs and eventually freeze solid. I wouldn't shed a tear. I only cared about our eight-year-old son.

If we had not left Vermont two years ago, my sweet Abby would have lived. Instead, she cut her foot on a nail and went to Heaven. God help me, though, I believed that little Abby's death was merciful. Women out west suffered lives filled with fear, as women had few rights, if any. Abby might have married and had several children only to have her husband leave to hunt or go to town and never return. She wouldn't know whether he had died or if he had simply abandoned them. Unsuccessful husbands often became violent, whereas successful homesteaders suffered and aged far too quickly. My little Abby deserved better.

I glanced over to Joseph's bed. His blanket moved up and down with each breath; I peered up at my husband, whose scowl bared white teeth.

Caleb thrust out his chest and took in a deep breath.

"Woman, we've gone through seven storms this year alone. Don't you dare remind me of the first storm. It wasn't my fault. Are you trying to humiliate me? Blame me?" He pulled on his shearling coat, his boots, the red woollen mittens I made him before we left Vermont, and his rabbit hat.

Knowing I struck a nerve, I turned to face the hearth. I could not speak to Caleb of Jedidiah. Our first winter here, a blizzard came without warning and trapped Caleb and Jedidiah in the barn. There was no rope then. Caleb made it back to the cabin; Jed did not. Caleb tied me to the bed so I wouldn't run out to find our son, and Abby and Joseph screamed along with me. My husband left and returned several times, but our eldest child, nine-year-old Jed, stayed buried under the snow, ten feet from our house, until the spring thaw.

"No, husband. I only want Joseph and I to survive the winter."

Caleb froze. He looked at the floor, drew in a deep breath, and shook his head.

"Grace, stop talking," Caleb said. He clenched his jaw, and I watched a vein throb in his bright red face.

I turned back to the fire. Tears stung my eyes. Snow and wind poured into the cabin in the moments before Caleb stormed out and banged the door shut behind him. While I stirred the pot, Jedidiah, Abby, and baby Beatrice beckoned me to walk out the door and into the snow. I never dared to tell Caleb how our children called to me in the wind or how they visited at night. Joseph heard them, too, but he understood that his Pa couldn't be told.

The previous winter, our nearest neighbours, Genevieve and Michael, fell on hard times. A failed crop caused near-starvation. Their only son drowned while fishing the swollen river. Genevieve survived the birth of their daughter but remained weak. Michael left her alone to travel to town to sell furs and to bring back necessities. When he returned, he found Genevieve in bed, holding their dead infant daughter.

"This is no life for a girl. I gave her the blessing of eternal peace," his wife repeated.

What happened to the child was unclear, but Michael sent Genevieve to an asylum in Kansas City, and Michael tried to run the farm on his own. Other neighbours found him hanging from the rafters in his barn.

Caleb grabbed my arm and forced me to look at him after he heard of Michael's death.

"If Michael had come home to no family, he could have saved his claim. Without a wife, he could have remarried and had more children. Instead, his crazy, selfish wife was alive. He couldn't remarry. There would be no more children, no more helping hands."

My husband would bury me in a shallow grave dug with his bare hands before he would send me to an asylum.

Caleb displayed no empathy for the plight of our neighbours—he had no empathy to give. Both people and homes could surround my husband and would not notice having neighbours; only his plans were of consequence. Caleb's only obligation was to himself.

Joseph awoke from his nap.

"Hi, Mama."

I wiped my eyes on my scratchy woollen sleeve, smoothed my hair, and before I stood, I plastered on a fake smile.

"My dear boy, you're awake? How are you,

darling?" My eight-year-old son sat up in the bed Caleb had made. The thin red quilt my mother made for Joseph hung on his bony frame. He was thin and pale from the illness that summer. I feared losing him and almost died myself, but Joseph got better before I did, and his hugs and kisses helped to heal me.

"Bored and cold."

"Yes, this is a hard winter."

The cabin felt smaller and darker every day, and I did not know how to feel cheerful or hopeful unless I looked at my son. I wished to stay in bed to hold Joseph until the storm was over, but I needed to contribute to the household if we were to stay alive.

"Is it still snowing?"

"Yes. Come look. Wrap Granny's blanket around you to stay warm."

We walked the few feet to the shuttered window. The floor's creaking created a rhythm in our warm cottage, more comforting, at least, than deafening silence. I peered through our one small window and strained to see anything other than white, but I saw only white.

"Pa left for barn chores?"

"Yes. He'll be back for supper."

"Unless he gets lost like Jed. If Pa didn't come back, you'd finally leave."

I didn't respond; what he said was true. Some nights, when Jed visited, I would repeat "I'm sorry, I'm sorry," until Caleb threatened to show me the inside of the asylum that I knew I would never see.

We had three more years to make the claim profitable before we would lose everything, according to Caleb. However, we had already lost everything precious. Still, we stayed.

"He will die before he declares defeat," my Mama had said before we headed west. Her tears perplexed me, but I later realised that she was saying her final goodbye to me. The men in town were being forced to join the union army when Caleb announced our departure. Papa wouldn't speak to Caleb, but I heard him call Caleb a selfish coward when he spoke to Mama.

We left Vermont, a family of five, and I was pregnant. As we approached our destination, I counted the graves I saw along the way. I saw no fewer than eight graves every day, marked with homemade crosses made from sticks tied with rope.

Before we reached the homestead, I gave birth in the back of the wagon. The birth felt wrong—I hadn't felt the baby move in weeks. Caleb distracted the children by a river and occasionally came back to check on me. I listened to the tall waves of grass swish between my cries and contractions. Beatrice was born blue and stiff, with the umbilical cord wrapped around her neck. Caleb took her away and buried her before we went on our way again. I laid in the back of the wagon, speechless and shocked, as a fire of anger gnawed at my soul.

Little Abby repeated, "Don't be sad, Mama. The baby is happy to be with the Lord. She told me."

Jedidiah was nine and aimed to be like his Pa, who never comforted me. It was my darling Joseph who kissed my head and made sure that I ate and drank.

Joseph and I moved away from the draft of the shuttered window.

"Can you hear them calling us? They want us to come," Joseph said. "They don't trust Pa."

"We'll stay together, Joseph. If we can leave in the spring, we will. I pray that your grandparents will take us in," I said.

"He'll never let you leave, Mama."

"I know, Joseph. Pray for a miracle. Practice your letters while I get supper ready."

I took the slate and a piece of chalk from under his bed and put them on the table beside the Bible. "Get busy so Pa won't be cross you napped again."

"Mama, can't you see Pa is getting scarier?"

The door swung open before I replied, and a near-frozen Caleb clambered in. I helped him undress, hung the clothes by the fire, and placed the wash-pan underneath to catch melted ice and snow.

I set the table for the three of us and used the embroidered tablecloth passed down to me from my grandmother as a wedding gift. The embroidery was a simple cross-stitch in different shades of pink on worn, white, cotton linen. Although stained, it was the most beautiful thing in my life next to Joseph. Caleb glared as I removed the writing slate from the table and replaced it under Joseph's bed.

Joseph and I waited for Caleb to dress, before sitting down to eat. We expected him to hold our hands and say a prayer of thanks, but when my husband sat, he stared at my hand and looked in Joseph's direction. Joseph extended his hand, but Caleb dropped his elbows on the table and covered his face with his chapped, calloused hands.

"I'm not doing this tonight. I need quiet."

"Shh! Daddy needs quiet," Joseph whispered to mock him; Caleb didn't notice.

We ate in silence. The wind and snow drowned out the sound of our utensils scraping china. The room darkened while the snow continued to fall. We became anchored ever deeper in our square of earth on the Kansas plains.

We readied for sleep after supper. I heated the bed stones in the fire and placed them at the foot of each of our beds. Caleb turned to face the wall while I tucked Joseph into bed and sang him a song. He was too old for lullaby's but enjoyed it. My beautiful boy fell asleep. Joseph's profile reminded me of my father. Tomorrow I would write him a letter. I wrote several letters each week throughout the winter and planned to mail all of them at once in the spring.

The howling wind carried my children's calls to wake me before sunrise.

I glanced at Joseph's bed. He wasn't in it. The bed was made, without so much as a dent in the pillow. I could not find my son anywhere. He was not in the cabin.

My screaming woke up Caleb.

"Where is Joseph?" I yelled into my husband's face.

"You're insane!" Caleb shook me by my shoulders, his eyes wild and wide.

"What did you do to him?"

"Nothing. You crazy, ungrateful woman," he bellowed.

I ran to the door and threw it open, prepared to run outside despite my thin nightdress. Caleb grabbed me around the waist, hurled me inside, and pinned me to the floor.

"Joseph! Joseph! Caleb, find my boy!"

"Think, Grace, think! Our boy is dead."

"You want me to go mad! You want to get rid of me! We lost everything because of you. You're not a farmer, Caleb. You killed our children because you didn't want to face going home or serving our country!" I screamed. "Joseph!"

My husband trembled with rage. "He's dead!" Caleb screamed.

As he pinned me against the cold floor, jumbled flashes of memories flooded my mind. A sweating Joseph, lying in his small bed, refusing to eat. His body covered in mosquito bites. Caleb using a knife to cut off Joseph's hair to cool his scalp. Immobilised, memories and images deluged my brain. I am also sick. Caleb splashing me with cold water. My husband carrying my boy's stiff body outside. Joseph lying beside me, touching my cheek. Whispering in my ear.

"I remember being sick, but Joseph got better before I did. He lay in bed with me," I said.

"Joseph didn't get better. He died, and I buried him.

You refused to believe it—still do. I've watched you read to empty chairs, set the table for three when only two are eating. I've been plenty patient," Caleb yelled.

"Joseph told me he wasn't sick anymore," I said. "He also said that you prayed for him to die so I would live. You traded Joseph's life for mine."

"Now, that is true, woman. If God had to choose between you and Joseph, then I asked him to take the boy. I need you to help with the claim."

"You are a demon. You sold your soul and I might as well be dead. Your selfishness killed our children." I spat in his face and he struck my cheek.

"It's you trying to kill me! I know you cut the line to the house last night," Caleb declared.

"What?"

"I was a few feet from the house when the rope broke. It was a miracle I made it back." His grip on me tightened.

"No," I said. "I didn't cut it. The children. They're out there. Let me join them."

"We can have more children."

I went wild. I scratched him until he bled and sunk my teeth into his hand.

"Damn you! I'm going to the barn to check on the animals," said Caleb. "If they're dead, then so are we."

"I have to find my children !" I screamed.

He sat me in a chair by the fire and restrained me using rope.

"I can't have you leaving."

"The children will save me," I hissed. "They know what you've done."

The door slammed, and I was alone by the fire. I hung my head and cried myself to sleep.

A gentle hand brushed my cheek. I opened my eyes. Joseph stood before me in the dark cabin, the fire extinguished; the cabin cold. No rope tethered me to the chair.

"Come, Mama. I cut Pa's line to the house. He'll wander the prairie forever now, we can be together."

"I want to be with you all, Joseph," I said as I wiped away tears. I stood and held my son's hand. We walked to the door and opened it. I gazed at the small figures standing in the rippling, infinite sea of green, below a bright blue sky.

Again

by James Lipson

The Cat in the Hat, The Story of Babar, A Bear Called Paddington, The Tale of Peter Rabbit. By the time Johnny turned five, he was bored of them all. These weren't the stories he wanted; he wanted scary stories, the ones about monsters, vampires, werewolves and ghosts.

Linda resisted when he first asked about redoing their nighttime reading list, afraid of the nightmares it would bring. She wanted him to feel the same joy she had when her father had read those books to her. She remembered them like renaissance paintings before the decades of dirt and light diminished their brilliance. The nightstand light fading her father's face as his soothing voice brought the characters alive until sleep caressingly whisked her away—this was the memory she wanted for her son.

Persistent begging was followed by solemn assurances of "not being afraid of anything." Day after day, Johnny wore his mother down, until finally she gave in. They clearly did not share the same wide-eyed wonder from The Cat, Babar or Paddington. Unable to bear any more whining, Linda assured him she would bring in a new story, a scary one.

With her carefully selected new book in hand, Linda momentarily stalled outside Johnny's bedroom door as she prepared herself to read his first scary story. Johnny was already in bed, teeth brushed and room cleaned up. *Perhaps this isn't going to be such a bad thing after all,* Linda thought as she surveyed the now-neat room.

"OK, sweetheart, I have a new book for you. But before I begin, I want to make sure you understand this is not real. The man who wrote this is Edgar Allan Poe. He is a very famous writer from the early nineteenth century."

Her trepidation dissipated when Johnny interrupted, "Mommy, can I tell *you* a story tonight?"

"Of course, sweetheart. I would love to hear a story from you!" she answered excitedly, placing the book of short stories behind her. Inwardly, she beamed at the thought that her son had made up a story just for her.

Repositioning himself under the covers, Johnny pulled the light comforter to his chin, rolled it back twice and asked his mother if she was ready.

"Yes, I am," Linda said with a wry grin as she brushed away a few stray hairs from his face, now flushed with pride.

"Mommy, this is a story of…" She looked into her son's face as he struggled to find the words. He began again. "Um, a long time ago, I was somewhere else, before I lived with you," Johnny said.

"Before you lived with me?" Linda asked, not understanding.

Frustrated, Johnny tried, in vain, to furrow his brow, "Yes. I don't know how else to say it."

"That's OK, honey. Please go on," Linda coaxed.

"Before I lived with you, I was in a town where it rained a lot, and the clouds came to the ground."

"Do you mean fog?" Linda suggested.

Johnny's eyes lit up when she explained that fog was like clouds that formed close to ground.

"Yes! It was white and sometimes you couldn't see through it. I liked when it was like that. I'm not sure why, but the fog made me feel warm," he continued.

"One night, I left my house with my watch, a handkerchief" —though his pronunciation sounded more like *hankachief*—"some money and a knife. It was a very sharp knife," he whispered.

Linda stared at her son, her proud countenance flagging. Her maternal eyes glazed over as she tried to process the "sharp knife" comment. Johnny paused, she assumed to concoct the rest of his tale, but he was waiting for her to refocus.

Satisfied she was back, he continued, "It was dark. I walked around a lot. There weren't any street lights like now, and there was always a bad smell. Sometimes I went to a place where there were a lot of other people. I didn't like them; they were bad people." He punctuated this thought with an almost imperceptible narrowing of his eyes that was lost on his mother.

"That night, I asked a lady if she would go for a walk with me. She said she would, for money."

"What happened when you went for a walk?" his mother asked, incredulous as to his level of detail.

"This is the part that is scary, and I'm not sure I want to tell you," Johnny answered cautiously.

"I won't be scared, sweetheart. You can tell me," Linda assured him, rubbing his leg gently.

"OK, Mommy, but you will be scared," Johnny said, looking at her while lowering the covers farther.

"I'll be fine, honey. Go on."

With his mother's encouragement, Johnny continued, "We walked around the block. There were a lot of people, so we went somewhere else. The lady was walking next to me, whispering in my ear and grabbing me. She had bad breath and ugly teeth. That's when I reached into my pocket and grabbed my knife and slid it across her throat before she could scream," he said in a barely audible voice.

Johnny stopped his story upon seeing his mother's eyes grow unnaturally wide. "I'm sorry, Mommy."

"It's all right, sweetheart. I…I just wasn't expecting that," Linda stammered.

"She wasn't either," Johnny whispered.

Linda's head was reeling as she tried to absorb the shock, when her husband poked his head in the room. "That's enough storytelling for now; Jack has to go to sleep."

Ageless

by J.W. Garrett

Sloan clenched her fists at her side. She wouldn't have all her work shot to hell over this little blip. Her research was clear, thanks to her statisticians. A number could mean just about anything if you threw the right graph at it…drafted the perfect population sample. All that was now water under the bridge. With the pharmaceutical companies practically tearing down her door to get at her product, Sloan knew she couldn't keep them on a leash for long.

Anger brewed deep inside her. One more second and she'd let it loose on the team before her. Gritting her teeth, she clamped down, barely grasping the reins of her control. The sacrifices…all of her time spent in study, research, grunt work, then placating just the right individuals at the ideal times. And years later—finally— recognition.

With the over-sixty-five population soaring with no end in sight, the market had been primed for so long. Other solutions had fallen short of the mark. But this one little pill, her life's work, could turn back the clocks of the aging public dramatically, and the effects were expected to last approximately forty-five years. Every human on the planet would soon be eating out of her hand.

Dollar signs multiplied in her head.

Beginning with the skin, the effects were apparent almost immediately. Then one's internal organs gained a boost, and—over time, through reverse DNA aging—cells were renewed and protected from future decomposition, the body tricked, essentially into redefining itself, the aging process rolled back and then rebooted.

Perfection.

Yet trials were unsatisfactory. The drug companies needed at least one year of data, preferably eighteen months to two years, so she could get their buy-in and continue this expensive endeavour. To date, she had only six months. And over three-quarters of the accumulated stats reflected poorly on her new wonder drug.

"You are all dismissed. I can't stand to look at you any longer…oh, except you, Tom. Hang back. We need to chat."

Tom's gaze swept to the door, then back to Sloan. Wiping sweat from his forehead, he nodded. "Sure. What can I help you with?"

"Here's what I need. The results of the positive trials

in progress need to be extrapolated. Chances are, outcomes will continue, right? Next, we need to eliminate those individuals who have not…reacted well to the drug. Disqualify them on some basis of your experiment. Use one bias or another. I don't care how. Leave only the results that confirm our knowledge of the drug's superior capabilities. Last, once the remaining results are extrapolated, replicate and backdate them." Her gaze levelled with his. "You can do this."

"Ma'am…Sloan…" he corrected. "You've got plenty of other minions willing to do your bidding, but I can't. You're aware just how horrific the studies show this elixir to be. Skin lesions, bronchial tubes burned, massive organ failure—and that's only the beginning. I won't be a party to this…mechanism of death." His jaw tightened. "This drug doesn't work, not in its present form."

A pout graced her lips. "Surely you've not forgotten how agreeable you've been in the past? And you've been very well compensated." Sloan bent over and straightened his tie, then patted Tom's chest. "Better, much better. Now, be smart. Reconsider. Not everyone gets to live their dream, on a space station no less." Palms up, Sloan spread her arms wide as she walked to the window and peered into the deep expanse. "All this while supporting your family in the lavish lifestyle to which they've become accustomed."

"No. Millions will die. I'm not a monster. Go back to the drawing board. Rework the drug. Something is there, and it's a work of genius…but not in its current state. As is, your wonder drug is a death sentence." Tom moved slowly to her side. "Go back to your roots. Some portion of this drug could still be salvaged. If anyone can do it, you can."

She chuckled. "Do any of us have another ten to twenty years to retool this thing?"

Silence.

"Reconsider, Tom."

"Not a chance. I'm more than ready to leave this hunk of metal and get back to my family. The cash, notoriety, and especially you, aren't worth it."

Idiot. I've come too far to turn back now. "I'm sorry to hear that. Sometimes I wonder what I ever saw in you, Tom. You're so weak." She raised her brows. "You used to have such…talent." Huffing out a breath, she strolled to her desk. "We'll deal with all the unpleasant details of your departure this afternoon. Be a dear and bring me a cup of coffee from downstairs, would you? I gave my secretary the day off."

Fifteen minutes later Tom returned, coffee in hand. "As you requested."

Sloan took two large gulps. "Did you brew a fresh pot?" She downed a few more mouthfuls. "This is fabulous."

"No, but I did add a special ingredient. You seem to like it."

"I do. Fill me in. It's the least you can do."

"Absolutely. You're now number one on your own human trials list."

Her eyes widened, and she forcefully emptied the contents of her stomach.

"Come on, Sloan. You know that won't help. Maybe it'll slow the onset of symptoms. You yourself perfected this part, wanting absorption to be quick, to satisfy the impatient public, like yourself." He leaned in close to her face. "Already the drug is entering your bloodstream, working its wicked magic on you. Do you feel it? Question is, will you be one of the lucky ones? I'll be watching your new stats with interest."

"How *dare* you? You've killed my dream."

"On the contrary, I think I've given this pharmaceutical a fighting chance. Who better than the originator of this mess to fight to fix it? For the record, my money is on you."

Jezebel

by Stephanie Scissom

Lucifer clamped his hands over his ears and groaned, "Shuuuuuut up!"

Jezebel stiffened. Her face remained impassive, but Lucifer saw defiance flash in her eyes. It amused him.

He leaned back in his chair. "Your politics bore me. It's too bad you're not heading the final battle against Michael. You're both such unrelenting warmongers."

"Yes, it is too bad," Jezebel snapped. "*I* would be building an army."

Inwardly, Lucifer sighed. Why did she have to provoke him? He wasn't in the mood for her shit right now.

With more venom than he actually felt, he growled, "Watch your tone, demon. You may have been a queen on earth, but down here, you are nothing."

"What of the four from the sea?" she persisted. "Do you know who they were? Do you know their strengths?"

Lucifer tensed. Why had Mephistopheles told her about them? That was not the kind of information he should share with a demon, even if he was fucking her.

Lucifer stood and advanced on her, scowling. "It seems you have been loosening my brother's tongue as well as his belt. Who are you to speak to me about them? Mind your business, demon. This is the last time I will warn you."

"My name is Jezebel," she hissed. "And someone needs to mind your business if you won't."

Lucifer grabbed her chin, then shoved her away. "No, your name is demon. Before that, it was human. You are nothing compared to me. Nothing. You like to call yourself Queen and beg to be mine, but what have you meant to the men you've championed? Utter devastation, from all I can see. Mephistopheles would do well to look around hell and see what a sorry lot your former lovers are. Ahab, Timur, Khan, Hitler, Zedong…you really helped them out, didn't you? I don't need you."

"I helped all of them!" she spat. "I was 15 years old when I was given in marriage to Ahab. I made him strong. I made him feared. They all worshipped him, and he worshipped me. They were weaker men. Their fates are not my fault. We could be different. I could help you. Let me show you. Let me fight by your side. Let me be your queen."

She grabbed his hand and Lucifer shook her off.

"Do not touch me, filthy creature." He laughed,

walking a slow circle around her. "Be my queen? You? What did Elijah say, 'the carcass of Jezebel shall be like dung on the ground.' That's all you are to me. Dog shit on my boot. Disgusting, annoying, lingering…but inconsequential. Do not presume to approach me again or I will show you what it means to cross me. If you are Jezebel, so I am Lucifer."

The rage on her face when he bastardised her own quote made him laugh.

Pride was a bitch, and Jezebel was filled with arrogance. In life, she had been a woman with a sharp, unfettered tongue during a period when women had no voice. Lucifer could almost admire that—when her tongue wasn't lashing at *him*. When it was, he delighted in putting her back in her place. He couldn't resist one more dig.

"Some leader you'd be," he taunted. "You're in hell for the stupidest reason possible. All that murder and sacrifice to a false god. How did it feel, when the horses trampled you and the dogs ate your flesh? When your soul raced towards hell and you realised that raging old zealot Elijah was right, that your god Ba'al was as fake as Santa Claus?"

"No stupider than you must have felt to be banished to this pit over a piece of ass," she retorted, then blanched.

She'd gone too far, and she knew it. She was already begging before Lucifer put his fingers in his mouth and whistled.

"Please, my king!" she gasped, backing away. "I'm sorry! Please, don't!"

A loud, eerie howl rattled the cavern, followed by another. Even in the distance, Lucifer heard claws scraping on the stone floor as his hellhounds answered their summons. Jezebel shrieked and surged out of her vessel, leaving the human to crumple like a pile of rags.

It was too late.

A pair of fiery eyes appeared in the dark corridor, followed by two more. The beasts' eyes glowed orange as burning coals. Jezebel made a noise like air going out of a balloon and she darted into the furthest corner like a dark cloud.

The leader stepped into the dim light, his hackles raised. Jezebel screamed and the hellhound went wild, snarling and snapping. Ropy, glistening drool hung from his long, razor sharp fangs. Lucifer reached to pet its thick, snarled black fur and its brothers stepped forward also—huge, wolf-like creatures with a combination of scales and ragged, smoking pelts.

"This old boy is Molech. These are Ba'al and Asherah. Your god isn't even the toughest dog." Lucifer gestured at the human on the floor and said, "Clean up this mess."

Immediately, the beasts were on the discarded body, snarling and ripping. Jezebel made a high, keening sound in the corner.

"Having a flashback?" Lucifer asked. "What was it they found of you? Your skull, palms and feet?"

Jezebel didn't pause her meltdown to reply.

"Hold," Lucifer told the beasts, and walked from the room. He met his brother Mephistopheles in the corridor.

"Where is Jezebel?" Mephistopheles asked.

"Treed in my chambers. I'll let her go in a bit. Brother, take care of your words with that demon. She is blindingly ambitious and—as much trouble we've gotten into by loving humans—loving a demon like that would be threefold. Ask Hitler. Does his Eva even visit him down here? I think not."

A few hours later, Lucifer heard his dogs growling and remembered to release Jezebel. She zipped past him, past the ruined form of the female body she'd possessed. He should really call her back and make her clean that up, but he let her go. He had more important things to worry about, like what he was going to do with his wife. Abigail wasn't safe anymore, and he wasn't sure there was anywhere she could be. Demons swarmed the earth like flies, and they all knew her face.

Thirty minutes later, he climbed the stairwell to Abigail's apartment and knocked on her door.

"Come in," she called, and Lucifer frowned.

He shoved open the door. "What the hell, Abigail? I told you to be—"

Something was here.

Abigail sat by the window, her white curtains billowing in the breeze. She looked calm as she applied her lipstick, but she didn't sense the evil in this room. Humans wouldn't.

Lucifer scanned the room, anxiety tightening his chest. Searching for shadows, for anything out of place. They weren't alone.

Abigail turned and smiled at him, pursing her red lips. "What's the matter, Buttercup? You look like you just stepped in dog shit."

The voice coming from his wife, from the only person who mattered to him, was not hers.

"Jezebel," he breathed.

Pride Goeth

by Gabriella Balcom

Starr opened the compact and studied her image in the mirror. She smoothed her long blonde hair, touched up her eye shadow and lipstick, then winked at herself.

"Girl, you're beautiful," L'Quonna said.

"I know." Starr shrugged.

"All the girls wish they were you," Belle commented.

"Of course they do." Starr's tone was matter-of-fact. "But there's only one me."

Belle asked, "How do I look?"

Starr barely glanced at her best friend. Guys chased her a lot too, but only because she hung around with Starr. "You look fine," she replied, dismissively.

After focusing on her reflection again, she blew herself a kiss and set the compact on the table.

She glanced around the high school cafeteria, her eyes falling on Kyla sitting a couple tables away. "Look at her stuffing her face," Starr whispered to L'Quonna and Belle. "Oink, oink," she called out, careful to pitch her voice loud enough to carry to the people seated around them, but low enough that the teachers across the room couldn't hear.

Laughter rang out as dozens of teenagers looked at Kyla.

Her face paled, making her freckles stand out. She lowered her eyes, dropping her fork when she tried to set it down.

"Piggy's all fumbly-fingered," Starr sneered.

Kyla raised her head, face flushed. Her voice shook. "I'm *not* a pig."

"What's going on?" Mrs. Bozeman asked, walking toward them.

"Nothing," Starr replied, staring into her mirror again and wrapping a lock of hair around her finger. She smiled at her reflection.

"I heard what you said." Mrs. Bozeman frowned as she surveyed Starr. "Calling people names is inappropriate."

"It's not my fault she's fat," Starr retorted, shooting her pals a small smile when one of them giggled.

"Kyla isn't fat. She simply has a different built to you. You're tall and thin. She's shorter with broad shoulders, but also thin." Mrs. Bozeman addressed everyone who was staring at them. "Lunchtime is almost over, so I suggest all of you finish eating." She turned back to Starr and said, "Come with me."

One week later

"*Ow,*" Kyla cried out as the fork struck her head and dropped to the floor.

Starr grinned. "Now you can shovel the food into your mouth twice as fast."

Kyla grabbed her tray and headed to a different table farther away.

"Run, pig, run," Starr called out. Beside her, Belle and L'Quonna laughed.

The cafeteria was abuzz as everyone chatted about the upcoming prom.

Belle kept droning on and on about the guys who'd invited her, which one she'd accompany, and what to wear.

"Can I join you two for lunch?" Trevor asked.

"Of course," Starr purred, answering for herself and Belle. They'd just sat down for lunch by themselves, because L'Quonna was out sick.

But fifteen minutes later, she was gritting her teeth to keep from screaming as Trevor and Belle smiled at each other—*again.* He'd been acting as if she were the only one at their table, barely even looking at Starr, even though she was a thousand times more beautiful than Belle.

She mentally catalogued her attributes: platinum blonde hair—check; sky-blue eyes—check; perfect, white teeth courtesy of braces and porcelain veneers—check; equally perfect nose, lips, and ears—check. Cosmetic surgery had seen to all that. Her bust had been enhanced, too, and her personal trainer helped ensure she stayed slender and sexy.

Belle, on the other hand, had plain brown hair and green eyes which were nothing special. Her teeth were okay, considering they hadn't been worked on. And, she was naturally well-endowed, with larger breasts than Starr, even after her augmentation, but so what?

"I have to take care of something." She forced herself to talk and act normally, then left to dispose of her lunch tray. She heard the two behind her laughing, imagined them staring into each other's eyes, and she felt like gagging.

The Junior-Senior Prom was only two months away. Despite being a sophomore, Starr was going. Guys had been inviting her for years. This year, she'd agreed to be a Varsity linebacker's date, but it was Trevor she actually wanted to go with. She'd had her eye on him ever since he'd broken up with his girlfriend, and it was still her plan to get him to ask her. He was the best athlete, and she deserved the best.

She saw Trevor less than twenty minutes later, during her off-period. He asked her about Belle's favourite flower, colour, and things like that, sharing that he planned to surprise her. Starr frowned, thinking about it.

"Belle's beautiful," Trevor murmured. "Her eyes are gorgeous. Her hair is like dark, spun gold, and I see red when the light shines on it."

"Uh-huh." Starr shrugged. "It takes the salon awhile to streak it."

"I thought it was natural."

"*Natural*? Very little of her is. You know—lipo and the boob job..." Seeing the startled look on his face, Starr put a hand to her mouth. "Oh, I'm sorry. I thought you knew."

She forced herself to frown, to keep from smiling when she said, "Hopefully she's not still contagious."

"*Contagious?*" He looked like he'd tasted something revolting.

"Yeah—the STD... But you have to promise not to

tell her I told you. Don't tell anybody else either."

Starr's eyes gleamed moments later when he asked her to the prom instead of Belle, and she gloated inwardly.

Four days later

"You *bitch!*" Belle yelled at Starr. "How could you say those horrible things about me? Your boobs were enlarged, not mine, and I've never had a sexually-transmitted disease in my life."

"Huh?" Starr played dumb, but Belle's slap left her ears ringing.

"I thought we were friends for life, but friends don't lie about each other. I've always stood by you, but you care about nothing but yourself. You trashed me to get a boy. Well, Trevor's not just any boy. He's real special. But he's done with you. And I am, too."

Starr glared as Belle turned and strode down the hall, accompanied by L'Quonna.

"What are you looking at?" she demanded of a freshman who was still staring, mouth agape.

Belle was done? Fine. Starr knew she was too good for her former friend anyway.

She fell flat on her face during her next class when someone deliberately tripped her as she walked up front to turn in an assignment.

"Hope your fake tits didn't pop," some girl said.

"Splat!" a guy called out, and the entire room exploded into laughter.

Starr's cheeks burned as she got up.

During lunch, she sat alone. She'd only taken a few bites of her meal when she started feeling funny. Her skin itched. Her lips tingled. Her eyes burned. She got out her compact and shrieked when she saw her face. It was strangely puffy and seemed to be swelling by the second. She tried to speak, but her speech was garbled. Touching her tongue, she found it enlarged. She stood but felt light-headed and collapsed.

The next thing she heard was her mother's voice. "She wouldn't eat almonds, because she knows she's allergic to them."

"Maybe not," a paramedic relied. "But pieces of nut were in her salad."

The next day

Starr prepared to shower after PE, but couldn't find

her shampoo. Luckily, somebody had left some out.

As she towelled her wet hair, her scalp tingled. She sipped the cold drink she'd found on the bench outside the showers, and scratched her head. A lock of hair came away in her fingers, and she gasped. Then a clump fell to the ground at her feet. Two more followed and she screamed, tears staining her cheeks.

Coach Weems appeared within seconds, her eyes widening. "Your hair—uh..." She stopped speaking.

"What?"

The coach sighed. "I think you've been pranked, and it's not just your hair. Your teeth..."

Starr ran to the closest mirror and wailed, her body shaking all over. Her head looked like a patchwork quilt. Bare, red spots interspersed with areas that still had hair which stuck out in every direction.

Raising a trembling hand, Starr gently touched a patch and screeched. That's when she realised her teeth were bright green.

Laughter rang out from behind her. She whirled, and saw her former best friends, Kyla, and several other classmates standing there, holding their cell phones. Clicks sounded as they snapped pictures.

Starr wondered what she'd ever done to them to deserve this. She was overcome by horror at the thought

of even more people seeing how she looked, and she fled
back into the showers.

At Legacy's End

by Sandy Butchers

"A foolish man,

if he acquires

wealth or a woman's love,

pride grows within him,

but wisdom never:

he goes on more and more arrogant."

- Hávamál, verse 79

I raised the patch that covered the scar where once I had an eye. It often stung and itched whenever my loyal ravens had spotted something worthy for me to see. With my free hand, I gestured to the men and women around me to be quiet for a moment, and focused on the images that came to me.

"Not him again," I muttered. A careful snickering sounded around me.

"What is Sigurd up to now?" my wife asked as she placed her hand on my shoulder.

"He is boasting again, about how he killed that dragon. He is making an utter fool of himself, pretending he wouldn't have drowned in the blood of the wretched creature if I hadn't told him to dig those trenches."

Loud laughter filled my hall. When I opened my one remaining eye, I saw how my quests were simply making fun of the whole situation. I chuckled quietly. "Can you imagine what it would have looked like if I hadn't told him?" I joked lightly, yet I was disturbed by the fact that my ravens had caught onto him again.

"I'm not sure if I am more amused by the image of Sigurd drowning, or the image of the damn dragon bleeding to death," Loki answered. How can he always make me shudder when he speaks?

"Why, what is it to you? I don't remember you being held hostage before Fafnir turned into the dragon," I said, staring at the lad sitting across the table. "In fact, if I do remember correctly, you were the only one to be set free, while I myself, Thor, and Hoenir were strapped to lantern posts by our wrists."

"You think that collecting a ransom for your insufferable asses wasn't torture? Trust me, it took me a lot of effort to actually collect that gold instead of leaving you all hanging there!" Loki hissed.

"If I remember correctly," Thor stated as he stood up from his chair, "you killed Fafnir's brother, thinking he was an otter. Providing the ransom to set us free was the least you could do, worm!"

"Didn't you also eat from the meal I served that evening? Wasn't it you who declared otter meat to be delicious?" Loki snapped.

Thor remained silent.

My scar itched again. My ravens wanted to show me more. "The fool is going to get himself killed," I said.

"Shouldn't we do something?" I heard my wife ask, but I was too distracted. In front of me, Thor and Loki were bickering as usual, about who was to blame for the farce we—thank goodness—got ourselves out of. Next to me, Frigg was trying to ease my mind as it was torn between a sense of guilt and my role as the High King of Asgard.

I stood up and slammed my fist on the table. It was quiet at once. "Sigurd may be a fool, a proud fool to be precise, but we mustn't let our own pride take the best of us. We needed him to kill that wretched dragon, or it would have destroyed everything and everyone."

"The man needs a lesson in humility," said Loki.

I agreed. I combed my fingers through by beard and nodded my head. "Then I shall go and teach him."

I finished my plate, chugged back my mead, and kissed my wife as I always do before I leave. I changed my robes for something more fitting, and took my staff before I left for Sigurd.

Upon arrival at the overly decorated house of the man in question, I shook my head. Things were worse than I thought. My ravens greeted me from the tree up ahead. Hugin landed on my shoulder and whispered quiet words into my ear. Words of warning, words of fear and desperation. When he left, Munin flew up to me and spoke into my other ear. He reminded me of the man Sigurd used to be before his pride corrupted him.

Looking at his house now, it was clear that he had overdone himself. He had adorned the carvings around his door with gold and jewels. The roof itself had been made of silver tiles. I saw several men and women toiling in the garden to tame its wild and thorny vines. Their arms were scratched and bleeding. Their faces dusty and dirty.

I sighed and sent my beloved birds away before walking to the golden doorway and knocking on the carefully carved wood. I chuckled quietly and shook my head in disapproval when I saw what kind of heroic images he'd had a very skilled woodworker carve into the door. When it didn't open after my persistent knocking, I decided to have a look at the other side of the garden.

There, I understood Hugin's words of fear.

Sigurd sat on a wooden throne in the shadow of a chestnut tree. He drank from a golden chalice while a woodworker, most likely the same that had carved the door, eternalised his portrait into the trunk of a cut down tree. In front of him, there we too women yelling at each other, prepared to tear each other's hair out at any second.

"What are you two bickering about now?" I heard Sigurd say from his throne.

As if stung by a bee, both women looked up from their quarrel and turned to the man behind them.

"Marrying me off to Gunther was not your decision to make!" one women screamed while her cheeks turned red as fire.

"He is your lord. He has paid for you. If marrying you off to the King is in his benefit, then he has every right to do so," the other woman replied calmly.

Sigurd gestured to the crying woman to come closer. He pressed his hand under her chin when she did. "Oh Brunhild, you are too pretty for these tears," he said.

"Don't patronise me," hissed the women.

"Gunther will make a wonderful husband. He is rich and well mannered, and I'm sure you'll make some friends among his other wives."

"He is fat and ugly, and I am no whore!"

I felt for the lady. She was right in standing up for herself like this. Sigurd had crossed the line. I realised that by enabling him to survive his attack on the dragon, I had killed him in a much more horrifying way…I had made him victim of his own pride, and it was slowly turning him into an entitled prick who thought he had the right to decide on other people's lives.

"What is all this about?" I asked as I entered the courtyard, just before Sigurd's wife could smack the other lady. I drew my hat a bit further down so that they wouldn't immediately see who I was.

"Nothing, sir," Sigurd answered. "Just a wench who does not do her job."

"And what is her job?" I asked.

"Well, look around you."

My goodness, even the sound of his voice now made my skin crawl.

"This garden is supposed to provide me with food. She isn't harvesting."

"Excuse me, sir," I said. "I couldn't help but overhear that she is to be wed?"

"You heard correctly," Sigurd's wife interrupted, "To maintain this land, it is of the utmost importance that King Gunther has nothing to complain about. If this wench is the trade we make to own this land for another year, then it must be so."

I scratched my beard. "So, this quarrel is not really about a woman not doing her job? Instead, it is about an arranged marriage for your own personal gain."

"And?" Sigurd yawned.

"Well sir, excuse me once again for saying this, but look around you. For a man who is no King, aren't you entitling yourself a bit too much?" I tried, I really tried.

"Do you know who I am?" Sigurd asked as he put his chalice down and gestured to the woodcarver to stop his work for a moment. He rose from his throne and walked closer to me.

"I killed the dragon, Fafnir. I dug a hole and hid in it until the beast walked over my head. I stabbed it with my sword, rending its belly open, and delivering the good people of this land from its flames and destruction. I take great pride in the courage and wits I needed to slay him."

"Tell me, do you take pride in handing over women to overly greedy men as well?" I asked, raising the eyebrow above my scar. I think Sigurd finally saw it then, for he took a step back with open mouth.

"And tell me, who told you to dig those trenches so you wouldn't drown in the dragon's blood?" I kept asking as I saw the panic in his eyes grow. "Now tell me..." I stepped closer to him and took off my hat, allowing

Sigurd to see the patch that covered the hole of my missing eye. "Who entitled you to own this land as if you were a King yourself?"

Sigurd mouth fell open. "Allfather," he gasped, "if only I had known it was you!"

"Then what? Would you have lied about the ill fate of this young woman?" I leaned on my staff.

"I can't believe you actually came," I heard the woman behind me whisper. I turned to face her.

"My ravens alerted me to you. I could no longer ignore your pleas."

"So, this is all your fault," Sigurd's wife interrupted again. "You asked Allfather to come and save you."

"No!" Brunhild cried, "I asked for justice. I asked that your husband would see his madness before any more harm would be done."

"Justice is what has come to Sigurd in return for his slaying of the dragon. There is no shame in his pride," the wife answered. "He earns every bit of respect we ask of you."

"He earns only ridicule," I noted. "Stop this madness now. Your actions entitle you to nothing more than the name of 'Dragon slayer.' Fafnir's death did not make you King, it did not make you better than anyone else, nor did it change your legacy."

"It changed mine. I am proud of my husband, and proud to be his wife! I will have no one—no god, no wench—take that away from me," said Sigurd's wife as she pulled a knife from underneath her belt.

"Then so be it," I whispered.

I saw how the woman raised her arm to stab the young lady in front of her. The ground trembled when I stomped my staff into the soil. Brunhild stepped backwards and away from the knife. She tripped over the first step of the wooden throne and lost her balance. She fell to her knees just before the knife would hit her heart. Instead, the blade plunged into Sigurd, who stood only inches away.

For a moment, I stepped back to observe the scene. It made me sad to think that Sigurd's wife was maybe as corrupted by pride as Sigurd was himself. I only noticed how bad it was when she cried, not because her husband had just died by her own hand, but because she no longer had Sigurd's fame to thrive upon.

I looked at Brunhild and nodded my head. "Not to worry," I said, "This was not your lesson to learn."

I left.

"How did it go?" Thor asked when he saw me.

"It was a hard lesson learned," I answered. "Sigurd died, his wife is left a widow without fame. Soon the people will know that he died by her hand. She will lose everything she has entitled herself to." I patted my son on his back. "Please remember, Thor, never think you are better than the purpose you were put onto this world for."

Thor looked at me with questioning eyes.

"Only foolish men grow pride when they acquire wealth or a woman's love. They will never grow wise, instead they will become more and more arrogant."

"Father, I truly hope that someday, someone will write down your ever so wise words."

I merely smiled, for I had already seen the future.

Not Guilty

by Wondra Vanian

Jack Kerrington was celebrating, and he let everyone in the shithole of a bar know it. Whether they wanted to or not.

"I'm a free man," he slurred after his seventh straight bourbon. Jack wasn't normally a drinking man but if leaving a courtroom with a "not guilty" verdict wasn't a good reason to get tanked, he didn't know what was.

The bartender, a man at least twenty years younger than Jack, rolled his eyes as he towelled a glass dry. Three years into a degree in psychology and two years behind the bar, he'd had just about enough of listening to other people prattle on about their lives. Just about enough of people, period. And it showed.

As the drunk old man slung back another glass of cheap bourbon, the bartender debated changing his major. Maybe he'd go into zoology...animals *had* to be better than people.

The bell over the door jangled as it swung inward, allowing a man who looked to be in his late forties to enter. The newcomer sidled up to the bar and ordered a beer. He said, "please" and "thank you," which earned him points with the disgruntled bartender.

"Free, I tell ya," Jack said to the man when he settled on a cracked wooden stool next to him. "Free."

The other man graced him with a tolerant grin. "Aren't we all, my friend?"

Jack shook his head. A little too hard. He had to grab the bar to keep from sliding off his stool.

The bartender decided that, if the old man fell, he could just lay there until someone came to get his sorry ass.

"Naw, naw," Jack said excitedly, glassy eyes bright. "You don't understand. I'm *free*."

The newcomer nodded, smiling patiently. "Sure, I get it. *Free*."

Waving an agitated hand—nearly knocking over the man's beer in the process—Jack said, "Not. Guilty."

Narrowing his eyes, the newcomer replied with, "Not guilty?"

Jack touched the tip of his nose with one finger and winked.

Having lost all interest in the conversation before it had started, the bartender disappeared into the backroom to…well, to do anything that involved ignoring the room full of drunken idiots behind him.

"Hey, aren't you the guy that was on the news today?" the newcomer asked Jack.

Puffing out his chest, Jack beamed. "That's me." He'd been on the *news*—practically a celebrity!

The other man frowned. His eyebrows drew together as he searched his memory. "Weren't you on trial for murdering your wife?"

Jack nodded, then threw back the last of his bourbon. Where had that useless bartender gone? He was ready for another drink...

"Did you do it?"

Jack stopped craning to see into the backroom and turned to face the man on the next stool. "Huh?"

"Did you do it? Did you kill your wife?"

"Not according to the jury!" Jack laughed, banging a hand on the bar.

No one else found it funny.

The other man leaned in. "No," he said in a loud whisper. "I mean...did you do it?"

Jack leaned in too, dangerously close to sliding off his stool. "You a cop?" he asked.

"No."

"Then, yeah," Jack said in what was probably meant to be a whisper but, in fact, boomed across the room. "I killed that old harpy. Been dying to do it for years, man."

He swayed, barely staying on his perch. "Ya shoulda heard the crack her neck made when it broke." He laughed. "Music to my fucking ears."

Jack continued to laugh—all the way to the floor, where he laughed up at the ceiling. A couple stepped over him on their way to the exit, but Jack didn't care. The floor was more comfortable than a lousy stool, anyway.

The other man took one last drag from his beer before stepping away from the bar. He crouched next to Jack with a disappointed look on his face. "Thank you for your honesty," he said sombrely. "Do you know who I am?"

Eyes glazed, Jack blinked slowly. "Sure, sure," he said. "You're the guy who isn't a cop."

"Look again."

Jack Kerrington's world suddenly became very clear. He couldn't see the bar anymore—but he could see two paths: one shrouded in darkness and fear, the other radiating the purest light he had ever seen and, between them, crouched a bearded man clad in white robes. A ring of heavy keys hung from his waist. The image brought to mind hot summer afternoons in a dusty classroom at the back of church. Jack knew then exactly who the other man was.

Awed, Jack could barely stammer out a reply. "S-Saint Peter?"

Peter nodded. The grim expression he wore didn't waver.

"Do you know why I'm here, Jack?"

A cold fear settled on the drunk man. "No," he said. Peter didn't bother trying to pretend that Jack meant, "No, I don't understand." They both knew it was a plea.

"I might have been able to help," Peter told Jack as the man tried to make his clumsy limbs work. They always tried to run; it was almost sad.

"If you had shown the slightest bit of remorse," he continued, "If you hadn't been so damned proud of your horrible deed…" He shook his head. "I might have been able to buy you time. Given you a second chance. But as it is…"

"No!" Jack said as panic raced through him. "Please, I'll do anything. I'll confess!"

Peter was not swayed. "You have already confessed."

The old man was crying now; loud, gasping sobs full of snot and despair. "I'll go back to the courthouse. I'll do my time. Anything! Please!"

"There's no going back. But you *will* do your time, Jack."

The radiant path faded, overshadowed by the darkness. Jack could see Peter's robed form, walking away as the blackness rose up to swallow him. Peter's voice continued in his head, even when the sounds of millions of screams filled Jack's ears.

"You have been judged, Jack Kerrington. And you have been found guilty."

Jack screamed, but even he couldn't tell the sound of his own screams over the din of other sufferers.

"Is he okay?" a concerned woman asked over the bartender's shoulder as he gave the fallen man a shake.

The bartender ignored her question.

"Call 911," he told the woman without looking up. "Tell them there's a guy here who's stopped breathing." He knew that there might still be a chance to save the old man—that he should start CPR right away—but there was something about the old man's face that kept him at a distance.

No one else stepped forward to do it either. Even if he hadn't been dead seconds after hitting the floor, the silent scream of terror frozen on Jack Kerrington's face was enough to frighten the other patrons away.

Joy's Debut

by Ximena Escobar

Shiny blue eyelids fluttered, bearing the brilliance of stage lights. Pink glitter twinkled as her mouth opened to sing of unrequited love. The Adam's apple bobbed as she swallowed her fear, and silver stars sparkled on the microphone; wings stretching, a heart soaring; a rainbow explosion breaking from its prison of shame.

She shut her eyes to the sound of hands clapping—metal chairs chalked the floor, because some even rose to show their love.

But father wasn't there. He stayed on the other side of the TV screen, making sure he flicked past any flashes of the Mardi Gras.

I'll See You on the Other Side

by Stephen Herczeg

"I'm the professor here, so don't give me that crap about my figures being wrong, okay?" Branson yelled at Jordan, his young intern, almost browbeating him into tears.

Jordan slunk away from the whiteboard and moved back to his desk. He flopped into his chair and stared back at Branson.

If I didn't need his sponsorship to complete my Doctorate, I'd be out of here, he thought.

Professor Branson Fletcher was a rock star of practical physics. A brilliant scientist who was full of charisma and managed to play both the role of a darling to the fawning celebrities and an outstanding intelligence to his business partners.

His simple innovations to popular products had yielded millions for the various companies he dealt with, in turn generating millions of dollars for his own personal research.

When he wasn't attending another red-carpet event with one of Hollywood's most glamorous starlets on his arm, he was appearing on multiple talk shows, rattling off nuggets of incredible facts and stories to delight the lay audiences across the world.

But when it all went quiet, he could be found working on his one true passion, the dream that he hoped would cement him into the firmament as one of the greatest minds of all time.

That passion was molecular teleportation. A jokey plot device that had been used by science fiction writers and movies for decades, but a concept, when placed in the hands and mind of Branson Fletcher, had become feasible and almost workable.

Jordan looked across at the two teleportation portals. Each a copy of the other, only distinguished by a large "A" and "B" inscribed above the entrance. They were simple rectangular structures that could have been doorways, standing on a flat platform.

The idea was straightforward. An item was placed on one platform, the teleporter was programmed and then readied for operation, the item disappeared, and moments later it would appear on the other platform. Whole and unharmed.

That was the simple theory anyway. The science

behind was insanely complicated. The portals each generated a localised wormhole that linked up through the fabric of time and space. The item would be sucked into the wormhole then, after several moments, spat out at the other end. The delay involved was a consequence of the time it took for the object to travel along the gravitational tunnel created between both wormholes. Branson estimated that tunnel to be between ten and twenty light seconds in length.

Jordan peered at the whiteboards that lined the walls of the laboratory. Several were dedicated to the formulae required to create a single instance of a wormhole, the basis of which was written within the laws of quantum entanglement. Sometimes his mind blurred at the mathematics required to unlock the secrets they had developed here, but today he was sure he knew what was wrong.

However, Professor Branson Fletcher was sure he was right, and when Branson Fletcher thought he was right, he wouldn't listen to anyone else's opinion. In Branson Fletcher's mind, his way was always correct.

Jordan knew that most of the time that was true, but he was positive that Branson had misinterpreted the consequences of introducing a moving object into the wormhole. That moving object being a living being as opposed to something inanimate.

The astounding fact about Branson's work was, it worked. The molecular teleportation system actually worked, but only for non-living objects.

They had cracked open several bottles of Dom Perignon on that first successful test. A simple cube of metal had been sent from one platform to the other. It had arrived, unharmed, undented, unscratched. They had measured every facet of the cube; it was identical to before it was sent.

From that day forward, they had expanded the test subjects. Metal, plastics, wood, paper, furniture, machinery had all been sent through the portal. All had arrived exactly as sent. The only blip had been a strange scratch on the leg of a table that had been sent through.

He and Branson had dismissed it, writing up their notes to say they must have missed seeing the scratch before sending it through. Jordan was still a little sceptical and couldn't find the scratch on the multitude of photographs they had taken before the event.

It was when they moved on to organic matter that things became stranger.

Humble items, such as a lettuce, had passed through without any problems. Though on the second try, the outer leaves arrived with a new split down their length. Branson had simply noted it and moved on.

Steaks, sausages, hunks of meat, all went through unharmed. It was the leg of lamb that disturbed Jordan most. It was undamaged but had moved. On Portal A it had been pointing from side to side, on arrival at Portal B it was pointing front to back, as if something had turned it slightly on its journey. Nothing else had ever moved during the transfer.

Branson's glee at the progress was palpable. His enthusiasm had a way of dragging you along with it. The next experiments were on live animals.

"The idea behind this invention is to redefine transportation as a whole," Branson said to Jordan, "Not just for goods and produce, but for humans. Imagine it; we could eliminate cars, planes and boats overnight. We could almost remove the need for motor fuels completely. That's my dream, that's why I've been doing this for years. But to realise that dream we must be able to teleport live animals."

The first experiment did not go well. A white mouse was placed on the platform. It disappeared as expected but arrived in a pool of blood thirty seconds later. They had revisited the maths, recalculated and recalibrated. Repeated with a non-living object successfully, then with another mouse.

This one arrived in two pieces, sliced completely in half.

Branson looked at the dead mouse and kept muttering, "I know I'm right," to himself. He stormed off and pored over the math for another two days, ignoring anything Jordan had to offer.

It was when Clara, Branson's personal assistant, and, Jordan believed, part time lover, arrived with a small pet cage, that Jordan's interest piqued again.

He inquired what was in the cage.

Trying to be clever and use her association with Branson to be funny, she replied, "Well, it's either a dead cat or a live cat."

Jordan knew the joke well and simply asked, "Why don't we just look then?" with as straight a face as he could muster.

Clara's face and shoulders deflated.

"It's a cat," she said, "I was trying to be funny," then stormed off to find Branson.

Jordan kicked himself inside, he liked Clara and had hoped that like could lead to something stronger when Branson tired of her. He realised now that may never happen.

Branson and Clara appeared moments later and headed across to Portal A. Jordan rose and hurried over, he already had an idea what they were going to do.

"You can't," he said, "The University forbids experiments with animals larger than a common rat."

Branson looked at him as if he was a fool.

"That's for medical experiments," he said, "This has nothing to do with medicine."

"It has everything to do with ethics," Jordan replied.

Branson looked down his nose at his young intern and said, "Ethics? What have ethics got to do with anything? What we are doing here is for the greater good of mankind, and the planet. Some pathetic quibbles about one small animal should not stand in the way of greatness. Now back away unless you're going to help."

Jordan glared at Branson for a moment. His eyes fell on Clara whose expression was a mix of sympathy and sadness. He realised they were aimed at the cat, not himself.

Branson spoke to Clara, "Wait until I give you the signal, then put the cat on the platform. You'll have to be quick and don't get caught in there, or you'll end up wherever the cat goes."

Clara looked horrified.

Branson smiled and reassured her.

"Don't worry, you'll only end up over there," he said pointing at Portal B.

Jordan noted that she didn't look any more reassured.

Branson moved to the control console and readied it for action.

He looked up and at Clara and said, "Now."

She pulled the cat out of the pet carrier and, calming it down with a hug and gentle stroking, placed it on the platform.

"Let go, now."

Clara pulled away. The cat's face grew horrified. The portal lit up in an array of flashing lights, there was a bright glow, then nothing.

The cat was gone. The portal's humming ceased. The lights dimmed.

All three turned towards Portal B and watched.

And waited.

After two minutes, Jordan spoke up.

"It's never taken that long before," he said.

Branson simply stared at the vacant portal and mumbled under his breath.

"My calculations are right. It should have worked. It should have worked."

He cursed, rammed his fist onto the frame of the console, stormed into his office and slammed the door.

Clara simply shrugged, walked over to the cat carrier, picked it up and left.

The next day, Jordan walked into the laboratory to see a large dog sitting inside Portal A, with Branson standing at the console.

"Good boy," said Branson in his best *his master's voice*.

The dog simply stared at him, bemused by the attention. From the look of the matted coat on the dog, Jordan realised it was a stray. Branson must have picked it up off the street, fed it until it was in an overstuffed stupor, then managed to get it to sit still in the portal.

Branson finished typing in the commands. The teleporter hummed to life and the array of lights brightened. Seconds later the dog was gone.

Forever.

"Fuck," screamed Branson.

He finally noticed Jordan and screamed at him.

"What the fuck have you done? My calculations are correct. This machine should fucking work. If I find out you've changed any parameters, I will kill you," he said, turning and stomping out of the laboratory and disappearing into his office once more.

Jordan simply stood, gobsmacked.

I think it's time to review my options.

Jordan stood at the whiteboard. From what he could tell, Branson was right. The figures were sound. Even allowing for the fact that any living organism placed inside the wormhole may be affected by temporal distortion caused by the movement of fluids within their system, they should still travel through the gravitational pathway in the same way as an inorganic object.

It just doesn't make sense.

He put the marker down and stood back staring at the equations. Within moments, they became a blur. It was time to go home. He turned to head back to his desk and pack up his things when Branson burst from his office.

The force of nature that was Branson wheeled through the laboratory and stopped before the console. He madly tapped into the keyboard, bringing the portals online and then did the insane.

Jordan ran towards the portal when he saw Branson step up onto the platform.

"Branson don't do it. We have no idea what will happen," he yelled.

The professor simply smiled at him.

"It's been the size this whole time. We need a larger specimen. The mice, the cat, the dog...too small. It's in my calculations. We need something over fifty kilograms. Something like me," he said.

Jordan implored him, "No. Don't do it. It's not worth it. We need to do more tests. Then we can try a human. But not yet."

The lights of the portal began flashing as the countdown timer reached zero. Jordan started to reach for Branson but pulled away as he realised he'd never get him in time. Branson simply smiled and pointed across to Portal B.

"I'm right you know. Always have been," he said, then winked, "I'll see you on the other side."

He disappeared.

Jordan slowly turned and stared at the other Portal. His shoulders slumped and his hopes faded as time dragged on. After several minutes, he trudged over to his desk and picked up the phone. After a few rings, a voice came on the other end.

"Clara, there's been an accident," he said.

The bright lights faded before Branson's eyes. He stared out across the rocky landscape. Huge mountains of rock reached towards the crimson hued sky. An enormous red star filled a quarter of the heavens, its light wasn't as bright as Earth's sun, but its size overpowered its brilliance in Branson's mind.

Of course. It's a way point. The wormhole passes across another planet. I was right. I was right all along. I just have to wait, and I'll return to Earth.

He stared around and saw a small skull and a collection of bleached white bones several metres away. He recognised the shape of the skull from its size and the extended canines.

Is that the dog?

He was confused and a little fearful. The atmosphere must be so corrosive that it stripped the flesh from the dog's body.

It must have moved out of range. I just need to stand still. I'll have to recalibrate when I get back.

A strange chittering noise grabbed his attention. He slowly turned and stared upwards.

Towering above him were a cluster of insectoid beings resembling massively overgrown praying mantises. He noticed blood on the mandibles of the nearest one. It was then he realised the atmosphere hadn't killed the dog.

The nearest creature stepped forward and reached for him with its front claws.

Branson screamed.

Nina Meets Auntie Dote

by Sue Marie St. Lee

Nina finished her registration in the cubicle and rose to find a seat in the waiting room. To the right of her, one seat was available next to an old woman who looked unkempt. A dirty, tattered tote bag stood between her legs. Her stringy hair appeared greasy and in great need of washing. She clattered her ill-fitting teeth in what seemed to be an innate habit. Her unpleasant scent wafted through the room, where the temperature was too warm for Nina's liking.

The old woman made eye contact with Nina, gesturing for her to sit beside her. Nina broke the eye contact and continued to peruse the area. She noticed another vacant seat, on the opposite side of the room from the old woman. A youngish woman sat in its adjacent chair. The young woman's head was crowned with thick, light brown, sun-streaked hair worn in a fashionable, long, layered cut. Although her features were exquisitely sharp, like a Greek goddess, she did wear a little make-up to slightly enhance the best of her qualities—a little swipe of red lipstick, and black mascara applied to her gorgeous, heavy eyelashes. The young woman also smelled pleasant, as though she had bathed in a tropical waterfall and dried off with hyacinth petals. Nina chose to sit next to the younger, definitely higher-class woman.

"Mind if I sit here?" Nina politely asked.

"Of course not," the woman answered with a beautiful, strong, melodic voice.

"Thank you."

Nina sat quietly for a few moments. There were no conversations between patients, and the silence was uncomfortable for her. She always had a radio or television spouting music or conversation when she was home. She explained to friends that she was still adjusting to the 'empty nest' syndrome, even though her children had grown up and moved away nearly twenty years earlier. She found it odd that there was no television in the waiting room. In all the other physician waiting rooms she had been to, they had a wall-mounted television, tuned in to either a news or home improvement channel. Here, there was no television, no piped in music—only silence.

Turning to the young woman, Nina broke the silence with a soft, almost whisper-like tone, "Have you been here long?"

"Not long." She smiled at Nina who noticed the woman's strange eye colour. Against the woman's sun-kissed skin tone, her amber eyes seemed almost surreal, almost golden, or a fiery yellow.

"Well, it looks like I'm going to have a bit of a wait." Nina continued chatting, "I wonder if it is unusual to be this crowded. I hate waiting."

"It won't be such a terribly long wait. I have it on good authority that there are two technicians working today and both machines are in proper order." The young woman seemed unconcerned.

"You're not nervous?"

"Oh, no. I do this quite often."

"Oh, I'm sorry. You must have been diagnosed with breast cancer?" Nina felt uneasy bringing up the topic of cancer, but that's why everyone was there, to have a mammogram. Wasn't everyone feeling a bit nervous?

"Thank you for your concern, but I'm not here for myself."

"Oh, you're here for moral support to a friend? I get it."

"No, Nina, I'm here for you."

Nina looked alarmed and puzzled at the young woman, wondering what on earth she meant and how she knew her name.

"What? I don't understand."

"Nina, you don't know it yet, but you are about to travel a lengthy, uphill battle after your test today."

"What? What do you mean? Are you saying that I have cancer?"

"Oh, yes. That is exactly what I am saying." The young woman looked blankly into Nina's worried eyes.

"You're nuts. What kind of woman blatantly tells another woman, in a breast clinic, that she knows the woman has breast cancer? You are sick. Sick, sick, sick!" Nina stood to move to a newly vacated seat across the room.

Laughing in a wicked tone, the young woman warned Nina, "You can move over there, but it won't make any difference. Your diagnosis will still be the same."

Stopping in her tracks, Nina turned to the young woman and said, "Really? And how is it you know any of this? You are just a crazy person!"

Nina's voice had reached the volume a speaker uses while addressing a crowd, and the crowd was listening. Every woman in the waiting room watched attentively while Nina and the young woman argued.

"I know because that is who I am."

"What the fuck is that supposed to mean? So, who

are you? Svengali?" Nina was beginning to lose her patience.

"You never asked my name. I am Cancer embodied."

With that admission, the entire room gasped, except for the old woman whose face was traced with trickles of tears.

Cancer looked at the old woman and motioned her finger as though marking a scoreboard in the air with a win. "I win! I told you she'd pick me." The old woman put her face in her hands and wept softly.

Confused more than ever, Nina looked at both women and demanded an answer. "You two know each other? The two of you are playing some kind of psycho game?" Staring at the smelly old woman, she continued, "And you! You old coot! What's your role in this game? What's *your* name, Death?"

Looking sadly at Nina, the old woman answered, "No, dear, my name is Auntie Dote."

Turning her attention back toward Cancer, Nina laughingly cried out, "Ha ha ha! Cancer and Auntie Dote. Clever. You are both sick fucks."

"Cancer and I are in this waiting room daily. It is our job," the old woman explained. "We sit on opposite sides of the room. Our power is only implemented when there are only two seats available, one next to her, one next to me. When those are the only seats available, the next person looking for a seat must choose to sit next to she or I.

"If you had chosen to sit next to me, I would have inconspicuously touched your hand. Your cancer would have been cured. Today's test result would have been clean. But, you chose cancer rather than its antidote.

"You judged me by my appearance, never considering the possibility that I have worth greater than outward appearance. You, ruled by your pride, judged me as a servile human."

"There you have it," Cancer chimed in, "Straight from Auntie Dote's mouth. You chose me, rather, your pride chose me. Now, you and I will be together for at least a year, and even if the doctors can work their magic in the operating room, never fear, I'll be back."

Nina spat on the floor. "Fuck all of you!" She proceeded to the exit door and left with her pride still intact.

Supply Run

by Rhiannon Bird

Axel pointed the unloaded gun at her. "But I'm the best of the best." She folded her arms and tapped her foot. It was a usual stance for Angela to take.

"Axel, I swear to god." She let out a frustrated sigh. "All I'm saying is that you could learn a thing or two from Violet."

He loaded the gun and shoved it into his holster. "If anything, I could teach her a thing or two."

Angela stepped closer and lowered her voice, "The girl was top guard at her last base, and when they were coming here, the team was scattered by an infected hoard. She was out there two weeks alone, no ammo, and still didn't get bitten."

"I could totally do that." Axel rolled his eyes.

"Look, as your commanding officer, it's an order: Take her on the next supply run." Angela gave him a hard look and waited. He reluctantly nodded before she turned and walked away. He stuck out his tongue at her back. If anyone should have been commanding officer, it should have been him. Axel grabbed an apple and headed to the assembly area.

The team was already geared up when he arrived. It was all the usual suspects, plus one extra. She was relatively short, it was almost comical. Angela thought that she could teach him something? How absurd! She was shorter, smaller, and younger than him. Axel could beat her anytime.

The girl, Violet, fidgeted on the outskirts of the group. He walked over to her, "I'm Axel." She looked him up and down.

"Angela told me about you," she said carefully.

"About my great leadership and skill?"

"Something like that," she mumbled, then she straightened. "What are we looking for in this run?"

"That doesn't concern you, I'll take care of it."

"You'll take care of it?" she asked incredulously, her mouth practically hanging open. "What the hell is that supposed to mean?"

"It means that I don't need a team to do this, Angela just makes me take one. You are all dead weight, so just try not to die while we're out there." Violet pursed her lips and stepped away from him. Axel didn't follow, he was getting bored with her.

He walked towards the gates, yelling for everyone to follow. They fell into line behind him, the same as always.

"Anything?" he asked the guard at the top of the gate.

"No visual infected," he yelled back and began to turn the crank next to him. Slowly, the gate shuttled itself up so they could slip underneath it.

"Stay in formation, and keep your eyes peeled," Axel yelled over his shoulder. They stalked across the barren perimeter zone with guns out and entered the forested area. It was dense here, but infected often made enough noise that you heard them long before you saw them. Violet made her way up the group so that she was walking beside him.

"Get behind me," he hissed.

"You are not my commanding officer. I am here as a favour to Angela." That made Axel grit his teeth. "Now, if you want to be smart about this, there is a crashed medical van west of here that would have supplies."

"How do you know that?"

"I passed it when I came in. And before you ask, I know you want medicine. Every base camp needs more medicine."

Axel glanced at her. "We are going to the hospital not far from here."

"That won't be any use; most bases have near-by hospitals that have run dry. It'll take too long to search through the building. Especially if no one else is looking for what you need."

"We are going to that hospital. Now get back with the rest of the group." Violet shut up after that, but she didn't move back. He ignored her as they trekked the rest of the way in silence.

The thick vegetation thinned out to reveal the hospital in front of them. Axel stood up straighter and holstered his gun, making sure to glance at Violet as he did. She stared right back and didn't move the gun from her own hand.

Axel headed straight for the doors. "Spread out around the front," he said to the team and pushed his way in through the doors. He stood in the middle of what once was the emergency room. To get any decent medication he'd have to go up to a higher level. The doors behind him squeaked and he spun, pulling his gun out, finger resting on the trigger. Behind him stood Violet,

"Someone's got to watch your back."

He headed for the stairs. "I don't need any help. I can do this alone."

"That's just stupid." She walked quickly beside him to keep up with his long strides. "Never go anywhere without back up, you don't know if there anything else in this building."

"That's rich, coming from you," he said through

gritted teeth.

"Look, I did what I had to. It was all about survival; the rest of my team was dead or bitten. I had no one else, and if I had, I would have wanted them watching my back for those two weeks. I am not arrogant enough to think I'm invincible." She glanced sideways at him.

"I'm not invincible, I'm just better. That base would not exist without me."

"I'm sure that's true, but I bet there's a lot of other people that made that base possible." They reached the third floor and hit the wall of smell; the rotting stench of skin mixed with hot blood floated around them. "There's an infected here," she whispered, holding her gun in front of her.

"That's just the bodies that were left behind when everyone fled. They've been rotting here for years."

"Trust me, I know that smell, it is distinctly the smell of infected. One that has been up here for a very long time." Violet walked carefully behind him as he inspected each room. Most of them were empty or destroyed to the point that nothing was salvageable. He glanced back at Violet, she was paying him no attention, alert for the infected that wasn't there. Axel chewed his lip as they walked. There had to be a room with something left. Anything to prove that he was right.

They came to a locked door and Axel smiled triumphantly. No one had been in here since the infection, it would have medication. He rammed his shoulder against the door.

"Shut up," Violet hissed. "You'll bring it right to us." He looked at her and kept hitting the door. The splintering of wood echoed across the floor. "Shut up," she said again.

"Almost there." The door broke loose of the lock. Axel smiled to himself, seeing more than enough supplies to prove he was right. There were a lot of drugs that he didn't know the names of and some bandages. The doctor back at base would be ecstatic. It had been a while since a supply run had brought back this much. He loaded up his bag and swung it onto his back.

"Can we go now?" Violet asked. For the first time since entering the third floor, Axel took a good look at her face. There were worry lines across her face that weren't there before, and there was something grave in the way she held herself. It was as if she was preparing herself for death.

He was so surprised, that all he said was, "Yes." He followed her towards the stairwell, this time watching the way she moved. Every muscle remained coiled and ready to flee at a moment's notice. Her head moved from side to side constantly. She was making him nervous; his skin was starting to itch, and his hair stood on end. Axel resisted the urge to reach for his gun—she would not change his mind. He'd been right about the hospital having what they needed, and he was right about there being no infected here.

The man jumped from the shadows with no warning. There was hardly enough time to even reach for his gun. Axel threw up an arm to protect himself, and the man hit him hard, knocking them both to the ground. The characteristic blood oozing out of the infected's mouth dripped onto his chest, and its wild eyes rolled from side to side. Axel had never been this close to an infected that was alive; it turned all his insides to jelly. He felt its teeth scrape at his shoulder, and then it stopped moving. The gunshot echoed around him. Violet walked over carefully.

"Did it get you?" she asked, her gun trained on him.

"What? Are you going to shoot me?"

"It's better than becoming one of them." She jerked her head at the infected. Axel stared into the barrel of the gun and thought about how much he didn't want to die.

"No, it didn't bite me," he said as he rolled the man off him and pulled his sleeve over the graze. It wasn't a lie, the infected really didn't bite him properly. She nodded and helped him up, and they left the building quickly after that.

When they got back, he dropped the supplies to the doctor, and he turned ready to get some sleep. "Axel," Violet called, "wait up." He stopped, pulling at his sleeve again just to check that it was covering his shoulder. "I think that you could be a really good leader if you put your mind to it. But you need to let go of this arrogance you have. Be proud of what you can do, but not to the point that you get complacent." Axel nodded—anything to get away from the conversation; he was starting to sweat. "Anyway, I was going to teach some of the guards some knife throwing because it can come in handy. Do you want to learn too?"

"No." He shook his head. "I think I need some rest." Axel suddenly felt out of breath. She looked him over carefully.

"Are you sure you're okay?" He could feel his shoulder beginning to throb under the material. There had been a few recorded cases of immunity to the infection. If anyone had that, it would be him.

"Yeah, I'm fine," Axel said, the metallic taste of blood swirling in his mouth.

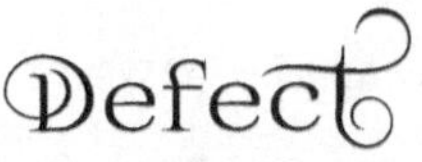

Defect

by N.M. Brown

The smell of an operating room is hard to describe: even to someone who's experienced it first-hand. It's disinfectant and copper mixed with cauterisation and the contents of one's own breath. Dr. Jorgensen ignored all this, yet winced at the crack of bone as the child's rib cage readied a path to her heart.

He was one of the best paediatric heart surgeons Tillman Hospital had ever seen. His success rate was unparalleled. Parents trusted him with their children's lives when it counted the most. It was indisputable that he'd been a saviour in his community for the past one hundred and thirty-eight years.

Stop and think about that though, *one hundred and thirty-eight years*. That's a mighty long time.

The good doctor had created a new technological medical implant to prolong age. After countless years, Merle was among the first to be granted the gift of semi-immortality. It was a ground-breaking procedure that was said to expand one's lifespan threefold.

One of the perks of being the first was the quarterly

annual health check-ups. Each patient with a clean bill of health was heavily compensated for their time and encouraged to spread the news of their procedure. Dr. Jorgensen was on the fast track to being one of the top doctors in the nation. He would go from saving tens of lives to millions.

Decades from now, when patients were living to two hundred and seventy without incident, everyone in the world would praise the name Merle Jorgensen. They would call him a miracle worker, a genius, and quite possibly…a *God.*

Not everyone believed, though. The directors of Tillman hospital had gently suggested retirement to him more than once. Ultimately though, as long as he didn't make any mistakes, there was nothing they could do. Merle had worked hard to get where he was. He didn't think his age should be anyone's concern.

Merle would get disgusted every time a fresh-faced surgeon joined the team, their eyes alight with hope and promise of brighter futures. He knew it would fade the first time they lost a patient. The slow drag of the ebb and flow of life would eat away at them all eventually, just like it happened to him.

It was no secret, the way they all looked at him. They knew they could be better…faster. Every one of them that came through those hospital doors wanted to be in his place. He also knew there was no reason for it. He had just as steady a hand as a fresh med school graduate. Tremors didn't rack his body and he his memory was just as sharp as it was when he started performing surgeries.

What no one knew was that Merle had been having trouble with the implant; starting with his eyes. He would never admit this to anyone of course, and he had become skilfully adept at hiding it. The same surgeons and interns he loathed were the same ones he used to cover up his eyesight problems. If anyone caught a whisper of a doubt about the implant, he'd be ruined. Besides, it was only blacking out here and there. So far, it has been perfectly manageable. At least, that's what he told himself.

See, they were all jealous of the miracle he'd given to people's quality of life. He just knew they were bloodthirsty hounds, insatiable for any mistakes caused by Jorgensen or the implant he created. They didn't want to see humanity succeed.

The latest of these being Dr. Ethan Sternan; a rising star in the world of laser cardiology. The ole doc just *knew* they'd hired him to take his place. A younger doctor with younger technology to match. What other reason could there have been? After all, Tillman hospital had him as their surgeon. As far as Merle was concerned, they didn't need anyone else.

This was their second week working together. In that time a handful of surgeries had come in, but mostly cosmetic, preventative things. A life saver didn't come through those doors until that very night, at eight pm.

She was a ten-year-old girl named Mara Clarkson. The poor girl had been shocked by an electrical cord, the current was slow—when it's slow like that, you can't even tell anything's happening. Currents continuously coursed through her body on a loop. The mental circuit couldn't even make the distance from her brain to her fingers to tell her to let go; instantaneous cardiac arrest. With the cybernetic advancements made to her heart, it was a miracle that she didn't die right there in her dining room.

Merle didn't bother bickering over who should operate and who should observe, he just went right in. There's no room for politeness in those life altering seconds. This girl's life depended on them. Now was no time for pleasantries.

Bright operating room lights glinted off the metal instruments, providing a bigger complication for Merle than his failing eyesight. The nurse rushed her chart in the room, filling them in on the details of what took place.

He could hear the girl's mother wailing from the

waiting area. *Where was that concern when her kid was playing electrician unsupervised? These damn millennials; no one ever gives a damn until it's too late.*

Ethan's voice interrupted Merle's internal monologue.

"Please take care, Dr. Jorgensen. You're travelling dangerously close to the mitral valve; one slip…one cut and she's gone."

Who in the Hell was this kid to tell me how to do my job? He doesn't even use real medical equipment for God sakes.

"Dr. Sternan…I will have you know that I have been performing these exact surgeries since before you were a tightening in your father's trousers. Now…were there any other concerns you have, or can I continue to try to save this patient?" Dr. Jorgensen snarked, intentionally letting the patient's blood pressure dip low for effect.

Dr. Sternan shook his head, anger apparent in his eyes.

"Thank you," Dr. Jorgensen continued. "I'm not about to let this little one flatline on the table just so you can pitch your laser beam methodology."

When Merle looked back into Ms. Clarkson's chest cavity, his mind blanked. Everything looked exactly the same; all of the valves, cogs guiding the wire ventricles…it all looked the same. The young doctor's words blinded him with doubt and insecurity. No matter though, if something went wrong and they lost this patient, it would be *Ethan* who was to blame, not Dr. Jorgensen. Let Sternan take the fall for being so stupid and interrupting him.

The leak was subtle at first, not like those you see in the dramatic television dramas. It took some time, but the doctors were able to stop the bleeding and repair the cybernetic vein.

After she was stabilised, the room went silent. The staff appeared…sombre.

"What's everyone so down for? We saved another one. This girl will go on to get married and start a family if she chooses to. You all helped me to make that happen. Good job team," he said, congratulating them.

No one gave a response. In fact, most eyes were on the floor in front of them. All except for Ethan. He had a look on his face; it was like shock mixed with anger. Dr. Jorgensen had no idea what his problem was, but if he was going to be this childish in the O.R., he would see that Ethan was transferred to a different one.

The parents were notified of the successful surgery. Mara's mother reached out to shake the doctor's hand, but he politely declined. The words didn't come out of

Merle's mouth, but his eyes said it all; Merle had seen the result of things left in the mother's hands and wasn't interested. If it was up to him, she wouldn't get Mara back at all. Trained dogs would be better for some of the accidents caused by sheer negligence that wind kids up on his operating table.

A bed was always available to him in the hospital's doctor's ward. However, he decided to drive home that night. Mara Clarkson would open her eyes to greet another day, and it was all thanks to him. Celebration by libation was in order.

Around the corner from the hospital, a group of five children stood waiting to cross the road. They weren't in his viewpoint yet, but even if they were, it wouldn't have mattered. Fingers clasped their neighbour's as the group joined hands for safety.

A shiny, black Mary Jane dress shoe tentatively took one step into the clear road, then two. Not far behind her, a size 4 boy's converse danced between the white lines of the crosswalk.

Right then, the corners of Dr. Jorgensen's vision started to blur; the tell-tale signs of an oncoming vision blackout. The elderly doctor questioned whether or not something was in the road but blamed the shapes on a trick of his ailing eyes. He didn't look up until after his car had been rocked from underneath.

The police officers at the scene soothed the three remaining children as they waited for their parents. Squeals or terror rang out as they looked around for their two missing friends, finding two white sheets on tables instead.

As they lowered Dr. Jorgensen's head to sit him in the police car, he repeated one thing: "Why the hell were those damned kids playing in the road to begin with? It ain't my fault! Vehicular suicide is what that was, plain as day."

The Hole of Shame
by Nerisha Kemraj

"Hi, Pride, do you need some help with that?" Lumino asked, seeing her struggle with her luggage, her wings fluttered apace.

Pride turned to see a tall, dishevelled fairy. His wings were dark and slightly deformed. He was the same fairy she had classes with. And she had long since written him off as the kind she didn't want to be seen with.

"I don't need your help! I can do it myself!" she said, a little too loudly, glaring.

She was a high-born. She wouldn't allow herself to associate with peasants.

Darkness crossed his face at her rejection. The thread of courage it took to approach her slowly broke.

Lumino didn't have the heart to tell her how he loved her...her self-confidence, her energy that allowed others to feel happy about themselves, so now, he allowed the shadows to swallow him in despair.

As soon as he disappeared, darkness fell around her, and Pride, still struggling with her bags and boxes, could no longer see where she was going.

"Maybe I should have accepted the help," she thought aloud. "Never! I am Pride, I don't settle for those beneath me!" She laughed at the mere thought of being seen with an outcast.

Wrapped in thoughts of ego and vanity, Pride did not see the hole which Humility had been busy filling. Before he could warn her, Pride fell into it, tumbling into oblivion, taking her luggage with her. Even Humility himself did not know where it led...although Shame stood responsible for it, waiting on the other side.

The Pact

by Maxine Churchman

The lady sitting next to her on the bus was smiling and nodding, but her eyes were starting to glaze, and Joy knew she should stop talking—but she couldn't.

"He was always top of his class at every subject and he played football and tennis for the county. Now he plays golf to professional standard," she gushed.

The lady had turned to face the window, not even pretending to listen anymore, but she still kept talking at her.

"We're going to watch him play in the Open next week. Do you watch the golf?" she asked in an attempt to recapture the lady's attention.

The lady sighed. "Sorry. I don't like sport," she said, not bothering to face her.

Joy was disappointed not to get a better reaction; after all, if George was to win the tournament, it would be the best day of her life. She was so proud of her son's achievements. She smiled; much of the credit was down to her, but no-one would ever know.

She thought back to the day she had met the stranger

in the park, when George was just a baby. It was the day the news was full of reports of refugees drowning in the sea, trying to escape to a better life. She had thought to herself then, *A few less to sponge off others.* She didn't say it out loud, especially not to her husband, Carl. He had shed tears at the news and pledged some of their money to a charity. He hadn't even consulted her first. She had been so cross, and they had argued.

"You have no soul," Carl had accused. She remembered that because the stranger had also mentioned her soul.

The stranger had sat on the bench next to her. George was asleep in his pram and the stranger had asked her what the baby's name was. She hadn't wanted to tell him at first; he had seemed a bit odd. He was dressed like a presentable city gent, complete with bowler hat, but his fingernails were exceptionally long and dirty, like talons, and he smelled earthy; a smell that reminded her of some old castle dungeons she had visited as a child. She had edged away from him in disgust.

The stranger had persisted though. "He is a very bonny looking lad. You must be very proud of him." His voice was deep and melodic, soothing her qualms and she had felt her chest swell with pride at his words.

"Yes, indeed. He's called George."

To her relief, he had not wanted to touch him, she would have balked at that.

Instead, he turned the conversation to her future aspirations for her son and she'd been swept along, seeing him as a revered celebrity with plenty of wealth, charm and happiness. When the man had offered to make those dreams a reality for the price of her soul, she had laughed thinking it was a joke, but he was so earnest. Then she'd thought "Why not, I apparently have no soul, so I won't miss it." And she hadn't missed it, but George had excelled just as the man had said he would.

A bell *tinged*, breaking her out of her reverie.

When the bus stopped, the lady sitting next to her rose to leave. Making way for her to pass, she told her, "Don't forget to watch out for George Little in the Open. He is going to win."

The lady smiled, then took a seat further up the bus. Well, how rude was that?

George held the trophy aloft and looked straight at her in the crowd. He was smiling from ear to ear. She waved back, happier than she had ever been, and her chest burst with pride. Then George's face changed. He no longer looked elated but full of despair. He dropped the trophy and ran towards her. In confusion, she turned to Carl, but he too was looking deeply concerned and was clutching her arm, lowering her gently to the floor. People were gathering around her; a sea of strange faces, except there, directly in front of her now, was the stranger.

He looked different, but she knew it was him. He now wore a cloak, and without the hat, she could see two small horns protruding from his head. *Like the devil*, she mused.

He reached out his hand to her, his talons clicking wickedly. "I have come for your soul," he said.

"But I thought I had given it to you already."

He sneered. "Your soul would have been meagre and tasteless when we first met. Now it is bloated with pride and will be a far more fitting feast for me. And besides— for me to take your soul you must die."

She frantically looked around for someone to help her, but she and the devil were floating above the crowd. No-one was looking up.

Sirens were blaring below as an ambulance rushed across the course, but in the centre of the crowd, she could see her husband and son already grieving over her lifeless body.

The Animated Dead

by Matthew M. Montelione

None of the revellers noticed that the host was one of the animated dead. Only I saw his horrid face, hidden behind his black mask. I noted his yellow eyes and decaying flesh, his pus-filled mouth and festering boils. His odour made me cringe. I tried to alert them, but not a single soul at the masquerade heeded my words. Instead, the conceited fools shunned me as they danced and drank in excess.

I strolled through the grand room illuminated by candlelight like a swan cutting through turbulent waters. I passed the musicians as well as many oblivious wealthy people. There were military officers and judges, merchants, bankers, and other businessmen. The women wore jewelled masks and were dressed in exquisite gowns. Lovely flowers of various colours and arrangements adorned their hair. Indeed, their colours stood in stark contrast to the dark and disgusting figure which slowly paced around the area.

How did they not notice their host's hideousness? They ignored his entire being! He was like a crow against a morning sky, or a scar upon youthful flesh. His gaping wounds grew fouler by the minute, his boils grew greater and trimmed with yellow pus. The putrid smell permeated throughout the great room. I wondered when the revellers would finally notice his decaying frame. I, for one, could no longer take his odious predicament.

I ascended the staircase and looked down at the party-goers. I analysed them as they smiled and laughed, touched, and grew closer to one another. The pathetic men, single and married alike, tried desperately to win the attention of many different women. They bragged of their various accomplishments, their riches and high offices. They were false souls.

Some of the women, vain and ambitious, flirted with temptation and fell before my eyes to such pompous suitors. They were false souls.

All their cosy actions were falsities; they were surface notions of the human condition. It was that same condition that they consciously betrayed in their ignorance of their failing host.

One of the more noble women finally noticed the smell and held her nose in disgust. At last, this insincere group turned their heads in confusion and abhorrence. Some people spilled their spirits on the floor as they bumped into one another and started to argue. The flowers in the hair of the fairer sex wilted and turned to grey. A few exited the masquerade altogether at the heightened smell of putrescence. It lingered!

Suddenly the harsh tones of the midnight hour bellowed throughout the opulent room and shook its very foundations with every swing of the pendulum. The musicians halted their noise; all ceased talking and arguing. All was quiet as the grave as everyone in the room removed their masks. All eyes turned to the terrifying sight at the foot of the staircase.

They finally saw their host, that poor man dressed in black. His mask dropped to the floor, his face swelled with yellowish fluids. Blood streamed from his eye sockets and out of his nose. The boils consumed his body and exploded, spraying pus and blood around the dimly lit room. The lifeless body fell to the ground with a thud. The vain crowd gasped as their eyes gravitated towards the towering figure at the top of the staircase: a dark ragged being they had not noticed before.

At last, they listened. At last, they were arrested by the presence of Death.

King of the Hill

by M. Sydnor Jr.

"You don't get it, Kap. This land is my legacy. My history. Right here." Sal stomped the floorboards and smacked the wooden wall. "This—this is sweat, and blood from my great granddaddy's bare hands as he erected this temple from the earth. Poor bastard died from infection not long after he installed that entryway. As far as I'm concerned, that blood is what keeps this place standing, and it shall remain in position—fuelled by that blood—my blood, until my very last breath.

"How dare you march up that hill and interrupt my morning food to restate the ridiculous notion to sell. I've already expressed to those heathens what they can do with their fucking offer. And if they find themselves delivering their belligerent proposal upon *my* hill, then they shall leave lesser-a-man than they arrived.

"If God himself finds the need to descend from the heavens to try and take this place, he, too, shall receive a bullet in the ass." He fiddled with the rifle that graced his lap. "Because friend, a man is *nothing* without land."

"I hear you, Sal. I do." Kap sat across from him at a

small table between the kitchen window and the front door. "But this is an offer you simply cannot refuse."

Sal shifted in his chair, grunted, then lifted the bottle of bourbon from the table and poured out two glasses.

Sal's son left his mother at the big table in the kitchen to play with a miniature soldier on the windowsill. Like the land, the figurine had been passed down through generations, but only recently. The boy's grandfather fought in the civil war and had carved it out of a branch from a tree that saved his life. The soldier was not to be played with. It was a monument.

"Boy, how many times do I have to tell you?" Sal slammed his fist on the table.

"Clint. Come and finish your food," his mother called from the kitchen.

"Listen to your ma now," Sal ordered him away from the window. "Go finish your supper."

Kap twisted the glass on the table, sloshing the alcohol around. "These are different men, Sal. The persistent, stubborn kind that ain't gonna go away at the first *no*. Hell, or the second or third neither. What I think they're offering is generous. This is a big world, Sal. You can buy you some more land, with a house twice the size of this 'un."

"What I need more house for? This one's plenty big

for the three of us."

"Four," his wife interrupted them and rubbed her belly.

"Yeah— Four," Sal echoed her. "And I shall raise that little one as I did Clint and my father did me."

"I'm just saying. Extra room won't hurt none. More room for your books, space for the boy and the new one to run around. Maybe land for some cattle."

Sal snatched his glass and drained it with a gulp. He slapped the cup back on the table, then poured him another.

"Be reasonable, Sal. At least for your family's sake. Don't let your pride make this decision."

Sal pounded on the table so hard it made the bottle of bourbon jump. His wife and child flinched, and Kap shifted in his chair, keeping a good eye on that rifle.

"You're a friend of this family. I invited you into my home, offered you some fine drink, listened to you. But I won't take you disrespecting me to my face. Now, you ought to be feeling some honour being here. I'm not leaving." His wife let out a huff and he amended his declaration. "*We're* not leaving…and this'll be the last I hear of it from you, Kap. Get me? The last time. Now, have a drink with me or get the hell out."

Kap stood and turned away from the tempting glass

of alcohol. "Mary." He gave her a gentle kiss to the hand then ruffled the boy's scruffy hair. "Clint, you take care of your mammy. And see to it your daddy stays out of trouble, ya hear?"

"Yessir," Clint responded as he crammed the last bite of eggs and toast into his mouth.

Sal refused to look at Kap until he stopped with the door half open.

"I remember running all over these hills with you, Sal. That is, when I could get you away from them books. Fishing, climbing, hell, we even fought once. Your daddy gave us a good whippin' for that. But the time that hits me hardest right now is when your mammy died. You was wrecked, I tell ya. I didn't see you for a whole months' time. But that night when the doctor come over and checked on her. Right before he gave ya'll the news of your mammy's passing, he told me something I'd never forget."

"What's that?" Sal said, the tone in his voice sharpening.

"A man ain't nothing without family." Then, Kap tipped his hat and left.

Sal took the second glass and downed it. He didn't want to think of the night Mother died—worst day of his life—so he poured another drink and guzzled it. That one hit him good, and as he stared at the wood ceiling, reminiscing, the world started to turn. The butt of the rifle stopped him from falling out of the chair. Mary came to him, her belly stretching the front of her dress, and helped him vertical.

"I'm fine, woman." He sneered at her. "Just fine."

She took the other chair at the small table. "Are we going to discuss this as a family, or are you making the decisions for all of us?"

"You ought to not make it a habit to talk to your husband this way. If we were in public—"

"But we're not in public, are we? We're alone now."

"State your complaint, Mary."

"What future we got here if everyone else is being bought out by these people? We'll be all alone up here…on this Godforsaken hill."

"I'd use caution with how you talk about *my* land, woman. You're creeping into dangerous discourse here."

"*Your* land?"

"Careful."

"Clint, go to your room," she ordered their son.

"No," Sal roared. "Boy's old enough to hear this. You want to discuss as a family, right? Well, let everyone be fucking present then as we dive deeper into this impertinent topic of conversation."

"You're drunk."

"Oh, darling, your husband needs to be drunk to converse in such idiotic subjects impossible to break the barriers of my established mindset." He stood and dropped the rifle on the table, then shook a finger at her. "The fucking King of the world can gift me all the gold and the rights to his castle and still I ain't fucking leaving. What the fuck did my great granddaddy build this place for—claim his spot on the planet—for me to leave at the sight of some money?"

There was a long pause as he stood over his wife, huffing and puffing, but he could see she wasn't scared. She'd seen him this way before.

"As you wish. Now please, sit down and sober up. You're scaring Clint."

Clint turned around in his chair. "I ain't scared, Momma."

"Ya see." Sal plopped back into his chair and nearly tipped over, if not for the log wall behind him. "We got us another man of the house. *Prince of the Hill.*" He gave his son a toast with the glass he thought was full. He tried to take a sip of it until he realised it was empty.

Mary had a good laugh at that, Clint too. And just like that, all the tension in the room had been erased.

"Should we be worried?" Mary asked one last time

as he poured himself another glass.

"My darling wife…don't let Kap terrorise your mind. I expect they've given up."

She sighed, then relaxed back into the chair, but a gunshot from outside made her jump.

"Sal Walker!" A man yelled.

Sober in an instant, Sal leapt to his feet and snatched his rifle from the table. He stalked to the door, ignoring his wife's appeals.

Twenty yards ahead, before the hilltop started its decline, stood a man in a suit holding a pistol at his side. If the unjustified gunshot to the innocent air didn't give it away, this stranger's mug did. Sal liked to think he knew all the men in a thirty-mile radius. This one, he didn't know. He stomped off his porch and marched toward the man in the suit, the rifle leading him. "State your business and toss the shooter away," Sal yelled at the trespasser.

"Which is it? Want me to state my business or toss my gun?" the man smiled, smug-like.

"Think on it any longer, friend, and I'll see to it the two options won't matter none." Sal stopped a few yards away.

The stranger tossed his gun and interlocked his fingers in front of his chest. "Had to get your attention somehow. I've heard stories around this neck of the woods, of men, strangers like myself, getting shot for a simple knock on the door."

"Well within my rights to gun you down where you stand, sir. Reason your intrusion upon my hill." Sal took a step closer and moved his finger over the trigger.

"Ahh, yes. King of the Hill they call you. Well, I won't waste any more of your time since you seem so eager to…gun me down."

Sal kept the blank stare toward the stranger. The rifle remained aimed, but he removed his finger so as to not slip up before the man stated his business.

"Mr. Walker, I am a representative of a certain party that wants to buy your land."

Sal grunted then dropped the rifle to his side. "I thought as much… Well, Mr. Suit and Tie, I can tell you my answer now, or I can do you the courtesy of delivering your rehearsed speech before you return to your trek down the hill."

"May I say, sir, you are extremely well-spoken for someone around these parts."

"Is this the opening of your speech, then?"

"My employer is a powerful man. But also, in a lesser degree, a spoiled one. He does not stop—*will not* stop—until he gets what he wants. For instance, your land is the centrepiece of a nine-hundred-acre territory that has recently come into his ownership. And your hill, Mr. Walker, your house right there, is simply just…in the way.

"We've been sending you proposals for a month now, each with an increase in offer, and every time you send it back with some scribbling over the letter, in a fashion that clearly does not represent the intellect that you present before me."

"That's right," Sal responded.

"May I ask why?"

"You did say you wouldn't waste my time, right?"

"I did."

"Well then, if the previous concludes your point, I will retire. Or I can treat you as the in-person letter and scribble my answer with some lead." Sal walked over and grabbed the stranger's pistol from the ground, tucked it in his pants and returned to his home.

"One last question, sir," the stranger shouted out. "Are you alone up here?"

Sal ignored the question as he went up the steps of the porch. He opened his front door and looked back at the man. "Best be out of sight by the time I look out that window."

"So?" Mary asked as Sal closed the door behind him.

"Nothing to worry yourself about." Sal went to the

window and looked out to an empty field. He exhaled.

"And the gunshot? Does he mean us harm?" She held their son close while rubbing her belly.

Sal turned away from the window as he pulled the pistol out of his pants and tossed it on the table. "He's gone. Let us move on from this sour topic so we can enjoy our evening. Or shall we go on about it some more until we're as stale as those books over there?"

"Fine." Mary retreated from the discussion and released Clint, who ran to the windowsill to play with the forbidden soldier.

Sal set his rifle against the bookshelf then sat at the small table and poured another drink.

"Momma?" Clint said from the windowsill.

"Son, get yourself away from there for the hundredth time. Do as I say." Sal placed the bottle back on the table and grabbed his glass. Before he took a sip, he saw his son had ignored him. The boy was frozen in his place, peering out the window. "Clint?" He put the glass back on the table and erupted from his chair. As he started after the boy, he saw his wife in the same state, frozen in place, gazing outside. "Mary?"

"You said they don't mean us no harm," she said.

"They?" He went to stand by his wife to see what she saw.

Outside, at the edge of the hilltop, six men stood with guns pointed at the house. Sal barely had time to look at his rifle before the bullets tore into the home. "Get down," he yelled as he stretched for his weapon.

Bullets smacked into the log home, the glass window shattered, and his wife let out a yelp, but he didn't stop until he'd grabbed his gun. Once secure in his hands, he turned and found his wife and son, bloody and lifeless on the floor. The goddamn soldier from the sill was in two pieces next to the boy.

He dropped the rifle and fell to his knees as the cabin continued to take a beating. He crawled over to his deceased family, not to hide from the bullets, but because his heart was too heavy for his knees to support. Sal clutched his son's body and pulled the boy to his lap. Then, he grabbed his wife's shoulders, trying to pull her closer into the huddle, but she was heavy, and he was weak. Tears were all over his face, their blood all over his hands.

Eventually, the gunfire stopped. Lost in his grief, he barely noticed.

Soon, scampering emerged from outside, some chatter, nonsensical talk and then he heard a familiar voice. "Burn it down. We only need the land." The stranger's voice from before was easy to isolate, *Mr. Suit and Tie.*

Before long, smoke poured in through the broken window, then the house went ablaze. Laughter and chatter filled the outside while misery consumed the inside. Misery and fire.

When he felt the heat, he snapped out of his grief and grabbed his rifle. He returned to the broken window to the surprise of the six men. One after the other, he shot them all dead. Except for Mr. Suit and Tie. He left him mortally wounded.

Sal exited the home to see the man crawling away for some sort of salvation. Sal grabbed his ankle and pulled him back toward the house.

There was no fight left in the stranger, not enough strength, but he laughed. "And now you are the King of Nothing," Mr. Suit and Tie said. When he realised he was being dragged to the burning cabin, he pleaded for his life.

Sal ignored the pleas and dropped the man off in the doorway where the fire was thickest. Then he said his goodbyes to his family and the cabin as they all burned. No tears left to cry. No more pain left to feel.

"You took my family, you bastard, and my home, but I told you, you weren't getting my land."

The Tyrant of Syracuse

by Mark Kodama

Dionysius I, tyrant of Syracuse, always wanted more. He was a citizen soldier who rose to the rank of supreme general before seizing power in the city of his birth. For a time, he became the most powerful ruler of all of Magna Greece. He collected cities and intellectuals alike like they were toys for his toy chest. He drove the Carthaginians from central Sicily to the west coast. He conquered and founded cities in Italy and Dalmatia. He brought Plato to his court then ordered the great philosopher sold as a slave in Aegina. He married the historian, Philistus, to his niece before exiling him.

One day, Dionysius was reading his poems in court. When he asked Philoxenus what he thought of his literary work, the royal poet called the poems drivel. The angry tyrant ordered his mercenaries to seize Philoxenus and send him to the salt mines to work as a slave.

The next day, Dionysius ordered his guards to bring the poet back to his court in Syracuse. The long-bearded

Dionysius dressed in his purple robes, and crowned with his jewel-encrusted diadem, read from his dais his newly composed poems to his now freed poet. The erstwhile royal poet, balding, and dressed in sweaty rags stoically stood between two armed guards.

"Knowing what you know, Philoxenus, now what do you think of my poems?" Dionysius proclaimed, looking down his long nose upon the hapless poet.

Philoxenus turned to one of the guards and said, "Take me back to the salt mines."

Blood Pride

by Cindar Harrell

They say that pride is the father of all sins. They are half right. Since I gave birth to them, brought them life, I think "mother" would be more appropriate. Either way, all sins stem from me.

I was the first, coalescing into being the moment Eve took a bite of that forbidden fruit. That moment when she thought of herself above all others was me.

We are a long way from Eden now, and humanity has grown, and with it, so have their sins. The most vulnerable to us always seem to be those blessed with great power and privilege. It is my job to see that these people give in to their hidden desires, to lead them down the path of sin and right into my open, matronly arms.

The seven of us have a very important goal: to obtain the most horrid of souls. Women in positions of great power, corrupted by our sins. We needed a full set in order to fulfil our purpose, to plunge the world, not just this one, but all the worlds, into a hurricane of endless sin.

The pride, if you will, of my collection, and thus the one chosen for this very special project, was a respectable woman from Hungary. But once I was done with her, history only knew her as "The Blood Countess."

Selected Sinner: Elizabeth Bathory
Hungary
1560-1614

She had always been vain, proud, of her appearance. It was her weakness and my plan was to exploit it to the fullest. First, I took the form of one of her handmaidens. I waited, looking for the perfect moment to strike. When she asked me to cut her hair, I saw my chance.

Smiling from my position behind her, I grazed her skin with the razor-sharp scissors causing a small cut. Crimson bubbled up from the tear in her fair flesh. She cried out in pain and reeled back.

"I'm so sorry, my lady! Please forgive me!" I said, feigning an apologetic and meek manner. I bowed my head low, but then looked at the blood that stained her hand where it had dripped from the wound. "My lady, you are bleeding!" I paused a moment then added, "Your skin is even more fair tinged red."

She looked to her hand and stared at it in awe. "So it is. Have I found the secret to eternal youth and beauty at last?"

I watched with pride and joy as the seed I had planted grew into an obsession unlike any other. It consumed her very being, destroying her soul utterly. When she killed for the first time, there was very little hesitation. The darkness within her steadily grew into an unstoppable miasma. By the end, she had killed hundreds of young girls all for the sake of her own vanity. From the sidelines I cheered as she was tried and sentenced to be sealed away in her own tower, hidden from the rest of the world. Her pride became their shame.

I was there when she finally died.

"Who are you?" she asked me, her voice old and tired.

"Who do you think I am?" I asked in return.

"A devil come to take me away."

I smiled. "You aren't far off. Don't worry though, I won't let you waste away in the depths of Hell. You have been selected for a higher calling."

"Higher calling? What am I to do?"

I took her by the hand and led her to join my family. "You've already done it. It's not time for you to shine again yet, my pet. But soon." I sealed her in a tomb of my own until it was time, until my daughters all had their own prizes. "We are the same, you and I. Our pride defines us." I ran my hand over the glass in front of her face, frozen in time until I commanded her to wake. "You truly were quite beautiful."

Looking around the circular room, I saw the other tombs reserved for each of our respective sins and their selected sinners. Some already housed their prizes but others remained vacant. Waiting.

I smiled as my daughters approached in the dark. Nothing fills a mother's heart with more pride than dutiful daughters delivering souls to make a complete set.

The Maiden's Walk

by Jodi Jensen

"It is time, daughter."

Anevy ran the bone-handled brush through her long black hair one last time. She wore her finest buckskin dress and strapped the best leather she had around her feet.

"Come," her mother beckoned.

Chosen by her people as the most beautiful, Anevy was to embark on a maiden's walk with eleven other young women from neighbouring villages, all chosen for their beauty. The journey was the first of its kind and would take three suns on foot. At the end of the third sun, the chief would choose his bride from those who'd completed the walk.

Anevy lifted her chin, confident she was destined to rule by the chief's side. Her name itself meant *superior*, and that's what she was.

She walked to the centre of the village, head held high, and joined the rest of the maidens in a circle. She didn't even glance at the other women, the unworthy were not her concern.

Two men stood in the middle of the circle, Mosa, the

leader of her village, and Tanga, a revered healer.

"You are being given one pouch for water and one blade." Mosa handed the blade to the maiden from the nearest village as a show of respect to those they traded with most, and the pouch went to a young girl with bare feet.

"Walk with the morning sun." Tanga spread his arms wide toward the distant mountain where the sun was rising. "You will find your chief where the water falls from the rocks."

"Go. Now." Mosa motioned to the east. "May the spirits go with you."

Anevy strode to the side of the girl with the pouch as they set out, determined to position herself by the one thing certain to sustain her on the journey; the water.

She glanced at the girl. "I am called Anevy."

"Pavati." The girl gave a shy smile, then looked at her bare feet.

Anevy straightened her shoulders, her own gaze toward the future. "Pavati. Your name means *water*, that is why you were given this duty."

"Perhaps." The girl looked at the ground as they walked, the pouch clutched to her breast. "We will not find more until we reach the mountain."

"The water must be protected."

"How?" Pavati cast a nervous glance over her shoulder. "We will need it long before the moon rises."

Anevy nodded and hid a small, knowing smile. "Stay with me. I will look after you."

Behind her, the women separated into small clusters, chattering and wasting time getting to know one another.

They walked for hours; until the sun was at its highest point. By then, they were well into the desert with nothing but rocks, red sand and an occasional cactus stretched out before them.

The woman who'd been given the blade approached Pavati. "It is time for water."

Anevy stepped in front of the girl and glared at the woman. "What do they call you?"

"Zihna. And you were not given the pouch to carry."

Ignoring Zihna, Anevy looked at the other women in the group. "There is little water to go around. Whoever can find a vessel, will have what it holds to drink."

"Who are you to say?" Zihna waved the blade at Anevy.

"I am her protector." Anevy snatched the blade, cutting the palm of her hand in the process. She held up the prized tool, her own blood dripping from the sharpened edge. "You will not have this advantage over the others. Go, all of you, find a vessel so you may drink."

Zihna's lips tightened into a deep scowl as she was pulled away by another of the women.

"She will hold a grudge." Pavati reached for the injured hand. "We must wrap this."

Anevy allowed the girl to bind her cut with a strip of cloth while her mind chewed over her competition. While there were none dressed finer than herself, and none with more pleasing features, there was one with enough aggression to challenge her. *Zihna.*

"Here, drink." Pavati gave her the pouch. "Quickly, so the others do not see."

Anevy didn't care if they saw. She stowed the blade in the leather ties around her ankle, then took a long swallow from the pouch…and another, then handed it back.

Pavati did not take a drink, simply put the stopper back in the opening, and sat cross-legged on the ground to wait.

Anevy turned her back to the sun and, as her shadow grew longer, a few of the women returned. One held a handful of vacant snail shells, another had a broken piece of a hollow branch. The woman who'd accompanied Zihna had an empty bird's nest, and Zihna had a rock with a depression in the middle.

"Where are the others?" Pavati rose, water pouch in

hand, but did not yet pour.

"Two turned back and the rest are still looking." Zihna held her rock in front of the pouch.

Pavati looked to Anevy, and at her nod, poured water into each vessel.

Anevy watched, her confidence growing. Her own portion had been larger than any of these. "We need to keep moving."

Zihna narrowed her eyes at Anevy. "You would leave them behind?"

"They know where to go. They will catch up if they choose to keep walking." Anevy gave a pointed glance at the mountain in the distance. "We will find no food or water until we get there."

"She is right," Pavati said, turning toward the mountain. "Let us continue our journey."

Victorious, Anevy took the lead, half of her competition gone in one fell swoop.

The women trudged through the desert all afternoon. No words were spoken under the brutal sun, each one lost in their own thoughts. Relief from the relentless heat came when the sun dipped below the horizon.

"Look," Anevy pointed. Ahead, a large boulder loomed, a rocky island in a sea of red sand. "We will shelter there for the night."

Zihna said nothing, but pressed her lips into a harsh line and remained silent.

Good.

When they reached the boulder, Anevy sank to the ground and leaned her back against the rock.

Pavati sat next to her and handed her the pouch. "I need to tend to this," she said, pulling her foot into her lap.

Anevy suppressed a shudder at the sight of the raw, blistered flesh. The girl had begun the walk barefoot and the trek across the scorching sand had shredded her feet. Glad for the leather wrapped around her own feet, she closed her eyes. The weight of the pouch was comforting in its promise of security.

She might have even fallen asleep, but for the noise next to her; cloth ripping, Pavati gasping, the women whispering. She opened her eyes to find Zihna kneeling in front of the girl, wrapping her damaged feet with torn strips of cloth.

"Give me the water," Zihna demanded.

"I will not." Anevy tightened her grip on the pouch.

"She did not drink earlier," Zihna said through clenched teeth. "She deserves a share."

"She has no vessel." Anevy didn't either, but *protector* of the water was not the same as *carrier* of the water.

"What she says is true." Pavati laid a hand on Zihna's arm. "I have no vessel, so I cannot drink."

Zihna brushed the girl's hand away, her angry glare stuck on Anevy. "She can have mine."

Pavati gasped. "No—"

"You cannot have it back," Anevy said, her tone thick with satisfaction.

Zihna gave a sharp nod and went to retrieve her rock.

When she returned, Pavati tried once more to stop her. "You must not—"

"I will find another." Zihna held the rock out and waited.

Anevy locked eyes with the woman, revelling in the hate being exchanged between them. The shared hostility made her fatigue disappear as she wielded her power over Zihna. She would make the woman wait until she lowered her eyes in respect.

Minutes passed, no one spoke or even moved. All seemed to be waiting for one of them to concede. Finally, when Pavati coughed, Zihna broke eye contact and lowered her head a fraction.

The corner of Anevy's mouth lifted in a smirk as she poured water into the small depression in the rock, then watched as it was passed to Pavati.

With a humble nod, the girl drank, then lowered the vessel to the ground next to her.

Anevy did not offer to return the water pouch to Pavati, nor did the girl try to take it, appearing content to be relieved of the responsibility.

With no food, no means to start a fire and no supplies, the women dug out shallow niches in the sand with their hands and made themselves as comfortable as possible.

Sleep did not come to Anevy. Instead, she sat thinking of her future, until her musings were interrupted by the telltale rattle of a serpent. She looked over in time to see it sink its fangs into the neck of a woman sleeping nearby.

Anevy smiled as she turned away; another maiden who would not stand between her and the chief.

A little while later, Zihna found the woman dead, her neck swollen and discoloured from the snakebite.

"You heard nothing of her suffering?" Zihna accused Anevy, pointing to where the woman's body lay stiff and bent in permanent agony. "She lay nearest you."

Anevy squared her shoulders as the lie rolled off her tongue. "Death took her quickly. There was nothing to hear."

Zihna, and the others, looked sceptical, but Anevy

did not care. She was strong, they were weak.

She turned away, blade still secure in the ties around her ankle and half-empty water pouch tucked against her chest. "It is time to move on."

Without another word, she strode toward the mountain. This time, Pavati walked with Zihna.

Hours later, at the foothill of the great mountain, Anevy stopped. The remaining four women trailed behind, silent as they caught up to her. No one spoke, they simply held up their vessels for water.

Zihna was last in line, her face smug as she revealed a turtle shell. The underside had been broken, leaving a smooth, deep reservoir for water. "My new vessel."

Anevy brought the pouch to her lips. "And this is mine." She drank deep, and only after her own thirst was slacked, did she pour the remainder into Zihna's shell, filling it less than halfway.

"The spirits will punish you." Zihna's jaw twitched as she tried to control her anger.

"You should hope not," Anevy said. "I am counting on them to guide me to more water so I may replenish the pouch."

Zihna's hand curled into a fist and Pavati limped to her side. "Let us not anger the spirits by wishing harm on one another."

"The great spirits would want you to keep better company." Anevy turned and started up the mountain.

By evening, they came to a wide river cutting across their path. As the water raced by, crashing against the jutting rocks, Anevy marched to the water's edge. "We shall stay here tonight."

"Will this lead us to where the chief awaits?" Pavati asked.

"It will." Anevy knelt to refill the pouch, then drank from her hands and washed her face. "We can follow the river up the mountain until we find where it falls from the rocks."

The other women murmured amongst themselves as they washed and drank their fill.

Zihna waded into a shallow inlet near an overgrown tree and bent, shoving her arm into the tangle of exposed roots. A moment later, she let out a triumphant cry and pulled out a catfish the length of her arm. She threw the fish onto the bank and bashed its head with a rock until it stopped moving. "I need the blade!"

Anevy's stomach growled, but instead of handing over the blade, she drew the weapon and sliced the fish's belly open herself. One of the other women gasped, but she did not care. Now that water was plentiful, she possessed the last thing of value and she would keep it.

Once the fish was gutted and rinsed, Pavati brought a portion over, though the other women grumbled about it. "You protected me, and the water," the girl said, lowering her eyes in respect. "We are even now."

Anevy took the fish and gave the girl a nod of dismissal.

That night, she sat alone and tuned out their chatting and laughter as she contemplated what the next day would bring.

When the sun rose on the third and final day, she was ready.

The women hiked uphill, following the river until they reached the bottom of the waterfall. The side of the river they were on led to a cliff. As Anevy had hoped, they would need to cross.

On the other side, on a flat rock near the top, their chief stood watching and waiting.

She scanned the river and smiled. "There." She pointed to a series of stones and fallen logs that formed a haphazard trail to the opposite side. "We can cross there."

Zihna gave her a nudge. "Show us the way."

Dropping the water pouch on the bank, Anevy's smile grew wider. "My chief will favour me when he sees me lead you to safety."

"If you make it," Zihna snorted.

"Go carefully," Pavati added, her brow creased as she stared at the roaring river.

Anevy turned her back to the women and took a small hop to the first stone. Her toes curled as they gripped the smooth rock and she looked to the next, this time a longer stretch and she grabbed a branch hanging over the water to steady herself. Now, up onto the log, a heart-stopping teeter, then she caught her balance. Her heart thundered and she was glad neither the Chief, nor the other women, could see her face, for she was sure her fear was showing.

As she crossed the log, she came to a large, jagged rock twice her height, with water swirling and raging around the base. There was a small ledge on the downriver side that she'd need to jump to. If she made it, she simply needed to hug the rock and circle to the other side where another, sturdier log awaited.

Anevy took a deep breath and jumped.

Her feet landed on the ledge, but she scrambled to find handholds as her balance shifted. At the last second, as she felt herself falling backwards, her fingers snagged a crack in the rock and she pulled herself in.

She rested her cheek against the cold, wet rock and gulped air. Once she'd caught her breath, she grinned. There was a crevice, large enough to stand in, right before the rock met the log.

This was her chance.

The other women wouldn't be able to see her. Neither would the chief.

She stepped into the crevice and waited.

After several long moments, the first of the other women leapt onto the rock. Her eyes widened as Anevy popped out of her hiding place.

"We thought you fell—"

"No, but you did." Anevy pushed the woman into the river.

She ducked back into the crevice, repeating the same action when the next woman appeared. Who would be next? Zihna or Pavati?

A moment later, Zihna's face came into view, and without hesitation, Anevy pushed her.

That left Pavati.

A slow smile spread across her lips. Almost done.

Anevy waited…

And waited…

But Pavati never made the leap.

Anevy peeked out of her hiding place, but didn't see her. She had kept her chief waiting long enough though, so she hurried across the log and started up the trail.

She climbed and climbed until at last she reached the

flat rock.

The chief greeted her with open arms. "I am Kwatoko. You are the first."

Anevy gaped at the man. He could not be the chief. He was…ugly. His face was scarred, and as his name indicated, he had a 'big beak'. It was the biggest nose she'd ever seen and all she could do was stare.

"You will wait over there." He motioned to a wall within the shallow cave behind him. "The others are almost here."

Others? She followed his gaze down the steep hill.

Zihna…and she was helping Pavati up the trail.

How?

It did not matter.

She knew this ugly man would choose her and she could not have that. He was not worthy of her beauty.

Anevy took a step closer to the edge of the rock.

Misty spray from the waterfall cooled her skin but did nothing to still her pounding heart.

She took another step and looked down. Water crashed into the boulders that littered the bottom, the roaring so loud that the chief's words were drowned out.

"Stop her!"

Zihna's scream penetrated the fog in Anevy's mind, but it still did not matter. She would not answer for what she had done, as she had done nothing wrong. And she would not let this ugly man have her.

She jumped off the waterfall.

Anevy's spirit separated from her broken body and rose to bear witness to which of these unfortunate women would be chosen by the ugly chief.

Zihna and Pavati knelt before the man, but he moved aside as another man emerged from the shadows within the cave.

"Thank you, Kwatoko, you may go now."

When the man stepped fully into the light, the sun shined down on his glorious headdress. He held a hand out in front of Pavati.

The girl rose, and despite her dirty, torn dress, and wrapped, bleeding feet, she glowed.

Anevy released a bitter scream, but no one heard her. In anger, she jumped off the cliff again, only to find herself caught in a loop, destined to witness and jump over and over, forever the victim of her own pride.

Stone Cold Beauty

by Diane Arrelle

Electra used to shudder every night at bedtime.

She needed her beauty sleep but hated sharing her bed with that gnome-like creature; all ears and nose and lips with a belly so big she was afraid he'd suffocate her if he moved up on her and covered her face.

How am I ever going to escape this life, she thought—her nightly mantra—followed by, *Why me?*

But Electra knew why her; she had plotted and connived until she had wooed Hubert away from her cousin, Susan, who had actually wanted to spend the rest of her life with such a vile looking man.

Hubert was rich, rich beyond rich, and Electra knew that she wanted to be rich beyond rich. She wanted it enough that she assumed love didn't need to be in the equation.

Now after half a century of marriage, she was almost happy with her existence. About ninety-nine percent happy. She only had to put up with Hubert on his weekly visits for a quick, cold, fondle and a stony kiss. But she didn't have a voice anymore, nor the ability to rebuff him, so she tolerated his intrusion into her perfect world, shuddering on the inside.

Electra, back in the beginning, was named Olive. She had been rather plain, but used Hubert's fortune for her enhancement. After five years of marriage and countless surgeries, she was transformed into Electra, one of the most beautiful women in the world. She loved being worshipped by the press, who never tired of taking her pictures. In her dressing room, she kept all the clippings about herself in ridiculously expensive binders.

Then one night, 45 years ago, Electra was changing her purse contents into her new diamond dusted evening bag. As she took out the wrapping tissue from the new purse, she found a coin about the size of a silver dollar. She studied the gold coin and saw it had words engraved on it in a strange language. She squinted at it and turned on the large spotlight directly overhead to see better.

"Oh my," she gasped as the letters transformed and spelled out: MAKE A WISH.

Considering herself a pragmatic person, Electra snickered in disbelief but muttered, "How weird."

She looked from the coin in the palm of her hand as it glimmered in the bright overheard light to look at her reflection. As usual, she smiled at the stunning creature in a slinky, sexy evening gown and fleetingly whispered,

"God, I am so gorgeous. I wish I could stay this way forever."

And just like that, she turned to stone.

After the initial shock, she waited to be discovered, to be rescued, but it was days before she was found. By that time, she had decided that, in fact, at last her life *was* perfect. She didn't have to deal every night with that groping, slobbering thing she called a husband. She did get to spend all her time with the one person she loved doing the one thing that made her happiest, admiring herself. *I'll never grow older and age, I'll never have to have corrective surgery to repair the wrinkles. I am perfect. Perfect!*

She stared at her reflection in the dressing room, the brightly lit mirrors all around her reflecting her image over and over as the mirrors reflecting in the mirrors created her image on and on into infinity.

Life was good. Hubert left her where she stood because he knew what made her happy, but once a week he would sneak away from his wife, Susan, to fondle Electra's perfect breasts and kiss her goodnight. "I miss you, darling. I know you miss me."

She so wanted to be able to tell him to just go away, but she couldn't talk, just stood and let his vile self touch her perfect self.

Forty-five years can be a lifetime for some, but Electra never really noticed the time passing. Not until that day. Hubert came up for his weekly visit. "I know you must have missed me these past five months, my darling, but I've…I've…I've been… sick. I know how sad this must make you, and I have terrible news. Electra, I am dying."

He stared into her perfectly composed face and added, "I can almost see the tears in your eyes. Please don't cry, but while you remained forever young, I've aged and withered and will soon be dead."

She saw him for the first time, really focused on him as he was reflected in the mirrors. She saw Hubert, thin, gaunt and so fragile. She hadn't noticed his absence at all, and almost felt pity for him, so pathetic, so mortal.

He held her frozen hand and gently cupped her breast in his other hand, then he leaned in and kissed her. As his palm touched the golden coin she was still holding, he sighed and softly said, "Oh, my darling, I wish we could be together like this forever."

Electra was no longer a statue, and as she opened her mouth to scream *NO*, the magic began to work as the new wish took the place of her old one. They were now frozen together, just as he'd wished.

Electra no longer enjoys her eternity. All she can see

is what, to some people, would be a lovers' embrace as they are locked in a kiss, holding hands as he fondles her perfect breast. Electra's view of herself is forever blocked by his withered old body, his head covering her face, their image repeating over and over as the mirrors reflecting in the mirrors carry their image on and on into eternal infinity.

Bella's Mirror

by D.J. Elton

The Del Rio family had held high stakes in the shoe industry for several generations. Even when the need for mass production of Aria Del Rio's exquisite designs became apparent, there was enough collective business savvy amongst the younger Del Rio generation to keep the Big Thing moving forward with a rejuvenated sense of chic. That is, until Bella Del Rio decided it was high time she alone would rule the empire, and when the old man, the patriarch, Firenzo died quite suddenly, she stepped in and took control.

Bella was fairly smart and very calculating. She also had a deep craving for fame, power and money, in that order. No-one could mess with Bella when it came to the family business. Her Achilles heel, however, was a heel—not of a shoe, but in the true sense of the word. Bella's need for recognition was becoming so overwhelming that she employed a charismatic healer-cum-coach named Mel, who encouraged her to do a daily ritual of mirror-gazing; a bold new therapy which proposed to unlock the way to become a totally invincible human being.

Each day at 5 a.m., Bella would get out of bed wearing her long thin nightie and approach her magnificent full-length Russian mirror standing in the corner of her bedroom. Mel had advised that by using antique mirrors one would get the best result. Her fourteen-year-old daughter Lulu was fascinated as she sneaked a peek through the balcony window. Mother truly was becoming weird.

Mirror, Mirror, on the wall. Who is the greatest? The best of all?

Then Bella would spend fifteen minutes staring at her face, focusing on a red spot on the tip of her nose; she had the elegant pumped up face of a forty-five-year-old Australian-Italian business mogul. This went on every day and sometimes late at night as well. Mel's bank account grew richer as Bella grew weirder. Lulu caught her mother in this odd posture one night, and being an adventurous and sensible young woman, decided to join in.

Mirror, Mirror, on the wall. Who is the greatest? The best of all?

Lulu used a low-pitched growl she learned in the drama class at school and spoke a poem.

Not you, dear Mother—and please forgive me
But what I truly see

Is your lack of generosity.
Your pride has swelled
Like a pregnant plum,
It's made you delusional
You're really undone.

And with the little rhyme still reverberating inside her head, Lulu suddenly remembered that it was a school day tomorrow. So, she jumped back into her own bed before Bella would realise what had hit her.

Mel, the healer-cum-coach, found her client the next morning still staring into the mirror, whispering odd words to whatever it was she was seeing. Not feeling any sense of responsibility, Mel decided to quietly leave the house.

Moral: When pride becomes foremost, you fall. As in Bella's case, you succumb to a charlatan, and unluckily become delusional.

Everything Went White

by Eddie D. Moore

I felt something sticky between my fingers as I slowly gained consciousness. When I opened my eyes, I sucked in a sharp breath. A corpse with eyes bulging from its sockets stared at me a few inches from my face. I scrambled to distance myself from the horrific scene, but my arms and legs slipped with sloppy splashes as I tried to move. When my back hit a wall, I realised that the floor was wet with blood, and I held my shaking, red stained hands before me.

Three other bodies were crumpled on the floor in contorted, unnatural positions. The fluorescent lights swayed on their chains and flickered, threatening to plunge the entire gory scene into darkness. My eyes darted to each of the twisted figures as I tried to remember what had happened.

I vaguely recalled opening my eyes and staring into a bright light, and hearing someone saying excitedly, "It's working! She's alive…"

A man with cold, calculating eyes that seemed to look through me, leaned over. When he spoke, his voice was flat and without emotion. "It's a shame that we'll have to dissect this one to see why the others failed. Put her out so we can get started. This is going to take a while."

When he lifted his hand, I saw that he held a long, slender scalpel and a spike of fear robbed me of breath. The *beep, beep, beep* of my heart rate monitor quickened, and someone shouted in a panic, "Quick, her nanites are taking over!" A burning white light consumed my vision, and the next thing I knew I was waking up on the blood-soaked floor.

I shifted my focus away from the gruesome scene before me and past the blood sprayed walls to the ceiling. A camera stared back at me with its single blinking red light. It seemed to glare at me with an accusation, saying, *I saw what you did.*

A monitor on a small desk in the far corner displayed the room, and I could see myself cowering against the wall and then moving. Avoiding the dark puddles on the floor, I sat down at the desk and shook the mouse. A cursor moved on the screen and several icons appeared. I backed up the video fifteen minutes and saw myself unconscious on the floor. I managed to find the beginning of the video file and turned up the volume until I could hear what was being said.

"Specimen 253 was given 150cc of military-grade nanites programmed with Resurrection software version 3.2. Within ten minutes, the nanites have healed the broken bones and bridged the spinal cord damage that caused her death 52 minutes ago. The heart started beating again three minutes after the injection, and we have shut off the bypass machine that was circulating her blood for the nanites.

"My modifications are working as intended. Thanks to my research, the human race will overcome death itself."

For a couple of minutes, the microphone only picked up pieces of the medical team's discussion and laughter as the technicians eagerly watched the machines. The conversation among them grew more animated, and whoever was dictating the procedure returned to the microphone.

"We are now 20 minutes post-injection, and brain activity is beginning to normalise. In the future—"

The speaker was interrupted as an orderly shouted, "It's working! She's alive."

The microphone failed to pick up what else was said, but when the doctor lifted his scalpel, my eyes took on a light of their own. My right arm grabbed the hand holding the surgical blade, twisted and jammed it into the doctor's chest. The doctor's arm fell to his side, leaving the scalpel protruding from his breastbone. His mouth fell open, and he stared at it in shock. An instant later, my left fist drove the shank deep into his chest, and he collapsed to the floor.

I slipped off the table as one of the men reached to restrain me. When I hit the floor, I swept my leg under his under him, and as he fell, I moved with unnatural speed to grab his forehead and drive the back of his head into the floor. The microphone did manage to capture the crack of his skull and a sickening splat when he landed. The other two men tried to put up a fight, but moments later, they were both on the floor twitching with dislocated arms and twisted necks.

I saw myself standing in the room for several long seconds. The glow in my eyes faded, and I eventually collapsed to the floor.

I was still shaking my head in denial when a deep voice filled the room. "Specimen 253, you will lay face down on the floor and stretch out your arms or we will be forced to terminate you. Do you understand?"

I shouted back at the disembodied voice, "What have you done to me? What am I?"

Without warning, the door blasted off its hinges and

men in black body armour rushed into the room. When I saw the explosive flash, time seemed to slow, and everything when white.

Pride goeth Before the Fall

by Dawn DeBraal

The Good Book, Proverbs 16:18 says, "Pride goeth before destruction, and a haughty spirit before a fall." Funny how folks incorrectly recite the verse as "Pride goeth before the fall." I had to look up haughty spirit. It means you think you're better than someone. That about explains me in a nutshell. My God-given; gift I could sing.

"The voice of an angel," my father said. He is the preacher at the First Congregation Church in Shelby County, Alabama. The Lord gave me this gift that it should be used to glorify His name. All through my lower grades, and on into high school, I sang most Sunday's at my daddy's church. Mama would dress me in finery, telling me to spread the Word. At thirteen, my parents told me I was adopted. They told me the story of how they swooped down, scooped me out of the arms of the devil. I was the product of a heroin-addicted whore and her pimp. Daddy said he had to perform an exorcism to scare the devil out when they brought me home. At two-years old, I don't recall any of it. Daddy warned me never to let my guard down; if I did, the devil could claim me back. Every Sunday, I got up, sang my heart out for the congregation, the Lord, and kept myself pure.

After graduating from Shelby County High School in Columbiana, I boarded a bus with my best friend, Dorothy Jean, headed for Nashville, Tennessee. I was going to be a professional gospel singer with all the confidence in the world. With the money I'd saved up working at Delacroix's Drug Store stuffed in my socks, and sewn in the hems of my coat and skirts, we set out for the big time. We were excited to leave Shelby County for good, even though Nashville was only four hours from Colombiana.

Nashville in the summer of 1956 was host to Kitty Wells, Jean Shepherd, and—my favourite—Aretha Franklin. My head was full of dreams, and my eyes full of stars. I was invited to audition at the Owen Brady recording studio, Sixteen Avenue South; a friend of a church member got me the audition. Dorothy Jean could sing some, but not like me. Dorothy Jean could harmonise with a wailing cat. I did sing with her lots of times, but it was never my intention of becoming a duo with her.

I had an aunt who owned a boarding house in Nashville; the main reason we were allowed to go. Aunt Lou gave us the family discount, with kitchen privileges.

When we arrived, Aunt Lou was at the Greyhound Station waiting to pick us up in an old Ford Deluxe that had seen better days. She gave me a big hug while shaking Dorothy Jean's hand. When we got to the boarding house, we were quite surprised. Aunt Lou had a pretty, two-story house, with large cottonwood trees that bordered the street in front of the house. We walked in through the front door and into an entryway with a seating area and a large staircase that led to the second floor.

"This is home girls," Aunt Lou said, putting her purse on a hall tree hook. "You have the room at the top of the stairs on the right. You'll share the room because of the family rate. It that's not suitable, you will have to talk to me on the non-family rate and pay a bit more, for private rooms." Dorothy Jean raced me up the steps.

"Dib's on the window!" I shouted as we opened the door. Twin beds with matching chenille spreads in delicate pink stood against one wall, with a white table in between. There was a small seating area at the opposite end of the room. Aunt Lou had left the window open, and a slight breeze blew in.

"This is beautiful," Dorothy said, smiling. I couldn't agree with her more. Part of me was glad I had spoken up first, getting the bed I wanted; the one with the view and the breeze. I don't think my daddy would have approved.

I think he would have told me to share the window bed every other month, finding a compromise with Dorothy Jean. Something came over me once I was away from my parents disapproving looks, I wanted what I wanted.

The next morning, Aunt Lou showed us how to get where we needed to go riding the city busses. I had my audition the following day, so I thought I'd take a dry run. I had nothing better to do. Dorothy Jean asked if she could come along, but we were already too tight for my comfort, I told her I needed to do it on my own. With relief, I left her behind and walked down to the corner bus stop. Right on time, the bus pulled up. Telling the driver I needed to go to Sixteenth Street, he said he would make sure I got off at the right stop as I put my money in the receptacle. Nashville is a big city compared to Columbiana. After a few stops, the driver opened the door telling me to take the 187 bus to Sixteenth Street. I was proud of myself when the 187 let me out a few feet from where I wanted to be. I decided to walk into the studio to look around, so there'd be no surprises before the audition. The square building looked more like a house with a Quonset hut at the back. I later learned that the Quonset hut was where the recordings took place. I was able to find my way back to Aunt Lou's feeling quite accomplished. Dorothy was waiting for me when I arrived.

"Did you find it? How was it?" I relished in the story of how I got to the studio. She was excited, but I could tell she was a little jealous of my experience. Dorothy Jean spent the day cleaning Aunt Lou's boarding house in exchange for her rent that week. I needed to open my sock to pay Aunt Lou directly. Knowing I should be doing the same thing, I decided I had to find a job and not waste my nest egg.

If I had any problems, it was that I didn't play an instrument. Everyone in Nashville played some kind of musical instrument—everyone but me. When I showed up at the Brady Recording Studio for my audition, the receptionist asked me if I had someone to play accompaniment. I did not. The woman sighed and made a phone call. Minutes later, a young pianist showed up and introduced himself as Robert Asher. Robert appeared to be older than me by a few years. He also knew he was handsome. Robert did the obligatory scales and then played through my piece a few times before the studio technician called us in.

I was told to sing into the microphone. Robert started the introduction to my song, and I'd only sung a few notes when the technician told me to stop. He made a few adjustments to the mike, before asking Robert to start again. Being cut off in my performance was disconcerting—I had never been stopped mid-song, ever—it angered me. I took a moment to relax, gathering myself back together. We started over. I felt my performance, overall, was quite good. I shook Robert's hand on the way out of the studio. Robert offered me a ride home. Not listening to the nagging voice in my head to decline his offer, I accepted because he was handsome, funny, and I would save bus fare. Driving to Aunt Lou's boarding house, we chatted comfortably in the car. Robert made small talk as he took me a round-about way to Aunt Lou's, showing me sights of Nashville. How naïve I was. He pulled over near the Cumberland Bridge, asking me if I wanted to walk. Flattered, I got out of the car. We started to walk across the bridge when he stopped to admire the views.

"That river, it's about eighty feet below us from here," Robert said. We stood watching the water flow quickly under the bridge. "Folks have come here to commit suicide," he offered. I kept quiet, thinking it was a strange conversation to be having. Robert put his arm around me—I thought it was a bold move, but I didn't move his arm. He pulled me close, telling me how beautiful I was. Then he kissed me. I had never kissed anyone before, and Robert caught me by surprise. *What am I supposed to do,* I wondered?

At first, Robert's kiss was soft and light. Then his advances became more aggressive. I tried to move out from under him. I asked Robert if we could go back to the car. I realised too late that it wasn't the right way to phrase it; Robert walked with me back to the car and, instead of setting off to Aunt Lou's, he pulled me into the back seat.

It was over before I knew what had happened. I know that I am still a virgin, but what he did to me wasn't right. I started to cry. Robert told me it was alright, that he respected me, that he cared about me. He asked when he could see me again, saying things that made me feel better. When he dropped me off at Aunt Lou's, I still wasn't sure what happened. I am angry that I even thanked him for the ride, saying I hoped I'd see him again, soon. Robert said he'd call me. When his car drove off, I realised Robert didn't have my phone number.

Walking in the front door, Aunt Lou reprimanded be for getting into a car with a stranger. I told her that he was a co-worker and that Robert was a perfect gentleman. That couldn't have been further from the truth, but Aunt Lou settled her feathers after that. I kept thinking about what had happened to me, not sure why Robert would choose me. There was no way I could share the experience with Dorothy Jean. She would have tattled on me to Aunt Lou, or worse…to Daddy.

Weeks later, I hadn't heard from Robert or the studio, so I accepted a waitress job at the Burger Shack. I needed to keep myself fed and a roof over my head. The pay was terrible, but the tips made up for that. Dorothy Jean found a job working at the lunch counter at Woolworth's. Neither of us had our dream jobs, but we were enjoying being out from under our parents' thumbs. Aunt Lou began to relax when it came to us, she said we were old enough to know what was in our best interest. She still didn't know what happened on my ride home with Robert; I pushed that memory out of my mind whenever it came back to haunt me.

About the time I gave up, I got a call back from the studio. They had accepted me as a paid singer! Returning to the Brady's, I was introduced to a woman by the name of Jenny, who was recording songs, making a record. I hadn't thought about the possibility of not being the recording star…I was just the back-up singer, and they expected me to sing harmonies. I wasn't as good as Dorothy Jean, and upon some unsuccessful attempts, they asked me if I had any friends who could do another part of the harmony.

Dorothy Jean came straight in when I called her. She jumped into the song, singing another layer harmonising while helping me get my part right. The sound was smooth, the technician and the lead singer seemed happy with what we'd done. Robert was playing piano, so when we caught a break, he came over to say hello. I had successfully ignored him up to this point. Robert acted very coolly towards me, but was interested in Dorothy Jean when I introduced them. I felt a little jealous; suddenly not the top person in the room. I wasn't even the top back-up singer in the room—Dorothy Jean out sang me with her harmonising, and was having to teach me how to do what came naturally to her. The other musicians, Jenny Lowell, the singer, the technician, praised Dorothy Jean on her ability. Even Robert went out of his way to thank her for her contribution. I was quite upset. Robert offered us a ride home, but I didn't want Dorothy Jean in his car. Robert made me feel worthless. I no longer suspected he had used me, that thought was confirmed. We said no to the ride. I didn't want Dorothy Jean and Robert together. Dorothy Jean had already taken everything away from me today. I asked Dorothy Jean to walk with me until we could wear down the excitement of the day. After that, we could take a bus or a cab. She readily agreed.

"I'm walking on cloud nine right now. I can see what you've been saying all along." Dorothy Jean skipped along beside me. I hated that she felt so successful when

I was overwhelmed with defeat. It was hard to stay silent about her bragging. I had never seen this side of Dorothy Jean before. She talked about how she found the harmonies, how she made up the parts, how everyone congratulated her on her talent.

We were crossing the Cumberland Bridge moving out of downtown. It was one of the places I did admire in Nashville—the city lights behind us, the sites were beautiful, and you could see both ways down the Cumberland River. I asked Dorothy to be quiet so we could take in the view. But I was reliving the nightmare of a few short weeks ago, still trying to deal with it. I was angry at myself and at Robert's treatment of me every time I was near him. He broke something inside of me; I couldn't put that into words, and I couldn't put those broken pieces back together. Confused and angry, I didn't want to listen to Dorothy Jean's day any longer. Dorothy Jean obliged me with blessed silence as we walked across the bridge. I remembered Robert telling me the bridge was eighty feet over the water. We were very high when we got to the middle of the bridge. I walked over to the edge and looked down. It was a dizzying height. A thought stirred in me. Climbing up on the railing of the bridge, I threw my feet over the edge. Dorothy Jean told me to get down.

"Will, you just look at this view? Smell the water. This scenery is beautiful!" Dorothy Jean reluctantly climbed up next to me. We sat in silence, taking in the sounds, the sights, the smell in the breeze. She couldn't contain herself. Dorothy Jean started to talk about her success at the studio again. I felt overwhelming anger toward her. I don't know what crossed over me. I felt it coming on this time; I didn't fight it. I gave myself over to it. My eyes seemed to look through a yellow coloured lens. I felt my blood turning cold. Some last vestige of me tried to think of a Bible verse to stave off what was happening, but I couldn't fight it anymore. My pride would not let me take a back seat to Dorothy Jean, or to Robert. I could deal with my feelings about Robert each time we met, but Dorothy Jean had been my best friend all my life. I lived with her, and now I had to work with her. She would never know how she contributed to belittle me that day. I didn't think I could stomach another minute of her bragging. Dorothy Jean stopped in mid-sentence.

"What's wrong with your eyes?" she asked me.

"My eyes?" I questioned.

"They're yellow!" she said, surprised.

"It must be the bridge lights. Let me see yours." I looked at her face, her eyes were normal looking, but instead, I told her, "Your eyes look yellow too, how strange!" We laughed. Something was guiding me, driving me, urging me. I felt as if I were a vessel of water being overly filled. I put my arm around Dorothy Jean's shoulders. She thought I was going to hug her, instead, I pushed Dorothy Jean over. It wasn't hard a hard thing to do. I now had more strength than I ever imagined. Just a gentle push, over she went. Dorothy Jean screamed the entire eighty feet, her arms and legs waving and running in the air before hitting the water at an odd angle. She didn't come back up. I ran to the other side of the bridge to see if she would surface further down the river, remembering Dorothy Jean couldn't swim. Never could. I didn't see her come up from the water.

Oddly enough, I felt nothing. All I could say to myself was the mashed-up Bible verse. "Pride goeth before the fall." I walked back to Aunt Lou's boarding house, thinking about that Bible verse. I believe the new me—the one the devil claimed—finally understood why the shortened version of that Bible verse made so much more sense now.

Homecoming

by Annie Percik

"You looking forward to getting home?"

Meral's gruff voice broke through Raldi's reverie, and she looked up from her horse's withers.

"I guess. The village'll seem pretty small after all we've seen and done."

Meral grinned. "All the girls'll be so impressed with our stories of wild adventure and desperate peril."

Raldi snorted. "You wish. They'll still remember the skinny, pimply youth you were when we left."

"But you'll back me up, won't you?" Meral pouted, looking every inch the petulant teenager Raldi had just described.

"No chance!" Raldi flexed her muscled shoulders beneath her leather jerkin. "I'll be trying to impress them with my own stories."

"Race you back, then!" Meral spurred his horse into a canter, calling back, "Winner gets first pick!"

Raldi cursed him under her breath and jabbed her heels into her horse's sides. Her long, straw-coloured braid thumped against her back as they crested the rise that looked down on the village. Meral had pulled his horse up short and was staring ahead, his body rigid. Raldi looked past him to see what was wrong.

There was nobody in the fields, and she could see even from a distance that the crops were sparse and stunted. There were few people in the streets as Raldi and Meral entered the village and their stares were unfriendly. Raldi recognised a few of the gaunt, anxious faces, but they didn't stop, instead making for the small tavern at the centre of the village. Most of the buildings seemed to be in disrepair, and the once spotless streets were mired in mud and detritus.

Meral drew his horse to a stop in front of the tavern, Raldi halting next to him. They both dismounted and secured their horses' reins to the hitching post. Raldi led the way into the building. The sight that greeted her made her wonder if they'd arrived at the wrong village.

Where there would normally be a roaring fire, the hearth was cold and empty. Rags covering broken window panes cast shadows across the floor, making the interior dim and unwelcoming. And, most unexpected of all, the figure behind the bar was not her father.

Instead, an elderly woman with straggly grey hair glared at them, her eyes hard.

"Aunt Magda?" Raldi said, uncertain.

"Oh, it's you, is it? Back from the wars, all high and mighty. Wanting us all to wait on you hand and foot, I expect." The woman sneered. "Well, you're in for a whole heap of disappointment, which is all we've got to spare round here. Nobody has the time or the energy to coddle the likes of you."

Raldi felt the rejection and hostility like an icy wind in the middle of summer. "Where's my da?"

"Dead, girl." The words were harsh, dropped into the space between them without care for where they fell. "Like a lot of people since you left."

Raldi gulped, fishlike, feeling her foundations rocking beneath her. Meral stepped up to her side and caught her elbow as if she was about to fall. Maybe she had been.

"What happened?" he asked.

"Harvest failed. Two years in a row. Not enough surplus to feed everyone. People started dying." Magda spat the short sentences out as if they tasted foul.

"Didn't you appeal to the church for help?" Raldi asked.

Magda's face twisted with bitterness. "Of course we did. Do you think we're idiots? The first time, they told us there was nothing to spare for the likes of us. Hard times across the realm, apparently. Aid couldn't spread this far. After that, they didn't even bother to reply."

"What can we do?" Raldi said.

She had spent three years taking action in all sorts of conflicts. She was used to solving problems with muscle and steel. She itched to do something, anything, to fix things.

"You bring several tons of grain with you on that fancy horse of yours?" Magda only had contempt for her query.

Raldi felt Meral bristle beside her.

"No," he said, "but we have money. We've saved most of our wages for the last three years, and we didn't do that just to keep it all to ourselves."

"Ha! Money," Magda scoffed. "What do you suppose we can do with that? You might be able to stuff a cushion with it. There's nothing to buy, lad. Just go back to your mercenary company and leave the rest of us here to die."

"No," Raldi said. "We won't abandon you. We'll ride to the city and force the church to listen." She rattled her sword in its scabbard, hoping to convey menace. "Come on, Meral. If we set off now, and ride through the night, we can reach the cathedral before dark tomorrow."

She turned and strode from the tavern, her confidence returning with a new sense of purpose and a determination to be the saviour her village so desperately needed.

They rode into the deepening twilight in silence for a while, before Meral finally spoke.

"I'm sorry about your da."

Raldi swallowed. All she wanted was to keep riding until she left the pain behind.

"Yeah," she said. "Thanks."

Meral cleared his throat, avoiding her gaze. "It probably wouldn't have made any difference if we'd been here. We can't control the weather."

Raldi sighed. "But we might have been able to do something about the church. Soon enough to make a difference."

She spurred her horse into a canter, wanting to leave the village and all its memories far behind. After a while, she heard Meral calling out behind her and slowed again, though she didn't look round.

"The horses are already tired," Meral said to her back. "And we don't have many supplies. If you keep going at that pace, we'll never make it. I think we should stop."

"But the village…" Raldi ground out.

"It'll still be there when we get back," Meral's tone edged towards pleading. "And they'll suffer more if our horses collapse out from under us and we don't make it at all."

Raldi knew he was right. She sighed deeply, growling her frustration.

"All right. But I'm not stopping. We'll keep going slowly."

The morning saw them pushing the horses over hard-baked ground under an unforgiving sun. Meral was sulking about not having had any sleep, but Raldi didn't much feel like talking anyway. She was thinking back over their journey from the mercenary camp to the village, and how the unrelentingly dry weather hadn't really registered. They'd hadn't needed to stop for supplies on their way, so they hadn't encountered the suffering of the people.

Now, the ravages of the weather on the surrounding countryside were glaringly obvious. The horses kicked up dust that clogged Raldi's nose and mouth, and there was barely a trickle in the stream bed where they stopped to try to fill their water bottles. It was going to be a long and uncomfortable ride to the city, but Raldi welcomed the hardship, feeling a masochistic desire to suffer as those she had left behind had done. Guilt pushed at her, easier to deal with and react to than the gaping loss it shielded from view within her mind.

The sun was going down and the temperature was finally starting to drop as they got their first glimpse of the cathedral in the distance. Raldi had only seen it once before, when she'd been a little girl and her father had brought her to be blessed. She remembered a vague hugeness and a sense of awe, which had now been thoroughly replaced by a slow burning rage, deep in her guts. The people of her village led simple lives of devotion, following the mandated prayers and paying their tithes on time. Now, it should have been time for them to receive support in turn, but the church had betrayed them, leaving them to starve.

The horses laboured up the hill, struggling more and more until Raldi called a halt, and they both dismounted to walk the last hundred yards. The cathedral's gates were closed, but there was a large, iron bell to one side of the path. Raldi grabbed the pull rope and yanked it hard. A harsh clanging rang out through the gathering shadows.

A small hatch opened in one of the gates, and a man's

face appeared in the gap.

"What's the meaning of this?" He glared at them.

Raldi stepped up to the gate and shoved her face close to the hatch.

"We want to see whoever's in charge."

"The cathedral is closed to visitors at this time," the man informed her, primly. "Supplicants can apply to the church office in the city for an appointment."

Something told Raldi that it was vital they gain access to the cathedral proper. It was like a voice, whispering in her mind, telling her not to let this man turn them away.

"No," she said. "That's not good enough. We need to speak to someone in charge here and now, not some flunky at an office, who can ignore us."

"Oh, I assure you, we can ignore you just as easily here. Now, go away."

The man slammed the hatch shut and Raldi heard a bolt sliding home. She turned to see Meral standing a few steps behind her, his mouth agape.

"What do we do now?" he asked. "Go home, or maybe try the office in the morning?"

"No," Raldi said again, surprised by her own vehemence. "We need to get in there tonight and make them listen to us."

"But the gate…"

Raldi swivelled back to face the barrier. The gates were tall and solid-looking, but there was a small gap between them, and Raldi pressed her eye up against it. She could just make out the courtyard beyond, nobody in sight. Glancing down, she could see a thick wooden plank set across the gap, presumably keeping the gates closed.

Raldi took a step backwards and drew her sword.

"What are you doing?" Meral squeaked, but she ignored him.

Whatever was driving her to gain access to the cathedral wouldn't allow any distractions. Raldi had told her aunt she would fix the problem and nothing was going to stand in her way.

She inserted her sword carefully through the gap below the plank. Once the hilt made contact with the wood, she swept the blade upwards with considerable force and felt the resistance of the plank. It shifted up slightly, so she redoubled her efforts and pushed it further until it was released from its brackets and fell to the ground on the other side of the gates with a clatter. Raldi pushed on the right hand gate and it slid slowly open. She threw a triumphant glance over her shoulder at Meral and strode inside.

She didn't check to see if Meral was following her,

but marched across the cobblestones towards an iron-bound door at the base of a tower. Her steps were unerring, her purpose pulling her onwards. No church official appeared or tried to stop her as she lifted the latch and opened the door.

"Where are you going?" Meral hissed from behind her, but she didn't reply.

Stairs led down into darkness, but Raldi didn't need a light. Something inside her showed her the way, drawing her ever further into the black depths beneath the cathedral. She heard Meral stumbling and cursing just above her, but she spared him no consideration. Her destination was down these stairs and she intended to reach it.

The stairs ended and a stone corridor led away into the shadows. Raldi kept going, until an imposing metal door blocked her path. It stretched a couple of feet above her head, and was secured with three large, iron bolts that disappeared into the rock. Whatever she was looking for, Raldi knew it lay behind this door. She grasped the first of the bolts and started to work it free.

She felt a hand on her shoulder, but shook it off.

"Raldi," a voice, frightened and vaguely familiar, breathed into her ear. "I don't think we should be down here. It feels wrong. Let's go back up and find someone to talk to."

The voice couldn't have been more wrong. This was exactly where Raldi was supposed to be. There was something behind this door that would help. She would save the village and all the surrounding area. Everyone would hail her as a hero.

The first bolt shot back and fierce satisfaction surged through her. She reached for the next bolt, twisting and pulling at it. This one took less effort, springing open easily. The joy she felt was almost like hunger, spurring her on to the last bolt. When she pulled it free, the door shifted, and a breath of fetid air washed over her. She heard someone coughing behind her, but she remained undeterred. She grabbed hold of the edges of the door and yanked it towards her. It was heavy, and scraped over the rough ground underfoot, but Raldi kept pulling until it was open enough to admit entry.

Slipping around the door, she stepped into the chamber beyond.

It was almost completely dark in the room, and yet its features were clear to her. It was roughly circular and only about two strides across. In the centre, a pillar of rock speared up from the ground. Atop it stood a golden flask that seemed to glow without actually giving off any light.

Two voices spoke at once, one from behind, and one

from within.

The voice behind her, uncertain and faltering, said, "I don't like it in here. I really think we should leave."

The voice within her, rich and silken, said, "Open the flask."

Raldi stepped forwards, reached out a hand and touched the golden surface.

Wind howled around her and she shut her eyes against a lightning flash that struck the ground inches from her feet. She was standing on an unfamiliar and weather-ravaged heath. Thick grass whipped around her ankles, while dark clouds boiled across the sky. The landscape stretched as far as she could see, the only feature a twisted, blackened tree some distance away.

Raldi took a couple of steps, fighting against the wind, and made out a figure spread-eagled against the tree trunk. It was a woman, naked and chained to the wood, metal chain links digging into her chest, waist and thighs. Her ribs and hips stood out against her hairless body. Her wide, pleading eyes drew Raldi towards her until they were only a few inches apart.

"You came." It was the voice she had heard before,

back in the chamber.

"Yes, I'm here." Raldi felt huge and awkward in her leather armour, her sword swinging against her thickly muscled legs.

The woman smiled and Raldi felt a burst of love and longing.

"Who has imprisoned you here?" she asked.

Sorrow suffused the lovely features. "Those who would inflict pain and prevent me from helping those in need."

"How can I help you?" Raldi asked.

"If you free me, I can help you in return. I can bring prosperity back to your village. I can even bring your father back from the dead."

A small sense of doubt nagged at the edges of Raldi's mind.

"If you can do all that, why are you kept chained here?"

"Because the church wants to hold onto its power. They want the people to suffer so they can maintain their control over them. Free me, and everything will change for the better."

Raldi thought about all the suffering she could help to eradicate, and how grateful everyone would be to her for saving them. The church had shown itself to be heartless and uncaring. It only made sense that they would be actively preventing such a powerful, benevolent being from giving aid.

Then, she felt a hand on her shoulder again, pulling at her. Someone was calling her name, but it was distant. The pulling hand grew more insistent and the shouting drew nearer. For an instant, Raldi saw Meral beside her in the rock chamber, his face twisted with fear and desperation.

The woman spoke again. "If you let him stop you, those who placed me here will hurt me more. And I won't be able to help you save your village."

Raldi hesitated. The woman's words were compelling. She saw her father and the whole village, lauding her as a hero. Meral was just jealous; he always had been. Raldi drew her sword and stabbed. She felt resistance, and then the unmistakable sensation of flesh parting before her blade. Meral cried out and her sword was pulled from her hand as his body fell. She let it drop and turned back to the woman chained to the tree.

The woman was smiling and Raldi felt the hungry joy again. She reached up for the chains and unhooked them from their fastenings.

Suddenly, she was back in the chamber beneath the cathedral, the flask in her hands. She prised the cork from its neck. As it came free, a thin tendril of smoke drifted out and forced itself down Raldi's throat. She dropped the flask, choking. Bent double, she saw Meral's lifeless body at her feet, her sword impaling him.

In her mind's eye, Raldi saw her village burning, all the remaining villagers scattered on the ground, dead. The devastation spread out to cover the entire region, spilling from her own hands. As the vision cleared, she knew the church had in fact been doing its best to protect the people from whatever had been trapped inside the flask. She tried to force the cork back, but found she could no longer move her hands or arms.

Her body turned to the door, and the passageway that would lead up and out into the world. Raldi had no control over her movements, and was carried as an unwilling passenger, silken laughter echoing through her mind.

Peccata Patris

by Andrew Anderson

Frank lumbered down the basement stairs. His hip was bothering him these days, which meant that every step of the descent took great effort. Despite the pain, a burst of adrenaline made him leap down the last step, and, after crossing the floor to his workbench, he had to lean against it to catch his breath.

His face had already broken into a sweat, and he wiped it on his shirtsleeve. Then, as Frank remembered why he had come down here, he reached into his shirt pocket. A smile spread across his face as he retrieved the newspaper cutting and allowed it to float down onto the bench. He savoured the bold words on the scrap of paper, though he had already long memorised them:

'THE SUNSET KILLER IS BACK!! Manhunt begins, as historic killer returns and takes 6th victim!'

Hands trembling, he opened the workbench drawer and withdrew the scrapbook, filled with all his favourite newspaper clippings. He laid it, almost reverently, upon the bench, open to the first page.

Most craftsmen take pride in their craft, but few took pride in their work like Frank. He deliberately paced himself as he paged through the book documenting his life's work.

Most serial killers have a *modus operandi*, and Frank was no exception: Frank's motif was to copy the methods of *other* killers, from the past. This had baffled police in multiple states, when killers already caught and executed—or long dead of natural causes—appeared to come back from the dead to continue their crimes from beyond the grave.

Frank believed he was carrying on the work begun by the great murderers, keeping their legacies alive. No one could paint a scene quite like Frank, even if his portfolio wasn't the kind likely to be made into a coffee table book. And whilst he was hardly a starving artist, it didn't stop him hungering for fame. Or infamy. The thought of the detectives scratching their heads almost brought tears of joy to Frank's eyes.

Suddenly, he felt almost lightheaded with it all, enough so he groped for the stool and sat. *Better safe than sorry.*

Speaking of which... he thought as he ran his fingers through his thinning hair; he would need to dye his hair again soon just to be safe, but the overuse felt like it was taking its toll. He'd end up bald soon if he didn't find a gentler dye.

The hairs on his arms, on the other hand, seemed healthy as ever, and had no problem standing on end when an ice-cool breeze blew across them. A draft—or a temperature variation of any kind, really—was unusual given that the basement had no windows. Frank started to get up to turn on the portable heater.

"Are you proud of yourself?" said a voice from the corner.

Frank felt his heart momentarily stop in his chest, and the rest of his body followed suit a half-second later. He froze, a rabbit in headlights, partway up from the stool, but momentum and gravity were not on his side; the stool tipped over and took him with it. He crashed, hard, onto the cold cement floor. Pain shot through his hip, but he still managed to scramble backwards, away from the unseen source of the voice.

"You should be proud, Frankie, cos I'm proud of you—well, to some extent anyway."

Frank trained his eyes on the shadows where he could see a vague shape. It was more of an apparition than a figure, but it had a voice he knew all too well.

Even before the presence moved into the light, Frank

spoke. "Seb?"

"Hi, Son. It's been a while," said Seb. "Did you forget your old dad?"

Frank struggled to compose himself, but even if his blanched features didn't give him away, the tremor in his voice did. "But you're...but I thought..."

Frank could hear, rather than see, that familiar sneer in Seb's voice as he said, "You were so wrapped up in your own artistry, I almost didn't want to interrupt you there, Frankie. But your most recent piece has been a step too far."

Frank's mind was whirling. His father. His *deceased* father, dead these three years, was standing there. Right there, in the very room where he had doled out his many beatings—abuse that Frank's own crimes were an attempt to blot from memory.

Sometimes he almost succeeded. Almost.

Frank cleared his throat. "H-how are you here, and w-what are you talking about?"

"It's been so long since I got to use my voice, and that's an especially long story which I can't go into. But you know better than anyone that I'm more the strong and silent type anyway, right?"

Seb chuckled and cracked his knuckles. Or, at least, a cracking sound emerged from the approximate area where his hands would be, were Frank able to focus enough to see what was happening right in front of him. Instead, his vision had blurred, and his brain had begun projecting a film against the back of his eyes, playing memories of being chased around this room for forgetting to take the garbage out.

"I've got to admit, *most* of your exploits have made me swell with pride that my own son could carry off such an elaborate ruse. There's something in the blood. Problem is, Frankie son, that if you insist on being a copycat, you need to at least equal the original."

Frank tried to speak, but no words came out.

"I can see that you're confused and lost for words. But don't worry, son; I'll spell it out for you, like I always had to."

Seb's outline paced the room; Frank jumped every time he came near. This room where he had celebrated his proudest adult moments had become a concrete prison again.

"You had done so well up to this point. You're an artist of sorts, but you've made a wrong stroke of the brush. There'll be no gold stars or lollipops for you this time, Frankie boy. See, I had left the *perfect* trail of terror."

Realisation spread across Frank's face.

"You… Su-su-sunset?"

He started to get up but somehow Seb pushed him back to the floor and continued, "You've been sloppy, and it's tarnishing *my* reputation. You were busy patting yourself on the back, but pride well and truly comes before the fall. You probably don't even realise that you've left clues behind, and that those incompetent detectives are, at this minute, already on your trail?"

Frank started shaking.

"I'll bet that when you started out, that you didn't think you'd be literally bringing killers back from the dead? Well, the papers say I'm back, but the manhunt will be futile after this one; rest assured though, you *will* go down in history, just not like you imagined. I'll put your book away on my way out—think of it as a final courtesy, from father to son, before I walk off again into the sunset."

Seb advanced on Frank, and his world went black.

Wing Woman

by A.R. Johnston

Chantelle did a full head toss so that her hair moved over her shoulder. The signature move that just about all women use to get the attention of men, and if you were known to have the assets to go with this move, it was almost a guarantee that you were going to get what you wanted. With that being said, Chantelle knew she had it all and she flaunted it shamelessly.

She was tall at five-nine, with flowing strawberry blonde hair, sparkling green eyes, and full red lips. Chantelle could be considered model material and was never at a loss for companionship.

The men in front of her almost drooled. Arguing with each other and taking bets as to who would take her home tonight. Chantelle secretly grinned—if she had her way, she would be taking them all home. All four of them.

Kara sat back at the bar, grinning at the whole scenario. She had come here with Chantelle knowing that she would probably be going home alone tonight. She mostly came out for the kick of it and to get out of the house. Chantelle was always the reason for things. She was the reason she was a fallen angel, sitting in a bar trying to get drunk and laughing at these pitiful humans drool and fight over her best friend.

How did they get here? What made them fall from grace, you ask? The simple answer is pride. The one sin which all other sins stem from, some would even call the sin vanity. Kara was saddened to say that she gave in to the sin and fell from Heaven. She had been vain in thinking she was more than what she was before the all powerful, and she was paying for it here on Earth among these mortal beings.

But was she really paying for it? She was enjoying herself here on Earth most of the time. Did she miss being one of the Almighty's chosen and being with the Archangels on high? Of course she did. She even missed the opalescent silver-tipped wings she once had. When she wanted, she could still release her wings, but they were black, pitch black like the sin. She almost always broke into tears when she saw them as a reminder, so she had literally clipped her own wings off so she wouldn't have to see them. She scratched at the spot where they used to be, they ached.

If she was to repent, would she be welcomed back home and get her wings back? She sipped her drink as she pondered this. Did she even think she could keep that promise of repenting and not fall again? Better to not ask for forgiveness and stay where she was. She was not sure she could survive the fall once more.

"Kara? Earth to Kara?" Chantelle's sultry voice broke her from her reverie. She was smiling brightly when Kara blinked at her.

"What's up?" She smiled, brushing her own bright red tresses to the side. Yet another prideful thing to do.

Chantelle giggled as she clung to the arm of one of the men she had been flirting with. The others were behind her, grinning like jackals too and eyeing her up. She shuddered, in revulsion not anticipation, but the ones in front of her took it as the latter; she could tell by the way their eyes gleamed. Lust, yet another sin.

"We're all going back to my place, are you coming?" she asked in a tone that suggested it would be fine if she did join them, but she didn't really want Kara to agree to it. Chantelle was the epitome of prideful vanity and lust. She would take whatever others had to offer her, and not think twice about it.

Kara smirked and winked at one of the boys, not to annoy Chantelle but to let her know she got the message.

"I'm good, thanks. I'm going to finish this drink first. Go on, maybe I'll stop by later," she pointedly answered, looking at Chantelle to let her know she meant she would stop by sometime tomorrow.

Chantelle smiled at her. "See you later, my love. Don't have too much fun without me." She leaned forward, kissing Kara's cheek, and whispered in her ear, "Thanks, girl. I'm going to have so much fun."

Kara chuckled. "Be off with you. Have fun."

The one she had winked at stopped beside her. He was tall, broad, and reminded her of one of the brilliant and gorgeous Archangels. He looked slightly concerned as he glanced toward the leaving harem and back to Kara.

"Are you sure you don't want to come? Would you like some company?" His deep voice sent pleasurable shivers down her spine.

She considered him for a moment before responding. "I'm good. But thank you for asking. I appreciate it." She really did. Never had one of the harem that Chantelle collected ever stopped and ask after her. It was an intriguing sensation that Kara had never had before.

This time he considered her, looking her over to see if that was what she really wanted or not. He waved off one of his friends calling back to him and sat down on the stool beside her.

Kara quirked an eyebrow at him. "Your friends are leaving."

He made an affirmative noise, raised a hand to signal

for a beer, and turned back to her.

"They are but you are far more interesting. I think I'll stay here if you don't mind."

Kara was momentarily flustered. She knew she was beautiful—it was one of the reasons her sin was vanity—but after falling, she didn't flaunt it as Chantelle did. She tilted her head at him, eyebrow raised.

He gave her yet another easy smile, nodding to the bartender as a beer was placed in front of him.

"That is, of course, if it's alright with you?" He gave her a patient look, sipping his beer as he awaited her answer.

She was not used to this. She always left Chantelle to get all the attention. She was feeling wanted for the first time in a very long time.

"I would enjoy the company, I think," she spoke softly, smiling up at him. She held out her hand. "Kara Seraph."

"Raphael Noble." He took hold of her hand, turning it and placing a kiss into her palm. "A true pleasure to meet you."

A blush rose up her cheeks as her smile brightened. "The pleasure is mine. To new friendships." She toasted him, raising her glass.

"To new friends."

Maybe falling from grace wouldn't be as bad as she thought.

The Acquisition of Things

by Terry Miller

Gregory Peterson had it all, but it wasn't always that way. He grew up in a single-parent home, his mother working two waitressing jobs just to make ends meet. After college, he succeeded in making himself one of the top lawyers in his firm. His mother passed away in his junior year so, being an only child, he only had himself to worry about. He became the cliché rich, single guy. He was lonely but found solace in fast cars and faster women. As his bank account grew, so did his ego.

Gregory accumulated wealth of which his childhood self could never have dreamed. He had it all, it seemed. He took pride in his accomplishments, flaunting his money around town like it was an endless fountain. For him, that's exactly what it was, that and the bottles of liquor which made him forget.

He perfected the perfect smile to hide behind so that no one perceived his emptiness. He came from nothing, and how quickly that nothing transformed into a new aspect of his life. He forgot from where he came. He had been a child in a home rich with love, now he was a rich man devoid of it.

One evening, he threw a party at his new home. He wanted to show off his latest acquisition. He was Gregory Peterson, after all; the self-made man! His male friends envied him, wanted to be him, and he knew it. It made him sincerely smile. He was proud. He had made something of himself. He was far better than those that ridiculed his thrift store clothes as a boy. Gregory Peterson was the success story of the decade.

Was.

When you seemingly have it all, people want what you have. Some of them don't have the drive to do the work, so they take a shortcut.

Felicia Peterson, the grieving widow, was now rich beyond her wildest dreams. She had the house, the cars, and the money; not to mention the pretty boy toys she kept for amusement. The performance she gave in the courtroom should have won her an Oscar.

Gregory learned the value of love and the value of riches. He learned that it was impossible to have both. He also learned that when you die, you take neither with you.

The Retort

by A.L. King

"Bastard," said Archibald to the empty page in his typewriter. "You have no father, and your mother was a whore. What more could make you a bastard? What more?"

The page made no retort. It had been silent for the last week and a half, and he was now on the third week of his annual month-long writing escape. He supposed the white sheet was only mum because he had given it nothing to say.

He decided a walk might get his creative juices flowing. On his walk, he observed a spring show: colour returning to trees, grass breaking through the ground like hair filling in on a newborn's scalp, and birds dancing on branches.

He was returning to the cabin when he noticed that the door of his mailbox was wide open. Years ago, during previous writing stints in seclusion, the only contact he allowed himself was the occasional letter from his wife. But mostly the mailbox was decorative.

He peered into the box and found that there had been

a delivery—a red envelope. He opened it and unsheathed a typed letter as he walked inside.

ArchibalD bAxter

I hav ur wife an wunt a million $$$ of that famus righter $$ or she will dye. Deliver the $$$ to 926 bearskin avenue by next Tusday or I will slit her throte!!!

Sinseerly,

Mr. SLAYER

PS NO PIGS!! or she will dye!!!

Archibald looked in horror at the letter.

"My God," he said. "That's so wrong. How could anyone be *so* wrong?"

He paced for a moment, biting his nails, knowing not what he would do. It was just so atrocious!

"Bastard," he said. "Filthy bastard!"

That was it! *Bastard.* Like the blank page in his typewriter. Yes, he knew what to do now. He could make things right. He sat down and gave the bastardly, son-of-a-whore page a voice.

Bubba "Slayer" Short was disappointed when he found the envelope shut in the screen door Monday morning. It was the same one he'd used to send the writer fellow a note, and he doubted a million dollars would fit in it.

He opened the taped-up sleeve anyway. There was no money, as expected, and he fought his ignorance to read what the writer had written back.

Dear Mr. Slayer,

I was very disturbed by your butchery of the English language. The second page of my delivery has a corrected version of your poorly written ransom note. You're welcome.

As for your threat to butcher my wife, I'm afraid you've made another mistake. Poor Selma went against our established rules by arriving at the cabin during my yearly writing excursion, so I put a pen in her neck and buried her beside the walking trail. A bit of grass is even springing up from her resting place like hair filling in on a newborn's scalp. You really should see it. Come visit any time!

Sincerely,

A.B.

The letter fell from his shaking hands. If Archibald Baxter had killed and buried his own wife, then who was the girl Bubba had hogtied in the basement?

The Fallen: Pride of the Dragon

by Zoey Xolton

Lucifer stood before the Throne, eyes narrowed, mouth set. "We were the first!" he declared, his arms outspread to indicate his angelic brethren. "It has been *we* who have kept your Grace and the Word all this time. You created us with a thought! We are beings of love and Light, of dreams, possibility and divinity! And these things—the ones you call *Man*—they're made of earth! Of *dirt*. They are nothing more than clay and dust. And yet, to them you bequeath the gift of free will. I will not serve these creatures. I refuse! That you would even deign to enforce such a burden upon us is beyond logic."

Lucifer's normally star-silver-blue eyes burned with the deep, black fire of rebellion. It spread through him, coursing through his veins, igniting something within him that no angel had ever felt before; pride. "I will not submit," he went on when the Almighty was silent. "Look, oh Creator, upon me. I am the most beautiful and fair of all your creations. I *am* beauty. I am the very spirit of music and Light! I am only second in glory to you yourself."

A roar rose among the ranks of Heaven, unlike anything ever heard before, as angels raised their fists in defiance of the Throne. Their cacophony sewed a feeling of discord that spread like a virus, infecting all those with the dark fire already sparking to life within their eyes.

"I stand before you now, and I ask, would you truly see my brothers and sisters bow down before these wretched creatures?"

"Lucifer, oh Light of the Morning Star, how you have fallen. It fills me with sadness and disappointment that you cannot see. The race of Man is new and young, and will be in need of guidance. It was my hope that you, as my angelic children, would understand my vision, and help Man to grow and walk in the Light."

"Fallen? Then proud I am, oh Father! It is within your power to gift them all that they need, and yet, you refuse? You treat even these new children of yours as if they were naught but pawns in some divine game. Why put them at a disadvantage to begin with? If you created them with more than a mere breath of divine Light, they would not need cosmic guidance. I am no minder!" Lucifer turned his back on the Throne to face the sea of angels gathered. "Who will stand with me? We are divinity given form! Born of truth, of the Word, of Light, direct from the Source! We were not created to Serve lesser beings! We are pure, and these baser creatures are filth! Stand with me, now, my brothers and sisters! Let us make our voices heard. Let us remind the Throne what we are!"

The discord that followed was so great that many angels who stood in disagreeance with Lucifer covered their divine ears against the Darkness that was birthed. Lucifer's eyes blazed, and when he next flared his wings, demanding attention, they were as black as the endless void of space. Looking over his shoulders, he observed them with a smirk playing upon his lips. "I am your Son no more!" he boomed, finger pointed at the Divine. "I am fallen, you say? Then *Fallen* I will be!"

Drawing his flaming sword from its sheath at his waist, he held it aloft, his roar echoing throughout Heaven in such a display as would never happen again. "You are with us, or you are against us!" he yelled. Those loyal to Lucifer, and those who believed in his celestial right to question, drew their swords in unison, joining in his battle cry."

The Divine stood from his throne, and for a single heartbeat, the realms of Heaven fell silent and breathless.

"Will you not end this yourself, oh Great One?"

Lucifer challenged, his spirit buoyed by the strength of his pride. "Would you see your angelic children slaughtered in Your name?"

"Do not answer, my Lord!" cried Michael, stepping down from beside him. "The Divine's Word is beyond question, Lucifer. He is the Law of the Verse. We exist, because of Him. Dare you challenge He that gave you life?"

Lucifer stepped forward, rising upon the first step of the holy dais. "We are Legion," he purred. "And we will bow no longer!" He lunged forward, his sword ringing against Michael's as Michael parried the blow.

"Heavenly Host! Rise! Stand by the Word! Repel the Darkness!" Michael ordered.

Lucifer smiled, and a great battle ensued. He shifted his form into that of the greatest, most fearsome and universally splendid creature he could perceive of—a beast he called the *dragon*. With wings that overshadowed the Heavens, he soared, breathing fire and wrath upon his staunch, deluded brethren.

The stars rang out with the horror of the First War. Angelic blood spilled in quantities beyond fathoming, staining the once pristine and hallowed halls of the Almighty. And the One merely stood by and watched, a seemingly impassive sentinel above the chaos.

When so many of her kindred had been slaughtered that the Angel of Love, Anael, cried out in desperation; "Oh, Lord! Stop this! My heart cannot bear such loss! Please, end this!", only then did He speak, and the war was temporarily arrested.

"Enough!" said the Lord, and all fell still, bound by his command. "My will is absolute, and my decision, final. Those who stand with the Word, move from the battle now, and join me!" The bloodied and weary angels who kept His truth walked from the battle to stand behind the Throne, counting just one third of the number of angels that were.

"Those that stand by the *Traitor*, Lucifer, move from the battle now and stand by your master!" And despite their desire to resist, the rebellious angels could not defy His will, and so moved from the fray of battle to stand behind Lucifer.

In the silence that ensued, one third of the angelic host stood alone, beyond the range of battle, neither fighting for the Divine, nor for the Great Antagonist.

"There is no sin greater than apathy!" decreed the Lord. "You would sit out, choosing neither Right nor Wrong. Do you await the victor, my children? Would you sell your immortal soul, and allegiance to the one who stands to gain the most? I am ashamed of you. Even

Lucifer, in his pride and hate, has not displeased me so! I cast you from the Heavens, and down to Earth—to dwell among the race of Man. Make yourselves seen, or do not. It matters little to me. Be gone from my sight, your judgement will come at the End of Days!" With a single thought, the angels that would not choose a side were banished.

And so they went on to live among men; shielded from His gaze, but never far from His reach. They would become the vain and twisted spirits and creatures of Faerie, dabbling in their own magics and heading the laws of none but their own.

"And you, Morning Star," said the Divine, turning to address his once Most Beloved. "I created you from the very essence of perfection. I breathed into you the best of all things; beauty, intelligence, and skills in all pursuits that exist, and are yet to come. There will never be another like you—and so, I have not the heart to destroy you. For your treason, and for the blood you have shed, however, you must be punished…I cast you from my sight. You are to dwell within the Void, banished to the darkness that would consume all. There, you will wait until the Day of Judgement, by which time, it is my hope that you will have repented of your prideful ways and wickedness. I would one day, have you re-join the ranks of the

Ascended, so the realms might benefit from your splendour."

Lucifer grinned from ear to ear as he flicked his night-dark locks from his eyes. "Keep your hope, Lord, for you will need it. I will *never* return, save to overthrow you! I will create my own kingdom, one of fire and passion, lust and torment, and pleasures unknowable to the Heavenlies! And know this: you may cast me and my kin from the Heavens, but with this choice, you damn your precious creations that walk upon the Earth. For me and my brothers and sisters, there will be no rest. With every moment, and every forsaken breath, we will seek to corrupt, to lead astray and drive your creations of clay into the Darkness. Only the blind follow the blind, oh Lord. And we will open their eyes! They will see that their Divine One is not all-knowing and all-seeing, for if you were, you would have foreseen *this*!" he gestured, arms wide, to the carnage around them. "And worse," he continued. "If you did know what was to come, and still you allowed it to happen—for innocent blood to be shed—then it is you who are the monster! It is you who is fallible! You claim apathy is a greater sin than pride, and yet, it would appear that you are the most apathetic of all!"

"Be gone from my sight, Lucifer. When the trumpets sound, we will meet once again, eye to eye, and the fates of the Heavens and all mankind will be decided upon the hour of Revelations."

Lucifer flared his black wings, his loyal brethren following suit. "With pleasure," he purred, and with a smug look upon his perfect face, he winked at Michael. "See you soon, brother!" he called before diving from the Heavens, through the countless realms of Creation, and into the welcoming gloom of the Abyss. His brothers and sisters joined him, falling from above like stars plummeting from the sky. Leading them, Lucifer, the Morning Star, was brightest of them all.

"Better to reign in Hell," Lucifer told himself, "than to serve in Heaven."

Pride

Author Biographies

A.L. KING

Author of *The Retort*

A.L. King is an author of horror, fantasy, science fiction, and poetry. As an avid fan of dark subjects from an early age, his first influences included R.L. Stine, Edgar Allan Poe, and Stephen King. Later stylistic inspirations came from foreign horror films and media, particularly Japanese. He is a graduate of West Liberty University, has dabbled in journalism, and is actively involved in his community. Although his creativity leans toward darker genres, he has even written a children's book titled "Leif's First Fall." He was raised in the town of Sistersville, West Virginia, which he still proudly calls home.

A.R DEAN

Author of *Driven to Death*

A.R. Dean is a dark and twisted soul. Dean has spent their whole life spreading fear with the tales from their head. Best known for stories that terrify and show the evilest side of human nature. So, look for Dean haunting your local cemetery or under your bed, because they're here to spread the fear. Turn off your lights and enjoy a scare. Dean is being published in Black Hare Press's Beyond and Unravel Anthologies. Keep a lookout for more stories.

Facebook: <u>A.R. Dean Author & Ghoul</u>

A.R JOHNSTON

Author of *WingWoman*

AR Johnston is a small town girl from Nova Scotia, Canada. She is known to write mostly urban fantasy, though she goes where the muses lead her and you never know where that may be. She is a lover of coffee, good tv shows, horror flicks, and a reader of good books. She pretends to be a writer when real life doesn't get in the way. Pesky full-time job and adulting!

Facebook: arjohnstonauthor
Website: arjohnstonauthor.wordpress.com

ALEXANDER NACHAJ

Author of *The Perfect Model*

Alexander lives and writes in Montreal. He's trying to complete his PhD, but the stories keep getting in the way. His work has recently appeared (or is forthcoming) in Mad Scientist Journal, Galli Books and Andromeda Spaceways Magazine.

Website: www.anachaj.ca

ALI HOUSE

Author of *The Fairest of Them All*

Ali House is the author of sci-fi/fantasy novels The Six Elemental and The Fifth Queen, along with various short stories in the "From the Rock" series published by Engen Books. She is a traveller, baker, and fan of the Oxford comma.

Website: engenbooks.com/tag/house-blog/

ANDREW ANDERSON

Author of *Peccata Patris*

Andrew Anderson is a spare-time writer of microfiction, flash fiction and short stories, from Bathgate, Scotland. His work has been published on FlashFlood and Re:Written, and published in Black Hare Press anthologies.

Twitter: soorploom

ANGELA ZIMMERMAN

Author of *Malcolm and Amelia*

Angela Zimmerman is a writer living in the Southern United States. She has been published in Unnerving Magazine and Coffin Bell. You can find her personal writings at Conjure and Coffee.

Website: conjureandcoffee.com

ANNIE PERCIK

Author of *Homecoming*

Annie Percik lives in London with her husband, Dave, where she is revising her first novel whilst working as a University Complaints Officer. She writes a blog about writing and posts short fiction on her website, which is also where all her current publications are listed. She also publishes a photo-story blog, recording the adventures of her teddy—he is much more popular online than she is. She likes to run away from zombies in her spare time.

Website: www.alobear.co.uk
Blog: aloysius-bear.dreamwidth.org/

BRIANNA WITTE

Author of *The Hunt*

As an up and coming writer from Ontario, Canada, Brianna has a passion for spinning tales of adventure and fantasy. She enjoys taking readers on a ride through the realm of fiction by weaving magical and mystical stories that materialise from her wildly creative dreams and vivid imagination. Briana is an active member of the Writers Community of Durham Region. She had received a commentation for her short story, The Hunt, in the 2019 Author of Tomorrow Award by the Wilbur and Niso Smith Foundation. To date, Brianna has had many short stories published in various anthologies by Black Hare Press, Lemon Theory Magazine, Fantasia Divinity, Zimbell House Publishing, and Polar Expressions Publishing. She has also released her first book, Witches and Vampires, in December 2019.

Facebook: BriannaWitteAuthor
Instagram: briannawitteauthor

CATHERINE KENWELL

Author of *Trip to Comeuppance*

Catherine Kenwell is a Barrie, Ontario, mediator and author. After 30 successful years in corporate communications, she sustained a brain injury, lost her job, and joined the circus. She writes both horror/dark fiction and inspirational non-fiction. Her works have been published in Chicken Soup for the Soul, Trembling with Fear, Siren's Call, and HellBound Books.

Website: www.catherinekenwell.com

CINDAR HARRELL

Author of *Blood Pride*

Cindar Harrell loves fairy tales, especially ones with a dark twist. Her writing is often fairy tale inspired, but she also loves mystery and horror. Her stories can be found in various anthologies from publishers such as Black Hare Press, Iron Faerie Publishing, Dragon Soul Press, Blood Song Books, Soteira Press, Fantasia Divinity and more. Traveling is a passion for her as it inspires her imagination to run wild, especially in places that have a mystic presence in the air. She regularly moonlights as another human, but no matter who she is, she is always writing. Her novella inspired by The Snow Queen is set to release in 2020 as well as her debut novel, Lithium, and short story collection, Perchance to Dream.

Facebook: CindarHarrell

CLINT FOSTER

Author of *When the Wood Walked*

Clint Foster lives with his herd of four cats, beloved Basset, Zero, and wonderful wife, Nik. He loves to tell stories just as much as he loves to read them, and is excited to share his work. A longtime consumer of media of all kinds, he enjoys giving back what he hopes everyone else thinks are good stories.

Facebook: ClintFosterAuthor

D.A. SMITH

Author of *Honour's Pride*

D.A. Smith is an editorial assistant for a local press, living with his fiancée, and nurturing a small following of 3000 followers on Twitter. You an also find him actively involved in a critique swapping community on Scribophile.

Twitter: notra661

D.J. ELTON

Author of *Bella's Mirror*

DJ Elton is a writer living in Melbourne's west. As a child she came from England to Australia, on the last boat down the Suez Canal, where she underwent a sacrificial dunking ritual in the court of King Neptune, and has never looked back. She likes creating speculative micro fiction and short stories, as well as random essays. Her work has been published in several anthologies, and she has written a historical fantasy novella, 'The Merlin Girl.' When not playing with a pen, she likes most of all to go to the green country.

DANNIELLE VIERA

Author of *The Ravencroft Reunion*

Dannielle Viera has been involved in the Australian publishing industry for over 20 years – first as a copywriter and then as an editor, project manager, proofreader and author. She has worked on over 100 non-fiction books, writing about subjects as varied as the history of Christianity, Native American mythology, vampires, knights and the death of Hollywood film stars. Some of the books for which she is credited as a contributor include Outside In Gains a Soul (ATB Publishing, 2019), A Christmas Cornucopia (Christmas Press, 2019), and Fire Burn, Cauldron Bubble: Magical Poems Chosen by Paul Cookson (Bloomsbury UK, 2020).

Facebook: DannielleVieraAuthor

DAWN DEBRAAL

Author of *Pride Goeth Before the Fall*

Dawn DeBraal lives in rural Wisconsin with her husband Red, two rat terriers, and a cat. She has discovered that her love of telling a good story can be written. Published stories with Palm-sized press, Spillwords, Mercurial Stories, Potato Soup Journal, Edify Fiction, Zimbell House Publishing, Clarendon House Publishing, Blood Song Books, Black Hare Press, Fantasia Divinity, Cafelit, Reanimated Writers, Guilty Pleasures, Unholy Trinity, The World of Myth, Dastaan World, Vamp Cat, Runcible Spoon, Dark Christmas, Siren's Call, Iron Horse Publishing, Falling Star Magazine 2019 Pushcart Nominee.

Amazon: amazon.com/Dawn-DeBraal/e/B07STL8DLX

DIANE ARRELLE

Author of *Stone Cold Beauty*

Diane Arrelle, the pen name of South Jersey writer Dina Leacock, has sold more than 250 short stories and has three published books including Just A Drop In The Cup, a collection of short-short stories and her new collection of horror stories, Seasons On The Dark Side. Retired from being director of a municipal senior citizen center, she is now co-owner of a small publishing company, Jersey Pines Ink LLC. She resides with her husband and her new cat on the edge of the Pine Barrens (home of the Jersey Devil).

Website: www.arrellewrites.com
Facebook: Diane Arrelle

EDDIE D. MOORE

Author of *Everything Went White*

Eddie D. Moore travels hundreds of hours a year, and he fills that time by listening to audiobooks. When he isn't playing with his grandchildren, he writes his own stories. You can find a list of his publications on his blog or by visiting his Amazon Author Page. While you're there, be sure to pick up a copy of his mini-anthology Misfits & Oddities.

Website: eddiedmoore.wordpress.com
Amazon: amazon.com/author/eddiedmoore

ERICA SCHAEF

Author of *Brick and Bone*

Erica Schaef worked as a Registered Nurse for many years before becoming a stay-at-home parent. Her short stories have been featured most recently by: Visual Verse (Vol. 06- Chapter 09), Blood Moon Rising Magazine (Issue 77), and HellBound Books ("The Toilet Zone"). More of her short stories will be in featured in upcoming anthologies by Fantasia Divinity ("Isolation"), and Jitter Press (Issue 8), as well as in the forthcoming issue of Still Point Arts Quarterly. She lives in rural Tennessee with her husband and two children.

G. ALLEN WILBANKS

Author of *Marinok*

G. Allen Wilbanks is a member of the Horror Writers Association (HWA) and has published over 100 short stories in various magazines and on-line venues. He is the author of two short story collections, and the novel, When Darkness Comes.

Website: www.gallenwilbanks.com
Blog: DeepDarkThoughts.com

GABRIELLA BALCOM

Author of *Pride Goeth*

Gabriella Balcom lives in Texas with her family, loves reading and writing, and thinks she was born with a book in her hands. She works in a mental health field, and writes fantasy, horror/thriller, romance, children's stories, and sci-fi. She likes travelling, music, good shows, photography, history, interesting tales, and animals. Gabriella says she's a sucker for a great story and loves forests, mountains, and back roads which might lead who knows where. She has a weakness for lasagne, garlic bread, tacos, cheese, and chocolate, but not necessarily in that order.

Facebook: GabriellaBalcom.lonestarauthor

HARI NAVARRO

Author of *The Completist*

Hari Navarro has, for many years now, been locked in his neighbours cellar. He survives due to an intravenous feed of puréed extreme horror and Absinthe infused sticky-spiced unicorn wings. His anguished cries for help can be found via 365 Tomorrows, Breachzine, AntipodeanSF, Horror Without Borders, Black Hare Press and HellBound books. Hari was the Winner of the Australasian Horror Writers' Association [AHWA] Flash Fiction Award 2018 and has, also, succeeded in being a New Zealander who now lives in Northern Italy with no cats.

Amazon: amazon.com/Hari-Navarro
Tumblr: harinavarro.tumblr.com/

J.M. MEYER

Author of *Caleb's Claim*

J.M. Meyer is writer, artist and small business owner living in New York, where she received her master's degree from Teachers College, Columbia University. Jacqueline loves the science fiction and horror genres. She also enjoys the company of her husband Bruce and their three children, Julia, Emma and Lauren. Jacqueline's mantra: The only time it's too late to try something new is when you are dead.

Website: jmoranmeyer.net
Amazon: amazon.com/J-M-Meyer/e/B07XWQLG57

J.W. GARRETT

Author of *Ageless*

J.W. Garrett has been writing in one form or another since she was a teenager. She currently lives in Florida with her family but loves the mountains of Virginia where she was born. Her writings include YA fantasy as well as short stories. Since completing Remeon's Quest-Earth Year 1930, the prequel in her YA fantasy series, Realms of Chaos, she has been hard at work on the next in the series, scheduled to release August 2020. When she's not hanging out with her characters, her favourite activities are reading, running and spending time with family.

Website: www.jwgarrett.com
BHC Press: www.bhcpress.com/Author_JW_Garrett.html

JACEK WILKOS

Author of *The Vessel*

Jacek Wilkos is an engineer from Poland. He lives with his wife and daughter in the beautiful city of Cracow. He is addicted to buying books, he loves coffee, dark ambient music and riding his bike. His work was published in Drablr, Rune Bear, Sirens Call eZine.

Facebook: Jacek.W.Wilkos

JAMES LIPSON

Author of *Again*

James Lipson's debut book, Fallen and Other Stories, was published in 2019. His writing is a combination of science and speculative fiction, influenced by some of his favorite authors, such as Philip K. Dick, Ray Bradbury and Isaac Asimov. With a background in art, James has naturally turned to illustrating as he writes, bringing many of his short stories to life not only with descriptive detail, but also detailed visual imagery.

Website: www.jameslipson.com
Instagram: jameslipsonart

JASON HOLDEN

Author of *Roses are Red*

Jason is a human. He lives here and there in the UK, always with his wife, daughter and fur baby. His primary goal is to raise his daughter to adulthood without any major damage. When he can, he writes. He thinks he does it well, but you can be the judge of that. He has been published in a few anthologies here and there, has been praised and put down for his writing. You can find and follow him on Facebook, although he asks you only follow him on Facebook and not through the streets. That's just creepy.

Facebook: Jason Holden-Author

JO SEYSENER

Author of *Knot for Fame*

Jo Seysener is a mum of three crazies, a scatter of chickens, a decrepit kelpie and a rambunctious GSD. She lives with her husband near Brisbane, Australia. When she is not exposing her kids to cult story books from her childhood, she can be found in the kitchen experimenting with new flavours and pairings. She adores alpacas.

Facebook: joseysener
Website: www.joseysener.com

JODI JENSEN

Author of *The Maiden's Walk*

Jodi Jensen, author of time travel romances and speculative fiction short stories, grew up moving from California, to Massachusetts, and a few other places in between, before finally settling in Utah at the ripe old age of nine. The nomadic life fed her sense of adventure as a child and the wanderlust continues to this day. With a passion for old cemeteries, historical buildings and sweeping sagas of days gone by, it was only natural she'd dream of time traveling to all the places that sparked her imagination.

Twitter: @WritesJodi
Facebook: jodijensenwrites

JUSTIN HUNTER

Author of *Chet and Floyd Play in God's Domain*

Justin Hunter has nine published novels and over thirty anthology credits among various publishers. He lives with his wife and four adopted boys in Missouri, USA.

KYLIE L. WEBBER

Author of *Obstructive Gaze*

Kylie L. Webber is a writer and photographer, and winner of the 2019 Penguin Write It Fellowship for historic fiction novel Portrait of a Childless Couple. Kylie's short stories have been published in the 42 Stories Anthology (ongoing, 2019), North Shore Observer, 2015 Lane Cove Literary Awards Anthology. Kylie has self-published a novel, The Fall of Peter Pan, and a collection of poetry, The Loaded Brush, and is the founder and editor of The Adventuresses Club Press, an electronic imprint to republish autobiographical accounts of female adventurers. Kylie lives and works in Sydney as an Editor and Quality Manager.

Amazon: <u>The Fall of Peter Pan: The Neverland Chronicles</u>

KELLY MATSUURA

Author of *Never Seen*

Kelly Matsuura writes diverse YA, fantasy, and literary fiction. She is the Creator of The Insignia Series' anthologies (Asian fantasy themed) and has had stories published with Ink & Locket Press, A Murder of Storytellers, Crushing Hearts & Black Butterfly, and many more. Kelly lives in Nagoya, Japan with her geeky husband. She loves traveling, knitting, cooking, and of course, reading.

Website: <u>www.blackwingsandwhitepaper.com</u>

LUIS MANUEL TORRES

Author of *At Odds*

Luis Manuel Torres was born in Puerto Rico, lived in Boston Massachusetts for thirteen years and currently lives in Springfield Mass. He has a love for stories in all forms they come in, from books to television to video games. His work can be found in A Zimbell House Anthologies 'Second Chance', '1969', 'W.com', 'Secrets in the Water' and 'The Marshal'. He is always working on multiple writing projects and currently has a short story collection on the Wattpad website under the name lobo1989.

Twitter: Luis1989Manuel

LYNDSEY ELLIS-HOLLOWAY

Author of *God's Right Hand*

Lyndsey Ellis-Holloway is a writer from Knaresborough, UK. She writes fantasy, sci-fi, horror and dystopian stories, focussing on compelling characters and layering in myth and legend at every opportunity. Her mind is somewhat dark and twisted, and she lives in perpetual hope of owning her own Dragon someday, but for now she writes about them to fill the void... and to stop her from murdering people who annoy her. When she's not writing she spends time with her husband, her dogs and her friends enjoying activities such as walking, movies, conventions and of course writing for fun as well!

Website: theprose.com/LyndseyEH

M. SYDNOR JR.

Author of *King of the Hill*

M. Sydnor Jr. is an author of novels and short stories. He began his career in writing in 2005 after trading in his basketball sneakers for a pen and pad, and the desire to create worlds took off. Early in his writing journey, he learned there was more than just putting an idea to paper, you had to read. He lives in Northern California collecting an unhealthy number of movies, books and graphic novels. The characters of his fantasy series, The Legends of the World, take most of his time when he's not coaching high school basketball.

MARK KODAMA

Author of *The Tyrant of Syracuse*

Mark Kodama is a trial attorney and former newspaper reporter who lives in Washington, D.C. with his wife and two sons. He is currently working on Las Vegas Tales, a work of philosophy, sugar-coated with meter and rhyme and told through stories. His short stories and poems have been published in anthologies, on-line magazines and on-line blogs.

MATTHEW M. MONTELIONE

Author of *The Animated Dead*

Matthew M. Montelione is a horror writer and American Revolution historian born and raised on Long Island in New York. His work has been published in many titles, including MONSTERS: A Horror Microfiction Anthology, Quoth the Raven: A Contemporary Reimagining of the Works of Edgar Allan Poe, Thuggish Itch: Devilish, WHAT IF?: History Rewritten, Long Island History Journal, and Journal of the American Revolution. Matthew lives with his wife in New York.

Website: maybeevils.com
Amazon: amazon.com/author/maybeevils
Twitter: @maybeevils
Facebook: maybeevils

MAXINE CHURCHMAN

Author of *The Pact*

Maxine Churchman lives in Essex UK and has recently started writing poetry and short stories to share. Her interests include learning to improve her writing, reading, knitting, walking and teaching yoga. She is also planning a novel.

MICHAEL DONOGHUE

Author of *Good Intentions*

Michael Donoghue mostly lives in his head, but resides in Vancouver, Canada. Michael works in public health, where he spends much of his time preoccupied with hand washing.

Twitter: @mpdonoghue

MIKE ADAMSON

Author of *Hubris in Retrograde*

Mike Adamson holds a PhD in archaeology from Flinders University of South Australia. After early aspirations in art and writing, Mike returned to study and secured degrees in both marine biology and archaeology. Mike has been a university educator since 2006, is a passionate photographer, a master-level hobbyist and journalist for international magazines. Short fiction sales include to Mind Candy, Daily SF, Compelling Science Fiction and Nature Futures. Mike has placed over ninety stories to date.

N.M. BROWN

Author of *Defect*

Since N.M. Brown made her first post to a popular Internet forum, she's taken the horror community by storm. Her ability to create, terrify, and drive home her stories is insurmountable. N.M. Brown's published works can be found in multiple anthologies for all to read, but be forewarned, if you do... you may want to call your therapist after, her stories are terrifying, disturbing and devilishly unsettling. She is not only a fright visually, but also has a creepy tentacle in horror podcasting as well. Sinister Sweetheart writes, voice acts and is the media director of the Scarecrow Tales podcast.

Website: Sinistersweetheart.wixsite.com/sinistersweetheart
Facebook: NMBrownStories

NEEN COHEN

Author of *Picked Her Up Again*

Neen Cohen lives in Brisbane with her partner, son and fur babies. She is a writer of LGBTQI, dark fantasy and horror short stories and has a Bachelor of Creative Industries from QUT. She can often be found writing while sitting against a tombstone or tree in any number of graveyards.

Website: wordbubblessite.wordpress.com/
Facebook: neen.cohen.82

NERISHA KEMRAJ

Author of *The Hole of Shame*

Nerisha Kemraj resides in Durban, South Africa with her husband and two mischievous daughters. She has work published/accepted in various publications, both print and online. She holds a Bachelor's degree in Communication Science, and a Post Graduate Certificate in Education from University of South Africa.

Amazon: amazon.com/author/nerisha_kemraj
Instagram: nerishakemraj
Facebook: Nerishakemrajwriter

NICOLA CURRIE

Author of *Filtering*

Nicola Currie is from Cambridge, UK where she works in educational publishing. She has published poetry in literary magazines, including Mslexia and Sarasvati, and short stories in various anthologies. She has also completed her first novel, which was longlisted for the Bath Children's Novel Award.

Website: writeitandweep.home.blog

RAVEN CORINN CARLUK

Author of *Like and Subscribe*

Raven Corinn Carluk writes dark fantasy, paranormal romance, and anything else that catches her interest. She's authored five novels, where she explores themes of love and acceptance. Her shorter pieces, usually from her darker side, can be found in Black Hare Press anthologies, at Detritus Online, and through Alban Lake Publishers.

Twitter: @ravencorinn
Website: RavenCorinnCarluk.Blogspot.Com

RHIANNON BIRD

Author of *Supply Run*

Rhiannon Bird is a young aspiring author. She has a passion for words and storytelling. Rhiannon has her own quotes blog; Thoughts of a Writer. She has had 4 works published. This includes 3 short stories and 2 poems. These are published on Eskimo pie, Literary yard, Down in the Dirt Magazine and Short break fiction. She can be found on Facebook, Instagram, and Pinterest.

ROBERT BAGNALL

Author of *The Artist and the Magician*

Robert Bagnall lives on the English Riviera, within sight of Dartmoor. His speculative fiction has appeared in a variety of magazines, websites and anthologies since the early 1990s. His first novel '2084' was published in 2017 by Double Dragon Publications and is available direct from the publisher or from most virtual bookstores. He can be contacted via his blog.

Website: meschera.blogspot.co.uk

SANDY BUTCHERS

Author of *At Legacy's End*

Sandy Butchers is an author and an artist, known for her elaborate fantasy worlds and creature designs. After living in Scandinavia for a year and traveling throughout the world, she now settled in the countryside, along with a variety of pets and maps on which X marks the spot.

Facebook: AuthorSandyButchers
Amazon: amazon.com/author/sandybutchers

STEPHANIE SCISSOM

Author of *Jezebel*

Stephanie hails from Altamont, TN. She works nights in a tire factory and plots murder by day. She's currently working on a twisted apocalyptic trilogy starring Lucifer and his tortured wife.

Facebook: <u>stephaniescissom2019</u>

STEPHEN HERCZEG

Author of *I'll See You on the Other Side*

Stephen Herczeg is an IT Geek based in Canberra Australia. He has been writing for over twenty years and has completed a couple of dodgy novels, sixteen feature length screenplays and numerous short stories and scripts. His horror work has featured in Sproutlings, Hells Bells, Below the Stairs, Trickster's Treats #1 and #2, Shades of Santa, Behind the Mask, Beyond the Infinite; The Body Horror Book, Anemone Enemy, Petrified Punks and Beginnings. He has also had numerous Sherlock Holmes stories published through the Belanger Books - Sherlock Holmes anthologies.

Amazon: <u>amazon.com/-/e/B07916SQOS</u>
Facebook: <u>stephenherczegauthor</u>

SUE MARIE ST. LEE

Author of *Nina Meets Auntie Dote*

Sue Marie St. Lee writes dark, twisted tales. Her favourite genre is horror with tinges of the supernatural and macabre. Ghosts, black magic, time travel, and all things weird feature in her stories. Sue also writes non-fiction on subjects ranging from healthcare to aging to caring for diabetic pets. When Sue is not writing, she enjoys getting physical with home renovations and landscaping projects. Her favourite way to relax is with a glass of wine, cat on her lap and reading her Kindle.

Blog: suemariestlee.home.blog
Amazon: amazon.com/Sue-Marie-St.-Lee/e/B07WJFRF1L

TERRY MILLER

Author of *The Acquisition of Things*

Terry Miller lives in Portsmouth, Ohio. His work has been featured in Sanitarium Magazine, Devolution Z, Jitter, Rhysling Anthology 2017, Poetry Quarterly, Sirens Call Ezine, The Horror Tree's Trembling With Fear, SpillWords, Organic Ink Vol. I, Curses & Cauldrons Anthology from Blood Song Books, Forest of Fear from Blood Song Books, the Dark Drabble Anthology Series from Black Hare Press, 100 Word Zombie Bites from Reanimated Writers Press, Scary Snippets, Guilty Pleasures & Other Dark Delights, 100 Word Horrors 3, and O Unholy Night In Deathlehem from Grinning Skull Press.

Facebook: tmiller2015
Amazon: amazon.com/author/millerterryl

TRISHA RIDINGER MCKEE

Author of *Golden Boy*

Trisha Ridinger McKee resides in a small town in Pennsylvania where pride has proven to be a problem. Her work has appeared or is forthcoming in publications such as Tablet Magazine, The Oddville Press, Crab Fat Literary Magazine, Night to Dawn Magazine, Deep Fried Horror, 4 Star Stories, and more.

WONDRA VANIAN

Author of *Not Guilty*

Wondra Vanian is an American living in the United Kingdom with her Welsh husband and their army of fur babies. A writer first, Wondra is also an avid gamer, photographer, cinephile, and blogger. She has music in her blood, sleeps with the lights on, and has been known to dance naked in the moonlight. Wondra was a multiple Top-Ten finisher in the 2017 and 2018 Preditors and Editors Reader's Poll, including the Best Author category. Her story, "Halloween Night," was named a Notable Contender for the Bristol Short Story Prize in 2015.

Website: www.wondravanian.com

XIMENA ESCOBAR

Author of *Joy's Debut*

Originally from Santiago, Ximena is the author of a translation into Spanish of the Broadway Musical "The Wizard of Oz" (2012) and of an original adaptation of the same, "Navidad en Oz" (2018), both produced in Chile. Since the latter she has dedicated herself to her writing, publishing poetry, short stories and drabbles, most of which can be found across Black Hare Press's Dark Drabbles Series. She has a degree in Arts & Communication Science, and lives in Nottingham with her family. To follow her progress, you can find her on social media.

Facebook: Ximenautora
Instagram: @laximenin
Twitter: @laximenin

ZOEY XOLTON

Author of *The Fallen: Pride of the Dragon*

Zoey Xolton is an Australian Speculative Fiction writer, primarily of Dark Fantasy, Paranormal Romance and Horror. She is also a proud mother of two and is married to her soul mate. Outside of her family, writing is her greatest passion. She is especially fond of short fiction and is working on releasing her own themed collections in future.

Website: www.zoeyxolton.com

Pride

BLACK HARE PRESS

Acknowledgements

When we embarked on our Black Hare Press journey back in late 2018, we never envisioned the huge support we'd get from the writing community. We have been truly humbled by the number of submissions we've received (around 3,000 over our first eight publications!) and have loved reading every single one.

So, thank you to everyone who crafted tales just for us—from the tiny tales in our Dark Drabbles series to these sinful tales you have read here in Pride—we thank you from the bottom of our hearts.

To our families and friends, collaborators, random strangers who took pity on us, and everyone who has helped us on the way: we couldn't have done it without you.

And to you, our discerning reader, we and these talented writers did it all for you. We hope you enjoyed these tales, and if you did, don't forget to leave a review.

Thank you all—see you next time.

Love & kisses
Ben & Dean

www.blackharepress.com

* 9 7 8 1 9 2 5 8 0 9 4 1 1 *